THE
KILLER
ON THE
BEACH

A ROBERT VANCE THRILLER

RICK VAN ETTEN

PROUD POINT PRESS
DES MOINES, IOWA

The Killer on the Beach

ISBN: 978-1-7348269-2-0

This is a work of fiction. While many of the locations and some of the businesses mentioned herein do exist, they are used fictitiously and to the best of the author's knowledge, none of the incidents described has ever occurred. Any resemblance to actual events or persons, living or dead, is entirely coincidental.

Published by
Proud Point Press
Des Moines, Iowa

Cover design by Jaycee DeLorenzo
Sweet 'N Spicy Designs

Praise for *The Killer in the Woods*, the first Robert Vance novel:

"More plot twists than a cyclone through an Iowa cornfield…Rob Vance puts a whole new spin on the idea of Midwestern hospitality." --Dave Carty, author of *Leaves on Frozen Ground* and *Red Is the Fastest Color*

"Perfect mix of suspense…hard to put down."
--Amazon Five Star Review

"An enthralling and finely detailed crime-turned-investigative story." *—The Eclectic Review*

"A real page turner…a very entertaining read." --Tom Carney, *The Upland Almanac*

Praise for *The Killer at the Lake*, the second Robert Vance novel:

"Reluctant vigilante Robert Vance is back. The prose is smooth and easy to read, with lots of local color. The tension ratchets up: the final third of the book had me reading past my bedtime." --Amazon Five Star Review

"Robert Vance does it again in his unassuming way. Thrilling and suspenseful follow-up to *The Killer in the Woods.*" *—*Amazon Five Star Review

ALSO BY RICK VAN ETTEN

The Killer at the Lake

The Killer in the Woods

In memory of

Lana J. Myers, 1946-2024
*Aunt extraordinaire and lifelong beachcomber at
heart*

and

Edward A. Lamb, 1964-2023
Friend and warrior

VANCE'S RULES
FOR CONTRACT KILLINGS

1.   No personal involvement…i.e., there must be no personal feelings whatsoever attached. This would cloud judgment.

2.   No collateral damage. Absolutely unacceptable; must remain true to purpose—righting a wrong, stopping a bully, etc. Eliminating bystanders/witnesses not permitted. Ditto letting an innocent person take the fall.

3.   Never keep a handgun after it's been used.

4.   No politicians (regardless of how much they might deserve it); too well protected; too much public scrutiny and investigation.

5.   No organized crime members. Flat-out too dangerous, and too much risk of touching off a gangland war that might result in innocents being killed.

PROLOGUE

The moon was a ghostly galleon tossed upon cloudy seas...
Alfred Noyes, *The Highwayman*

THE MOON, MORE THAN three-quarters full, was just visible above the dunes when Sara Lawson parked her dark green Subaru Forester at one of the graveled turnouts on the street that ran parallel to the beach. As she exited and locked her vehicle she could hear the roar of the surf from beyond the dunes and she wondered if a king tide was in the offing. She hoped not, as the tide could threaten some of the turtle nests, those built lower on the dunes and closer to the beach.

Sara Lawson was a tall, slender woman with ash-blonde hair that fell just below her shoulders. She was seventy years old and had been widowed three years earlier when her husband Albert, a lifelong smoker, had succumbed to a heart attack. The couple was childless. Sara was a lifelong resident of the area and her sister Jane lived just a few miles away.

It was a few minutes before eight o'clock on a warm evening in early June and she and Jane had agreed via text earlier that day to meet at this parking area, one of the public ones not requiring a permit. Although the dunes blocked her view of the ocean, Sara could hear the sound of the tide increasing in volume. Curious as to how high the tide was and whether her worries about the turtle nests were justified, she decided not to wait for her sister. Jane would see her vehicle when she arrived and could catch up to her on the beach, Sara decided.

Signs posted every fifty yards or so warned people to stay off the dunes—erosion was a constant worry—or be subject to arrest and a $500 fine. Sara walked a few yards from the parking area to one of the wide wooden stiles erected to provide a walkway over the dunes. She mounted the steps, paused for a moment at the top to scan the beach and the ocean before her, then descended to the beach.

The surf was rolling in powerfully but so far it was retreating before reaching the base of the dunes. Sara wore a simple, pale blue cotton sundress and she paused just long enough to remove her flip-flops and lace the fingers of her left hand through their straps. On the top of her right foot, just above the instep, was a blue, half-dollar sized tattoo of a sea turtle.

Carrying her flip-flops, Sara continued on toward the water for another twenty yards or so to the edge of the surf, then turned at right angles and began walking parallel to the dunes. She loved walking barefoot on the beach on warm summer evenings. The damp sand beneath her soles, the salt spray in the air combined with a cooling breeze off the ocean and the moonlight overhead made for a feeling of such peace, almost enchantment, that Sara sometimes forgot, if only momentarily, that she was on a mission.

That mission was monitoring the nests of the sea turtles. She knew of a turtle nest about one hundred yards down the beach and she wanted to check it and make sure it hadn't been disturbed.

Sara had always loved the giant turtles and since her husband's death she had devoted herself to their protection. She was a volunteer at the Paige Green Sea Turtle Rescue and Rehabilitation Center in Surf City, North Carolina, a few miles south of her home in Schnock's Harbor, and along with several dozen other volunteers she helped locate and mark the turtle nests and regularly checked them for signs of hatching.

The nest she was now walking toward was one of the earliest of the season and while she doubted the hatchlings had begun to emerge, she wanted to make sure. She also wanted to confirm that the nest, marked with several posts, hadn't been destroyed by vandals or late-night beach revelers. It sometimes happened and Sara was both enraged and saddened when it did.

As she continued down the beach she glanced at the moon overhead and recalled a line from a poem read in high school that described the moon as a ghostly galleon. She couldn't recall the title of the poem or its author—it had been more than fifty years since she had read it—but she had always remembered and loved that description. A galleon, she knew, was an old-time sailing ship, and the nearly full moon did resemble such a vessel with its sails full and billowing. And yes, there was something apparition-like about it as well.

She turned her attention back to the dunes, looking for the posts that marked the turtle nest. The nests were typically dug several feet up the sides of the dunes, or even on top of them, which helped protect them from being washed out by a high tide. When she first learned this, Sara thought it remarkable that the turtles instinctively knew they should dig their nests on higher ground, but then she realized they hadn't survived for millions of years—far longer than mankind—by locating their nests haphazardly. It was no different, she decided, than the hatchlings knowing from the moment they emerged from their shells and dug their way out of the sand that they should scramble their way across the beach and into the water.

Once in a while, however, a turtle did lay her eggs in a nest dug on the beach or low on the side of a dune. When this happened and the volunteers found the nest, they were permitted to carefully remove the eggs—which might number more than one hundred—and relocate them to a higher elevation.

Sara sometimes wondered if the turtle that made such a nest was a first-time mother, one lacking in experience, and she hoped that in subsequent seasons the turtle would locate its nest in a more auspicious place. Knowing, however, that once the turtle laid its eggs it didn't return to the nest—and therefore would never know if the eggs had successfully hatched—Sara realized the turtle also had no way of learning from its mistake and choosing a better location for its next nest.

She also admitted to herself that this line of thinking was more than a bit anthropomorphic. The entire breeding, nesting and hatching sequence was hard-wired into the turtles'

DNA, and the fact that the turtles had survived for all these millennia was proof enough of their capacity for survival. The occasional ill-chosen nest location wasn't going to doom the species.

But mankind might.

There were seven species of sea turtles and all of them were endangered, some critically. Though she found the idea repugnant, Sara knew the turtles were hunted for their meat and their shells, and the nests were sought for their eggs. The turtles were federally protected in the U.S. but this wasn't the case in many other countries, where harvesting the turtles was permitted. Poaching and illegal trade in turtle meat and shells was also widespread throughout the world.

Then there was the matter of pollution.

Jellyfish were a primary food source for the turtles, and small pieces of floating plastic were often mistaken for jellyfish by the turtles and eaten, usually with fatal results. Turtles also frequently became entangled in nets or discarded fishing gear—again, often fatally—a phenomenon known as bycatch. And of course, the occasional oil spill poisoned turtles and their nests as well, as did all sorts of other chemical pollutants.

Sara was determined, for a long as she lived, to do everything she could to help the turtles survive.

She quickened her pace when she saw the posts marking the nest ahead. Then she broke into a jog when she saw, unmistakably, what was colloquially referred to as a turtle boil. She couldn't help grinning.

The baby turtles were hatching.

The sand covering the nest was churning as the hatchlings emerged, giving the nest the appearance of a pot of boiling water and thus, its nickname. Sara knew that the first hatchling emerging from its shell triggered all of its siblings to do likewise, simultaneously. Clawing their way free of their sandy covering, the hatchlings immediately began clambering down the side of the dune and scrambling toward the surf.

Sara clasped her hands together and uttered a heartfelt, "Oh!" Although she had seen this same occurrence many times previously, she was—as always—totally captivated. The hatchlings were about three inches long and one would have fit perfectly in the palm of her hand, but she knew she shouldn't touch them, much as she longed to. With their huge dark eyes and tiny flippers, Sara thought there was nothing more irresistible than the baby turtles. She hoped her sister would get here in time to see them.

Then she heard it.

It was the angry snarl of an ATV being driven at high speed, and it was coming from behind her. She quickly turned back to face the way she had come, and she could see the ATV's twin headlights rapidly bearing down on her.

Her first thought was the safety of the hatchlings.

She began waving her arms and shouting "No!" even as she realized the driver wouldn't be able to hear her over the sound of the machine's engine. The ATV, a black and yellow Polaris RZR XP 1000 White Lightning, rocketed toward her and she continued waving her arms, hoping the driver would swerve and miss the baby turtles that were just now beginning to stream past her feet. She prayed the driver would swerve toward the surf and not toward the dunes, as the latter would see the ATV crushing the procession of baby turtles just as they came down off the dune.

The driver of the ATV—he was helmetless, and Sara could see his red hair in the moonlight—showed no sign of swerving or slowing. Instead, he stomped the accelerator and bore down on the frantically gesticulating woman. The RZR boasted 114 horsepower—more than some compact cars— and a top speed of nearly 80 miles per hour. It was kicking up a huge plume of sand in its wake and the roar of its engine was almost deafening. The driver hunched lower over the steering wheel, grinning and hoping to give the woman a good scare. He expected her to jump from his path. But if she didn't…his grinned widened.

Sara stood her ground and continued to wave and shout.

Unnoticed by either of the humans, another person— Sara's sister Jane—appeared at the top of the dune just in time to see the ATV close the last few yards to Sara. In one terrible instant Jane took in the scene and knew what was about to happen. She saw the driver stretch out his left arm just before he reached Sara and his forearm caught her at the neck as he shot past, the ATV missing her body only by inches. She dropped instantly and the driver roared on down the beach without slowing.

Jane screamed and ran down the side of the dune. Losing both of her flip-flops in the sand, she raced across the beach to her sister, who lay motionless in the moonlight. Jane sobbed and sank to her knees when she reached Sara. Only then did Jane notice the hatchlings scrambling past her on their way to the water.

She saw several lying crushed and motionless in the tracks made by the ATV. She sobbed again and said, "Oh God, no!" as she gently lifted Sara's head and shoulders from the sand to cradle her in her lap. She stared down at Sara's lifeless eyes for a moment then raised her head to look down the beach in the direction the ATV had taken.

There was no sign of the vehicle or its driver. The ATV had vanished around a bend in the dunes and Jane could no longer hear its engine.

But a slight noise beside her caused her to drop her gaze back down to the sand. One of the hatchlings, partially crushed by one of the ATV's tires but not yet dead, was still struggling and attempting to follow its siblings to the water. It continued pushing feebly with its tiny flippers but after a moment its mouth opened spasmodically and it died. Jane sobbed again.

The other hatchlings continued scrambling toward the water, streaming past the kneeling woman and her dead sister. Through her tears Jane saw one of the hatchlings clamber over Sara's bare foot, the one with the sea turtle tattoo above the instep, and continue on its way to the sea.

PART ONE: DISCOVERY

*Everyone is a moon, and has a dark side which he never
shows to anybody.*

Mark Twain

Chapter 1

I HADN'T KILLED ANYONE in nearly a year, and I was enjoying my retirement.

I've been a contract killer—a hit man—for about thirty years. But that's actually a sideline, not my primary occupation; for about the same length of time I've worked in magazine publishing. For the last twenty of those years I was the editor of an outdoor sporting magazine, a "hook and bullet rag," titled *American Wingshot*.

I retired from that position the previous December. After editing thousands of features and columns, and writing hundreds of articles and editorials myself, I felt it was time to step down. I realized I was no longer bringing much to the table and the magazine would benefit from some new blood. I submitted my letter of resignation to my publisher, Bill McKenzie, on November 1.

McKenzie asked me to stick around until a new editor was hired so I could help with the transition. I agreed to do so. My actual final day of employment was December 15. I considered retirement my Christmas present to myself, ten days early.

I'm a lifelong upland bird hunter, so in many ways my position as editor of *American Wingshot* had been a dream job. I can't deny that leaving it after twenty years didn't come with some regrets, but again, I knew it was time to go. And unlike a lot of retirees, I wasn't worried about how I was going to keep myself busy. I live with an eight-year-old German wirehaired pointer named Preacher, which pretty much guarantees that a sedentary lifestyle is not an option. Anyone with a high-energy sporting dog can confirm this.

Iowa's pheasant season always ends on January 10, so Preacher and I logged quite a few days afield in those first weeks after I retired. The possession limit of roosters is twelve, and we finished the season with a full freezer. Most of those birds would end up grilled over indirect heat (charcoal;

I'm a purist) over the next few months when I invited my lady friend, Daryl Nelson, to join me for a wild game dinner.

Daryl and I have been involved for a little over a year and a half. She's an op-ed writer for the *Des Moines Register* and it was one of her columns that caused me to contact her initially. I was impressed with her writing and I sent her an email complimenting the column. That led to a couple of lunch dates, then a dinner date at Skip's, one of my favorite restaurants here in Des Moines. A goodnight kiss in the parking lot after dinner marked the real beginning of our relationship, a relationship that was marred by only one critical factor…make that a *hugely* critical factor.

Daryl knew nothing of my second job.

My last assignment—or non-assignment, actually; more on that in a moment—some ten months earlier had caused me to do some serious soul searching. Daryl was a straight shooter and I felt increasingly guilty about keeping such a vital part of my life hidden from her. But then again, how do you tell someone—especially someone with whom you've become intimately involved—that you occasionally kill people?

I struggled with this for weeks as I investigated, albeit reluctantly, the death of a friend, a woman I knew from walking Preacher at Maffitt Reservoir. The woman's name was Hannah Wilkinson and she owned a golden retriever named Maisie that she also walked at the reservoir. We occasionally met there and walked together…that is, until the morning I found her drowned in the lake.

The police and the ME ruled Hannah's death a suicide, but her nineteen-year-old daughter Jessica was convinced Hannah had been murdered. Jessica quickly zeroed in on a guy named Greg Fletcher, believing he was a sexual predator who had lured Hannah into the water one evening and forcibly drowned her.

Subsequent events and a pile of circumstantial evidence proved Jessica was correct.

With the help of good friends Rachel and Al James, I had sent Fletcher to a watery grave himself. I did this not only to avenge Hannah's death but also to protect Jessica, as I had good reason to believe Fletcher was planning the same fate for her that he had visited upon her mother. I couldn't stand by and allow that to happen.

Which is why I characterized this as a non-assignment. No one had gone through the usual channels (responding by email to my rather innocuous online ad hinting at what I do) and hired me to kill Fletcher. Jessica herself had no idea I was a hit man, nor did she ever learn of Fletcher's ultimate fate. I performed this hit pro bono, so to speak.

Further adding to the paradox, killing Fletcher also violated the first of my five inviolate rules about contract killing: no personal involvement. Ordinarily I try to remain completely detached when I accept an assignment and plan the target's fate. Personal involvement carries the strong likelihood of clouding one's judgment when, conversely, a cool head must prevail. But because of my friendship with Hannah and her daughter, I'd had to bypass this rule.

Fletcher's death had occurred in early August. It was now the following June and I'd taken no additional assignments. My online ad was still running but I'd had only a few half-hearted inquiries that hadn't developed into anything solid. And I'll admit, I wasn't particularly interested anyway. The retirement bug had bitten hard and I was enjoying coming and going as I pleased, not having to meet deadlines and keeping my days largely unstructured. I was seriously considering retiring from my contract killing gig as well.

I could afford to do so because it has never been about the money. I have an abiding hatred of bullies—this stems from an incident in high school that haunts me to this day— and injustice. I don't kill people because I need the income, and my fees are decidedly modest. I have never charged more than $10,000 for a hit; sometimes much less.

No, it's not about the money. Instead, I kill people to make things right. My targets are those individuals who relish inflicting pain and have made the lives of others unbearable, or in some cases, have destroyed those lives completely.

When this happens, I'm sometimes sought by those who feel they have no other recourse, or by someone who wants retribution for a murdered loved one—retribution that our sketchy criminal justice system often fails to deliver.

I don't consider myself to be some gallant crusader, however. I'm actually pretty average. I don't have an extensive military or espionage background, no special combat skills or any high-tech weaponry. Think of me as the kind of guy who might be standing behind you in line at the grocery store or sitting at the table next to yours in a favorite restaurant, the sort of fellow you'd not give a second glance, and you'll have an accurate impression. I look like who and what I am—a recently retired senior citizen just hoping to enjoy his remaining years peaceably.

Besides allowing me to enjoy those years with fewer hassles, retiring from contract killing would also provide a major additional benefit. It would ease the guilt I was feeling about keeping that part of my life a secret from Daryl. Sure, a lie of omission—and admittedly, this one was a whopper—is still a lie. But at least I would no longer have to go to great lengths to conceal my activities from her when I accepted an assignment; wouldn't have to tap dance around what I was up to as I planned to kill someone. And maybe, just maybe, I'd get lucky and that part of my past could remain hidden.

That's wishful thinking, of course. Even the best-kept secrets usually find a way to come to the surface, and when they ultimately do, their impact is often far more devastating than if they'd been made known earlier on. I realized that the likelihood of my being able to keep Daryl in the dark forever was probably very slim. How she would react and what she would do when she learned the truth, I really couldn't predict. Or didn't *want* to predict, anyway.

But this much I did know. Given the level of intimacy and trust we'd achieved in our relationship, she deserved better of me.

Chapter 2

THE MAN SMILED, LIFTED HIS wineglass and said, "Cheers."

The woman sitting opposite him did the same. They clinked glasses lightly and both took a sip.

It was a Wednesday evening in early June and the man and woman were sitting in a booth in Biaggi's Ristorante Italiano on University Avenue in West Des Moines. Because it was midweek the restaurant wasn't crowded. Nevertheless, they both kept their voices low, not wanting their conversation to be overheard. And perhaps not wanting to draw attention to themselves, as well.

They were a good-looking couple. The man, recently widowed, was in his late forties, trim and handsome, and the woman, though a few years older than her companion, was an attractive brunette. Both were reasonably well known throughout the metro; he was a prominent attorney and she was a widely read journalist who had once been nominated for a Pulitzer.

They had met at a political fundraiser some six months earlier, struck up a conversation and then, after some initial hesitation on both of their parts, slipped into a relationship. Given their respective positions and the corresponding recognition factor, they had of necessity kept their affair under wraps. Most of their previous get-togethers had been limited to weeknights at either her house or his. It was only now that they were beginning to cautiously "go public," which was why they had chosen a restaurant in West Des Moines rather than someplace downtown.

"Here's to a better summer than last," the man added.

"Amen to that." The woman took another sip and shook her head.

The man rotated his wineglass in his fingers, thinking. Then he added, "What a crazy time that was. I mean, one coincidence after another. You couldn't make this stuff up."

"No, you couldn't," she agreed. "It all reminds me of a Tom Clancy quote."

"Really? What did Tom Clancy say?"

"He said, 'The difference between fiction and reality? Fiction has to make sense.'"

The man laughed. "That pretty well covers it. And I'd agree, there's a lot about last summer that doesn't make sense. I mean…look at us. Who could have predicted any of what happened, beginning with Rob finding my wife's body?"

"I know. And then the two of us meeting several months later. I've thought a lot about that also. The whole thing is just…crazy."

They sat in silence for minute, then the woman asked, "That guy your daughter believed killed Hannah…Greg Fletcher? He disappeared, right? Did the police ever find out what happened to him?"

"No," said the man. "They never did. To use an archaic expression, it appears he flew the coop."

The woman laughed. "That's archaic, all right. But do you really think that's what happened, that he just decided to disappear? That he managed to vanish without a trace?"

The man shrugged. "I don't know what other explanation there could be. His brother filed a missing persons report but apparently the police never turned up any leads."

"You don't think…" she hesitated, then continued, "that Jessica might have been right? That maybe he did kill Hannah and that's why he disappeared?"

The man shook his head. "No, I just don't believe that. Her death was ruled a suicide and there was never any real evidence that it was anything else. But I'll admit it's suspicious that he disappeared so soon after Hannah died. Another crazy coincidence along with all the others."

"And there was no evidence of foul play?" the woman asked.

"No indication one way or the other," the man replied. "As I recall, they found his vehicle sitting in his driveway and his house was locked. Nothing inside the house was disturbed or out of place; no signs of a struggle. His wallet and keys were missing so it's assumed he took those with him, wherever he went. That's about as much as I was able to find out. The cops haven't exactly been forthcoming—I think they just want the matter closed—and I didn't want to pry too deeply."

"What about a cell phone?"

"Missing also. No signal so it's assumed he turned it off. No way to trace it."

"That's just weird. To be able to disappear so completely, I mean. Especially nowadays."

"I agree. But he worked at the airport, remember, so I guess it's conceivable that he might have had some inside knowledge on how to get out of Dodge." The man laughed. "Or out of Des Moines, anyway."

The woman laughed also. "Maybe. But if he flew anywhere there would be a record. Unless he used another name."

"That's possible," the man said. "The only other explanation is that he was abducted, but again, there's no evidence of that happening."

The woman smiled and said, "That would also raise the question of who abducted him. And why."

The man laughed. "Well, I'm sure it wasn't Jessica, if that's what you're thinking," he said. "Although she probably would have liked to. And then tortured him at length."

The woman laughed also. "How's she doing?" she asked.

"She's doing okay. I talked to her on Sunday and she said her summer classes were going well. She'll graduate next spring."

"Wow," the woman said. "She's really done well after losing her mother like that…what an awful thing to have to deal with at her age. Or any age, for that matter."

They were interrupted by the arrival of the server with their entrees, chicken marsala for the man and steak de burgo for the woman. The server placed their plates in front of them and asked, "Is there anything else I can get you right now?"

"I think we're fine for the moment," the man replied,

and the woman nodded in agreement. They were sharing a bottle of chardonnay so there was no need to order another round of drinks.

"Well, then, enjoy!" the server said, smiling, as she withdrew from their table.

The man smiled across at his companion again. "Speaking of Rob…have you given any more thought to when you're going to tell him?"

"It will be soon, I promise," she said. She reached across the table and squeezed his hand. "I'm not trying to delay or drag things out."

"I know that," he said. "And after everything that happened, I agree that we needed to let the dust settle." He glanced around the restaurant. "I'm glad we can at least be seen together in public. Or start to be seen, anyway."

"I am too."

They both picked up their utensils and began eating. After a minute the man said, "Mine is very good. How's yours?"

"Mine's good also."

The man took another bite of chicken, chewed and swallowed, then said, "Let me ask you one more question, then I promise I'll drop it."

The woman smiled and said, "Okay."

"When you tell Rob, how do you think he's going to take it?"

The woman shook her head and laughed slightly. "Not well."

"Not well?"

"Oh, I mean, he's going to be surprised, and I'm sure he'll be upset. But…I don't think he'll do anything crazy."

"No?"

"No. I mean, we're all adults and I've never gotten the sense he was the type to fly off the handle. Sure, he likes to hunt and all that, but I don't think he's really the violent type. Not toward other people, anyway. He's generally pretty laid-back."

"Well, that's good to know," Craig Wilkinson said.

"I'm more worried about you than I am for myself."

"You can relax," Daryl Nelson replied. "I don't think either of us has anything to worry about."

"ARE YOU GOING TO TELL ROB?"

Al James glanced at his wife as he posed the question. They had just left Biaggi's and were walking across the parking lot to Al's vehicle, a gleaming black Chevy Silverado.

"Of course I am," Rachel James replied. "I've been friends with Rob a lot longer than Daryl. She's a friend—or she *was*, anyway—but she doesn't have the kind of history Rob and I have. I can't stand the thought that she's cheating on him." She shook her head and added, "The bitch."

They reached the Silverado and climbed in. Al cranked the ignition.

"Do you think Rob will believe you when you tell him?" He shifted into reverse to back out of the parking space.

"Of course he'll believe me. He trusts me and I trust him. He knows I wouldn't make something like this up."

She paused, then held up her cell phone. "Besides, I have proof. I got pictures."

Chapter 3

I RENT SEVERAL P.O BOXES THROUGHOUT the Des Moines metro, all in the name of my innocuous-sounding LLC, a bogus copy-editing and proofreading service. (Before my retirement I also had a P.O. box reserved for magazine correspondence and submissions, but I'd allowed the rental on that box to lapse several months earlier.) It's to these boxes that checks, made payable to the LLC, are sent upon completion of an assignment.

Let me back up a bit and explain how this whole system works. I've already mentioned that I run an online ad—again, innocuous-sounding—that hints (just barely) at my contract killing gig. So far I've avoided joining the Dark Web—the logistics of which would most likely defeat me anyway—and now that I was seriously considering retiring from that gig altogether, doing so was a moot point.

After responding to the ad, potential clients are taken through an initial series of "blinds" that lead to several additional email exchanges, a second series of baffles. Only after passing through these baffles—which I use to evaluate the sincerity and trustworthiness of the client—will I then provide them with a P.O. box number and the simple instruction to send me, via regular mail, a phone number. I insist they follow this procedure.

Why snail mail to a P.O. box? Because, all the complaints about the USPS notwithstanding, it's still a lot safer than any kind of online correspondence. Sure, messages can be encrypted and de-encrypted, but that's yet another pain in the ass for a semi-Luddite like me. (Some of my friends would dispute the "semi" in the previous statement.) Firm believer in the rule of KISS that I am, I've employed this system successfully for quite a few years now. I'll also admit that I've been damned lucky—no one from any law enforcement agency has ever attempted to contact me…at least, not to the best of my knowledge.

Once I receive the client's phone number, I call him or her on a burner, and if they ask my name, I give them something simple like John, Joe or Tom. All subsequent contacts will be made with the same burner, which I destroy as soon as the assignment is completed and I've received their check.

Although I wasn't currently expecting a check and had no pending assignments, nor any recent inquiries, I nevertheless make a point of checking the P.O. boxes once or twice a week, mostly just to clean out the accumulated fliers, ads and other promotional junk mail. It's amazing how much of that crap you receive, and I've often thought that if environmentalists were really serious about protecting our forests, they would lobby to outlaw junk mail. Fat chance of that ever happening.

On a Thursday morning in mid-June I made the rounds of the boxes—they're scattered throughout the city and the trip usually takes me about an hour and a half to complete— but found nothing of interest in any of them. That wasn't surprising because, as I said, I had nothing pending. As I drove home I reflected that I could probably start letting the rentals on most of these boxes lapse as well. I wouldn't be needing them if I retired from my moonlighting gig as a hit man, and there was no point in continuing to pay the rental fees.

WHEN I GOT HOME it was almost 11:00, a little too early for lunch although my stomach was growling. I had enough coffee left over in the pot from earlier that morning to fill a mug, which I did. I nuked it for a minute, added a dash of milk from the fridge, then headed back to the bedroom that serves as my office.

As I passed through the living room, Preacher was sprawled on the sofa in what I jokingly referred to as her roadkill pose. She was sleeping on her back with her belly completely exposed and her neck and head twisted to one side at an impossible angle and her four long legs sticking up crookedly in the air. Her whiskered lips had also drooped away from her jaws, showing their mottled pink undersides and exposing her teeth in what looked like the rictus of death.

Despite her morbid appearance I couldn't help smiling. "You look ridiculous," I said. She opened one eye and thumped the sofa a couple times with her docked tail. I shook my head and continued on to the office, still smiling and reflecting that one of our dogs' primary purposes in life was providing comic relief. Preacher was a master.

While the coffee had been nuking I'd noticed the red light blinking on the handset phone in the kitchen. It's one of several remote sets throughout the house that are linked to the old landline phone and answering machine in my office, the one I'd used for many years for magazine-related business. Friends and family members knew the old landline number was still the best number at which to reach me, as I'm not always the most conscientious about keeping my cell phone turned on and at hand.

I set my coffee mug down on my computer table and sat down in my desk chair. The window on the answering machine showed a lighted red digital 2, indicating I had two messages. I punched the play button.

The first message was from Daryl. "Hey, babe," she said. "I know we were planning to have dinner at Skip's tonight but I think I'd better beg off. I woke up this morning with a headache and an upset stomach and I haven't been able to shake either one. Might have caught a bug so I think I'd better cancel. Sorry."

Well, crap. Daryl and I had a standing dinner date on Thursday evenings, our way of getting a jump on the weekend. I was disappointed that I wouldn't be seeing her but I hoped the bug she caught wasn't anything too serious. I'd probably give her a call after lunch to see how she was feeling.

The second message was from Rachel James. "Hey you," she said, employing our standard greeting. "I know you usually get together with Daryl on Thursday evenings, but if by chance you don't do that tonight, I was wondering if we could get together for beers on your deck. I have something I need to share with you."

Well, yours truly intrigued. I wondered what it was

that Rachel wanted to share that was so urgent she wanted to get together on a night I ordinarily would have been out with Daryl.

I also couldn't help reflecting on the coincidental timing of the two messages. Daryl cancels our dinner date and Rachel follows with a suggestion that we have deck beers if I'm not getting together with Daryl. What were the odds?

Or as they say on social media, WTF?

Chapter 4

HAVING BEERS ON MY DECK is a longstanding tradition between Rachel and me. I don't recall exactly how the tradition got started, but I do know we've solved many of the world's problems while sitting on deck chairs and drinking a few cold ones…pardon the obvious hyperbole. But over the years we have addressed any number of personal issues, both hers and mine, and have often come up with workable solutions or at least valuable insights. Even when solutions elude us, just getting the issues on the table helps as a venting exercise, especially when accompanied by beer.

I should also add that the plans for many of my assignments have been discussed and fine-tuned during these sessions.

I'll freely admit that Rachel is a better strategist than I am. She's quick to wade through—and in many cases eliminate—the niggling "what if's" that I tend to get bogged down in, and she has the ability to focus with laser-like precision on the essentials.

Besides being a brilliant planner, Rachel is also my source for pharmaceuticals whenever I need something to subdue a target. I have no idea where she gets the drugs; I've never asked and I never will. I will tell you that her day job is nothing healthcare-related, so I know that's not her source. Beyond that, I'm clueless. And that's okay.

After listening to her message about wanting to meet for deck beers that Thursday evening, I called her back on her personal cell. She answered on the second ring. "Hey you," she said, sounding atypically non-committal.

"Hey you," I replied. "Got your message about possibly getting together tonight for deck beers. Believe it or not, I had a message from Daryl just before yours, saying she wasn't feeling well and canceling our dinner date. So yeah, we can do deck beers if you'd like."

There was a momentary pause before Rachel answered

and I wondered if something in her workplace had distracted her. Then she answered in a tone that sounded almost business-like. "Yes, let's do that," she said. "Seven-thirty okay?"

"That'll work," I said. "See you then."

"See you then," she echoed.

I hung up wondering at her curiously unemotional tone. I told myself it was my imagination, that she was probably just preoccupied with some work matter.

RACHEL ARRIVED PROMPTLY at seven-thirty, accompanied by Alexander the Great, her huge, handsome Saint Bernard. They had walked from home, which was just a few blocks away. "Hey Alex," I said as I opened the gate across the driveway. He responded with a wave of his plumed tail as they walked through and I closed the gate behind them.

We rounded the corner of the house and headed toward the deck. Before mounting the steps Rachel leaned over and unsnapped Alex's leash. He trotted out into the back yard to mark one of the huge soft maples. From inside the kitchen Preacher barked, letting us know she wanted to join the party.

Rachel and I climbed the three steps to the deck. I waved toward one of the Adirondack chairs and said, "Have a seat and I'll let Preacher out and grab us a couple beers."

I couldn't help thinking Rachel's smile looked rather wan as she said, "Thanks." Something definitely seemed to be troubling her.

I opened the door and stood aside as Preacher rushed out to greet Alexander. She didn't bother with the deck steps—she seldom does—but launched off the edge of the deck and hit the ground running. She met Alexander halfway across the back yard and they went through the usual sniffing and getting reacquainted routine, accompanied by plenty of tail wagging. Because of her coquettish behavior around him, I've long suspected Preacher has a crush on Alexander. There's no question he's a magnificent beast.

I stepped into the kitchen, opened the fridge and snagged two bottles of beer, a Miller 64 for Rachel and a Blue

Moon for myself. I uncapped them and headed back out to the deck.

I handed Rachel her 64 and she thanked me. She was wearing gray gym shorts and a black V-neck t-shirt and I noticed as I sat down opposite her that she was still wearing her black Chuck Taylors. This was a little unusual—it was a warmish evening and ordinarily the first thing Rachel did upon sitting down for deck beers was slip off her shoes. That she hadn't done so suggested she was awfully preoccupied and/or she was feeling defensive about something, not willing to expose any more of herself than necessary.

I raised my bottle of Blue Moon in a halfhearted toasting gesture and smiled in an attempt to put her at ease.

"What's Al doing this evening?" I asked, hoping to get the conversational ball rolling.

"Oh, he's at the Eagles watching a race with some of his buddies."

I knew Al was a big-time NASCAR fan. I nodded and said, "Cool." It was a little lame but the best I could come up with. I noticed Rachel fidgeting in her chair, rotating her bottle of 64 in her hands. Then she raised it and took a long pull.

I decided to press the issue. "In your message this morning you said you had something you needed to share." I gave it a moment then added, "What's up?"

She gave me a long searching look. Then she looked out at the back yard where Alexander and Preacher were frolicking. After a moment she looked back at me and I thought I saw the glint of tears in her eyes. Rachel is not a crier by nature except under the most extreme circumstances and I immediately knew something bad, really bad, was in the offing.

"Just tell me," I said softly. I fervently hoped there hadn't been a tragedy in her family, or that she and Al had had a serious falling out.

She shook her head. "I'm not sure how," she said.

I took a deep breath. "Take your time," I said. "Come at it any way you want."

She drew a deep breath also. "Okay," she said. She

held up her cell phone and I could see an image on the lighted screen but couldn't make out the details. Then she dropped the phone again like she was having second thoughts about letting me see whatever it was.

She drew another deep breath. "Okay," she said again. "Al and I had dinner at Biaggi's last night." She paused, then added, "We saw someone we recognized."

"Okay," I said, mystified.

She held up the phone again. "I got several pictures."

"Who was it?" I asked, wondering who they possibly could have seen that would leave Rachel so shaken.

She didn't answer. Instead, she shook her head like she regretted what she was about to do. Then she handed me her phone so I could see the image.

Chapter 5

I had to take off my glasses to see the image in detail. That's something I now have to do whenever I want to be able to focus on something up close, whether it's read a book, work at the computer, sign a charge receipt at a restaurant, whatever. Yes, I'm a candidate for bifocals but so far I've resisted, probably because I don't want to give in to yet one more sign of aging.

I laid my glasses on the small wooden table next to our chairs and took Rachel's phone.

The photo showed a couple sitting in a booth at Biaggi's. I've eaten there plenty of times myself, often with Daryl, and I immediately recognized the décor. The photo had been taken at an angle from maybe twenty feet away, most likely from another booth across the aisle, and I also immediately recognized both people in the photo.

The man was Craig Wilkinson, the husband of Hannah Wilkinson, the woman I had found drowned at Maffitt Reservoir the previous summer and whose death I had later avenged. He was facing the camera and smiling across the table at the woman who was his dinner companion.

The woman was Daryl Nelson.

Daryl was facing away from the camera but her face was in three-quarter profile. There was no mistaking her strong jawline that always made me think of actress Marcia Gay Harden, nor the dark bobbed Kris Jenner-style haircut she had begun wearing several months earlier…right around the time I was in the middle of the whole Hannah Wilkinson business, in fact.

I stared hard at the photo, taking in all the details.

Wilkinson was wearing a navy suit with a white shirt and a tie with red and blue stripes. Some of his lawyer garb, no doubt. Daryl was wearing a sundress that I immediately recognized because it was one of my favorites, a bright aqua floral design on a black background.

They were sharing a bottle of wine, most likely chardonnay, Daryl's favorite. I couldn't identify their entrees but guessed Daryl had probably ordered steak de burgo, her usual choice at Biaggi's. Daryl's right arm, closest in the photo, was stretched out across the tabletop and the man's left arm was outstretched also. They were clasping hands.

This was obviously more than a professional meeting.

My mind reeled at what I was seeing but Rachel's voice got through to me.

"Rob, I'm so sorry," she said, and I heard a break in her voice.

I nodded. I didn't trust myself to speak. Then I used a forefinger to swipe across the screen, right to left, to scroll to the next image.

It was similar to the first but they were no longer holding hands. Daryl had picked up her fork and the man was using his knife and fork to cut something on his plate. He was still smiling, obviously happy with the way the evening was proceeding.

I scrolled again. The third photo was similar to the second, with both of them eating and obviously enjoying themselves. In the fourth photo, which must have been shot a little later, they were sharing a crème brulee dessert. They were both smiling, and they both had their spoons in the bowl at the same time.

Rachel had done a good job of documenting Daryl's betrayal.

I couldn't think of it as anything else. The photos spoke for themselves. I blew out a harsh breath and shook my head. Rachel leaned forward and reached over to put her hand on my knee. She squeezed gently and said, "Rob, I'm really, really sorry. But I thought you should know."

I nodded. I still didn't trust myself to speak. And it would have been difficult to say anything anyway, given the large, painful lump in my throat.

I set Rachel's phone on the table, face down. Rachel removed her hand from my knee and leaned back. I looked up at her. She wiped her hand across her eyes and said, "I hate being the one to tell you this." She looked down at her phone and shook her head. "Or show you."

I took a deep breath. "No, that's okay," I said, my voice coming out in something of a croak. "I appreciate you letting me know." Another deep breath. "Knowing is always better than not knowing."

Rachel nodded. "That's what I thought too," she said.

"I take it Daryl never saw you?"

"No, they were already there when Al and I came in. Our booth was across the aisle and a couple back from theirs. She never turned and looked back in our direction. I recognized her by her haircut. And the man was focused on her; he never looked over at us. Or at least, never more than a glance. He didn't notice me shooting the pictures. And we left before they did."

In spite of myself, I couldn't keep from smiling slightly. "Good detective work," I said.

A wan smile from Rachel. "Thanks."

We sat in silence for a minute or so. I picked up my Blue Moon and managed to take a swallow. Rachel did the same with her Miller 64. She set the bottle back on the table and then said quietly, "There's more."

"More?"

She nodded. "But I'm not sure you'll want to hear this."

"It's okay," I said. I couldn't imagine what could be worse than what I had already learned.

"This was Al's idea," Rachel said, and I wondered if she was somehow trying to deflect from what she was about to tell me. I decided she wasn't; Rachel was not one to shirk or attempt to shift responsibility.

I nodded. "Go ahead."

Rachel leaned forward again. "Okay," she said. "We got out to the truck and Al said, 'Let's see if Daryl's car is here.' So we drove around the parking lot until we found her blue Corolla."

"Okay," I said again, beginning to suspect where this might be going.

"We parked a little ways down from her car and waited. About ten minutes later they came out of the restaurant and started walking toward her car. They were walking really close to each other. She was kind of hanging on his arm."

I blew out another sharp breath. I was thinking of the many times Daryl and I had walked across a parking lot in the same manner.

Rachel said with a trace of alarm, "Are you sure you want to hear this?"

"Yes," I said.

She sighed. "We watched as they walked up to her car. When they got there…" she hesitated and I thought I saw her shudder slightly. Then she added, "Let's just say they parted with more than a handshake."

I nodded. I had already guessed this was what was coming. And again, I couldn't help likening it to the many times Daryl and I had parted in similar fashion, beginning with our first dinner date at Skip's.

"Then what?" I asked after a moment.

"Then she got in her car. He leaned in to give her one last kiss, then he walked over to his car parked a few spaces away."

"Let me guess," I said. "A white Cadillac Escalade."

There was no mistaking Rachel's surprise. "That's right," she said. "How did you know that? Do you know this guy?"

"Oh yeah," I said. "I know this guy."

Chapter 6

"How do you know him?"

"His name is Craig Wilkinson." I gave it a moment for the name to register with Rachel, and not surprisingly, it did, almost immediately.

"Ah," she said. "He was Hannah Wilkinson's husband." She said it with certainty, not asking.

"That's right," I said. "I first met him the same day I found Hannah's body. He and his daughter came by my house that afternoon to pick up Maisie, their golden retriever. I brought her home from the lake that morning so she wouldn't be impounded."

"Ah," Rachel said again. She smiled. "That was nice of you."

I nodded. "That's how I know what kind of vehicle he drives. He called me a few days later to ask me to be a pallbearer at Hannah's funeral. I saw him at the funeral, and that was the last time. But I saw Jessica several times later at the lake. You know all about that."

"Right."

We sat in silence for a minute or two. Then Rachel asked, "What are you going to do?"

Damn good question.

I gave it a moment's thought then answered honestly. "I'm not sure," I said.

She gave me one of her long searching looks, trying to fathom what I might be thinking. Then she said, "Rob, please don't do anything crazy."

I couldn't help laughing. Well, a little, anyway. "Crazy?" I said. "Me?"

Rachel didn't laugh. "You know what I mean," she said.

Yes, I knew what she meant. And her concern was justified. Rachel knew me better than just about anyone; knew my long history as a contract killer. She couldn't be faulted for wondering if I might already be thinking of exacting revenge on Craig Wilkinson, or Daryl, or both.

I shook my head. "No, I'm not going to do anything crazy," I said. "I'm not that stupid." Even as I said it, I hoped it was true. I also hoped Rachel believed me.

Rachel was continuing to stare at me, probably trying to determine if she could trust what I had just said. Finally she shook her head and said, "This is just unbelievable. After everything you went through last summer after finding Hannah's body…what are the odds that Daryl would connect with her husband?"

"Something beyond astronomical," I said. "But it's one more example of that old saying, that Des Moines is just a large small town."

"Right."

We sat silently for a couple minutes, taking an occasional drink of our beers. Preacher and Alexander climbed the steps to the deck and sprawled in front of us. My mind was still reeling as I tried to assimilate everything I'd just learned, but I also felt curiously numb.

I shook my head again and sighed heavily. "Thank you for letting me know. Like I said, knowing is always better than not knowing. No one likes to be played for a fool."

Rachel nodded. "That's right. And that's why I thought I had to tell you." She stretched her legs out and toed off her Chuck Taylors without untying the laces. I guessed that she probably felt more at ease now that the bad news was on the table.

"I appreciate that you did," I said. "As for what I'm going to do about it…I guess I'll start by talking to Daryl." I sighed again. "I'll try not to lose my cool; just let her know that I know and then see what she says."

"She'll probably try to deny it."

I nodded. "You're right; she might. If she does, what do you suggest?" I really didn't want to cite Rachel and Al as my source, but I wondered if there was any way to avoid doing so.

Rachel eased my concern. "I'm okay with you telling

her that we saw her," she said.

"Really?"

"Yes, really. Knowing what I know now, I don't care what she thinks of me. Or of Al. If you need to tell her that we're the ones who caught her, go ahead." She hesitated, then added, "I can even send the pictures to your phone if you want. She'd have a hard time denying anything if you show her those pictures."

Call me vindictive but I couldn't suppress a smile at the thought of confronting Daryl with the photographic evidence and watching her squirm. I gave it a moment's consideration then shook my head. "No, that's okay," I said. "I don't want those images on my phone. If I tell her you and Al saw her, that should be enough to convince her that she's been caught."

Rachel nodded. "Yes, that should do it. But she's probably also going to be pissed. She won't like the idea that she's been found out. That's definitely going to put her on the defensive, and she'll be angry."

"BFD," I said. "She may be angry, but I'll be angrier. And with good reason."

"That's understandable but just promise me—*promise me*—you won't lose your cool."

"I promise."

Another long look from Rachel, then we both picked up our beers and finished them.

"Ready for another?" I asked.

"Yes," Rachel said.

I picked up our empties and stepped back into the kitchen.

RACHEL STAYED FOR ANOTHER HOUR, during which we killed two more beers apiece. We didn't say a lot during that time, but I couldn't help thinking Rachel was watching me to make sure I was going to be okay. It was about 9:00 and almost dark when she set her empty 64 bottle on the table and said, "I probably should get going."

"Are you okay to walk home? I can drive you if you'd

like." Even as I spoke I wondered if Alexander would fit in the cargo space of my Equinox on Preacher's thick dog pillow. I guessed he would, but it would be tight.

"I'm okay to walk," Rachel said. She bent over and untied her shoelaces and slipped her shoes on. "In fact, it will do me good." She looked up and smiled as she retied the laces. "And Alex will protect me."

"I'm sure he will," I said.

Rachel finished and stood up. She picked up Alexander's lead and said, "C'mon, Alex, time to go home." He stood up and stretched and Rachel snapped the lead to his collar. "Thanks for the beers," she said.

"You're welcome. And…thank you again. For everything."

"I'm sorry it was such bad news."

I nodded. Rachel leaned toward me and gave me a one-armed hug while she held Alexander's lead with her other hand. "Are you sure you'll be all right?" she asked.

"I'll be fine," I said. "Please text me and let me know you're home."

"Will do."

We walked down the deck steps and I opened the driveway gate. Rachel and Alexander walked through and I closed the gate behind them. Rachel turned back toward me with another wan smile. "Bye," she said.

"Bye," I said.

I watched them walk down my driveway, the streetlight directly across the street causing them to cast long shadows behind them. As they turned toward home, a thought suddenly occurred to me.

Thank God I had never told Daryl about the killing.

Chapter 7

I'M SURE I DON'T HAVE TO TELL YOU that I spent a sleepless night after Rachel departed and I eventually turned in.

As she had promised, Rachel texted me when she and Alexander got home. Her text read: "Home safely. Again, very sorry for the bad news. Please take care and let me know if you need ANYTHING." She ended the message with a hugging emoji.

I replied, "Glad you're home. Thanks again for letting me know about Daryl. I'll be okay." I couldn't think of anything else to say, so I sent the text then logged off and turned off my phone, wondering if I would, in fact, be okay.

I put the phone on the charger, then I sat down at the kitchen table and sat in silence for the next hour while my mind attempted to come to grips with what I had learned.

The sense of betrayal was overwhelming. The woman I had always believed to be a straight shooter had turned out to be anything but. That alone felt like a sledgehammer to the gut, but compounding the feeling of betrayal was the realization that I had been duped. As I'd said to Rachel, no one likes to be played for a fool, but that was what Daryl had done. God only knew how long she had successfully kept me in the dark while she happily carried on with another man.

Another man. The husband of the woman whose body I had found and whose death I had avenged. Christ. As the old saying goes, you couldn't make this stuff up.

I wondered about the timing. I recalled one of the last conversations I had with Hannah Wilkinson before her death. We had run into each other at Maffitt Reservoir and walked our dogs together, and she confided that she was going through a divorce and suspected her husband was having an affair.

Was Daryl the other woman?

I had no way of knowing—and would quite possibly

never find out—how long Daryl had been involved with Craig Wilkinson. I thought back over those times Daryl had canceled a get-together with me, claiming an upset stomach, a headache, a looming deadline, an event she had to cover for the *Register*. And I, willing to give her the benefit of the doubt and never suspecting any duplicity, had blithely accepted her excuses.

What a fucking idiot.

And yet…

Living in a constant state of suspicion, of constantly doubting and questioning your partner, was no way to build and maintain a relationship. (I couldn't help thinking of that Terry Stafford song, "Suspicion"…yes, I was old enough to remember when it was a hit.) Relationships are built on trust and sharing, not on secrets and doubt. Nurturing that trust was the responsibility of both parties. I had believed Daryl and I were equally committed to that objective.

Which, I suddenly realized, made me the world's biggest hypocrite.

That realization whacked me upside the head as I sat at the kitchen table trying to make sense of everything I had just learned. Daryl had betrayed me, yes, but wasn't I equally guilty of betraying her trust by keeping a critical part of my life—the killing part—a secret?

Which was the bigger sin?

AT A FEW MINUTES AFTER TEN Preacher barked softly at the back door, asking to be let inside. I'd actually forgotten she was still outside and I stood up guiltily. I crossed the kitchen to the back door and let her in. She walked over to the counter where the box of Milk Bone dog biscuits were kept and stood there expectantly, wagging her docked tail. I opened the box and handed her a biscuit. She crunched it down noisily then trotted out to the living room and jumped up onto the sofa, settling in for the night.

I mechanically started going through my usual bedtime routine, rinsing out the coffee pot and filter basket and upending them in the strainer in the kitchen sink. I considered having a nightcap—something stronger than a beer—but decided against it. I was still feeling the effect of the three beers I had had with Rachel, and going to bed drunk after learning of Daryl's infidelity seemed awfully cliché.

I also realized that regardless of how much I drank, I probably wasn't going to sleep. My brain was in overdrive and I knew it would probably remain so for most of the night. Hundreds of questions and scenarios were already coming to mind and I knew there would be no shutting them out.

Foremost among those scenarios were the ones involving intimacy between Daryl and Wilkinson. I couldn't block the images that my mind kept conjuring up. It was the ultimate exercise in self-inflicted mental torture.

Nor could I stop speculating about the details of the affair. How had they met? How long had they been involved, and when exactly had it begun? (I realized these were two variations of the same question.) How often did they get together and hook up? Did Wilkinson know that Daryl was also involved with me or had she somehow managed to keep that from him?

The last question sent my mind off in another direction, and I almost welcomed the distraction, such as it was. Daryl knew nothing of my killing Greg Fletcher. But she did know the details of Hannah Wilkinson's death, that I was the one who had found Hannah's body and had been questioned by the police initially, that Hannah's daughter Jessica had become convinced Fletcher had killed her mother, and so on. We had discussed this several times and—yet another ironic coincidence—had, by chance, even had dinner a couple times with a DMPD detective named Madeline Madison and her romantic partner, a personal trainer named Beth Palmer. Madison was one of the detectives who had questioned me the morning I found Hannah's body.

Given all of this, I couldn't help wondering whether Daryl had ever mentioned me to Craig Wilkinson, and if so, exactly what she had told him. "Oh, by the way, Craig, I'm also sleeping with the guy who found your wife's body floating in the reservoir. Hope that's not a problem for you."

Unlikely, that.

I MIGHT HAVE DOZED a time or two during the night, but if so, it was only briefly. Mostly what I remember from that night was the endless parade of images moving through my mind, almost like a video loop stuck on play. That and checking the large illuminated green numbers on the digital clock that sits atop the low dresser opposite the foot of my bed. I tried to keep my eyes closed but still found myself looking at the clock every few minutes.

At just past 5:30 Preacher came into the bedroom and whined, letting me know she needed to go outside. I was already awake so getting up was no problem…in fact, I welcomed the excuse to get out of bed. We walked out to the kitchen and I let Preacher outside, then I started a pot of coffee. The lack of sleep had me moving on autopilot and I knew the day ahead was going to be a very damn long one.

While the coffee was brewing I turned on the television in the living room to catch the weather. The predicted high for the day was 82 degrees and there was no rain in the forecast. As soon as it began to get light, Preacher and I would head out to the lake for our early morning ramble. It's something we do every day unless there's a sluicing downpour, and I hoped the exercise would help banish some of the thoughts and images still lingering from my sleepless night.

Fat chance.

Chapter 8

A FORMER COLLEAGUE HAD A FAVORITE expression he repeated whenever he caught a break: *Once in a while, you get plain old dumbass lucky.*

It means, of course, that every so often, through no effort of your own, fortune smiles on you in a big, unexpected and (quite possibly) undeserved way.

On the morning after I learned of Daryl's betrayal, I got dumbass lucky not once, but twice.

It was barely daylight when Preacher and I left the house to drive out to Maffitt Reservoir, some ten miles southwest of the city. I hoped that by getting out to the lake extra early we would miss any of the other regulars, those folks who, like us, started their day with a walk at Maffitt.

Some of these people had dogs, and Preacher and I were known to all of them just as they were known to us. I didn't know the last names of many of these folks, nor did they know mine, but we knew each other's first names—and the names of our respective dogs—and we always exchanged greetings and occasionally stopped to visit for a few minutes. It made for a pleasant start to the day.

But this morning I was in no mood to visit with anyone. And that's where I caught my first break, or got dumbass lucky, so to speak. I didn't run into any of the other Maffitt regulars.

Not even Tim Sullivan, the fellow we had nicknamed the Mayor of Maffitt. Tim is a retired short-order cook, a few years older than me, and he walks at Maffitt every day, rain or shine or sub-freezing temperatures. Only on the very bitterest days—say, in January or February when it's below zero with a minus-twenty windchill—does he fail to venture out.

Tim always has a cheery word for everyone, and he's usually happy to stop and chat for a few minutes on a variety of subjects, including any wildlife he's recently seen or any improvements and other work being done on the reservoir property. He often stops to talk to the Des Moines Water Works employees and grounds people he encounters, so he's probably the best informed of all of us regulars, at least in terms of what's going on at the reservoir.

I didn't see Tim's truck, an older red Ford Ranger, parked in its usual spot when I drove across the dam at the north end of the reservoir and turned into the west entrance. Since retirement Tim had been coming out to the lake later in the morning, no doubt enjoying the chance to sleep in after his many years of having to rise well before dawn to prepare for the breakfast rush.

I drove down the gravel roadway to the first parking turnout, maybe a quarter-mile from the gate. I pulled in and parked and killed the ignition, then got out and removed Preacher's ramp from the long box on the back seat of the Equinox. I unfolded the ramp and positioned it against the rear bumper. I opened the hatch cover and Preacher trotted down the ramp. This was a routine we'd been using for about two years now, after our veterinarian told me to stop letting Preacher jump in and out of the vehicle to reduce the stress on her joints.

I refolded the ramp and placed it atop Preacher's dog pillow in the cargo space. I closed the hatch, hit the button on my key fob to lock the vehicle, and we set off down the roadway. The morning was quickly gathering light and growing warmer. I planned to walk Preacher as far as the canoe launch, where she could splash around in the water to cool off. I hadn't bothered to bring along one of her retrieving dummies but figured I could probably find a stick to toss for her to fetch a few times so she could get in a little swimming as well.

We followed the roadway around to the canoe launch and Preacher immediately trotted down the gravel slope and waded out into the water, gulping some as she went. I poked around in the brush next to the gravel and came up with a stick about ten inches long and maybe an inch and a half in diameter. Perfect for playing fetch, which would keep my mind occupied—well, partly—with something other than

Daryl's infidelity. I was still struggling to keep the endless parade of images and questions at bay.

I lobbed the stick about twenty yards out into the water and Preacher marked the splash. She launched toward the stick, swimming powerfully. German wirehairs are considered a versatile sporting breed, expected to retrieve waterfowl as well as hunt and point upland birds, and Preacher was adept at both tasks. She wasn't quite as proficient in the water as a Labrador, but she was nevertheless a strong and enthusiastic swimmer.

Preacher grabbed the stick and turned to swim back to me. As she did, it occurred to me that we had been engaged in the same activity at this same spot when, almost a year earlier, Hannah Wilkinson's golden retriever, Maisie, had come running up to me carrying one of Hannah's athletic shoes. Maisie had subsequently led us back to the spot along the lakeshore where I found Hannah's body floating in the water, triggering the sequence of events that culminated in my killing Greg Fletcher.

I shook my head as I bent to take the stick from Preacher and lob it out into the water again. I couldn't help thinking that the chain of coincidences, the latest of which was Daryl's affair with Hannah's husband, was nothing less than incredible. Astonishing, even.

So what was to be done?

That was the question that kept coming to the forefront of my mind. My first knee-jerk reaction—that of wronged romantic partners everywhere—was to retaliate. Once the initial shock of learning about Daryl's infidelity subsided, I instinctively wanted to lash out and hurt the people who had hurt me. But, tempting though the impulse was, I knew I couldn't act on it.

First, I knew I couldn't bring myself to harm Daryl in any way. Confront her, yes. Put an end to any further association, yes. But physically harm her? I knew I couldn't do that; didn't even want to.

Craig Wilkinson was another matter.

Yes, there was a part of me—a big part—that wanted

to hurt him, wanted to inflict physical pain, or worse. It was an instinctive reaction, and I didn't try to deny it.

But I knew I couldn't do it for two reasons.

The first was simple self-preservation. While I had thirty years of experience in killing people and getting away with it—i.e., not leaving any incriminating evidence behind—I knew that if Craig Wilkinson met with a sudden and unexpected fate, or even a serious injury, I would be one of the first people, maybe *the* first person, the police would investigate.

I didn't know if Daryl would voluntarily dime me to the cops as a possible suspect, but it wouldn't take much digging to uncover her affair with Wilkinson and follow up accordingly. If they asked Daryl if she knew of anyone who might have a grudge against him, she would probably offer up my name… that is, if I had already confronted her and let her know that I knew of her affair. Which I was planning to do sooner rather than later.

For obvious reasons, I didn't want the police to investigate me or take too close a look at my life.

The second reason I couldn't harm Wilkinson was directly related to his daughter, Jessica. During the previous summer, despite our forty-five-year age difference, Jessica and I had become good friends while she attempted to gather evidence that her mother had been killed by Greg Fletcher. She had confided in me several times and had, in fact, eventually convinced me that Fletcher had murdered Hannah.

Killing Craig Wilkinson would deprive Jessica of her only surviving parent. I couldn't do that.

Nor could I inflict serious bodily harm on Wilkinson, however much I might want to. My friendship with Jessica simply wouldn't allow it. There had been enough trauma in her life the previous summer. I wasn't going to compound that trauma by injuring her father now.

Retaliation was off the table.

Chapter 9

WHEN WE GOT HOME FROM THE LAKE I fed Preacher her morning meal—I'm a firm believer in feeding my dog two smaller meals a day, rather than one large one, to reduce the risk of gastric torsion—then I headed back to my office and logged onto my computer. I checked my email for messages and found the usual assortment of promotional crap, everything from offers for senior life insurance to a new non-addictive sleep aid product. I couldn't help thinking I could have made good use of the latter the previous night.

There were also a couple of political jokes from a long-time friend and former co-worker named Marcia Thompson. The jokes put a smile on my face, but only briefly. I deleted the lot, then sat back in my chair and stared at the screen.

I was at a loss as to how to spend my day.

Some six or seven months earlier I would have had editing tasks to keep me busy, and I would have welcomed them. Now, I had nothing pressing upon which to focus.

So of course my brain resumed its mind-fucking exercise concerning Daryl's infidelity.

The big question that now kept coming to the fore was "Why?" Why had she become involved with Craig Wilkinson? Was it simply a matter of an undeniable mutual attraction they couldn't resist acting upon, or were there other underlying factors? I had believed Daryl and I were on solid footing and equally committed to our relationship. I'd had no sense there was any dissatisfaction on her part, nor had there been any on mine. We had seemed compatible in every respect. But even more than compatible, we were happy.

Or so I thought.

So why had she done what she had done?

I wrestled with this for maybe twenty minutes, shifting my gaze from the computer screen to the window at my side that looked out on my back yard. I didn't find any answers in either place.

I finally stood up and headed back out to the kitchen to nuke a mug of leftover coffee. Preacher was sleeping on the sofa in the living room as I walked through, but not in her comical roadkill pose.

Not even my big bristle-coated housemate could lift my spirits just now.

I HAD JUST RETURNED HOME after making a run to my bank to withdraw some cash for the weekend—yes, I'm one of those Baby Boomers who still uses cash for most purchases, and why are you not surprised—when my landline phone rang.

Caller ID told me it was Daryl.

"Hello there," I said, trying to keep my voice light and not betray what I was feeling.

"Hi there," she replied. "How's it going?" She sounded perfectly normal, but then, why wouldn't she? She had no idea that I knew of her affair.

"Not bad," I replied. "Just got home from the bank." I hesitated, then added, "How are you feeling?"

"Much better, thanks," she said. "I don't know what the problem was yesterday but I felt a lot better when I got up this morning. I think I'm still going to take it easy this evening, though; don't want to push my luck. But I wanted to know if you'd like to come up for dinner tomorrow night. I was thinking of making salmon."

My first inclination was to yell "Liar!" when she made the comment about taking it easy this evening. But instead I just said, "That sounds good, if you're sure you're up to it." As I spoke, I thought, *here's the opening you were looking for. You just got dumbass lucky…again.*

"I'll see how I feel in the morning and call you if anything changes," Daryl said. "But otherwise, let's plan on it. Say, around 6:30."

"Okay, sounds good," I repeated.

"All right then. Talk to you later."

"Talk to you later."

I hung up wondering what she and Craig Wilkinson might have planned for tonight.

DARYL'S CALL CAME THROUGH at about 11:00. It was a little too early for lunch when we hung up but I was still at a loss as to what to do with myself for the rest of the day. I had mowed the lawn a couple days before so that didn't need to be done. I finally decided to wash the Equinox at the car wash on Southwest 9th Street. It offered both automatic drive-through lanes and DIY bays. I always opted for the latter, preferring to do the washing myself with a pressure wand.

As I was backing out of my driveway I had a sudden thought. Before his death, Greg Fletcher had lived just a few blocks away. (The fact that he was a neighbor of both Rachel James and myself had, in fact, figured into the plan we came up with for his demise.) I hadn't driven by his place for months and for some reason now I decided to do so.

His house, like most of the others on his street, was a ranch with a one-car attached garage. It was gray with white trim and a row of neatly trimmed juniper bushes along the front beneath a large picture window.

I remembered that Fletcher had driven a dark gray Dodge Durango. There were no vehicles in the driveway when I drove past, suggesting that whoever now owned the place was at work. I wondered if the house had been purchased by a single person or a family.

I shook my head as I headed on up the street toward County Line Road. What the hell had this little detour been about?

I had a sudden disquieting thought. Was Daryl's infidelity punishment for my killing Fletcher, and for all the other killings I'd done over the years? Was it also punishment for having kept this part of my life a secret? Was the pain I was now feeling from her betrayal—an aching, overwhelming hollowness—payback for having betrayed her trust?

I found myself remembering the last conversation I'd had with Jessica Wilkinson the previous summer. Shortly before she returned to UNI for the fall semester, we had run into each other at the reservoir and walked our dogs together. During our walk she had commented that she hadn't seen Greg Fletcher for quite a while. I had thought to myself, *and you won't*, knowing he was already dead.

Jessica had gone on to say she believed in karma and that even if she wouldn't see it happen, she was confident Fletcher would ultimately be punished for killing her mother. She didn't know, of course, that the punishment she was hoping for had already occurred. Nor did I tell her.

I did say, however, that I believed she was right.

That was as close as I came to telling her that Fletcher had already suffered the fate she was wishing upon him. I didn't elaborate, for obvious reasons, not the least of which was that informing her would have made her at least somewhat complicit.

It now occurred to me that over the years I had become, of necessity, very good at keeping a lot of people in the dark.

Once again, I wondered if the heartache I was experiencing because of Daryl's betrayal was payback for all of my secrecy and for all of the lives I'd taken. To be sure, I had always believed my targets deserved their fate. But…

Was this how karma worked? Did I deserve what I was now feeling?

Or in simplest terms, had I brought this pain on myself?

Hell if I knew.

Chapter 10

After washing the Equinox and stopping at the Subway in Stefon Plaza on Army Post Road for a six-inch ham and turkey breast sandwich—for which I had little appetite and could barely choke down—I came home and settled myself on the deck with John Sandford's latest "Prey" novel. A long afternoon stretched ahead of me and, restless though I was, I couldn't come up with any other physical activity to keep myself busy.

The temperature had climbed into the low 80s, just as predicted, and I considered taking Preacher back out to Maffitt Reservoir for another run. We could walk the shoreline so she could get into the water to cool down if necessary, but I decided against it. At the moment I was still feeling haunted by the previous summer's events at the reservoir, and I didn't want to trigger another round of speculation as to whether my role in those events might have somehow caused, or at least contributed to, Daryl's betrayal.

I made myself comfortable in one of the deck chairs and opened the novel.

And read no more than a page before my mind began to wander.

The same images and thoughts that had kept me awake most of the night began churning through my mind again. Try as I might to focus on something else—the book or anything else handy—I couldn't stop thinking about Daryl and Craig Wilkinson, how their affair had begun, how long it had been going on, and how Daryl had played me for a fool all the while.

I did, however, come up with one consoling thought.

Tomorrow evening I was going to turn the tables on her.

Eventually I dozed off sitting on the deck with the book open on my lap. That's probably not surprising, considering I had barely slept the night before, but I still felt a little sheepish when I woke up with a start some forty-five minutes later.

I glanced around guiltily, wondering if any of my neighbors had seen me. I told myself it didn't really matter if they had, that I needn't feel ashamed of falling asleep while sitting in the sun on my own backyard deck. I also had to admit that the nap had afforded me a measure of peace for a short while; I mercifully had been spared any further thoughts or dreams about Daryl and Wilkinson.

Now, however, those thoughts returned full force.

I slammed the book shut and glanced at my wristwatch. It was just past two o'clock and I decided another trip out to Maffitt was in order, after all. As I stood up I remembered a line from one of John D. MacDonald's Travis McGee novels, something to the effect that any depression could be cured if you could keep the person moving around enough.

I wondered if the same was true for heartache.

WE STAYED AT THE LAKE for nearly two hours.

I drove into the park on the east side of the lake and followed the winding paved roadway all the way around to one of the graveled turnouts down by the water. I pulled in and parked and got Preacher unloaded, then we headed down to the shoreline. A picnic table sat under several big oaks on the high bank above the water, and I took a seat at the table while Preacher found the pathway down to the sandy shore.

I sat on the bench closest to the water, facing outward toward the lake and leaning back with my legs outstretched and my elbows on the tabletop. There was very little breeze and the water was glassy smooth. I saw a couple of kayakers near the center of the lake and a family of Canada geese, the parents and eight half-grown goslings, resting maybe thirty yards out from shore.

I let my gaze move across the water to the opposite shoreline, maybe a half-mile distant. Along the shoreline beneath a grove of pine trees I could just make out a large, tan granite boulder.

It was near this boulder that I had found Hannah Wilkinson's body floating in the water nearly a year ago.

I sighed at the recollection. What a chain of events that discovery had unleashed. Events that now seemed still to be ongoing. I turned my thoughts to tomorrow evening's dinner with Daryl.

I wondered if she had any intention of telling me anytime soon about her affair with Wilkinson, or if she was just hoping to keep it under wraps and continue to play me indefinitely. I also wondered—this was the big question— how I was going to broach the subject.

I fully intended to do so at some point. Before the evening ended, I vowed she was going to know that I knew of her infidelity.

I pondered this for some time, rehearsing various lines in my mind. I admitted to myself that I wanted to shock her with the revelation and then try to keep her off balance as I followed up, hoping to get answers to at least some of my questions.

One of my favorite authors is Joe R. Lansdale. I'm a big fan of his novels featuring Hap Collins and Leonard Pine, two roughneck good ol' boys in East Texas, and I smiled as I recalled the title of a recent book in the series, *The Elephant of Surprise*. I loved the play on words, and that's what I was hoping to take advantage of tomorrow evening when I confronted Daryl—an elephant-sized surprise.

At the same time, I also hoped I could keep a cool head and not lash out recklessly. I didn't want my anger—and there was certainly plenty of that, along with my pain—to get the best of me. I wasn't worried about hurting Daryl, at least not physically, but I didn't want to lose control and start raving at her, either. The cooler and more detached I could remain, the better.

I took a deep breath and watched as Preacher prowled the shoreline below me. She spotted the goose family and waded a few yards out into the water toward them. But then she stopped and stood belly-deep in the water, studying the geese but not advancing any further. She let out a soft "woof" but the geese were unimpressed and made no effort to swim away. After another moment Preacher turned and waded back to the shore, apparently deciding they weren't worth pursuing.

Interesting standoff.

I looked out across the water again. The kayakers were paddling toward the south end of the lake. Preacher climbed back up to the bank and trotted over to lie down in the grass next to me at the picnic table. I glanced at my watch and saw it was 3:15. I could feel another round of drowsiness coming on, and I welcomed it.

My chin dropped to my chest and I dozed off again.

WE LEFT THE LAKE at a couple minutes after four. Driving home on the bypass that skirts the south side of Des Moines, I thought about what I was going to do for dinner. I still had very little appetite and I was in no mood to cook anything. But spending the evening at home with nothing but my thoughts to keep me company—okay, Preacher would be there, but she wasn't much of a conversationalist—held little appeal, either.

I thought of Skip's or Johnny's Italian Steakhouse, both of which were on Fleur Drive and only a few minutes from my house, but there was one big problem. They were favorites of Daryl's and mine, and we were well known in both places. If I showed up by myself it wasn't unlikely that a server or bartender would ask me where my partner was. I didn't want to have to field that question, and I certainly had no intention of getting into any kind of explanation…at least, not yet. Nor was I going to make excuses on Daryl's behalf.

I gave it a little thought and finally decided on Charlie's Barbecue in West Des Moines. Daryl was not a big fan of southern barbecue—one of the few things on which we had agreed to disagree—and we had been there only a couple times together. On the other hand, I was a regular so no one would think it unusual when I came in alone. I often had dinner there by myself—I always sat at the bar—before heading over to Half Price Books, a couple miles west of the restaurant on University Avenue.

Besides the restaurant's proximity to the bookstore, there was another reason for my patronage.

The manager was a tall, good-looking brunette named Anita. She was in her early forties and often tended bar, so over the course of several years and numerous conversations we had become friends. She always greeted me with a hug when I arrived and gave me another when I was leaving.

Anita possessed a smart mouth—make that a *very* smart mouth—and more than a modicum of snark. At the same time, she was a sympathetic listener and wouldn't hesitate to offer her insight on any issue I might raise. While I wasn't ready to share the story of Daryl's infidelity with her just yet (and maybe never), I thought some banter with Anita might give my spirits the boost they so sorely needed.

Then maybe, just maybe, I would have better luck sleeping tonight.

Chapter 11

DINNER AT CHARLIE'S BARBECUE DID indeed lighten my mood, at least temporarily.

When we got home from the lake I fed Preacher her evening meal then took a quick shower and put on a clean pair of khaki cargo shorts and a steel-blue polo shirt. I left the house at a few minutes after 5:30 for the drive out to West Des Moines and I walked into the restaurant about twenty minutes later.

Anita came around from behind the bar and greeted me with her customary hug. I took my usual seat at the end of the bar nearest the door and she returned to her position behind the bar. There was one other customer sitting at the bar a few stools away, a guy about my age wearing a Hawkeye t-shirt, shorts and a Chicago Cubs baseball cap.

Anita leaned her elbows on the bar top and asked, "What's new?"

I smiled and said, "SSDD." Not the most original response, admittedly, but about the best I could come up with under the circumstances.

She smiled and said, "I know the feeling. What are you drinking?"

"Blue Moon."

"Short or tall?"

"Tall."

I watched Anita draw the beer and add a thick orange slice to the rim of the tall glass. She set it down in front of me. I took a long pull, then I set the glass down and plucked the orange slice off the rim. I squeezed its juice into the beer, then I dropped the slice into the glass. I remembered reading somewhere that you shouldn't do that because there was no telling what nasty things might be lurking on the skin of the orange, but I was feeling reckless.

Anita asked me if I needed a menu and I said no, that I already knew what I wanted. I ordered one of my favorite entrees, a combo platter of catfish fingers (yes, that's what they're called; they're deep-fried, finger-sized strips of catfish) with fries, coleslaw and a corn muffin.

I still didn't have much of an appetite but just being out of my house and among people was helping me put my thoughts about Daryl and Craig Wilkinson on hold. I figured I would eat what I could and take the rest home with me. If I didn't eat the leftovers for lunch tomorrow, I'd leave them out at the lake the following day for the raccoons and possums. Conservationists and biologists discourage feeding wildlife like that, but I doubted I would upset the natural order too badly with my transgression.

I took another pull of my Blue Moon and caught Anita studying me and wearing a slight frown. I smiled and said, "What?"

She said, "Something's troubling you. I can see it all over your face."

So much for keeping my heartache hidden.

I GAVE ANITA A VERY abbreviated version, saying only that a major rift had developed between Daryl and me and that it was unlikely our relationship would recover. I told her it was something that had happened just recently but I did not go into any of the details about Craig Wilkinson or even mention that there was a third party involved. Anita nodded thoughtfully as I was talking and I had the distinct (and uneasy) feeling that she was filling in the blanks on her own and doing so accurately.

But to her credit, she didn't probe for details.

My catfish fingers combo platter was delivered and provided a welcome diversion from our conversation. Anita left her station behind the bar and went off to handle a complaint made by some unhappy customers and I began eating, hoping that when she returned we could talk about something besides my love life.

I was about halfway through my catfish fingers when Anita returned, shaking her head and muttering, "Some people."

"Did you get everything straightened out?"

"Yes, although I was tempted to tell them to go fuck themselves." Anita was not above dropping the occasional f-bomb and I could commiserate. When I was still editing the magazine I'd been similarly tempted when I took the occasional phone call from an irate reader who was usually upset about something misread or inconsequential. "*Really* tempted," she added.

I laughed. "You're a paragon of restraint," I said.

She rolled her eyes. "Oh yeah, right. Restraint is my middle name."

"I've always wondered what the R stood for," I said, and we both laughed.

I LEFT CHARLIE'S carrying a takeout box with about half of my French fries and a couple of catfish fingers. It was a few minutes past seven o'clock and when I climbed into the Equinox and cranked the ignition I wondered what I was going to do with myself for the rest of the evening. I decided sitting on my deck with another beer and the John Sandford novel was about as good an option as any. There would be enough light to read for at least another hour.

As I pulled out of the parking lot I had a sudden disquieting thought. It occurred to me that by the time I got home it would be almost exactly twenty-four hours since Rachel James had sat on my deck and showed me the photos on her phone of Daryl and Craig Wilkinson.

That realization gave rise to another thought—or idea, rather—that was equally disquieting.

I considered driving past Daryl's house in Beaverdale to see if Craig Wilkinson's white Escalade was in the driveway.

I resolutely put the thought aside. Or tried to anyway.

I told myself I was not going to succumb to the temptation to become a stalker. I was not going to start cruising past Daryl's house hoping to find evidence of Wilkinson visiting her. Nor was I going to drive past Wilkinson's house in the River Oaks development west of

Maffitt Reservoir, looking for Daryl's blue Corolla.

I had stalked many targets over the years—and had done so successfully without getting caught—so I had plenty of experience, but this was a different matter entirely. I vowed I was not going to do any of the foolish things that spurned lovers so often do. Once again I reminded myself to keep a cool head and not allow myself to do anything rash.

I headed south on 22nd Street toward Ashworth Road. I would take Ashworth east to 63rd, then head south again toward Army Post Road and eventually my home in Greenfield Plaza on the far south side of Des Moines. I would bypass Beaverdale and would not turn west toward the reservoir and River Oaks.

Twenty minutes later I pulled into my driveway and sighed with relief for having stood firm on my no-stalking resolution.

The deck and another Blue Moon were calling my name.

Chapter 12

I ARRIVED AT DARYL'S HOUSE in Beaverdale at 6:30 Saturday evening with a bottle of her favorite chardonnay, Kendall Jackson, in hand.

Crazy, right?

Earlier I had considered showing up empty-handed, but that would have been somewhat unprecedented. I had almost always taken her a bottle of wine when she invited me to her house for dinner, and not doing so now might have raised a question in her mind. She would have been too polite to say anything, but I didn't want to give her any reason to suspect something was amiss. Of course, something most definitely was.

I figured the price of the KJ was inconsequential if that was what it took to keep her off guard—especially since this was the last time I would ever be buying a bottle for her. So call me a devious bastard.

Daryl gave me a big smile when she opened the door to greet me. She was wearing a black t-shirt, white shorts and black flip-flops, and God help me, I couldn't help thinking that she looked lovely in a summer-casual sort of way. She said "Hi!"

Even as I felt the knife twisting in my gut, I managed to smile when I handed her the wine. "Hi," I said in return. *How many times had she greeted Craig Wilkinson in a similar manner?*

She thanked me for the wine and turned to lead the way into the house. We usually ate in the kitchen rather than her dining room, and I was fine with that. "Something smells good," I said.

"Oh, thanks. We're having baked salmon with stir-fry veggies and rice pilaf. Hope that's okay."

"It sounds great." *Chill*, I kept telling myself.

Ivy, Daryl's golden tabby, greeted me with a loud meow. She had stationed herself near the oven, no doubt attracted by the smell of the salmon. From past experience I knew Daryl would give her a bite or two.

"There's Blue Moon in the fridge," Daryl said. "Help yourself. Oh, and there are frosted mugs in the freezer."

"Thanks," I said, crossing to the refrigerator and grabbing a bottle. I took a mug from the freezer and felt a sudden twinge at the realization that such amenities would soon be ending. I drew in a deep breath, uncapped the bottle and poured the beer into the mug.

Daryl already had a glass of wine sitting on the counter next to the stove. I lifted my mug toward her and said, "Cheers. And happy Saturday."

She picked up her glass and smiled as she clinked it lightly against my mug. "Happy Saturday," she said.

Could I have been any more duplicitous?

BEFORE HEADING UP TO DARYL'S I had spent most of the day trying to keep myself busy. After taking Preacher for our usual early morning run at the reservoir I mowed the lawn (although it hardly needed it) then trimmed some bushes and piled the trimmings in the fire ring in my back yard. After they had dried for a few days I would burn them; one of the advantages of living in Greenfield Plaza, just south of County Line Road, was that residents were not subject to many of the ordinances of the city proper and we could still burn branches and leaves.

While doing the yard work I let my mind wrestle with how the coming evening was going to play out and how I was going to raise the subject of Daryl's affair with Craig Wilkinson. I rehearsed a few lines, usually beginning with something like, "Oh, by the way…" followed by dropping the bombshell. I also tried to anticipate how Daryl was going to react and what she might say in response so I could have my own replies ready.

I also reminded myself that imaginary conversations almost never take place as planned, and that all of my speculation was just that—speculation and nothing more—and my rehearsed lines would probably be of little use.

After lunch I settled myself on the deck again with my John Sandford novel. I considered calling Rachel and inviting her over for a beer but decided against it. Her weekends were usually taken up with family matters; her daughter Summer lived in Johnston, just north of Des Moines, with her two sons, Gabe and Sam, and they often visited Rachel on Saturday. I didn't want to intrude on their get-together, much as I would have liked to get Rachel's input and advice on how to handle the evening's looming confrontation.

I gave up on the novel after twenty minutes. This was no fault of the author's; Sandford has long been one of my favorites and I've always enjoyed the escapades of Lucas Davenport and Virgil Flowers, but just as the day before, my mind kept wandering and I couldn't shake my restlessness. I finally decided to hell with it and went inside to rouse Preacher from her nap on the sofa.

Another trip to the reservoir was in order.

DARYL WAS A GOOD COOK and the baked salmon was excellent, moist and not overdone. But in spite of its flavor I had to struggle to eat it, finding it necessary to wash down almost every bite with another drink of Blue Moon. Ditto the stir-fry veggies and the rice pilaf.

If Daryl noticed, she didn't comment.

Our conversation followed its usual course. We took turns recapping our previous week's activities, which in my case consisted mostly of yard work, outings to the lake with Preacher and repainting the peeling frame of the side door of the garage. I had repainted the doorframe the previous summer as well but apparently I hadn't primed the wood sufficiently because the paint peeled again after a few months.

Ah, the exciting life of a retiree.

Daryl described a city council meeting she had attended and reported on for the *Register* but I had a hard time paying attention to what she was saying. My mind was racing ahead, knowing that our pleasant evening was about to be derailed in a major way, and I would be doing the derailing.

For one brief moment I considered saying nothing

about Daryl's infidelity and just continuing to play the clueless boyfriend.

Where this thought came from I couldn't say, aside from the natural aversion most of us feel toward confrontations. But I quickly put the thought aside, telling myself that the issue had to be faced, and the sooner the better. Feigning ignorance of her actions was nothing less than cowardice, I thought, and I needed to get the issue on the table if for no other reason than to salvage my self-respect. Or attempt to salvage it, anyway.

I looked up from my plate—I had just taken another forkful of salmon—to see Daryl studying me with an expression that combined curious with concerned.

"What?" I said.

"Is something bothering you, Rob? You look really upset about something," she said, and I immediately recalled Anita making a similar comment at Charlie's Barbecue the previous night. I was obviously doing a very poor job of masking my emotions.

I blew out a hard breath and laid my fork across my plate. "As a matter of fact, there is something bothering me," I said.

Daryl's expression softened and she said, "Tell me what it is."

I drew a deep breath, leaned back in my chair and squared my shoulders.

"So," I said, "how long have you been fucking Craig Wilkinson?"

Chapter 13

MY ELEPHANT-SIZED SURPRISE had the hoped-for effect.

You've heard references to the color draining from someone's face when that person experiences a shock. I saw it firsthand when I laid my crudely worded question on Daryl. Yes, the crudity was intended to add to the shock, and apparently it worked.

Daryl sat back in her chair almost as if she had taken a punch. (In case you're thinking otherwise, I kept my hands flat on the tabletop.) She drew a deep breath and her eyes widened. And within no more than a second or so, her face was almost chalk white.

"Well," I said. "How long?" I kept my voice level, not wanting to betray any anger. Or any emotion whatsoever, actually. Once again I reminded myself to keep a cool head.

Daryl drew another deep breath. "How did you find out about him?" she asked. Her voice sounded a bit unsteady, but I thought it was interesting that she hadn't tried to deny what I said. She had also avoided answering my question.

"You were seen," I said. I hesitated, then added, "And photographed."

The color began returning to her face. "What, you have people following me?" There was no mistaking the anger in her voice. Just as Rachel predicted, Daryl had immediately become defensive. Or gone on the attack, rather.

"Of course not," I said, now struggling to keep my own anger under control. "You were just careless. Next time you have dinner at Biaggi's, you might want to check your surroundings."

She blew out a harsh breath and looked away. She shook her head then looked back at me. Her face was now flushed. "So who saw me?" she asked, her voice only slightly less agitated.

I hesitated again, but I recalled Rachel's comment

about not caring if Daryl knew who had seen her and reported on her dalliance. And because this was going to be the last time I ever had dinner at Daryl's—I was determined to end our relationship tonight and cut off all further contact—I decided there was no reason to hold back.

"Rachel and Al," I said. "They had dinner at Biaggi's Wednesday night also."

"So naturally they shot pics of me and immediately ratted me out." Again, there was no mistaking the anger in her voice. "I don't believe this," she added disgustedly. "This town."

"What?" I said. "You're blaming the town because you got caught?" I didn't try to hide my sarcasm.

She didn't answer. She shook her head again and kept her eyes averted. After a moment she picked up her wineglass and took a drink. She set the glass down and faced me again.

"I can't believe they shot pictures," she said. "Let me guess. It was Rachel who shot the pictures."

I nodded but didn't otherwise confirm her accusation. "I saw the pictures and it was obvious this wasn't any kind of business or professional meeting," I said. "And that you and Wilkinson are more than just friends."

"Christ."

"I don't think He was involved."

She ignored my sarcasm and kept shaking her head. "I don't believe this."

I couldn't help smiling grimly. "You keep saying that. For what it's worth, I've had a hard time believing it also. But for different reasons."

She sighed deeply. "So now you know. What happens now?"

"Nothing happens now," I said.

"Nothing?"

"Nothing further between us, I mean," I said. "Our relationship ends right here, right now."

She sighed again. She said nothing for a minute or so, apparently gathering her thoughts. "I was going to tell you," she finally said, her voice much softer. "I just…wasn't ready."

"Oh? And when do you suppose you might have felt…ready?"

My mockery earned me a long direct look but she said nothing.

After another minute of silence I said, "You still haven't answered my question."

"What question?"

"How long have the two of you been involved?" This time I worded it a little more tactfully.

"What difference does that make?" On the defensive again, her voice rising.

I shrugged. "I guess it doesn't, really. Just curious is all. But I'm guessing this has been going on for a while, at least."

She sighed again. "About six months. We met right after the first of the year."

"Where did you meet?" I expected her to be evasive again but she wasn't.

"At a fundraiser for Representative Sorensen."

"Ah," I said. "And the two of you…what? Just clicked?"

"No, it wasn't like that. He approached me and we started talking. But we didn't exchange numbers or anything. Then he contacted me at the *Register* a couple days later. I told him I was already involved with someone but he was… persistent."

"So you eventually caved."

Another deep sigh. "I eventually agreed to meet him for lunch, yes."

"Boy, does that sound familiar."

"What can I say? My curiosity got the best of me."

"Your curiosity."

"Yes, my curiosity, all right? He was interesting. And fun to talk to. I won't deny it."

"And all the while you knew he was Hannah Wilkinson's husband. Her widower."

"What does that have to do with anything? I mean, beyond the fact that it was a crazy coincidence?"

"It was crazy, all right," I said. "I guess…I don't know." Now it was my turn to try to gather my thoughts, which seemed to be scattering in all directions. "Did you tell him? About me, I mean? About us?"

"Eventually I did, yes. And he couldn't believe the coincidence, either. Especially since you were the one who found Hannah."

I shook my head. "Wow." I couldn't think of anything else to say.

We sat in silence for another minute, then she said softly, "Rob, I'm sorry. I know that sounds lame, but I never meant to hurt you. Things just got out of hand. I never meant for that to happen."

I bristled at her last remark. "Of all the excuses, or rationalizations, that people come up with, that one is by far the lamest," I said. "And the most insulting."

"It's not just an excuse. It's true."

"No, it isn't true. You want to know why?"

"Why?" Humoring me, her exasperation obvious.

"Because at some point you made a choice. You said yes when you could have said no. Or at the very least, you went along with something when you could have turned away. At that point, you damned well meant for it to happen. So trying to pretend otherwise, like you had no say in the matter, is just bullshit." I knew I was letting my anger get the best of me, something I had vowed not to do, but I figured at this point there was no reason to hold back.

She considered what I said for a moment, then said angrily, "All right! Yes, I made a choice. So I guess you could say I meant for it to happen. But it wasn't something I went out looking for."

"Oh, that makes me feel so much better."

"What can I say? It happened. I can't change that. Should I have told you sooner? Yes. But even if you don't believe it, I still care about you. I didn't want to hurt you." She hesitated, then added, "And I was still enjoying our time together. I didn't want that to end. So call me selfish."

"Wow. I'll say."

"I'm sorry. I don't know what else to say. But I am really sorry."

I couldn't think of a reply that wasn't sarcastic or worse, so I said nothing.

We sat in silence for a minute or two. Beneath the table, Ivy meowed loudly and in spite of ourselves, we both laughed.

Daryl smiled wanly. "She doesn't like discord."

"Most of us don't." I wasn't going to be sidetracked by a noisy cat.

Daryl sighed and shook her head again. "Rob, I'm really sorry. I know I've already said that, but it's true. I am really, really sorry. I know I should have told you sooner. And I'm sorry that you found out…the way you did."

I nodded. "It was a shock, all right. I can't deny that."

"I'm sure it must have been."

I didn't reply. I wasn't going to be sidetracked by her attempt at empathy, either. I also realized that I probably had said everything that needed to be said. Prolonging the conversation would accomplish nothing, I thought.

After a moment I pushed away from the table and stood up. "I need to get going," I said.

Daryl stood up also and gave me another long, searching look. I could see her eyes filling with tears. "I'm really sorry," she said. "About everything."

I nodded. "So am I. About everything." The painful lump in my throat I'd felt when talking to Rachel a couple nights earlier had returned. I wanted to get the hell out of there before either one of us broke down completely.

Daryl looked down at the table. She picked up her napkin and used it to wipe her eyes. Then she made what struck me as the most inane remark imaginable, given the circumstances.

She pointed to my plate and said, "You didn't finish your salmon. Do you want to take it with you?"

"Give it to Ivy," I said, and I took myself out of there.

I WAS NO MORE THAN FIVE MINUTES from

Daryl's house, driving south on Beaver Avenue and coming up on Westminster Presbyterian Church, when I suddenly had to pull over. I swerved into the church's parking lot and shot across to the far side. I jammed the Equinox into park and jumped out, leaving the engine running as I headed for the thick row of bushes alongside the parking lot.

I barely made it to the bushes before bending over and vomiting. I stood with my hands on my knees for several long minutes, my head reeling. Then I managed to stand up and take a few deep breaths. I wiped my hand across my mouth and stepped back. I took another few steps and bent over again to wipe my hand in clean grass.

I returned to the Equinox and climbed in, thankful no one—especially any cops—had witnessed what I had just done. I sat for another minute, taking more deep breaths and trying to steady myself for the rest of the drive home.

I hoped God would forgive me for sullying the grounds of a place of worship.

PART TWO: DISTRACTION

If a fellow is spoiling for a fight, Fate is ever prone to send him one.

Albert Payson Terhune

Chapter 14

For the next week the reminders ate me alive.

There was no escaping them. Songs on the radio in the Equinox reminded me of Daryl. Just seeing the place she always sat on the sofa when we watched television—that is, if Preacher didn't happen to be sleeping there—reminded me of her. The pair of fuzzy slippers she kept in my bedroom for those times when she stayed overnight. The small collection of toiletries she kept in my bathroom closet. Even the wineglasses she drank from when I made her dinner.

No matter where I looked, indoors or outside, I saw items or places that reminded me of her.

I tried to remove as many of these reminders as I could. Obviously I wasn't going to get rid of the sofa or the wineglasses, but I did bag up the toiletries and the slippers. Curiously, however, I couldn't bring myself to dispose of them, at least not yet. Instead, I took the bag down to the basement and stashed it on a shelf in a far corner. I'm not sure why I did this, except that some small part of me just wasn't ready to completely let her go.

Pathetic, right?

But I did stand firm on another matter, and that was allowing no further contact.

Daryl called me three times during the week following our Saturday night confrontation. Each time I checked Caller ID before answering and didn't pick up when I saw she was the caller. She left a message each time, and they were all similar. She began with an apology, saying she was very sorry about everything and she hoped we could get together at least one more time so she could clarify a few things and perhaps part more amicably. She ended each call by asking me to please call her back, which I never did.

I wondered what the hell she thought she could clarify—the photos Rachel had shown me had spoken for themselves—or how any further discussion could lead to a more amicable parting. I saw the whole matter as a straight-forward case of Daryl cheating on me with Craig Wilkinson and getting caught. I couldn't imagine what Daryl could say that would change my feelings about that.

End of story.

ACCORDING TO A PHILOSOPHY PROFESSOR whose class I attended in college, the best way to deal with unwanted reminders of anything was not to try to suppress or ignore those reminders but simply acknowledge them and let them fade away on their own. He believed trying to suppress the reminders often had the opposite effect and served only to keep them at the forefront of our minds. Better to just roll with the punches, he advised, and eventually the reminders would diminish and ultimately disappear.

Sounds good in theory, but not so easy to put into practice, especially in the short term.

I kept myself busy with as much physical activity as I could. I took Preacher to the reservoir at least twice a day and sometimes three times—early morning, after lunch and again in the evening. Depending on how hot it was—this was Iowa in the summer, remember—we sometimes skipped the after-lunch or evening outing. But twice a day became our minimum, and of course Preacher was happy to go out to the lake as many times as I would take her.

When we weren't at the lake I did yard work and took care of any other household tasks that needed attention or I could dream up. And while thus physically occupied, I also engaged in my usual mental exercise of relentlessly analyzing everything I'd learned and everything Daryl had said, probing for additional answers or information I was unlikely to find.

I did come up with one answer, however, and that was based on Daryl's claim that she had been involved with Wilkinson for about six months; that they had met at a political fundraiser shortly after the first of the year. Assuming she was telling the truth—for some reason I was inclined to believe her, maybe because she hadn't had much time to fabricate her response—this told me that she wasn't the woman with whom Hannah Wilkinson had suspected her husband of having an affair.

Hannah had voiced this suspicion during one of our last walks together at the lake, shortly before her death. After Rachel showed me the photos of Daryl and Wilkinson, I remembered Hannah's comment and wondered if Daryl could have been the other woman. But given the chronology, I was now reasonably certain that woman couldn't have been Daryl, as she and Wilkinson hadn't met until months after Hannah's death.

Which told me what, exactly? That Wilkinson was something of a player, perhaps, and Daryl was just the latest in his string of conquests?

Even if I was correct about this, what good did knowing it do me? Or maybe more specifically, how could I use it to my advantage?

I had already determined I was not going to retaliate against Daryl or Wilkinson, at least not in any direct physical way. (Wilkinson would never know how lucky he was that I had established a friendship with his daughter, and that this friendship was serving as a buffer to keep him protected.) Still, I thought knowing Wilkinson might be a serial philanderer could eventually prove useful. I wasn't sure how just yet, but I felt it was a nugget of information worth tucking away.

In the meantime, one other thought kept recurring during all my mental gymnastics. It was the same thought I'd had the night Rachel had alerted me to Daryl's affair.

Thank God I had never told Daryl about the killing.

The guilt I'd felt previously over keeping that part of my life hidden from her was diminishing by the day.

ON FRIDAY, SIX DAYS after confronting Daryl, I made the rounds of my P.O. boxes. I hadn't done this in a little over a week—the last time was the Thursday when, later that evening, Rachel had shown me the pictures from Biaggi's— so the boxes were crammed full of the usual assortment of promotional junk that I immediately discarded.

That is, all except one item.

In the box I rent at the UPS store on Fleur Drive I found a regular white business envelope tucked in among all the ad fliers. The envelope was addressed to my LLC, and although the handwritten return address didn't include the sender's name, I was nevertheless reasonably sure I recognized the address in Schnock's Harbor, North Carolina.

If I was correct, this was something totally unprecedented. Unless I was mistaken, the letter was from a former client, one from four or five years earlier.

Never before had I received such a follow-up.

Chapter 15

I FISHED MY POCKETKNIFE OUT OF MY CARGO SHORTS as I crossed the parking lot from the UPS store to the Equinox. I opened the smaller blade and used it to slit open the envelope, then I closed the knife and dropped it back into my pocket. I climbed into the Equinox and after settling myself in the driver's seat I pulled out the letter and unfolded it.

It was a single sheet of standard white printer paper bearing just a few typewritten lines. The salutation simply said "Jim" in quotation marks, followed by a colon, and I couldn't help smiling. I was fairly certain the writer intended the quotation marks humorously or perhaps a bit sarcastically, an acknowledgment of the fact that Jim was not my real name, but only the one I had provided when we had conducted our previous business.

The message read: *If this is still a correct address and you still offer proofreading services, please contact me at the number below. You helped me four years ago and I hope you can do so again. If you received this message in error, simply discard it. I apologize for any inconvenience. Sincerely, Jane Trehorn.* The signature was handwritten and was followed by a phone number with a 910 area code.

I recognized the writer's name and I remembered completing an assignment for her some four years earlier. I smiled again at her reference to my having helped her. If you could call permanently eliminating a husband with a long history of violent physical abuse helping someone, then yes, I had helped her.

I wondered what kind of help she needed this time. Or more specifically, who the target might be.

Then I had another thought, this one far more disturbing. I wondered if perhaps this was a set-up, something to lure me in. If maybe her husband's death—a mugging gone wrong while he'd been jogging on the beach near their home late one evening—had been investigated more fully and the police had eventually zeroed in on his widow. Maybe they had traced the ten thousand dollars she had paid me and had promised her leniency in exchange for her assistance in nailing me.

I didn't know enough about the law to know whether this would constitute entrapment if I replied to her query and agreed to complete another similar assignment. I guessed it probably wouldn't, as long as I didn't actually kill anyone. If the police were using Jane Trehorn just to get me to tip my hand, there wouldn't be an actual target. But if I replied to Jane that I was still offering the services about which she had inquired, that might constitute a confession of sorts. I would be admitting, albeit indirectly, that I had killed someone for her previously.

A bitterly ironic thought suddenly came to mind. Craig Wilkinson could no doubt answer my question about entrapment.

I shook my head and put the thought aside. I was about as likely to ask Craig Wilkinson for legal assistance as I was to have my bald scalp tattooed with daisies.

Nevertheless, I had to admit I was intrigued. Was Jane's message legit? To respond, or not to respond? (Sorry, Hamlet.)

As if I didn't already have enough mind-fucks to contend with.

BY THE TIME I SEATED MYSELF at the bar in Skip's that evening I had changed my mind about responding to Jane at least a half dozen times.

I had wrestled with the question all afternoon. I had taken Preacher back out to the reservoir after lunch and tossed her knobby retrieving dummy into the water ten or twelve times and she'd happily plunged in each time and fetched it back. She was still dancing around, eager for one more throw, when I told her that was enough. It was another warm afternoon with the temperature in the mid-80s and I didn't want to overdo it, her enthusiasm notwithstanding.

We returned to the Equinox and after getting Preacher

loaded up, I sat in the driver's seat with the windows open, gazing out at the water for a few minutes. I thought again about the fact that Jane's letter was unprecedented. In all my years as a contract killer I had never received a similar follow-up, asking if I was still in business, so to speak, and willing to take on another assignment.

That alone made her letter suspect.

But then again, if she had a serious problem with someone—the kind of problem that could only be solved by taking that someone off the board—wasn't it natural to suppose she might reach out? I had, as she stated, "helped" her previously and maybe, just maybe, she was desperate enough to need my help again.

If this was the case, I also couldn't help speculating about whom that someone might be.

Of course I had no way of knowing, or even coming up with a reasonable guess, without contacting her. A second husband, maybe? Had she remarried and ultimately discovered her new husband was just as abusive as the first one? Marriage counselors and psychologists would attest that people in abusive relationships often repeat the same patterns of behavior and move from one such relationship to another. Had that happened here?

Again, I had no way of knowing without contacting her. But was it worth the risk?

We all know what curiosity did to the proverbial cat.

OPTING TO HAVE DINNER at Skip's was a calculated risk.

It had been almost a full week since I had confronted Daryl about her cheating. I remembered once reading somewhere that the length of time it takes to get over a failed relationship is directly proportional to the length of the relationship. That is, if a relationship lasted X number of years, it would necessarily take X number of months (or maybe years) to completely get over that relationship after it ended.

The only problem was, I couldn't remember the

specific figures. Was it fifty percent of the original relationship's time? Or twenty-five percent? Ten percent? I couldn't recall, and I wasn't going to bother researching the matter.

But I realized that a week was not nearly long enough to expect to be completely over my relationship with Daryl. Our relationship had lasted about eighteen months and even without the specific equation at hand, I knew it was going to take weeks, or maybe months, to put it completely behind me. Or at least reach the point where I was no longer troubled by painful reminders every time I turned around.

Hence a bit of apprehension about having dinner at Skip's.

Daryl and I were regulars at the restaurant—remember, our first serious dinner date had taken place there—and we were always recognized by the bartenders and most of the servers. It wasn't unlikely that if I showed up solo, I might be questioned about Daryl…specifically, why she wasn't with me. That was a conversation I wanted to avoid.

On the other hand, because we *were* so well known, I could feel reasonably comfortable about coming in alone and sitting at the bar without feeling too self-conscious. If anyone asked about Daryl, I could probably deflect, saying she was busy (which, I thought sarcastically, she might be, if she was spending the evening with Wilkinson) or something to that effect.

I decided to risk it.

Chapter 16

My favorite bartender, Biancia, was working and she smiled at me when I came in and sat down. The bar at Skip's is a square-cornered U-shape, and I found a seat at the back corner farthest from the door and next to the walk-through the bartenders used to access the bar.

Biancia ("The second i is silent; what can I say, my mom liked lots of vowels," she'd once told me) is a tall, slender brunette with a smart mouth and big dark eyes behind big, round, dark-framed glasses. Like all of the bartenders and servers at Skip's, she was dressed in black. Not surprisingly, she asked, "Where's Daryl?"

I shook my head and replied, "Under the weather." I told myself one small lie was as good as another.

"Sorry to hear that," Biancia said. "Blue Moon?" She knew me well.

"That'll work," I said as Biancia turned to one of the coolers beneath the register to pull out a bottle of Blue Moon. I was pleased she hadn't asked for any more details about Daryl's alleged illness.

Biancia uncapped the bottle and placed it on a cocktail napkin on the bar in front of me. She grabbed a frosted glass and added an orange slice to the rim. She set the glass on another cocktail napkin next to the bottle and said, "Menu?"

"Sure," I said. I was leaning toward blackened salmon, one of my favorite entrees at Skip's, but I hesitated, remembering that Daryl had served salmon the previous Saturday evening. Then I thought, what the hell. I hadn't eaten much of it, and Daryl's wasn't blackened. Maybe it was time to start confronting the reminders head on.

Biancia placed the menu in front of me and I gave it a quick scan while she turned away to help other customers. She turned back to me a couple minutes later and said, "Know what you're having?"

"Yes," I said. "I'll go with the blackened salmon."

"Sides?"

"Au gratin potatoes and salad with creamy parm."

"Got it," Biancia said, smiling. "Your usual."

"Right."

I nursed my Blue Moon until the salad was delivered, then I dug in. I was surprised to find myself actually hungry. The bar and dining rooms were crowded and a little noisy—not unusual for Skip's on a Friday night—and I wondered if just being out among people, all of whom appeared to be enjoying themselves, was having some kind of beneficial effect on my psyche. I suspected it was; I told myself this certainly beat moping at home and trying to force down a meal for which I had little appetite.

Plus, there was Biancia. Remaining in a funk when in her presence was unlikely; I always enjoyed watching her banter with her customers and tonight was no exception. Most of the folks seated at the bar knew her and called her by name, and she did the same in return. It kept things lively and I believed I could feel the positive energy in their exchanges, snarky in a good-natured way.

My salmon was served just as I was finishing my salad. A young couple, probably in their early thirties, was seated next to me. The woman, an attractive blonde, was closest to me and as Biancia set the plate down in front of me, the woman said, "Oh, that looks good."

"It always is," I said, smiling. I was feeling better by the minute about coming to Skip's.

"Well, enjoy!" she said, giving me a nice smile in return.

Biancia was smiling at me also. "Do you need anything else, Rob?"

"No, I think I'm good," I said, reflecting that this was probably the first time I had used that word to refer to myself in over a week.

THE BLACKENED SALMON WAS EXCELLENT as always, and I was happy I had chosen it and had not allowed myself to be spooked by it reminding me of Daryl.

I was just finishing the last couple bites when Biancia propped her elbows on the bar and leaned toward me. Her dark eyes were huge and intense behind her glasses. "So," she said, "what's on your mind?"

She caught me off guard. "What?" I said, the best I could muster.

"You look really thoughtful, like you're wrestling with something or trying to solve a problem." Good Lord. I wondered if I now had a digital read-out on my forehead, continuously streaming my thoughts like the scroll at the bottom of a television newscast.

I laughed. "It's that obvious?"

"Very."

"Well…as a matter of fact, I am trying to reach a decision about something." I realized I needed to be extremely careful here. Biancia, of course, knew nothing of my contract killing.

"Care to share? Maybe I can help you decide."

I laughed again. "It's kind of a personal matter," I said. "But in a nutshell, I heard from someone today after not having any contact for several years. I'm trying to decide whether to reply." *So far, so good*, I told myself. I hadn't said anything too revealing.

Biancia's smile grew wider. "An old girlfriend?" she asked, jumping to the obvious conclusion.

"No," I said, smiling also. "More like a former business acquaintance." *Be careful, guy!*

Biancia arched her eyebrows. "If it's just business, what's the problem?"

"Well, it could be a little risky."

"How so?"

"That's where the personal stuff comes in," I said, deflecting. I wanted to steer this conversation in another direction. I was sorry I'd said as much as I had.

Biancia gave me a long, searching look, then she smiled again, actually more of a grin. With classic bartender intuition—and I would have bet big money Biancia was even more intuitive than most—she apparently realized I had said as much as I was going to say about the matter.

She said, "Well, you know what they say. The only risks you regret in life are the ones you didn't take."

I laughed. "Is that what they say?" I'd heard variations of that line many times over the years.

"Yes, that's what they say," she said, still smiling as she turned away to attend to other customers.

I WAS STILL THINKING of that line as I drove home after dinner.

I knew the line—or at least the thought behind it—was pretty much universal. I also knew that I shouldn't read too much into the fact that Biancia had cited it. Still, I couldn't help thinking she might have provided the answer I'd been looking for.

I continued pondering this as I pulled into my driveway and hit the remote to open the garage door. I pulled into the garage, turned off the ignition and climbed out of the Equinox. I crossed the garage and hit the button next to the overhead door to close it. Then I stepped through the smaller side door, pulling it closed and locking it behind me.

I climbed the three steps to the deck and crossed it to the back door. I unlocked it and went inside to the kitchen. I grabbed another Blue Moon from the fridge and glanced over at Preacher, sprawled on her rug. "Outside?" I asked. She got to her feet, stretched, then walked over to the back door, tail wagging.

I let her outside and followed her out onto the deck. Preacher trotted down the steps to make a circuit of the back yard. I settled myself in one of the deck chairs and thought about calling or texting Rachel James and inviting her over for deck beers, but I decided against it. I could run the whole Jane Trehorn scenario by her and get her thoughts on whether it would be risky to reply. But while I always valued her opinion, I generally tried to avoid bothering Rachel on the weekends, knowing she was usually busy with family matters.

I sighed and took a long pull on my Blue Moon. I

thought again of Biancia's comment, that the only risks you regretted in life were the ones you didn't take.

I realized that while the statement might be considered axiomatic, it wasn't really true. Plenty of people had taken risks, suffered disastrous results and undoubtedly regretted their impetuosity. I smiled as I recalled those videos I'd seen of Darwin Award winners.

Still, I was tempted.

I WAITED UNTIL 10:00 the following morning—11:00 in North Carolina—to call Jane Trehorn.

After Preacher and I returned from the lake and I fed Preacher her morning meal, I went back to my office and pulled a new burner out of the bottom drawer of the file cabinet. I plugged it into the charger and waited an hour, killing time answering emails and poking around online. Then I disconnected the burner from the charger, picked up Jane's letter from my credenza and punched in her number.

She answered on the second ring. "Hello," she said, and although it had been four years, I thought I recognized her voice. She had just a trace of a southern accent.

"Hello, Jane," I said. "This is the fellow you called Jim."

Chapter 17

A MOMENT OF SILENCE, THEN JANE laughed and said, "Well, hello there. You must have gotten my letter." Yes, I definitely recognized her voice.

"I did," I said. Once again I reminded myself to be careful. So far I had admitted to nothing except receiving the letter she had sent me, but I wondered if that was already admitting too much.

"Thank you for getting back to me," she said. "I wasn't sure if that address was still valid, but I decided to give it a try. I didn't have any other way to reach you."

"I still have that P.O. box," I said. Another guarded admission.

"And are you still offering the same services?"

Oh boy. There it was, the $64,000 question. If this was a set-up, my next answer might really seal my fate. Correction: it would *definitely* seal my fate.

I tried to avoid replying directly to what she had asked. "You said you needed help again," I said. "Can you be a little more specific?"

She hesitated a moment, and when she spoke I thought I heard a break in her voice. "My older sister was killed recently," she said. "I'm certain I know who did it but I'm also certain he will never be brought to justice. That's why I reached out to you."

I took a deep breath and exhaled. Then I took the plunge.

"Give me the details."

MAYBE IT WAS THE CATCH in her voice that convinced me her query was legitimate, not part of an elaborate scheme by the police to ensnare me. Then again, maybe I was just being a damn fool and letting myself be suckered. Either way, I realized I was approaching this with an oh-what-the-hell attitude that was a far cry from the caution

I usually employed in these matters. I wondered if all the conflicted feelings I'd been wrestling with since learning of Daryl's cheating had made me reckless.

I suspected that might be the case.

I also realized that by asking Jane for the details I had crossed a line from which I couldn't retreat. If the police were listening and hoping for confirmation that I was a killer for hire, I had pretty much just given them that confirmation.

I heard her draw a deep breath. Then she said, "My older sister's name was Sara. She was eight years older than me and had just turned 70. She lived here in Schnock's Harbor just a few miles from me, and she was a widow. Her husband Albert died three years ago.

"Since that time…well, actually beginning several years ago before Albert died, she has…had devoted herself to sea turtles."

"Sea turtles?"

"Yes. She loved them and was very protective of them. She was a volunteer at the Paige Green Sea Turtle Rescue and Rehabilitation Center in Surf City, which is only a few miles from here, and she got me involved with the Center also. It was an ongoing hobby, I guess you could call it, that we shared. Except for Sara it was really more of a passion. I enjoyed it, but she lived and breathed it every day. And it got her killed."

"Okay," I said, wondering how Sara's devotion to sea turtles could have resulted in her being murdered.

Jane continued, "So about two weeks ago we had agreed to meet on the beach one evening to check for turtle nests. It's a little too early in the season for any baby turtles to be hatching and the known nests are flagged when it's getting close to the hatching date, but we like to monitor the nest locations prior to that to make sure they haven't been disturbed.

"We planned to meet at about 8:00, just at dusk, because we try to be careful about revealing the nest locations to any random people who might be on the beach. The turtles are protected by law, but that doesn't guarantee vandals won't destroy a nest if they find one. So we tend to be circumspect when we check the nests."

I smiled at her use of the word circumspect. Not many folks would drop that word into a conversation, but Jane did so deftly. "Go on," I said.

"I was running a few minutes late. I parked in one of the parking areas next to Sara's Subaru and saw she must have gone on to the beach without me, as she wasn't in her vehicle. That's when I heard it." She paused and I thought I heard her draw another deep breath.

"Heard what?" I prompted.

"An ATV. It was really roaring and it sounded like it was on the beach. I couldn't see it because there's a tall dune between the parking area and the beach, but it was really loud. So I hurried to the top of the dune and just as I got to the top, I saw it bearing down on Sara. She was about a hundred yards down the beach from where we'd parked, and the ATV was coming up from behind her, really fast."

Jane paused for a moment before continuing. I guessed this was difficult for her, but she was doing a good job of painting a word picture of what she had witnessed. I was having no trouble imagining the scene as she described it, even though I had no idea what her sister looked like. "Then what happened?" I prompted again.

Another deep breath. Then, "I saw Sara turn back toward the ATV and start waving her arms, trying to get the driver to stop or swerve…at least I think that's what she was doing. Between the sounds of the ATV and the tide coming in, I couldn't hear her but I think she must have been yelling also. She was waving almost frantically and somehow I knew, I just knew, that there must have been hatchlings on the beach she was trying to protect."

I assumed hatchlings were baby turtles, but I didn't ask. I didn't want to interrupt Jane's narrative.

"But the driver didn't stop or slow down, and he didn't swerve. He just went roaring up to her, almost like he was deliberately trying to run her down."

"Did she try to get out of the way?"

"At the last second I saw her try to jump back, but it was too late. The driver stuck his arm out straight and caught her at the neck as he went by. I think in football they call it a clothesline or clotheslining."

Yes, that's what they called it in football, and I was impressed that Jane knew the term. I saw the scene vividly in my mind as she described it. And although I was sure I already knew the answer, I asked, "And your sister…?"

"She just crumpled. That's the only way I can describe it. She just kind of crumpled to the beach and lay there in a heap. By then I was running down off the dune toward her and I'm sure I was screaming. And—I know this is going to sound awful—I knew my sister was dead even before I got to her. It was the way she went down so suddenly and then didn't move. I knew she was dead."

Neither of us spoke for a moment, then I asked quietly, "What about the ATV? Did the driver stop?"

"No. He didn't even slow down. He went tearing on down the beach and disappeared behind some dunes about a half mile down."

I blew out a hard breath. "I'm very sorry for your loss," I said. I couldn't think of anything else to say, or ask, at the moment.

"Thank you," Jane said. She hesitated, then added, "What I said before, about knowing who killed Sara? I'm sure I know who the driver was, even though he didn't stop and I only saw him at a distance."

"How do you know that?"

"The moon was almost full that night and there was enough light for me to see that he had flaming red hair. That, plus the fact that I've seen him driving the same ATV on the beach a bunch of times before. I'm positive I know who it was."

"And who is that?"

"His name is Gaston Stevens. He's the son of one of our state representatives. Congresswoman Maggie Stevens."

Chapter 18

I HAVE FIVE INVIOLATE RULES TO WHICH I adhere when it comes to my contract killing assignments. Maybe I should say to which I *try* to adhere, because recently I have broken a couple of those rules.

Avenging Hannah Wilkinson's death the previous summer saw me violating Rule Number 1, which stipulates no personal involvement. Although it wasn't a contract killing in the strict sense—no one actually hired me to kill Hannah's killer—it did require plenty of personal involvement.

I guess that means my five inviolate rules aren't quite so inviolate after all.

The fourth of these rules stipulates the target cannot be a politician, no matter how much he or she might deserve it. A political assassination will bring all of the most powerful investigative forces to bear, even if said politician was relatively low-ranking. It's hard enough these days to stay at least a jump or two ahead of the local and state police agencies. I have no desire to cross swords with the FBI, the NSA, the Secret Service and God only knows who else.

But there is nothing in my five rules about the family members of politicians.

Of course that carries a high degree of risk, as well. Even minor politicians usually have quite a bit of clout and they would undoubtedly apply all sorts of pressure and call in multiple favors to see their family member's killer brought to justice. Killing a congresswoman's son was guaranteed to unleash an absolute tsunami of investigation that would almost certainly lead to my apprehension.

That is, unless the killing could be made to look like an accident.

"A CONGRESSWOMAN'S SON."

"That's right. And a known hell-raiser, through and through. He's been in and out of trouble lots of times. A case of Mama's Boy can do no wrong."

"So the congresswoman is super-protective and uses her influence to keep him in the clear."

"That's right."

I gave this a moment's thought, then I said, "Let's back up a minute. I'm sure you reported your sister's death that night?"

"Yes. I called 911 from the beach. While I was still sitting there in the sand holding Sara's head in my lap, in fact."

I heard her voice break again.

"And then what happened? I'm guessing they responded pretty quickly?"

"Yes. They were there within minutes. The police, the fire department with their ambulance and EMTs, lots of people and vehicles. The beach was swarming...I halfway expected the Coast Guard to show up as well."

"And then...?"

"The police tried to get me to give them a statement about what I'd seen. To their credit, they were very kind and patient with me. I know I was almost incoherent, at least at first. I couldn't stop crying."

"That's understandable. Were you able to give them a statement?"

"Eventually, yes. Like I said, they were very patient with me. I didn't want to leave Sara but they kind of gently led me away while the EMTs were attending to her...body. There was a lady officer named Robbins who took charge and she walked me away. She's the one I talked to."

"You told her what you'd seen?"

"Yes. She—Officer Robbins—recorded what I said. She asked me to repeat several things, including my description of the ATV and the driver."

"I'm sure you told them you thought you knew who the driver was?"

"No, not that I *thought* I knew. I told them I *did* know who the driver was, that I recognized him by his red hair and seeing him riding his ATV on the beach a bunch of times before."

"You gave them his name?"

"Yes."

"And did they follow up on that?"

"Yes. They talked to him later that night, in fact. Officer Robbins called me the next morning to tell me that, and that they were still investigating the incident but she thought it was likely that he was going to be arrested."

"Really!" For some reason I found this surprising, probably because of what Jane had said about the congresswoman and her influence. Or maybe because I found it a little curious that Officer Robbins had volunteered this information before an actual arrest was made. Whatever.

"Yes, she said the charge was likely to be manslaughter, and in fact that's what it ended up being. When they talked to him, he claimed he hadn't seen Sara until he was almost upon her, and that he was going too fast to stop so he tried to swerve and reached out to try to push her out of the way. The cops saw some bruising on his arm from where he had clotheslined her and he said she had panicked and jumped toward him, rather than away, and that's why he hit her neck instead of her shoulder."

"Interesting. And the police believed him?"

"I'm not sure they believed him, but I don't think they had any evidence to the contrary."

"Except for your statement as to what you had seen."

"Right. So it was basically my word against his."

"Right," I agreed. I thought for a moment, then asked, "So where is he now?"

"Oh, he's out on bail, waiting for his trial, which won't start until sometime early next year. In the meantime, he has to wear an ankle monitor and not leave the state, but otherwise he's free as a bird. Walking around like nothing happened and it's all just a big mistake or misunderstanding that will eventually blow over."

"Wow." It was all I could think of to say. Based on what Jane had just told me, I already didn't like the guy, even though I actually knew very little about him beyond her description. But I did know his type—a spoiled rich kid whose parents always covered for him so that he basically grew up knowing few restraints and that he could essentially get away with anything.

"I'm sure that can't be easy," I finally said. "Seeing him walking around free, I mean."

"You got that right. Schnock's Harbor is a small community...well, you probably remember that. So I see him every so often, usually hanging with some of his buddies. They're all pretty much the same, spoiled rich kids with way too much time on their hands. Plenty of time to get into trouble, in other words." I smiled slightly at her confirmation of my initial impression.

Her comment also raised another question in my mind. "How old is this guy…you said his name is Gaston?"

"That's right. He goes by Gas or Gast, I'm not sure which. He's twenty-six."

"Does he have a job?"

I heard her snort. "You gotta be kidding," she said. "He doesn't work. He doesn't have to. Like I said, he spends his time hanging with his friends, dreaming up ways to get into trouble."

"Drugs?"

"I don't know, but it wouldn't surprise me. At the very least they probably smoke weed. I know they like to get drunk. Gaston's been charged a couple times with DUI, but you can guess what happened there. A slap on the wrist and nothing more."

"Okay," I said. "I'm getting the picture." And I was. The big question that remained, however, was whether I could trust Jane's account of what had happened. I was inclined to give her the benefit of the doubt, partly because we had done business previously and all of her claims at that time had proven true—my own investigation had established that her husband *was* the abusive son of a bitch she said he was, which left little doubt in my mind that he deserved the fate I had delivered.

I was also convinced by the sincerity of Jane's account of her sister's death. There was no question that she was speaking from the heart and fervently believed that she had seen Gaston Stevens deliberately run down and kill her sister.

But I quickly reminded myself that eyewitness testimony is often unreliable. A dozen witnesses can report on the same incident and give a dozen different versions, and each of those witnesses is convinced his or her account is the one that is accurate. In simplest terms, different people see things differently, especially if there is a personal element involved. Witnessing the death of a loved one is as personal as it gets.

So it was possible that Jane's account wasn't completely accurate. It was natural to want to blame someone for the untimely death of her sister, and Gaston Stevens, readily identifiable by his red hair and ATV, coupled with his reputation as a troublemaker, made the perfect suspect. Maybe, just maybe, the incident had occurred as he had claimed and Sara's death was an accident.

Maybe, I told myself, Gaston Stevens was the one who deserved the benefit of the doubt, at least until I could determine otherwise.

"So," Jane was saying, "Will you consider looking into this?"

I hesitated a moment, then that what-the-hell attitude asserted itself again.

"Yes," I said. "I'll look into this."

Chapter 19

THAT MEANT I WOULD SOON be making a trip to North Carolina.

Whenever possible, I prefer to do my own investigating when I take an assignment. Clients occasionally offer to help with this investigation, and in some cases—albeit rarely—I have taken them up on this, mostly by allowing them to fill in some of the blanks regarding the target's background. But I generally try to keep the client's actual involvement to a minimum. I'm a firm believer in that old saying, "loose lips sink ships," so the less the client knows of my actions, the better.

Also, as I've already mentioned, I never accept an assignment unless I'm convinced the target deserves to be taken off the board. This means I have to rely on the client's account of the target's transgressions, at least initially. Then, after listening to and evaluating the client's claims—and verifying they are valid—I have to develop a course of action. At this point I do sometimes seek outside assistance. Rachel James frequently plays a key role in nailing down the best way to complete the assignment and do so with minimal risk to myself.

I concluded my conversation with Jane Trehorn by saying that I needed a couple days to consider everything she had told me, and that I would contact her again soon. (I didn't tell her that I would be doing an extensive online search to confirm the details of her sister's death and Gaston Stevens' arrest.) She inquired about my fee—she laughed slightly when she asked if, like everyone else, I had raised my prices—and I laughed also and told her no, that the standard rate still applied. She said she looked forward to hearing from me, and I assured her again that I would be in touch soon.

Then we hung up and I sat there at my desk for a couple minutes wondering what the hell I had just gotten myself into.

MY ONLINE SEARCH CONFIRMED that Schnock's Harbor resident Sara Lawson, age 70, had died some two weeks earlier, just as her sister had described. Jane had told me Sara's last name as we were concluding our phone conversation, and it was a fairly simple matter to find her obituary on the website of O'Brien's Funeral Home in Schnock's Harbor. I also found several articles posted on the websites of area newspapers that provided details on how she had died. These also matched Jane's account.

From the obit I learned that Sara had no children, had been preceded in death by her parents and her husband Albert (which Jane had already told me) and was survived by her sister, brothers Bruce and Edward and their wives and several nieces and nephews. I wondered if the fact that Sara was childless had in some way contributed to her devotion— Jane's word—to the sea turtles. I suspected that was probably the case.

The obit also included a photo of Sara. She was an attractive woman with a wide smile, strong jawline and shoulder-length blonde hair…or at least I guessed it was blonde. The photo was in black and white so her hair might have been silver or gray, but she definitely wasn't a brunette.

Not surprisingly, I also found quite a few articles detailing Gaston Stevens' arrest and being charged with involuntary manslaughter for Sara Lawson's death.

These matched Jane's account as well. Much of the content of these articles, however, was focused on Gaston's mother, Congresswoman Maggie Stevens, her background and political career. Although her son was the one charged with a crime, the congresswoman was obviously deemed more newsworthy by the writers of the articles. That she had a son charged with killing someone was certain to attract the attention of many readers, especially in this, an election year.

Once again, I wondered what I had gotten myself into.

AFTER VERIFYING JANE'S ACCOUNT of her sister's death, I started thinking about how next to proceed. I considered driving to Schnock's Harbor but quickly dismissed the idea. From my home in Des Moines it was a little over 1,200 miles to the North Carolina coast, so it would take me nearly two full days, with an overnight stay somewhere along the way, to reach the seaside town.

I knew this because four years ago, when I had completed the previous assignment for Jane Trehorn, I *had* driven down there. It was a real haul, and while I had made quite a few trips as long or longer when I was editing *American Wingshot* magazine—usually to participate in an advertiser-sponsored hunt at some posh lodge—I wasn't particularly eager to do so again.

On the other hand, the big advantage to driving was that I could take along any necessary items I might need to complete the assignment…specifically, anything I wouldn't feel comfortable, or couldn't risk, checking in my luggage. Topping that list: an ice-cold firearm.

My third inviolate rule mandates never keeping a handgun after it has been used. Hanging onto a handgun after using it to commit a violent crime—that is, shooting someone—is the ultimate folly, and I always dispose of such guns in the same way. I disassemble them, then toss the pieces in different directions into a body of water—preferably a river, the deeper and swifter the better.

I currently had an untraceable handgun I'd purchased some eighteen months earlier but never used. My source for these firearms is a pawnbroker named Gerald Matthews who has a shop on the south side of Des Moines. I've never heard anyone call him Gerald or Jerry, and I always address him as A.C., an abbreviated form of his nickname, A.C.T.C, which stands for As Cold as They Come. I have occasionally heard him called Cold, which strikes me as a nice play on words, matching both his personality and the merchandise in which he occasionally deals.

Over the years I've purchased quite a few untraceable handguns from A.C. Although he has no doubt wondered why I'm such a frequent repeat customer, he's never asked. In the same vein, I have never asked him where he gets those guns I buy from him, nor will I.

The firearm I'd purchased from A.C. and still had on hand was a .357 Colt Python with a six-inch barrel—nicknamed a "Snake Six" by firearms aficionados—with a stainless steel finish and black grips. I'd taken it along on an assignment in Illinois but hadn't fired the gun…in fact, I'd used the target's own nine millimeter Glock to complete the assignment, staging his death to look like a suicide. I'd brought the Colt back home with me, figuring I might need it sometime in the future, and it was locked in my gun safe.

I wondered if I might need it in North Carolina.

There's an old saying that it's always better to have a gun with you and not need it rather than to leave the gun behind and then find yourself wishing you'd brought it. I didn't want to make that mistake so taking the Colt to North Carolina would necessitate driving. I wasn't going to check an ice-cold—read, highly illegal—firearm in my luggage and risk being questioned about it. Which I almost certainly would be. That would, to put it mildly, bring a very abrupt end to my trip.

Although it was still very early in the planning stage, I reminded myself that I was hoping to make Gaston Stevens' death look like an accident and thereby head off overzealous investigations by various law enforcement agencies. At the moment I had no idea how I was going to arrange such an accident; I would need to get down to North Carolina and do some serious recon to come up with the best—i.e., most believable—scenario.

But I was reasonably certain if such a scenario was to look like an accident, it wouldn't involve a gun. The Snake Six would stay at home.

Chapter 20

THE AMERICAN AIRLINES FLIGHT from Des Moines to Charlotte was about an hour and forty-five minutes and I arrived in Charlotte at 2:10 in the afternoon. My layover was a little over an hour, which gave me time for a beer before catching my connecting flight to Wilmington. I stopped at one of the concourse lounges and settled myself at a small corner table. Blue Moon wasn't listed among the beers on the drink menu so I opted for a Goose Island IPA.

While drinking my beer I checked my cell for messages. The first was from Rachel wishing me luck and telling me to be sure and let her know if I needed anything; that she would be happy to make a quick trip to North Carolina to help me strategize and/or provide whatever I might need to complete my assignment.

She ended her text with a wink emoji, which I interpreted as a reference to the drugs she had supplied me on many previous occasions…and was apparently quite willing to supply me with again. If I was correct about this, she was a lot more willing to risk flying with an illegal substance than I was with an untraceable handgun. I smiled at her boldness—not that I was all that surprised—and took another sip of beer.

My second message was from Mike Stevenson, the good friend and hunting companion with whom I had left Preacher. Mike and I have known each other for quite a few years and we frequently hunt together each fall for both upland birds and waterfowl. Mike has a young yellow Labrador named Rusty and we had spent the previous summer on training sessions to get both dogs accustomed to working with each other in the field.

The training sessions paid off and we had enjoyed a successful season. Preacher and Rusty got along well and Mike's message was brief, saying that Preacher had settled right in and made herself at home after I'd dropped her off the previous evening. I smiled again, guessing that Mike's two daughters, and probably his wife as well, were spoiling her. I knew she would be in good hands until I returned; I had kept Rusty at my place a couple of times under similar circumstances when Mike and his family had gone on vacation.

After reading Mike's message I turned off my cell, dropped it into my briefcase and pulled out the burner I had been using to correspond with Jane Trehorn. I logged on and checked it for messages. I had one from Jane.

"I'm making jambalaya for dinner," her text read. "Call me when you get to your hotel and I'll give you directions to my place."

I texted her a quick reply: "Will do. Jambalaya sounds great!"

I logged off the burner and dropped it into my briefcase. I finished my beer, paid the check and left a healthy tip, then I wandered down the concourse to gate C12, where I would board my forty-minute flight to Wilmington.

OKAY, I SUPPOSE I have some explaining to do.

Having dinner with a client was something I had never done before, either in the client's home or in a more neutral setting. Even meeting a client in person was something that had happened only a couple times previously, and one of those times was an accident, a case of our almost literally bumping into each other. I typically go to considerable lengths to make sure I remain anonymous to clients and, for obvious reasons, that my face is unknown to them.

I've already mentioned that once I accept an assignment I try to keep contact with the client to a minimum, and I do the majority of investigative work by myself, especially as it relates to the plan I come up with for completing the assignment. I don't divulge any of the details of my plan to the client, knowing he or she will find out in due time—either through the media or from one last burner call from me—that the job has been done. Then it's a simple matter of the client sending me a check for services rendered, and that concludes our business once and for all.

Except in this instance.

Never before had a former client contacted me to ask if I would consider taking another assignment. Jane Trehorn's request was, as previously noted, entirely unprecedented. But after verifying her account of her sister's death and the subsequent arrest of Gaston Stevens, I had called her a second time and told her I would agree to fly down to North Carolina and at least investigate the matter a little further.

This second phone call lasted a lot longer than I expected.

Jane was noticeably pleased to hear I was tentatively accepting the assignment. I warned her that I wasn't making any promises just yet, that I would need to get the lay of the land and do a little more digging before I could decide for certain. She laughed when I said this and said she understood. Then she added, "So when should I expect you?"

I'll admit, she caught me off-guard.

"Well," I said, trying to keep from stammering, "I haven't booked my flights yet, so I can't say for sure when I'll be there. But…as a rule, I don't meet with clients in person. It's safer for both of us if we remain…removed."

"I understand," she said. The she laughed again and added, "But rules are meant to be broken, and I might be able to help with your investigation." Was I detecting a slight flirtatious note in her voice?

I told myself to stand firm.

"I appreciate the offer," I said. "But I really prefer to handle things on my own. Like I said, it's generally safer for both of us that way." I hesitated, then added, "The less you know about me or how I'm going to take care of things, the less chance there is of you ever being implicated in any way." Even as I said this I realized it probably sounded lame. Or at the very least, evasive.

Jane wasn't fooled.

"What you mean is, if you keep me in the dark there's less chance of me letting something slip or screwing something up that might get you caught," she said. Another laugh.

I couldn't help laughing also. "Okay, call me paranoid," I said. "But I haven't survived this long by being careless. I always try to err on the side of caution and that includes keeping my plans close to my vest."

"I understand," she said for the third time. "But I still think I could help you get the lay of the land, as you called it, and be useful. Maybe even point out Gaston Stevens to you. If nothing else, I could show you around and help familiarize you with the area."

"I've been there before," I reminded her.

"I know that. But that was four years ago. Things in Schnock's Harbor haven't changed that much, I admit, but I'd still be happy to help you in any way that I can." Another pause. Then: "I don't really have anything else going on at the moment." This time I thought she sounded a bit wistful.

I hesitated and a curious thought intruded. I found myself trying to picture what Jane looked like, based on the sound of her voice. I wondered if Jane resembled her sister. If she did, she was definitely an attractive woman.

God help me.

I pulled my thoughts back to the matter at hand and said, "Tell you what. Let me give it a little thought and get my flights booked, then I'll get back to you. Okay?" Thinking, *could my stalling be any more obvious?*

Again, she wasn't fooled. "Now you're just trying to put me off," she said. "But in case you've forgotten, I would remind you that Schnock's Harbor is a fairly small community. If you show up and you're here for more than a few days, you're likely to be noticed. I don't know how you managed to keep yourself hidden the last time you were here, but you might not be so lucky a second time."

I laughed. "And how would meeting you keep me from being noticed?"

"That's easy. It's called hiding in plain sight. If anyone saw us together and asked, I could say you were a friend or relative who was visiting. They wouldn't give that a second thought, especially with my sister dying so recently. Well, they might be curious as to the nature of our relationship, at least a little, but let them wonder. I'm sure they wouldn't come up with your real reason for being here."

I sighed. "Has anyone ever commented on your persistence?"

"Oh yeah," she said, and now there was no mistaking the mischief in her voice. "All the time."

I laughed. "Okay," I said. "You wore me down. I'll book my flights and let you know when I'm getting in. We can maybe meet for dinner, anyway, and see how it goes."

"Deal," she said.

I couldn't quite believe what I had just let myself get talked into, and I was already having second thoughts. But I could at least meet the woman for dinner, I thought. It was unprecedented, but probably no great harm would be done.

"Okay, I'll talk to you soon," I said. I wanted to wrap things up before I did anything else foolish.

"One more thing before you go," she said.

"What's that?"

She laughed. "Do I have to keep calling you Jim?"

Chapter 21

NO, SHE DIDN'T HAVE TO KEEP calling me Jim. Trying to continue that masquerade over dinner struck me as ridiculous, especially since she obviously knew Jim wasn't my real name.

I laughed and told her my name was actually Robert and I went by Rob, not Bob. She laughed in return and said she would do her best to remember that, and she was going to hold me to my promise to have dinner with her. I reiterated that I would let her know when I would be arriving, then we said our goodbyes.

I smiled but shook my head as I ended the call. I had the uneasy feeling that things were already spiraling out of my control, and I reminded myself to proceed with caution and not become reckless. And above all, not to be taken in by Jane's seeming flirtatiousness. I knew my break-up with Daryl was much too recent for me to be making sensible decisions about getting involved with another woman…assuming, that is, that Jane was in fact coming on to me.

I snorted as I realized how ludicrous this line of thinking was. To the best of my knowledge, Jane had never seen me during my previous time in Schnock's Harbor, and she knew me only as a man who killed people for money. There was no reason to suppose she would find such a person attractive, especially when she had never laid eyes on me. I'd be the first to admit I'm no George Clooney or Brad Pitt.

A more likely explanation was that she was simply curious. I smiled again as I realized very few people could say they had ever had dinner with a hit man…at least, not knowingly. (Yes, Daryl immediately came to mind.) Maybe Jane just wanted to see what someone in my—ahem—profession looked like, someone to whom she had already paid $10,000 and was planning to pay that sum again.

That had to be it, I told myself. She was curious, nothing more. I also told myself to get a grip.

But then again, why had she offered to show me around

Schnock's Harbor? Why was she so insistent on helping me? She had mentioned that she didn't have anything else going on at the moment, which meant…what? That she was bored and thought assisting in eliminating her sister's killer might be exciting? Or—worse yet—fun?

I snorted again, thinking that the last thing I should be considering was allowing a family member to participate in a contract hit—especially someone who was eager for revenge and whose thinking was undoubtedly clouded by grief. Letting such a person play a role in an assignment was almost a guarantee of disaster.

I took a deep breath and told myself to chill. Having dinner with the woman committed me to nothing. I had already warned Jane that I couldn't promise to take the assignment until I had dug into the matter a little further. Our dinner would simply provide us with the chance to get better acquainted—admittedly, something I'd never done with any previous client—and then I would take my leave, investigate Gaston Stevens, and decide whether he deserved the fate Jane believed he had coming. If so, I would tactfully decline any offers from Jane for additional help and I would handle everything on my own, like always.

Matter resolved, I told myself.

Have I ever mentioned that I tend to overthink this stuff?

IT'S ABOUT A ONE-HOUR DRIVE from the Wilmington airport to Schnock's Harbor, and I spent most of that time replaying many of the thoughts—read, misgivings—I harbored about the advisability of having dinner with Jane Trehorn. I told myself for the hundredth time that just because I'd never done anything like this with a client before, there was no cause for alarm; that this was going to be nothing more than a casual dinner date and I could insist on going it alone afterwards.

That she would know what I looked like…well, again, that was almost entirely unprecedented, but given the nature of our business, I felt I could trust her with this knowledge. I was reasonably confident she would never identify me as the person she herself had hired to commit a crime.

So call me foolhardy.

At the Wilmington airport I collected the car I had rented from Enterprise, a two-year-old, midnight blue Chevy Impala. I stowed my large bag—packed mostly with t-shirts, polo shirts and cargo shorts—in the trunk, tossed my battered steel gray briefcase on the passenger seat, and cranked the ignition. I followed the signs out of the terminal to Route 17, the four-lane highway that runs parallel to the coast and passes Topsail Beach, Surf City and North Topsail Beach before coming to Schnock's Harbor, just south of the Camp Lejeune Marine Corps base.

I had a room reserved at the Hampton Inn and I pulled into the parking lot at a few minutes after 5:30. The four-story red brick structure looked like Hampton Inns everywhere and I remembered that a previous target, an attorney named Frank Reynolds, had stayed in one in Macomb, Illinois, a couple years earlier. I had stayed next door at a Best Western and had followed Reynolds into the woods early on the second morning of deer season and completed the assignment there.

Such are the reminiscences of a contract killer.

I retrieved my luggage from the trunk of the Impala and, wheeling it with one hand and carrying my briefcase in the other, I entered the lobby and checked in. The clerk behind the counter was a tall good-looking blonde with a friendly face and a tiny diamond stud in her right nostril. When she handed me the registration form I caught a glimpse of a small heart-shaped tattoo on the underside of her left wrist. Her nametag told me her name was Stacy.

"You're in room 224," she said with a smile as she handed me two magnetic key cards. "The elevator is just down the hall to the right."

I thanked her and headed off to the elevator. I glanced at my wristwatch and saw it was now 5:45. I needed to call Jane and get the directions to her place, and I wanted to grab a quick shower and change clothes before driving over there for dinner.

I wondered if her jambalaya was as good as Skip's.

"THIS IS JIM…er, Rob," I said in a rather lame attempt at humor when Jane answered her phone on the second ring.

To her credit, Jane laughed, and I gave her points for being a good sport. "I thought it was about time I should be hearing from you," she said.

"I got in about twenty minutes ago," I said. "Wanted to get settled here at the Hampton before heading your way." I didn't tell her I had just showered and was standing in my room in my underwear. TMI, definitely.

"Let me tell you how to get here," she said.

"Actually, if you just tell me the address I should be able to find it. There's this app called Google Maps…"

She laughed again. "Yes, I've heard of that." She told me her address and I jotted it down on the notepad next to the lamp on the nightstand.

"Got it," I said. "About how far away are you from the Hampton? Timewise?"

"I'd say no more than fifteen minutes; probably not even that long. That is, if you don't get lost." I thought I could still hear a trace of laughter in her voice.

"I'll do my best," I said. "One more thing. I hate showing up for dinner empty-handed. Do you have a favorite wine, and is there someplace between here and your place I can stop to pick it up?"

"That's very kind of you," she said, "but the truth is, I already have a pitcher of margaritas ready. So don't worry about showing up empty-handed. And in case you don't like margaritas, I also have beer."

I laughed. "I like margaritas *and* beer," I said. "It sounds like you have the whole beverage thing covered."

She laughed again. "Then the only remaining question is, do you prefer your margaritas with salt, or without?"

"With," I said.

"Good answer," she said. "I'll see you soon."

"See you soon," I echoed. I hung up thinking, a woman who has a pitcher of margaritas waiting. Plus beer. Oh, be still my heart.

So much for proceeding with caution.

Chapter 22

JANE'S ESTIMATE ON HOW LONG it would take me to drive from the Hampton Inn to her house was right in the ballpark. I made it in twelve minutes.

It was a pleasant drive with light traffic, and the residential area in which she lived quickly reminded me that I was no longer in the Midwest. Huge spreading live oaks were curtained with Spanish moss, and palmettos were visible in almost every yard, along with the occasional palm tree.

It was just past 6:30 when I pulled into Jane's driveway. Her house was a red brick ranch with white shutters and trim and a large screened front porch. A crushed shell walk, flanked on both sides by red azalea bushes, curved from the driveway to the porch.

I followed the walk to the porch, walked up three steps and pulled open the screen door. I stepped onto the porch and saw a hanging bench swing and three cushioned all-weather chairs to my right. A small table stood next to the chairs.

I crossed the porch to the inside front door and rang the doorbell. I still felt a little sheepish about showing up empty-handed but I told myself not to worry about it, that I was just following Jane's instructions. It was a humid, warmish evening—I guessed the temp was in the low eighties—and I was wearing khaki cargo shorts, a lemon yellow polo shirt and a pair of tan sandals. I hoped I wasn't underdressed for the occasion.

I needn't have worried. Jane answered the door in peach colored shorts, a V-neck white t-shirt and buff-colored leather flip-flops. Glancing down, I noticed a small blue tattoo on the top of her right foot but I couldn't make out the design and I didn't want to stare. I smiled at her and said, "Good evening."

"Good evening, Rob," she said, smiling also. "C'mon in." She stepped aside and motioned for me to enter. I followed her into the living room, which was decorated in a seashell and beach motif. The house was air conditioned, comfortably cool with no trace of the outside humidity. A large ceiling fan revolved slowly overhead, adding a slight breeze that amplified the coolness.

Still smiling, Jane gave me a long searching look and I couldn't help wondering if she was comparing my appearance to whatever she had thought a hit man might look like. I spent the moment doing a comparison of my own. Yes, Jane looked a lot like her older sister. Tall and slender—I guessed she was probably five-eight or five-nine—with the same strong jawline. The most noticeable difference was that her hair was darker than Sara's had appeared to be; Jane's was strawberry blond, trending toward auburn, with just a few silvery gray strands. Her eyes were a beautiful sea-green, which—given her proximity to the ocean—I found especially fitting.

"It's good to meet you," she said. "Thank you for coming."

"Thanks for the invitation," I said. "It's good to meet you also." I hesitated, then added, "Something smells awfully good!"

She laughed. "The jambalaya is simmering so we can eat in just a few minutes," she said. "In the meantime, can I interest you in a margarita?"

"Absolutely," I said.

"Follow me," she said, turning and leading the way to her kitchen.

THE JAMBALAYA WAS EVERY BIT as good as that which is served at Skip's. Maybe better.

We ate at Jane's kitchen table and by the third bite I could feel my scalp beginning to perspire, which reminded me of another passage in a Travis McGee novel. Commenting on the chili made by his best friend Meyer, McGee noted that Meyer didn't believe any chili was spicy enough unless it immediately brought tears to one's eyes. I thought the same could be said of Jane Trehorn's jambalaya.

I loved it.

Ice-cold kickass margaritas—Jane didn't stint on the tequila—and large squares of homemade cornbread were the perfect accompaniments to the fiery jambalaya. After spending most of the day traveling, I was hungry and didn't have to feign having an appetite. I dug in and found that the apprehension I'd been feeling about meeting a client in person and having dinner with her had vanished.

Well, mostly, anyway. I reminded myself not to let my guard

down completely. But there was a vivacious quality about Jane that made it hard for me to remain wary. I found myself wanting to open up to her.

To her credit, she didn't immediately start probing with questions or comments about what it was like to be a contract killer; didn't lead off with anything like, "So, tell me what it's like to kill people for money." (Definitely not your standard dinner-table conversation.) But I couldn't help thinking that such thoughts had to be lurking somewhere in the back of her mind.

Instead, she asked the usual stuff people ask in these situations, whether I'd had a good flight from Des Moines, and so on. Typical ice-breakers, in other words.

"The flights were fine," I said. "On time and clear skies; no bumpy weather." I took a sip of my margarita and added, "Speaking of which, what's the forecast here for the next few days?"

"We're supposed to have good weather, with no rain until the weekend. Temps aren't going to be bad, either, mid-eighties during the day and down into the sixties at night. That's fairly mild for this area in the summertime."

"That sounds good," I said. "I noticed a nice breeze as I was walking up to your porch."

"I'm only about eight blocks from the ocean here, so there's almost always a good breeze," she said.

"Nice," I replied. "By the way, you have a beautiful home."

"Oh, thanks. As you can tell, I love the beach and the ocean and everything related."

"Have you always lived here? Or in this area, I mean?"

"Yes, I'm a native Tar Heel," she said, laughing. "And yes, I've always lived in the area. What about you? Are you a native Hawkeye?"

I laughed in return, mentally giving her props for knowing Iowa's nickname. "No, I'm not, as a matter of fact," I said. "I'm originally from Illinois. I lived in the Chicago area for thirty some years before I moved to Des Moines. I've been there for a little over twenty."

"Why did you move?"

"New job," I said. "I was hired as editor of *American Wingshot* magazine, and at the time it was owned by a company in

Des Moines. It was sold a few years later to a New York-based outfit, but the new owners asked me to stay on as editor and they set me up to work out of my home. I wound up staying for another sixteen years. I just retired last year right before Christmas."

She smiled and said, "That must have been nice, working out of your home for all those years."

"It was," I said. "You couldn't beat the commute. When I started my workday, all I had to do was carry a cup of coffee from the kitchen back to the bedroom I use as an office. Took me all of about thirty seconds."

Jane laughed and said, "I don't mean to pry, but I'm guessing you live alone?"

"That's right. Well, actually, I do have a roommate. An eight-year-old German wirehaired pointer."

Jane gave that a moment's thought then said, "I'm not a hunter, but my dad and my brothers were. I'm guessing you must be also?"

Here we go, I thought. *Now for the questions about being a hit man. Be careful!*

"Lifelong," I said. "I grew up hunting with my dad, my uncle and my cousins. So editing *American Wingshot* was pretty much a labor of love. As you'd guess from the title, it's a magazine about bird hunting." I hesitated, then added, "In the trade, outdoor magazines like that are called hook-and-bullet rags."

Jane laughed and nodded. "Hook-and-bullet rags," she said. "I like that. I'll have to remember it."

I realized belatedly I had been doing almost all of the talking—so much for guarding my words—and was probably becoming boorish. "What about you," I asked. "Do you work?"

"No, I'm retired also," she said. "I was a public schoolteacher for twenty-five years. Fourth grade."

"Really!" I said. "My dad taught sixth grade."

"Small world," Jane said, and we both laughed.

"Yes, it is," I agreed.

We took another drink of our margaritas, and that's when the conversation turned serious.

Chapter 23

AFTER SETTING DOWN HER margarita glass—Jane used the large goblet style—she studied it for a moment, rotating it with her fingers. Then she raised her eyes to mine and gave me a slight smile.

"So I have to ask," she said, "does the fact that you're a lifelong hunter relate to your other occupation?"

"I suppose it does," I said. *Careful!* I told myself again. "At least somewhat. There are certain skills that are…useful. But it's not like that old Richard Connell short story, *The Most Dangerous Game.* I don't…do what I do just because I'm looking for a chance to match wits with my targets."

Jane frowned slightly and said, "Targets?"

"For want of a better word."

We sat silently for a minute and I found myself regretting, big time, the turn the conversation had taken. But I reminded myself that Jane was the one who had raised the subject, and she had hired me once before and was hoping to do so again. She was hardly blameless in the current situation and if she didn't like my choice of words, well…

After a moment she nodded and smiled slightly. "I suppose that's as good a word as any. I'm sure you have to retain a certain amount of detachment."

I nodded. "Yes, I do," I said. "In fact, I have a rule to that effect. No personal involvement." Good Lord, here I was, spilling my guts again. *Shut the hell up*, I told myself.

Jane was still smiling. "Does that rule include not having dinner with the people who hire you?"

"As a matter of fact, it does. I'll admit, this is a first."

Her smile grew wider. "I hope you're not going to tell me that now that I've seen your face, you'll have to kill me."

I laughed. "I don't think that will be necessary."

She made an exaggerated sigh and, still smiling, said, "Whew. That's a relief."

"SHALL WE TALK ABOUT Gaston Stevens?" Jane asked.

"Sure."

After finishing dinner and clearing the table, we had adjourned to Jane's front porch. We'd brought our margaritas with us and I was feeling more than a slight buzz. I realized the alcohol was loosening my tongue, and I reminded myself again to be careful and not become chatty. *Good luck with that*, I thought wryly.

Jane had settled on the hanging bench swing, leaning back at an angle on one end. She'd kicked off her flip-flops and she was sitting with her ankles crossed and her legs outstretched along the seat. I was struggling a bit to keep from staring at those legs. I saw her smiling at me and I guessed she knew all about my struggle.

I was sitting in one of the chairs at an angle to the swing. Jane was cradling her margarita glass in both hands. I had set my glass on the small table and I told myself to leave it there for a while.

"So," she said after a moment. "I already told you that he's the son of a congresswoman, Maggie Stevens. And he's been in and out of trouble all of his life. Some juvenile delinquent stuff when he was younger. Vandalism, shoplifting, then a couple of DUIs when he got older and started driving. Plus some disorderly conduct charges, public intoxication, that sort of thing. But he always gets off with a slap on the wrist."

"And you think that's going to happen again."

"I think it's almost a given."

"Well, you might be right. But a manslaughter charge is a lot more serious than any of those other offenses. It's going to be a lot tougher for him to walk away from that, even with his mother's influence."

Jane leaned forward in the swing and placed her glass next to mine on the table. Then she locked eyes with me and there was no mistaking the seriousness of her expression. "You don't know Maggie Stevens," she said. "If she wants her son exonerated, she'll find a way to make it happen."

I had no immediate response. Jane was right; I didn't know Maggie Stevens. But based on everything Jane had told me, I had no trouble believing that the congresswoman would stop at nothing, or almost nothing, to protect her son.

"Do you think she'll try to have the charges dismissed?" I asked after a moment.

"Oh, I'm sure she has her attorneys working on it right now. If they can find a way to get the charges dropped, they will. Otherwise, if it goes to trial, they'll do everything they can to try to prove Sara's death was an accident, that Gaston was trying to push her out of the way like he claimed. It'll be his word against mine, and I'm sure they'll do everything they can to discredit me."

"I'm sure you're right."

"Plus, the fact that he was charged with involuntary manslaughter, not murder or even voluntary manslaughter, is already in his favor. Even if he's convicted, he'll probably get off with a very light sentence. Maybe no more than a few years, or, God forbid, even a suspended sentence."

I took a deep breath. "Okay," I said. "I hate to ask this, but are you *sure* it was Gaston you saw that night? You mentioned his red hair, but it was after dark, right? How positive are you that it was him?"

"Absolutely positive. The moon wasn't quite full, but almost. So there was actually quite a bit of light. Plus, I recognized the ATV he was driving. It's a Polaris something or other. Razor, or something like that. Black and yellow, with a roll cage. I've seen him on it several times and so have a lot of other people."

"Okay," I said. There was obviously no shaking Jane in her conviction that it was Gaston Stevens she had seen run down her sister.

"You're forgetting about something," Jane added.

"What's that?"

"When Gaston was arrested, he didn't deny what had happened, or that it was him on the beach that night. He just claimed it was an accident, and that Sara had panicked and jumped in front of him. So my being able to ID him is almost moot. He's already admitted to being there."

Right. I suddenly felt like a total fool for overlooking, or forgetting, something so obvious. And for sounding like I might be doubting, or at least questioning, Jane's account.

Obviously, the margaritas had hit me even harder than I'd thought.

"I just wanted to make sure *you* were sure about all of this," I replied, and even as I said it I realized how lame it must have sounded. "Sorry if I sounded like I doubted you."

Jane studied me for a moment, then she smiled and said, "It's okay. And I understand why you have to be sure about these things. You wouldn't want to kill someone on somebody's say-so and then find out later that they were mistaken. But I know what I saw that night. It was Gaston Stevens, and what happened was no accident. He ran my sister down deliberately."

"All right," I said. "I'm convinced. And not just because he admitted to being there." Sheesh, could my attempt at damage control have been any more obvious?

"Thank you," she said. "For believing me." If she suspected I was humoring her, she was at least giving me the benefit of the doubt. She leaned back in the swing and shifted slightly, uncrossing her ankles as she did so. She stretched out her right leg and rested the heel of her bare foot, the one with the tattoo, on my knee. She smiled again and said, "Can I have a foot rub?"

I laughed and said, "Sure."

TALK ABOUT UNPRECEDENTED.

Not the foot rub itself. I had done the same for Daryl plenty of times after dinner, usually while we were watching television or a DVD of a favorite old movie. In fact, I couldn't help thinking this was almost eerily ironic and coincidental, coming so soon after my break-up with her.

But it certainly sent my resolve to remain detached and keep client contact to a minimum right out the window. I could feel my sense of apprehension returning. *What the hell are you doing,* I asked myself.

Jane, on the other hand, seemed completely comfortable with the proceedings. She sighed and leaned back on the swing. She closed her eyes and said, "Mmm, that feels good."

I smiled and—thinking again of Daryl—reflected, *well, I've had lots of practice.* But I didn't want thoughts of Daryl to intrude on this moment. I said, "Tell me about this tattoo." I could now see it was a sea turtle, and I traced its outline with a fingertip.

Jane laughed but kept her eyes closed. "Oh, that was Sara's idea," she said. "I told you she was devoted to the turtles, and when we started volunteering at the Paige Green Rehab Center, she talked me into it. We went into the tattoo place together and got them at the same time."

"I like it. It's cute."

"Thanks." She hesitated a moment, then added, "It reminds me of Sara every time I see it." I thought perhaps I detected a slight catch in her voice.

"Sorry if I brought up a painful memory."

"Oh no, not at all. I loved volunteering with Sara and it's a fond memory, not a painful one."

"Okay."

We slipped into a comfortable silence for another ten minutes or so. Then I patted her foot and said, "Time for the other foot."

Jane shifted in the swing and put her left foot on my knee. She laughed and said, "If you ever decide to stop killing people, you could get a job as a foot masseur."

"Always good to have a backup plan," I said, and she laughed again.

I TOOK MY LEAVE at about ten o'clock. After the foot rub, we carried our now-empty margarita glasses back to the kitchen, then I told Jane I was beginning to feel the effects of the day's travel and I needed to get back to the hotel. She said she understood and walked me back to her front door.

We faced each other for a moment, a bit awkwardly,

then Jane smiled and said, "Thanks again for the terrific foot rub."

"You're welcome," I said. "Thank you for the wonderful dinner. And those kickass margaritas."

She laughed. "Speaking of which, are you sure you're okay to drive back to the Hampton?"

"I think so." I wondered what she would have said if I had answered in the negative.

"All right," she said. "Want to give me a call when you get there? Let me know you're home safe?"

"Okay, Mom," I said.

She laughed. "Just do it," she said. Then she put her hand on my chest and with a gentle push she sent me on my way.

THERE WAS LESS TRAFFIC on the drive back to the Hampton, and I made it in ten minutes. When I got back to my room I picked up my cell phone and punched in Jane's number from memory. She answered on the first ring.

"Hello?" She sounded a little hesitant or uncertain.

"Back at the Hampton, safe and sound."

"Oh, Rob," she said. "I'm sorry. I didn't recognize this number."

Then I realized I'd called from my personal cell, not the burner I had been using with her.

Wow.

I'd have liked to blame the margaritas, but I knew better.

I was definitely slipping.

Chapter 24

ANOTHER SLEEPLESS NIGHT.

Well, partly, anyway.

Ordinarily I'm not one of those people who has trouble sleeping in a strange bed; I can usually drop off pretty much anywhere if I'm tired enough. And actually, I did sleep, but fitfully. I would doze off for an hour or so, then wake up and check the illuminated numerals on the small clock radio on the nightstand. I would drift off again, then wake up again and repeat the exercise, maybe doing a mental calculation on how many minutes had passed since the last time I'd looked.

Not exactly a restful experience, for sure.

When I did sleep, my brain remained in overdrive, attempting to process and make sense of what had happened earlier. I kept telling myself—yes, I had an unending internal dialogue going—that having dinner with Jane Trehorn was no big deal, unprecedented though it was. The food was good, the conversation was lively and, for the most part, fun; and no real harm had been done, even though—Jane's joking comment about me having to kill her came to mind—she had seen my face.

But there was also the matter of her attractiveness.

I couldn't deny I found her to be very good-looking. I've already mentioned there was a vivacious quality about her as well, and it was combined with a certain earthiness—as suggested by her casual request for a foot rub—that I also found appealing.

So of course, I couldn't help wondering what she might have thought about me.

She had seemed completely at ease throughout the evening, and I had to wonder how many people would have felt the same if they knew—as she did—that they were having dinner with a contract killer. Once again, thoughts of Daryl and the secret I had long withheld from her came to mind. I would never face that dilemma with Jane.

What the hell?

Was I already imagining a relationship with this woman?

I told myself I seriously needed to get a grip. Ours was a pending business arrangement, nothing more, and I would do well to remember that. There was no reason to suppose Jane was interested in anything beyond seeing her sister's killer brought to justice.

I also told myself I was far too old to be engaging in romantic fantasies, especially when my previous relationship had ended less than two weeks earlier. Getting involved on the rebound with another woman—and a client to boot—was the very last thing I should be considering.

Coming up with a game plan for eliminating Gaston Stevens, and accomplishing that task with minimal risk to myself, was where my thoughts should be focused. The entire situation with Daryl might have made me reckless, but it wasn't too late to correct course.

So…matter resolved.

Right.

THE NEXT MORNING, I had just finished showering and was pulling on a clean pair of cargo shorts when my cell phone rang—my personal cell, not the burner I'd been using with Jane. My first thought was that it was probably Rachel James, calling to see how I was doing, how my dinner date with Jane had gone (yes, before leaving Des Moines I had confided to Rachel about this) and so on.

Then I did a quick calculation on the time difference. It was 7:30 here in North Carolina, which meant it was 6:30 in Iowa. I was pretty sure Rachel wouldn't have called me this early.

The phone rang again. I crossed the room to the nightstand and picked up the phone. Caller ID told me it was Jane.

My slip-up from last night was coming back to haunt me.

"Hello?"

"Good morning, Rob. I hope I didn't wake you."

"No, I've been up for a while." I told myself this wasn't a fib, as I'd been up for about 15 minutes. "What's up?"

"Well…I offered to show you around Schnock's Harbor and I wondered if you'd like to have lunch today. I know a great little place called the Crab Shack. It's pretty rustic and it's actually in Surf City, but that's only a few miles from here and the food is really good. I think you'd like it."

"Well…okay. Sounds good." The previous evening's margaritas, followed by such a restless night, hadn't left me at my sharpest and I couldn't think fast enough to come up with a good reason to decline her offer.

"Great! How about I pick you up at, say, 11:30?"

"I'll be ready."

"See you then!"

Margaritas, hell. Who was I kidding? I just wanted to see her again.

I WAS WAITING OUTSIDE the Hampton when Jane pulled up in a dark green Subaru Forester. I climbed in and said, "Good morning."

"Good morning," she replied. "How was your night?"

"Fine ," I said. "Yours?" I buckled my seat belt and we pulled out of the hotel parking lot onto Highway 210.

"Oh, mine was fine also." She laughed. "After the margaritas and the foot rub, I was nice and relaxed. I dropped right off…well, after we talked, I mean."

"That's good." After telling her my night had been fine—okay, a small lie—I didn't want to go into all the restlessness I had actually experienced. So I added, "You said this place where we're going is called the Crab Shack?"

"Right. It's in Surf City. That's also where the Paige Green Turtle Rehab Center is. I thought after lunch we could swing by there."

"That sounds good." Even as I spoke I realized none of this was getting me any closer to Gaston Stevens, or to coming up with a plan for his elimination. I considered voicing this thought but decided against it. For the moment I was happy just to be having lunch with Jane.

Then reality bit. *Get a grip*, I told myself again. *You're not here on vacation.*

"This is a nice ride," I said, trying to keep the conversational ball rolling.

"Oh, thanks. It's actually Sara's…I mean, it *was* Sara's. I'm using it because my Jeep Cherokee is in the shop." She paused, and when she continued I detected a wistful note in her voice. "Well, I guess actually it *is* mine, or it will be when her estate is settled. I was Sara's next of kin, along with our two brothers, so I'm inheriting a lot of her things, whatever she didn't will to our nieces and nephews."

"She didn't have any children?"

"No. And neither do I."

She didn't elaborate on this point and I thought it best not to ask. But after a moment she said, "Our two brothers, Bruce and Edward, both have kids…well, they're adults now. But of course when they were younger Sara and I spoiled them every chance we got." She laughed. "I think we were always competing to be their favorite aunt."

I laughed also. "Of course you were. Sibling rivalry."

"Right. And now that Sara's gone, I guess I win by default." She paused a moment, then laughed nervously. "I'm sorry. I can't believe I just said that."

"No worries, and no need to apologize. I'm sure they're going to miss her."

"I'm sure they already are. Missing her, I mean. Which reminds me—we're having her celebration of life tomorrow afternoon at the Paige Green Center. I'd love to have you attend."

"I'd be honored," I said.

What other answer could I have given?

THE CRAB SHACK WAS EVERYTHING Jane had described. The exterior was decidedly unpretentious—with its weathered white siding, "shack" wasn't far off the mark—and the inside was, as Jane had mentioned, rustic. Well-worn wooden booths painted red, exposed ceiling beams and pipes, large wooden ceiling fans, classic rock and roll playing on the sound system.

I loved it.

And the food was every bit as good as Jane had claimed. She had a shrimp burger and I had a blackened catfish sandwich with fries and coleslaw. Our server was a middle-aged blonde with a weathered, canny look about her, and after we gave her our order and she walked away, Jane laughed and said, "Catfish?"

"What can I say, I'm a native Midwesterner," I said. "My grandfather loved fishing and catfish were his favorite. I have a lot of happy memories of fishing with him when I was a kid."

She laughed again. "Sounds like an ideal childhood. Right out of *Tom Sawyer*."

I smiled. "Ideal might be a stretch, but yes, my childhood was pretty good."

She thought for a moment. Then: "Last night you mentioned hunting with your dad and your uncle and cousins, but you didn't say anything about any brothers. Or sisters. Are you an only child?"

"Don't hold that against me."

She laughed. "I'll try not to."

"Thanks." –

Chapter 25

THE PAIGE GREEN SEA TURTLE Rescue and Rehabilitation Center was a beautiful facility, and there was no question its staff and volunteers were totally dedicated to their mission of ensuring the perpetuation of sea turtles worldwide. Their enthusiasm was contagious and after spending an hour there with Jane following our lunch at the Crab Shack, I was almost ready to volunteer myself and do whatever I could to help such magnificent creatures survive and flourish.

Our visit also bolstered my appreciation of the commitment to the turtles shared by Jane and her sister, and why the circumstances of Sara's death had been especially devastating for Jane. And it further explained Jane's determination to see Sara's killer brought to justice…not that her determination needed any additional explanation or was the least bit in doubt.

We entered the Center and paused for a moment in the front hall before a gorgeous floor-to-ceiling mural depicting all sorts of colorful underwater sea life, turtles and fish alike. The mural was titled "Sea of Wonders" and as I stood gazing at it I couldn't help uttering a soft, "Wow." I'll admit I felt somewhat overwhelmed.

"It's beautiful, isn't it?" Jane smiled beside me.

"Breathtaking is more like it."

She laughed and said, "Want me to shoot a pic of you in front of it?" She pulled her phone from the pocket of her shorts.

I almost said yes, then thought the better of it. "Umm, better not," I said. I lowered my voice a notch and added, "I'm supposed to remain below radar, remember?"

Jane picked up on the implications immediately. She nodded and said, "Ah, got it." She stuffed the phone back into her pocket.

As she did so, a tanned, dark-haired young woman

approached, calling out as she did so. "Hey, Janie! Good to see you!" She stopped before us and gave Jane a quick hug. Then she looked my way, smiled, and said, "Who's this?"

"This is my friend Rob," Jane said. "Rob, this is Julie Thompson, another volunteer."

"Nice to meet you, Rob," Julie said, sticking out her hand. I shook with her, noting the strength of her grip and that her hand was dry and more than a bit callused. Whatever Julie did for the rehab center or elsewhere, I was willing to bet it involved manual labor. I guessed she was somewhere in her late twenties to early thirties.

"Nice to meet you also, Julie," I said.

"Rob's visiting for a few days and I wanted him to see the center," Jane said. "Is there a tour going on?"

"One just started a little while ago," Julie said. "Do you want to catch up to them?"

"That would be great if it's not a problem."

"C'mon. I think they're in the Turtle Bay."

We followed Julie as she led us through the main hall and into a large room filled with water tanks, some of which were nearly the size of an above-ground swimming pool. Each of the tanks had one or more turtles swimming in it. A group of nine people, adults and children plus a tour guide, were watching from a ramp above the tanks. "This is where turtles are rehabbed before they're returned to the ocean," Jane explained. "It's called the Turtle Bay because that sounds better than Sick Bay."

I laughed. "That makes sense."

We joined the group on the ramp and gazed down at the turtles swimming beneath us. They varied in size and one of the smaller turtles, a little larger than a dinner plate, appeared to be missing its right front flipper. I asked about it and Julie replied, "Yes, that's Gracie. She was caught in a fishing net and by the time she was rescued, her flipper was so badly mangled, probably from struggling to free herself, that it had to be amputated. But she's coming along fine now and getting good at swimming with only three flippers. We're still hopeful she can be returned to the sea."

I couldn't help shaking my head at Gracie's misfortune. But I also felt a surge of admiration for the people who were dedicated to her recovery and for their tireless efforts on behalf of Gracie and all the other turtles in their care. I couldn't deny I found their commitment inspiring.

THE TOUR LASTED another twenty minutes or so and concluded at the facility's gift shop. *Good marketing*, I reflected, but I kept that thought to myself. Given the nature of all non-profit conservation organizations and their never-ending need for funding, the turtle rehab center couldn't be faulted for operating this additional revenue source.

We spent a few minutes browsing the merchandise, which, not surprisingly, consisted almost entirely of turtle- and ocean-related items. We passed a rack of t-shirts bearing the rehab center's logo—which prominently featured a sea turtle—and Jane insisted I pick out a shirt for myself. "I'll buy," she said.

"You don't need to do that."

"I want to." She grinned. "Something to commemorate your visit."

A visit that will probably end with me killing someone, I thought. *Is that really something we should commemorate?* But again, I kept this dark thought to myself. Jane was obviously enjoying showing me around and I had to admit—again—that I was also enjoying the time I was spending with her.

I selected a dark blue t-shirt with the logo in a lighter blue. Jane laughed when she saw me pull an XL off the rack. "Extra large?" she said. "Really?"

I laughed in return. "I like them roomy," I said.

"Okay," she said. She began digging in her handbag for her wallet and we headed to the register.

AS WE CROSSED the parking lot to Jane's Forester, I started tallying up everything Jane had spent so far on my "visit," as she termed it. Last night's dinner at her house and today's lunch at the Crab Shack. (I had offered to pick up the tab for the latter but she refused, saying she was paying because she had invited me, rather than vice versa.) And now a souvenir t-shirt from the rehab center's gift shop.

All of this in addition to the fee she was planning to pay to me after I avenged her sister's death by killing Gaston Stevens.

My misgivings concerning this whole unlikely scenario returned full force.

Today's outing had been fun, but I realized I was once again letting my thinking be clouded by Jane's attractiveness and my own enjoyment at being with her. This was, quite simply, no way for a contract killer to act...or, more pragmatically, to conduct business. I knew I was on very dangerous ground here, and I would do well to start distancing myself from my client.

I wondered how to go about doing this.

"What did you think of the center?" Jane asked as we settled ourselves in the Forester's seats. She cranked the ignition and immediately turned the AC to high. She had left the SUV parked in the sun and its interior was the proverbial oven.

"Very impressive," I said. "It's a beautiful facility, and the people are obviously dedicated to what they're doing." I laughed and added, somewhat lamely, "If I were an injured sea turtle, this is where I'd want to be, and these are the people I'd want taking care of me."

Jane smiled but didn't laugh. "It's all pretty inspiring, isn't it?"

"Yes, it is," I said, recalling my earlier thought when we'd been watching Gracie and the other turtles.

"Then maybe you can understand why Sara and I were so committed to this, and why her death hit me so hard."

I wondered now if our visit to the center had been a deliberate tactic on Jane's part intended to further convince me that Gaston Stevens deserved the fate she was paying me to deliver. If so, the tactic had been successful.

"Yes," I said. "I understand that."

Chapter 26

IT WAS JUST PAST 2:30, North Carolina time, when Jane dropped me off at the Hampton Inn.

We hadn't talked much during the drive from the turtle rehab center back to the hotel. Jane seemed to be concentrating on her driving and I was still wrestling with how to put some distance between us. Offhand, I couldn't come up with a plausible way to do this without alienating her. Which, I admitted to myself, I didn't want to do.

Still, it was a reasonably comfortable silence, the kind enjoyed by, say, old friends who don't feel the need to keep up a constant line of chatter. I was fine with that, and apparently, so was Jane.

But when we entered the hotel parking lot, she pulled into one of the vacant spaces opposite the building rather than using the semi-circular drive-through to drop me off like I was expecting. She shifted the Forester into park and turned in her seat to face me. She smiled and said, "Hey. This was fun."

I smiled in return. "Yes, it was. Lunch was great, and the turtle center is…" I hesitated, then added, "remarkable. I'm glad I got to see it. Thanks for taking me."

"You're welcome. I'm glad you enjoyed it." She studied my face for a moment, her expression turning serious. Then: "So what happens now?"

I wasn't sure how to respond. Was she asking what the next steps were regarding Gaston Stevens? Or was the question of a more personal nature, hinting at the possibility of a developing relationship?

I played it safe and, after a moment, opted for the former.

"I really need to start focusing on Gaston Stevens," I said. "I need to get a look at him, first of all, and get a feel for where he spends his time and what he does, that sort of thing. Then it will be a matter of coming up with a plan to cross paths with him and take some action."

"Like I said before, I might be able to help you with some of that."

I shook my head. *Here we go*, I thought. "No," I said. "I appreciate the offer, but like *I* said before, it's probably best if I handle this part by myself. The less you're involved, the safer you'll be if anything goes sideways."

"I'm not worried about my safety," Jane said. "And whatever you do, don't patronize me." There was no mistaking the anger in her voice.

I sighed. "Okay," I said. "Sorry if that's what it sounded like. But…what you're hiring me to do has the potential to blow up in my face, or our faces, rather. There's always that possibility anytime I take an assignment, and this particular situation carries an even bigger risk, given the fact that his mother is a congresswoman."

"I know all of that."

No, you really don't, I thought. *You've never killed anyone, and you don't have any firsthand knowledge of how many things could go wrong.* Then I reminded myself that she had, in fact, been through this exercise once before. True, I had handled the hit on her husband by myself, but she was the one who had set those wheels in motion. As the old saying goes, this was not her first rodeo.

I also reminded myself that Rachel and Al James had played an active role in my last assignment, and in addition, I had asked for help from a computer geek in Chicago named James Collins, plus his two hacker buddies. The fact that the assignment was one of my own choosing—no one had actually hired me—was of little consequence. The simple fact remained I wasn't quite the lone wolf operator I fancied myself to be. At least, not any longer.

I wondered if my age had something to do with my increasing reliance on others.

I realized Jane was waiting for a response. Trying to put the onus back on her, I said, "What exactly is it that you think you can help me with?"

She smiled and said, "For starters, I know where he spends a lot of his evenings."

"And where is that?"

Her smile turned into a grin. "I'd rather show you than tell you."

"Why is that?"

"Because if I tell you, you'll go there by yourself, without me." She sounded triumphant.

Now it was my turn to get angry. "Jane, this isn't a game," I said. "My time down here is limited, so I need to find Gaston Stevens and put together a plan as quickly as possible." I didn't say the rest of what I was thinking, namely, *I don't want you tagging along and possibly slowing me down. Nor do I want to be responsible for watching out for you and keeping you safe.*

"Besides," I added, "if you're with me at whatever place you're talking about, won't he recognize you if he sees you? If he does, there goes any chance I have of going unnoticed."

She gave this a moment's thought. "Okay," she finally said. "You're probably right about him recognizing me. I can see why that would be a problem, especially if he turns up dead so soon afterwards. I might be questioned, and they might ask me who the guy was I'd been seen with recently."

"That's right. And I'd prefer you not being put in the position of having to cover for me. Like I said, the less involved you are, the better. For both of us."

"All right," she said. "I get it. But how are you going to recognize him if I don't point him out?"

"Trust me, I've had a lot of experience at finding people and making sure I've identified them correctly; that's where the internet comes in handy. I'm sure he's on social media, so there are bound to be pictures of him, and you already told me he has flaming red hair. Is there anything else you can tell me about him? Anything else that will help identify him, like a tattoo, maybe?"

She gave this some thought, then said, "No, I don't think he has any tattoos. At least, not any that are large or noticeable. Nothing on his arms, anyway." She laughed. "I can't speak to what might be under his clothing."

I laughed also. "Okay, so no help from the tattoo standpoint. Anything else that might help me recognize him?"

"Well, his two best friends, or the guys he usually hangs with, are Grady O'Neill and Dave Sonderheim. The three of them go everywhere together, or it seems like that, anyway."

"Anything distinctive about either of them?"

"Well, now that you've mentioned it, Dave Sonderheim *does* have tattoos. In fact, he's almost covered with them, or as much as I could see. He has full sleeves on both arms, and several big tats on his legs as well. I've never seen him without his shirt, but I'd guess he has some body art also."

"Okay, that helps. He should be easy to recognize. So all I have to do now is find a guy with flaming red hair who's hanging with another guy covered with tats."

Jane laughed again. "Piece of cake," she said.

WE TALKED FOR ANOTHER ten minutes or so, during which Jane told me the name of the bar that was, in her words, "their favorite watering hole." This was the place I would be likely to find Stevens, and his two buddies, on most nights.

"It's called the Dive Bar, and it really *is* a dive bar," she said. "But the name is kind of a play on words, because of lot of divers, scuba divers, hang there."

"Gaston Stevens…is he a diver?" I was already considering possible scenarios in which he might have an accident.

"Not that I know of. He and his buddies do a little surfing, maybe, but I don't think he's into scuba diving."

"Okay," I said. *Scratch that idea.* "Where is this Dive Bar? I'm guessing it's probably somewhere nearby?"

"Yes, it's only a few minutes from here, in fact. Want to drive by and take a look?"

"No, that's okay. I'll find it," I said. "But I am curious about something. How is it that you know where Gaston and his buddies hang out? Have you been following them?" I laughed as I said this, realizing that suggesting she had been tailing Gaston, private eye style, probably sounded a little farfetched.

But it actually wasn't. The same James Collins whose

help I had requested had done that a couple years earlier, following the attorney who murdered his sister until he, Collins, had gathered the evidence he used to convince me of the attorney's guilt. I wouldn't have been all that surprised if Jane said she had been doing the same.

But she hadn't. "No," she laughed. "I haven't been following him. But I dated a diver for a couple months and we used to see Gaston and his buddies in the Dive Bar. They were there almost every time we were, so unless something has changed and they've started doing their drinking and hell-raising elsewhere, I'd say that's where you're likely to find them."

"Okay, got it," I said. I couldn't help feeling curious, and maybe a bit jealous, about the diver she'd mentioned dating, but I didn't ask. Apparently she was no longer seeing the guy and I told myself it shouldn't matter to me anyhow.

I suddenly found myself wanting some time to decompress and mull over everything we had discussed. Also, as much as I enjoyed Jane's company—and there was no denying that I *did* enjoy it—I wanted to start easing her out of the picture as quickly as possible, at least as far as Gaston Stevens was concerned. This looked like an opportune time to do so.

"I should let you get going," I said. "Thanks again for lunch and the tour of the turtle center." I laughed and added, "And for the t-shirt."

"My pleasure. And fyi, I'd suggest having dinner again tonight, but I'm getting together with my brothers to go over the arrangements for Sara's celebration of life tomorrow. You know, make sure we have everything taken care of, that sort of thing."

"I understand. And no worries about dinner. I can find something on my own."

"Okay then. Remember, you're invited to the celebration. It's at 1:00 tomorrow at the rehab center."

"I'll plan to be there."

Chapter 27

MY ROOM WAS A COOL, DARK cave when I stepped into it.

Housekeeping had come and gone during my absence; the bed was tightly made, the wastebaskets had been emptied and fresh towels had been hung in the bathroom. The person who had tended my room had picked up the two five-dollar bills I'd left as a tip on top of the dresser, tucked under a note on the hotel's notepad. She had left a note of her own thanking me. It was signed "Tanya" and was accompanied by a hand-drawn smiley face.

The blinds were closed and I guessed this was intended to aid the air conditioning by blocking the afternoon sun that otherwise would have been streaming through the west-facing windows. I snapped on a light and moved over to the bed, tossing the plastic bag with my souvenir t-shirt onto the armchair in the corner. I sat down on the bed and kicked off my topsiders. Then I laid myself back on the bed, folded my arms across my chest and stared up at the ceiling, wondering what my next move should be.

I didn't wonder for long. Within three minutes I was asleep.

I WOKE UP about forty-five minutes later. The clock on the nightstand said it was 3:37. I continued to lie there for another couple minutes, staring up at the ceiling. I didn't find any more answers there than I had before I fell asleep.

I sat up and shook my head, trying to clear the cobwebs. I had wanted some free time away from Jane and now that I had it, I wasn't sure how to proceed. I was planning to visit the Dive Bar she had told me about in hopes of getting a look at Gaston Stevens, but that wouldn't be until later in the evening. I had several hours to kill in the meantime.

I thought about calling Mike Stevenson to see how Preacher was doing, but I realized Mike would be at work and

Preacher was probably getting along just fine. If there had been any problems, Mike would have called me.

Rachel would also be at work. She was keeping an eye on my house and bringing in my mail—she's the only person besides myself with a key to my place—but again, if there had been any problems she would have contacted me, either by text or with a call. I also reminded myself I had only been gone for a little over one day so it was unlikely any kind of crisis had occurred.

Then, inexplicably, I found myself thinking about Daryl.

She too would undoubtedly be at work, not that I was thinking of calling her. But I couldn't help wondering if she was still seeing Craig Wilkinson; if now that I was gone from her life their relationship had progressed even further. She no longer had to worry about keeping anything hidden from me, so that would facilitate matters, green-lighting their affair. I bristled at the thought.

I shook my head again. *Don't go there*, I told myself. *There's no sense speculating about any of that, and besides, what difference does it make?*

Indeed.

I ENDED UP on the beach.

It was a short drive from the hotel and I cruised along the street paralleling the beach until I found a public parking area, one that didn't require a permit—presumably one you had to pay for—to park. The houses on the street, opposite the dunes on the ocean side, were usually three or four stories, often in pastel colors and built on stilts in case of flooding. They had names like After Dune Delight, Shore Feels Good, Sea Renity and Loggerhead Lounge. I smiled as I read them, the last one reminding me of the turtles I'd seen at the rehab center earlier that afternoon.

I pulled into the graveled parking area and turned off the Impala's ignition. I donned a khaki bill cap and as I climbed out and locked the vehicle, it occurred to me that if I were back in Iowa I might very well be doing something similar—specifically, walking at Maffitt Reservoir. The reservoir is my go-to place when I need to clear my head, or as Herman Melville said in *Moby Dick*, "Meditation and water are wedded forever."

The big difference—aside from the fact that I was at an ocean and not a lake—was that if I were at Maffitt I would be accompanied by Preacher.

The whimsical thought crossed my mind that someone in this area should operate a concession where you could rent a dog for, say, an hour to accompany you on a walk. I mean, there are such rent-a-bicycle concessions, so why not?

Yes, I recognized the impracticality of this idea.

But that's kind of the way my mind was working as I wandered down the dunes until I came to a wooden stile that provided access to the beach. Signs warned people to stay off the dunes or be subject to a $500 fine. The signs also explained this was to protect the dunes from erosion and asked the public's support in this effort by using the stiles.

I mounted the steps of the stile and paused at the top for a moment, taking in the beach and the ocean before me. Big waves were rolling in and making quite a bit of noise in doing so, an unmistakable reminder of the ocean's vastness and power. Another line from *Moby Dick*, the final clause of the last chapter, came to mind: "…and the great shroud of the sea rolled on as it rolled five thousand years ago."

A great shroud indeed. Considering my reason for being in North Carolina, I found the metaphor especially apt.

I descended to the beach and started walking. I'd taken only a few steps before my topsiders were filled with sand, so I paused to remove them. Then, carrying them in my left hand, I continued on.

The afternoon was warm but a strong breeze coming off the water offset the heat and kept things pleasant. I was wearing cargo shorts and I had exchanged the pale blue polo shirt I'd been wearing for a t-shirt before leaving the hotel, but I hadn't thought to dope up with sunscreen and I realized I was probably courting sunburn. At least the cap would protect my scalp.

People were scattered along the beach but it wasn't crowded, this being a weekday. A few folks were beachcombing, stopping occasionally to pick up seashells or driftwood, and several children in swimsuits chased each other in and out of the surf, accompanied by a lot of laughing and yelling, while their parents cautioned them to be careful. The children, of course, paid little attention to the warnings.

I ambled along, alternating my gaze between the rolling surf and what lay ahead of me on the beach. Five brown pelicans in a tight formation, looking eerily like a squadron of World War II bombers, flew low over the water, their wingtips almost touching the wave crests. I hoped I might see one of them make a sudden dive for a fish, but it didn't happen. I watched them until I could no longer make them out against the water and they were lost in the distance.

Seeing the pelicans awakened something predatory in my nature. I started thinking about Gaston Stevens.

I wondered if I would be lucky enough to see him at the Dive Bar later that evening. According to Jane, Stevens and his buddies were regulars so it seemed like a fairly good bet. Of course, there were probably a hundred reasons why they might not be there on this particular night, but for want of a better place to start, I would give it a shot. Offhand, I couldn't think of a better plan.

Thinking about Stevens also caused me to start reviewing last night's after-dinner conversation with Jane. I wondered if I was anywhere close to the place where Sara Lawson had been killed. Jane hadn't specified exactly where it happened, so I had no idea if Sara had been killed on this beach or somewhere else. I also realized that it probably didn't matter, but I always like to gather as many details as possible because sometimes the stuff that seems insignificant can ultimately prove helpful.

I continued to mull all of this over and I walked for probably a good mile or so before turning back. My daily outings with Preacher have kept me in reasonably good shape but I wasn't used to walking in soft sand and my calves were beginning to ache. To make the walking a little easier I moved out to the firmer wet sand at the edge of the surf. As always, I was momentarily surprised at how cold the water was—the ocean is *always* cold—when a small wave broke over my feet.

I headed back toward the car, hoping I'd recognize the stile I had crossed to get down to the beach. The stiles were located every few hundred yards and looked almost identical. I realized belatedly I should have noted the landmarks near the one I had used, but I hadn't paid much attention to them.

One more sign of age-related absentmindedness, no doubt.

Chapter 28

THE DIVE BAR WAS INDEED a dive bar, just as Jane said. Like the Crab Shack where we had lunch, the bar's exterior was weathered white siding that desperately needed paint. The interior was similarly run-down, with well-worn wooden booths and an equally worn bar with wooden stools. The walls were hung with mounted saltwater gamefish plus a huge manta ray, mottled black and white, that covered almost an entire wall. None of the mounts, including the ray, were in good condition, but I suspected neither the proprietors nor the clientele were particularly bothered by this.

In spite of its general shabbiness, the bar seemed to give off a positive vibe. Most of the customers were young to middle-aged—I guessed I was one of the oldest persons present by a good ten years or more—and everyone seemed to be enjoying themselves in a laid back, friendly fashion. A Jimmy Buffett song was playing on the sound system, and there was nothing threatening in the air.

This was a relief. Based on Jane's description, I'd been anticipating a somewhat rougher crowd and the kind of place where the occasional fight might break out over a disputed pool shot or simply looking someone in the eye—or at someone's girlfriend—for a moment too long.

But the patrons of the Dive Bar appeared to be an amiable bunch, and I got the impression most of them knew each other. They were about evenly divided between men and women and there was lot of laughter. Everyone was dressed casually, with t-shirts and shorts and flip-flops predominating among both sexes.

Except for my well-worn topsiders I was dressed similarly and I hoped I wasn't too conspicuous. I put a harmless old geezer smile on my face and hoped I might pass for an aging beach bum or something similar. I had indeed picked up a bit of sunburn during my walk on the beach that afternoon, and with my beard now showing a lot more salt than pepper, I didn't think this was too much of a stretch.

The beard, by the way, was Daryl's idea. I had been wearing it for almost a year now. I'd initially balked when she showed me a photo of actor Corbin Bernsen and encouraged me to start wearing a short-cropped beard like his. At the same time, she recommended having my thinning hair buzzed short so I could avoid slipping into comb-over territory. I eventually acquiesced and after adjusting to seeing myself BWB (bald with beard) I had to admit her suggestions had been good ones. I especially liked the low maintenance aspect.

I shook my head to rid myself of thoughts of Daryl. I moved over to the bar and settled myself on an empty stool. A cute brunette wearing a powder blue t-shirt with a white dolphin on it was to my right; a young blonde guy with a lot of freckles was to my left. They both looked my way when I sat down and the brunette smiled and said, "Hi." The guy nodded and smiled but didn't speak.

I nodded and smiled in return. "Good evening," I said. The bartender, a burly bald fellow in a sleeveless gray t-shirt, approached. A barbed wire tattoo circled both of his powerful biceps. He smiled also and said, "What'll it be?"

I did a quick scan of the beer taps and didn't see Blue Moon. But I spotted a suitable substitute. "Dos Equis," I said.

"Sure thing," he said. "Lime?"

"Yes, thanks."

He drew my beer, added a lime wedge to the glass and placed it in front me. He smiled again and said, "Here on vacation?"

So much for passing myself off as an aging beach bum or someone local. I wondered if the bartender had detected a Midwestern accent in the few words I'd spoken. Or maybe it was just that I was a face he hadn't seen before.

"Yes," I said. "Just in town for a few days." I wanted to deflect any further questions about where I was from. I did a quick glance around and added, "This is a nice place you have here."

"Thanks. We like it. My name's Steve." He extended his hand and I shook with him. I wasn't surprised that he had a strong grip.

"Rob," I said.

"Good to meet you, Rob," he said. He moved away to fill more drink orders.

I took a pull of my beer, then I sat back and took another look around the place. Two couples were shooting a game of eight ball on the pool table at the back of the room, near an old-fashioned glass-sided popcorn machine. The bin beneath the popper was about half full of popped corn and a stack of paper boats sat next to it. Every so often a patron would go over and open the glass doors and use a metal scoop to fill one of the boats with popcorn, then carry the boat back to his or her table or place at the bar.

All that was missing from this convivial setting was a young guy with lots of tattoos, accompanied by another fellow with flaming red hair and an ankle monitor.

EARLIER IN THE EVENING I had eaten dinner at a nearby Mexican restaurant called Agave Azul. I ordered carne asada, served with sides of rice and refried beans, and a margarita. The latter, of course, immediately reminded me of the previous evening at Jane's place and I spent most of the meal thinking about her. Why are you not surprised.

I kept telling myself not to read too much into her friendly gestures and to keep focused on the matter at hand, the assignment for which she was hiring me. I was due to fly back home in four more days so I couldn't afford to waste time on romantic fantasies, Jane's attractiveness notwithstanding. I really needed to clear my mind and concentrate on Gaston Stevens and how I was going to eliminate him.

Never before had I had to deal with such a distraction.

I knew, or thought I knew, anyway, that some of this was due to my lingering feelings about the whole Daryl situation. When I could force myself to think objectively about what had happened, I knew I was far from being over her involvement with Craig Wilkinson. It still stung, hugely, and I knew that was likely to continue for quite some time.

As such, I didn't want to fall into the old cliché of a

rebound relationship, even if Jane was willing.

I had a sudden disquieting thought, or two of them, actually. I wondered if my attraction to Jane, and my desire to get involved with her, was perhaps an attempt on my part to get back at Daryl. Was I just seeking to even the score?

Even more disturbing, I also wondered if my agreeing to take on the Gaston Stevens assignment was in some way an attempt to diffuse the anger I felt toward Craig Wilkinson, i.e., for reasons I've already mentioned, I couldn't retaliate directly against Wilkinson, so was I making Gaston Stevens a surrogate target for that anger?

God help me if that was the case.

I STAYED AT THE DIVE BAR for about an hour and a half. I learned that the cute brunette's name was Annie and she was a sophomore at UNC-Chapel Hill, where she was majoring in marketing and communications. She lived here in Schnock's Harbor and was home for the summer break.

The blonde fellow on my left was named Ken. When he told me this I couldn't help thinking of a certain doll's boyfriend, but I kept that thought to myself. He appeared to be about the same age as Annie and I wondered if by sitting down between them I might have spoiled any hopes he'd had of hitting on her. I hoped not, but c'est la vie. At any rate, the three of us had a friendly conversation and I knew I would be leaving the bar before they did, so maybe Ken would regard my departure as the signal to make his move.

While we talked I momentarily considered bringing up Gaston Stevens and asking if either of them knew him, but I immediately dismissed the idea, realizing I couldn't come up with a plausible way to do this without tipping my hand. Thanks to Steve the bartender it had already been established I wasn't a local, so any interest I betrayed in Stevens was bound to be noticed. Plus, if either of them did know him, they might mention to him that some old dude with a beard had been inquiring about him. Not good.

I finished my third Dos Equis and signaled to Steve that I was ready to cash out. Gaston Stevens and his buddies were no-shows, at least as of 10:15, and I sensed that Annie, Ken and I had pretty much run out of things to talk about.

It was time to cut my losses and head back to the hotel. I disliked knowing that in my first attempt to get a look at Gaston Stevens, I'd struck out, big time.

Maybe Ken would have better luck with Annie.

Chapter 29

IT WAS JUST PAST 10:30 WHEN I got back to my room at the Hampton. I undressed and was headed for the shower when my cell phone rang. Caller ID told me it was Jane.

As I picked up the phone I couldn't help reflecting that she seemed to have an uncanny knack for catching me on my way to or from the shower. But I didn't share this thought. Instead, I said, "Hey, there."

"Hey, there," she replied. "I hope I didn't wake you."

"Nope, I just got back from the Dive Bar," I said.

"Any luck?"

"No, sorry to say. I struck out. I was there for about an hour and a half, and Gaston and his buddies were no-shows."

"Oh, sorry about that."

"No worries. I can try again tomorrow night."

"Hmmm. Let me think about that and see if I can come up with another idea." She paused for a moment, then said, "What about checking out where he lives?"

I'd already thought of this, but I didn't say so. "Do you know where he lives?" I asked. I was willing to bet she did.

"As a matter of fact, I do. I don't know the address offhand…I mean, I know the street but I'm not sure of the house number. I've driven by it a few times. I could take you by it tomorrow after Sara's celebration, if you'd like."

"That would work," I said. "In the meantime, I keep forgetting to ask you if he has a girlfriend. You mentioned his buddies, but…"

"I don't know if he does or not," Jane said. "I kinda think he doesn't, at least not someone steady." She laughed. "Do people still use that term?"

"Beats the heck outta me. But I know what you mean. And you don't think he does?"

"Well, not that I've seen. Like I said, he usually hangs with those two guys I told you about. Or at least that's what he was doing whenever I saw him at the bar."

"Okay, that helps. For the moment we'll assume he doesn't have a girlfriend." I laughed. "At least not someone steady."

She laughed also. "Is knowing that helpful?"

"It could be, yes. If nothing else, it should make it a little easier to catch him alone. If we can cut him away from his two buddies, that is." As soon as I said this I realized that by saying "we" I had just implied Jane was going to be part of the action. Oops.

Whether Jane picked up on this, I wasn't sure. But I would have guessed she did. Then another thought occurred to me.

"Okay, while we're on this subject, I'll go ahead and ask," I said. "You say he usually hangs with the same two guys…" I hesitated a moment and Jane read my mind.

"You're wondering if he might be gay."

"That's right," I said.

"I don't think so. In fact, I'm sure he's not. Whenever Matt and I saw them in the bar, they were usually hitting on the girls there. Whether they were successful, I couldn't say; I didn't pay that much attention. But no, I don't think he or his buddies are gay. Does that really matter?"

"No, it doesn't. But like I said before, it's better to know this stuff than not know. The more you can find out about a target, the better. You never know what detail might prove useful."

"There's that word again. Target."

"Sorry."

"Don't be," she said. "We talked about the detachment last night. I shouldn't have mentioned it."

"No worries," I said. Thinking, *so Matt is the name of the diver you used to date.*

WE TALKED FOR A FEW more minutes and I asked Jane how the meeting had gone with her brothers that evening.

"Oh, fine," she said. "We just went over everything for the celebration tomorrow, checking off the items on the list and making sure we have everything covered. I think we're good to go."

"That's good," I said. "And you said it's at 1:00 at the turtle rehab center?"

"That's right. I'm planning to go over about an hour early to help set up. We have a photo montage to display, some decorations to put up, refreshments to set out, that sort of thing."

"Do you need any help with that?" I realized that unless I intended to start bird-dogging Gaston Stevens on my own tomorrow morning, I would have several hours to kill before the celebration.

"Well…thanks. My brothers and their wives and I can probably handle it, but if you want to help, sure. Want me to pick you up?"

"No, that's okay. I'll just meet you there about noon." I wanted my own wheels so I could break away if I felt like it and not have to depend on Jane for transportation all afternoon.

"Okay. Thanks."

"Sure. No problem."

There was a moment of silence, then Jane said, "Good night, Rob."

"Good night, Jane."

I put my phone on the nightstand and headed for the shower.

IT WAS JUST PAST 11:00 when I climbed into bed. I tried to read for a few minutes—I had brought along a trade paperback of John Connolly's latest Charlie Parker thriller—but my mind kept wandering. As usual, I replayed the conversation I'd just had with Jane, but nothing especially significant jumped out. Well, except that I now knew the name of the diver she'd dated. His first name, anyway.

I put my bookmark in place and set the book on the nightstand. I turned out the light then lay there in the dark, hands clasped behind my head, staring up at the ceiling. I knew sleep wasn't going to come easily.

My mind was wrestling with all the unknowns. I'd learned a few things, yes, but not nearly enough to begin formulating a plan for eliminating Gaston Stevens. I was still hoping to make his death look like an accident but other than possibly staging a hit-and-run in the parking lot of the Dive Bar—and that would be extremely hard to pull off without getting caught—I couldn't come up with anything. I just didn't have enough information, and the clock was ticking.

I admitted that some of this, maybe most of it, was my own fault.

Much as I liked Jane, I knew it had been a mistake to have dinner with her last night and spend so much time with her today. Yes, it had been fun. And yes, I was looking forward to seeing her again. But none of that was getting me any closer to completing the assignment.

Or was it?

Jane was planning to show me where Stevens lived. I probably could have found this out on my own, either by searching it myself or by contacting James Collins and asking him to run it down for me. But since Jane had volunteered...well...

I reminded myself again that this wasn't a game or a vacation, and I shouldn't be using the assignment—a contract kill—as a means to get romantically involved with someone. A man's life was on the line and while Jane had pretty well convinced me he deserved to die, I hoped I wasn't taking advantage of that just to pursue a relationship with her. Or, as I had reflected earlier, that I wasn't redirecting my anger at Craig Wilkinson toward Stevens. Neither was acceptable.

I sighed deeply and closed my eyes. Maybe when I saw where Stevens lived, something would suggest itself. If not, I'd just have to keep digging.

And, as much as possible, do it on my own.

Chapter 30

THE NEXT MORNING, FOLLOWING YET another restless night, I found myself back on the beach.

I drove to the same parking area I'd used the day before and I crossed the dunes at the same stile. I was hoping another long walk might help me clarify my thinking about Jane Trehorn and Gaston Stevens. If nothing else, I thought the exercise would do me good, and once again I found myself missing Preacher.

It was about 8:30 when I got to the beach. I had taken advantage of the complimentary breakfast at the hotel, and now, wearing a fresh t-shirt with yesterday's cargo shorts and my usual khaki bill cap, I set off down the beach in the opposite direction from which I had walked yesterday.

I had gone only about fifty yards when I heard someone calling my name. Surprised, I turned and saw Jane walking briskly toward me, or as briskly as anyone can walk wearing flip-flops in soft sand. She smiled and called out again, "Hey, Rob!"

So much for a solo walk to clear my thinking. But I couldn't help smiling in return.

She paused just long enough to kick off her flip-flops and pick them up. I'd already done the same with my topsiders. She started toward me again and I waited for her to catch up.

"Good morning," she said as she reached me, sounding just a bit winded. She was wearing white shorts and a coral-colored t-shirt and a bill cap of her own, light blue. Her strawberry blonde hair was pulled into a ponytail through the opening at the back of the cap.

"Good morning," I said in return. I laughed. "Fancy meeting you here."

"I saw you crossing the stile just as I pulled in to park. I wanted to get in a walk this morning before the celebration this afternoon. I come here quite a bit, actually."

"I was here yesterday afternoon myself," I said. "It's a beautiful area."

"Yes, it is." She hesitated, then asked, "Shall we walk together, or were you wanting to be alone with your thoughts?"

Well, yes, that's what I had intended. But now that she was here…I'm sure you can guess my response.

"Sure, let's walk together," I said.

"YOU SAID YOU COME here often?" I asked. Once again I wondered if this was the beach where Sara had been killed.

"Yes, several times a week, at least. I'm actually a little late this morning. I usually try to get here by seven or seven-thirty but I had to make a couple of phone calls. Needed to double-check with the caterer and make sure everything was taken care of for the celebration this afternoon, that sort of thing."

"Everything copacetic?"

"Yes, I think so. Fingers crossed, anyway." She laughed. "You said you were here yesterday afternoon?"

"Yes. I drove over after you dropped me off at the hotel." I didn't mention that I'd napped in between.

"I love this beach. Like I said, I'm here almost every day. Sometimes twice. I come back in the evenings a lot of times also."

"If I lived in the area, I probably would too." I hesitated then laughed and added, "The only thing missing is a dog."

"A dog?"

"Right. I take my dog out to a lake for a run every morning. Weather permitting, that is. So I kinda feel like something's missing if I'm walking without a dog out in front of me."

"I get it." She laughed again. "I hope my company will suffice in a pinch."

"No worries on that score. You're definitely a better conversationalist." This earned me another laugh and a backhanded whack on the arm.

We walked in silence for a minute or two, then Jane asked, "Do you still want to check out where Gaston Stevens lives, later this afternoon?"

"Sure, if it's not going to be too much trouble. I mean, I can probably find it myself if you have family stuff to attend to after the celebration."

"No, after the celebration we'll have to spend a little time cleaning up, but otherwise, I should be free after that. We don't have anything else planned."

"Okay, then yes; let's check out his place. Is it someplace nearby?"

"Yes, it's not too far from here. That's the thing about Schnock's Harbor and Surf City and Topsail Beach…everything's within easy driving distance."

"I take it, then, that he doesn't still live at home. With his mother the congresswoman, I mean."

"No, he has a place of his own. But she doesn't live far from here, either."

"Got it. I'll be interested in seeing his place."

Jane grinned and said, "It's a date, Nate."

I laughed and replied, "Can't wait, Kate." Thinking, *Rob, what the hell are you doing?*

WE WALKED ON, staying in the soft sand at the base of the dunes and skirting the occasional patches of sea grass that grew along the edges. We had just passed one such patch, maybe a half mile from our starting point, when Jane suddenly gave me a hard hip check that would have done an NHL defenseman proud. It sent me reeling to the side a couple of steps.

"What the…" I started to say, surprised and annoyed, when I saw Jane making a quick jump to the opposite side.

"Sorry," she said, pointing to the spot on the ground between us. "But you were just about to step down into that nest of fire ants. Trust me, that is not someplace you want to put your bare feet."

I recovered my balance and bent over to look at the ant

nest. Sure enough, the ground was mounded and disturbed, a mixture of sand and soil maybe eighteen inches across, and the ants were hurrying back and forth busily doing whatever it is ants do.

"You might want to step back another foot or two," Jane was saying. I glanced up and noticed she was keeping her distance from the nest.

I took her advice and backed up. But I bent over again for another look at the ants. They were about a half-inch long with dark red heads and darker brown bodies. I straightened up and said, "I've heard of fire ants but I've never seen them before. I take it they're bad news?"

"Oh yeah," she said. "Very bad news. Let's keep moving." She started walking away and I fell back into step beside her.

"Thanks for rescuing me," I said.

She laughed. "Sorry about the bump, but it was the quickest way to keep you from stepping on them. And like I said, that's not something you want to do."

"Are they really that dangerous?"

"They can be. They not only bite; they also sting. And their venom is toxic. You'd have been burning and itching for several days, at least."

"Wow. Thanks again," I said.

"You're welcome."

WE WALKED ANOTHER HALF-MILE or so before Jane stopped and glanced at her Smartwatch. She sighed and said, "We should probably start heading back, or I should, anyway. I'd like to stay longer but I need to get home and shower and change for the celebration. But if you want to keep going, that's fine; I'll just see you there later."

"No, I'm about ready to head back also. I need to shower and change too. Which reminds me…I'm guessing attire for the celebration is casual? I didn't bring a coat and tie."

Jane laughed. "Yes, it's casual. You'll see a lot of shorts and flip-flops, I'm sure. I'm wearing a sundress and my brothers said they're going to wear khakis and Hawaiian shirts, and we'll probably be the most formal ones there. You don't need to dress up. Imagine you're going to a party on the beach and dress accordingly."

"I can do that," I said. "I'll still plan to get there early and help you with the set-up."

"Thanks, I'd appreciate that."

"No problem."

We turned and headed back to our vehicles. This time we got past the fire ant mound without Jane having to deliver a hip check.

Chapter 31

SARA LAWSON'S CELEBRATION of life was well attended.

I didn't do a head count, but I guessed more than a hundred people—the majority of whom appeared to be dressed for the beach, as Jane had predicted—gathered beneath the large open-sided tent that had been erected in a grove of palm trees next to the parking lot at the turtle rehab center. Long tables had been set up inside the tent, along with a podium and microphone, and several large fans kept the air moving under the tent to help offset the afternoon's heat and humidity.

I had arrived at a few minutes after twelve to help with the set-up, only to find that there was very little for me to do. The caterers Jane had mentioned, a four-person crew consisting of two women and two men, all dressed in khaki shorts and white polo shirts bearing their company logo, were handling almost everything. They unloaded the tables and chairs from two large panel trucks and placed them in position, then began bringing out food platters and beverages and arranging them on two tables at the end of the tent opposite the podium.

It was an organized and efficient operation, and as one of the women passed me on the way to the food tables, bearing two large platters of mini sandwiches, I smiled at her and commented, "I'd guess you've done this sort of thing a few times before."

She smiled in return and said, "Oh yeah, a few times." And kept right on moving.

Jane was at the front of the tent, setting up a three-sided photo montage on a table next to the podium. The table was decorated with seashells, driftwood and—of course—several impressive figures of sea turtles. One of these appeared to have been carved from mahogany and I guessed it might weigh close to fifty pounds. There was also a beautiful aquamarine urn, trimmed in gold, that I knew must contain Sara's ashes.

"Need a hand with anything?" I asked as I approached. Jane was wearing a pale yellow sundress with large white flowers. She was also wearing white sandals and had a white flower—an orchid, maybe?—pinned over one ear.

She turned and said, "Oh, hi! I think I've got it, as long as it doesn't blow over." She moved a piece of driftwood closer to a bottom edge of the montage board as a prop.

I studied the montage for a moment. There were dozens of photos, most of which showed Sara with friends or family members and many of her on the beach. There was no mistaking the fact that she and Jane were sisters.

"You and your sister looked a lot alike," I said.

Jane laughed. "We were told that all the time. In fact, people who didn't know us very well sometimes got us confused and called us by the wrong name. I got called Sara a lot, and vice versa."

"I can see why."

"Sara loved it, because she was eight years older. I think the fact that people sometimes thought she was me made her feel younger."

I laughed. "There's that sibling rivalry again."

A tall man with graying blonde hair approached. One glance was all I needed to recognize him as one of Jane's brothers. "That looks very nice," he said to Jane, nodding toward the montage and decorations.

"Thanks," she said. "Rob, I'd like you to meet my brother Bruce."

Bruce smiled and said, "Good to meet you," extending his hand.

"Good to meet you also," I said as we shook hands. He had a firm, dry grip. He was dressed just as Jane had said he would be, in khaki slacks and a Hawaiian shirt, ivory-colored with dark green palm trees. I wondered if Jane had mentioned me to him previously, and if so, what she had told him.

"Rob and I just met recently," she said, answering my question. I also thought, *well, that's true enough, in that we never actually met in person until two days ago.* "He's visiting from Iowa," she added, and I winced inwardly, wishing she wasn't being quite so forthcoming.

"Really?" Bruce said. "Whereabouts in Iowa?"

"Des Moines."

"Ah, I have a good friend who graduated from Drake." I smiled. "Small world."

"Yes, it is. Are you from Des Moines originally?"

"No, Illinois. I lived in the Chicago area for thirty some years."

"Ah," he said again. "What took you to Iowa?"

"Job change."

"I see. What is it you do?"

"I'm actually retired," I said. "But I was a magazine editor for more than twenty years." Glancing past Bruce's shoulder, I saw Jane biting her lower lip to suppress a smile. There was also no mistaking the mischief in her eyes.

"Really? Let's see…there's a big publisher in Des Moines, isn't there?"

"Right, Meredith Corporation. But I worked for another company, Trimedia. I was the editor of *American Wingshot*, a magazine about upland bird hunting." Bruce nodded and before he could ask any more questions, I asked one of my own. "What about you?" I wanted to steer the conversation away from my background.

"Oh, I'm in commercial real estate," he said, and I nodded, wondering what to say next. Jane saved me.

"Rob's here on vacation," she said. "We met at the Crab Shack yesterday and ended up having lunch together. Then we ran into each other again on the beach this morning. We started talking about sea turtles and I invited him to the celebration so he could see the rehab center."

Bruce laughed and said, "Got it." He nodded toward me and added, "Janie is Schnock's Harbor's unofficial version of the Welcome Wagon."

I laughed also, going along with the joke, but thinking yet again that this much personal involvement with a client— and now her family—was proving to be a big, big mistake.

THE SERVICE BEGAN at a few minutes after one. A casually dressed non-denominational minister—I'm guessing that's what he was—stepped up to the microphone and opened with a prayer that included a Scriptural passage referencing the creatures of the land and the sea, and man's responsibility, as steward of the earth, toward those creatures. He tied this directly to Sara's devotion to sea turtles and said her devotion exemplified God's mandate.

He then read the eulogy—most of which I already knew from reading Sara's obituary—then he invited everyone present to come forward and share their favorite memories of her. Jane was the first to respond.

She shared an anecdote from childhood, describing an incident when she, six years old, had caught Sara, fourteen, trying to suck the pimento out of an olive at a holiday meal with lots of relatives present. Sara had lost the pimento and it had fallen into her lap. She had quickly grabbed the pimento and popped it into her mouth, then looked up guiltily to see Jane watching her.

They both laughed, realizing no one else at the table had seen what had happened. Then they proceeded to giggle almost uncontrollably for the rest of the meal, despite their parents repeatedly asking them what was so funny and admonishing them to settle down. Afterwards, they both received a severe scolding for their rudeness and were grounded for a week. They never told their parents the reason for their giggling.

"The kicker was, we kept that joke alive for many, many years," Jane concluded. "Every time we had a big family get-together, Sara and I would try to pass the relish tray to each other for the entire meal, asking each other if we wanted more olives. And of course, we'd crack up every time we did this, much to our parents' dismay. And that's how I remember Sara best, always laughing, always ready for a joke and, at the same time, the most loving, devoted big sister I could possibly have ever had."

Jane's comments drew laughter and a round of

applause, and as she returned to her seat she glanced my way and gave me a smile.

Bruce was the next person to get up to share a memory, and at that point my mind began to wander. I started replaying our earlier conversation and examining it for any possible slip-ups on my part. Everything I had told him about my background was true and—I hoped—relatively innocuous, but I still felt uneasy about having said so much. On the other hand, I'd been caught off-guard and really hadn't had much choice when he began asking me questions.

Getting caught off-guard is something a hit man should not let happen...make that *never* let happen.

I also replayed Jane's part of the conversation. She had given her brother a version of the truth, albeit a rather heavily edited—and substantially altered—version.

No, I wasn't here on vacation. And no, we hadn't met for the first time at the Crab Shack, as she had implied. Nor had we talked about sea turtles during our walk on the beach that morning, and that wasn't when she had invited me to Sara's celebration of life.

Wow. Talk about revisionist history.

Chapter 32

ANOTHER TEN OR TWELVE PEOPLE, including several volunteers from the turtle rehab center, got up to share memories of Sara after Bruce finished, but I paid little attention to what they had to say. I was still wrestling with how Jane had explained our friendship to Bruce, and how we had met. She hadn't strayed *too* far from the truth, but still…

I tried to tell myself that it was no big deal; that once our—ahem—business was concluded, I would be on my way and in all likelihood, that would be that. We would have no further contact and I would return to Iowa and pick up my life as before, spending my days taking Preacher out to Maffitt Reservoir, tending to yard work and other projects around the house, and just generally enjoying the low-key lifestyle of a retiree. And, oh yes, continuing to avoid having anything to do with Daryl Nelson.

Could it be that simple?

Of course not.

AFTER SARA'S FAMILY MEMBERS and friends finished sharing their memories the minister directed everyone to the food tables at the back of the tent. Attendees formed a long line and began filling their plates with goodies, everything from finger sandwiches to relishes and cheeses, fresh fruit and cupcakes decorated with miniature candy seashells.

I joined the line and scanned the crowd. Jane and her brothers—I hadn't yet met Edward, but I recognized him by his blonde hair and his resemblance to Jane and Bruce—and their wives were circulating among the people, stopping to chat for a few minutes here and there. Several younger adults, whom I took to be Jane's nieces and nephews, moved with them.

I had almost reached the food tables when Jane sidled up to me. "Can I cut in?" she asked, smiling.

I smiled in return. "Of course."

"Just kidding. I need to keep mingling. But I wanted to say hi again. What did you think of the service?"

"Very nice. I loved your story about the olives."

"Oh, yeah, that's become a family classic. Like I said, it was a running joke between Sara and me forever. She loved keeping it alive with all kinds of reminders. I have a set of kitchen towels with olives printed on them that Sara gave me one year for Christmas."

"Funny."

"Yes, well…" Jane's expression turned wistful and she added, "I'm going to miss her."

"Of course you are."

She drew a deep breath and said, "I should go mingle a bit more. I'll catch you later."

"Sounds good."

"LATER" TURNED OUT to be almost an hour after our talk at the food line. After eating, the guests sat around in small groups and Jane and her siblings continued to make the rounds, exchanging small talk and thanking them for coming.

I ended up sitting by myself near a bunch of young folks who were all wearing t-shirts bearing the rehab center's logo. I guessed they were probably volunteers and this was confirmed when one of them greeted me by name.

"Hey, Rob," a young woman called out, and I recognized Julie, the volunteer I had met when Jane and I toured the rehab center the day before. She waved and I nodded and returned her wave. "C'mon over and join us," she added.

This was a dicey moment. I glanced around quickly, hoping I wasn't being too obvious but wanting to see where Bruce was and if he might have heard Julie's greeting. I spotted him sitting with his back to us several tables away, talking to a half dozen other people.

I breathed a sigh of relief. He hadn't heard Julie, which might have caused him to wonder—and perhaps ask—how I knew her if, as Jane had implied, this was my first visit to the center.

Call it a bullet dodged.

I got up and moved over to sit closer to Julie and her friends. As I pulled out a chair and sat down, Julie said, "Everybody, this is Rob. He's a friend of Jane's." This was followed by a chorus of hellos and how are ya's and I smiled again and said, "Nice to meet you all."

I recalled what Jane had said about hiding in plain sight and I realized that might be what was happening. Julie and her friends were, in effect, giving me perfect cover. All I had to do was sit here and make small talk and attempt to blend in.

Not my forte, admittedly, but I'd give it my best shot.

JANE RESCUED ME some thirty or forty minutes later.

She came over to the table and was greeted warmly by everyone, several of whom made comments similar to what I had said, telling her how much they had enjoyed her olive story. She laughed and thanked them and then she turned to me and said, "How are you doing?"

"I'm doing fine," I said. "How about you?" I suspected she probably wanted to bring the proceedings to a close and take some time to decompress. At least, I knew that's how I would be feeling in similar circumstances.

"I'm fine," she said. "We should be wrapping things up shortly. I'll need to help with the clean-up but that shouldn't take long. Do you want to stick around, or…"

"Actually, I was thinking of heading back to the hotel and changing," I said. I'd worn khakis and another polo shirt to the service—I hadn't brought any Hawaiians—and I wanted to get into shorts and a t-shirt to get some relief from the afternoon's heat.

"That's fine," Jane said. "How about I swing by and pick you up in, say, an hour or so?"

"That would be great," I said.

"Ooooh, hot date!" Julie said, obviously eavesdropping.

Jane and I both laughed and I thought, *babe, if you only knew.*

Chapter 33

"NICE SHIRT!" JANE SAID AS I climbed into the Subaru a little over an hour later.

I laughed and replied, "Thanks. A friend bought this for me." After grabbing a quick shower when I returned to the hotel, I had put on clean cargo shorts and the t-shirt Jane had bought for me in the turtle rehab center's gift shop the previous day.

Glancing over at her now, I saw that she must have gone home and changed also. Instead of the yellow sundress she had worn to the service, she was wearing light khaki shorts and a mint green t-shirt and her usual flip-flops. The white orchid she'd worn over her ear was missing and her bill cap was on the console between us.

"Sorry I couldn't spend more time with you at the celebration but I kinda needed to make the rounds and talk to as many people as I could," she said. "I hope you weren't uncomfortable or didn't feel too out of place."

"Not at all," I said. "The service was lovely and Julie introduced me to her friends, so hey, no problem."

Jane laughed. "Yeah, Julie. She's something of a character but I'm glad she saw you and called you over to their table. They're a good bunch of kids."

"Yes, they are," I agreed as we pulled out of the hotel's parking lot and headed off to check out Gaston Stevens' digs.

GASTON STEVENS LIVED in a gray bungalow with white trim, a wide screened porch and a detached two-car garage. The door of the garage was open and as we drove past I could see a bright red Mustang and a black and yellow Polaris ATV—presumably the one he'd been driving when he ran down Sara Lawson—parked inside. Sitting in the driveway closer to the house was a black Dodge Dakota pickup.

A rich kid and his toys, I couldn't help thinking. *Living in a house his parents probably bought for him.* I remembered what Jane had told me about him not working.

"He must be home," Jane said. "I've seen him driving that truck a few times so I'm sure it's his, not one of his buddies'."

I nodded. "Good to know." By then we had passed the house and were about halfway down the block. The neighborhood was similar to Jane's, with palm trees, palmettos and live oaks growing in the yards. And just as Jane had said, it was probably no more than fifteen or twenty minutes from the turtle rehab center or Jane's own house.

"Do you want to go by it a second time?" she asked.

"Yeah, let's risk it," I said.

We circled the block and just as we were making our second pass, Gaston stepped out the front door and onto his porch. Because of the screening I couldn't see him very well but I could make out his red hair. He also appeared to be shirtless and wearing only a pair of baggy shorts, the kind surfers call jams.

"That's him," Jane said. To her credit, she didn't slow down but kept the Subaru moving at the same pace. We cruised on down the block and she asked, "What do you think?"

"Not sure," I answered honestly. I hadn't seen anything about the house that suggested a plan for his elimination, but then I hadn't really expected to. Still, it was good to get a fix on the place and the type of vehicles he drove.

"What do you want to do now?"

I laughed. "I'm not sure about that, either," I said. "Any suggestions?"

"Want to go back to the beach?"

"Sure."

WE PARKED AT THE SAME PLACE I'd parked previously. *I'm becoming a regular*, I thought, recalling that Jane had said she frequently came to this beach also. After climbing the stile we headed in the direction I'd taken my first time here, opposite the direction of the fire ants.

Jane had put on her bill cap before we climbed out of the Subaru, and I did the same with my cap. I had remembered to grab it from where I'd left it on the front seat of the Impala before we left the hotel, and I was thankful I'd done so as we ambled along in the late afternoon sun. The heat also made me glad I'd changed into shorts and a t-shirt.

We walked in silence for a couple minutes until Jane suddenly said, "Look! There must be a bait ball out there!" She was pointing to a flock of birds maybe a hundred yards out over the water, circling in a tight formation and occasionally dive-bombing the surface.

"What's a bait ball?" I asked. I had never heard of such a thing.

"It's a concentrated school of small fish just below the surface of the water. They tighten up when they're being pursued and attacked by predator fish. The old safety in numbers strategy, I guess. But then the birds spot them from above and start diving on them." As she said this I saw another bird make its dive. I was pretty sure it came up with a fish.

"Wow," I said. "Very cool." The predator in me silently congratulated the bird on its catch.

Jane laughed. "Well, not for the fish. But yes, it is something that's cool to see."

We watched for another couple minutes or so until the bait ball apparently moved out into deeper water and the flock of birds—Jane told me they were herring gulls—began to disperse.

"Fishermen watch for bait balls also," she said. "They know that where there's a bait ball, there are likely to be larger predator fish nearby, the kind they want to catch. So if they spot birds working a bait ball, they head their boats in that direction."

I couldn't help laughing. "You know a lot about bait balls," I said.

Jane laughed also. "Well, I should," she said. "After all, I live here."

"Good point," I conceded.

I wondered if anything I had just learned about bait

balls could be applied to a plan to eliminate Gaston Stevens.

WE WALKED ON for another ten minutes or so, then my curiosity got the best of me.

"I want to ask you something," I said, "but it's a sensitive subject. Painful, even."

Jane gave me a searching look then said, "Okay. I'll consider myself warned."

I drew a deep breath then plunged ahead. "I can't help wondering…is this the beach where Sara…"

"No, it's not, thank goodness. I told you that this is one of my favorite places, and if Sara had been killed here, that would have ruined it for me." She hesitated then added, "Sara was killed about five miles north of here, and I haven't been back there since that night."

"That's understandable. And…I'm sorry I brought it up. I was just curious, but that was thoughtless of me."

"It's okay. And under the circumstances, I can understand why you'd be curious."

"Well, like I said, I'm sorry to have brought it up."

"It's okay," Jane repeated. Then she smiled and said, "But now I get to ask you something of a sensitive nature."

I laughed. "I guess that's only fair."

"Actually, personal might be a better word than sensitive. Or maybe it's both."

"Okay," I said. "Now *I'll* consider myself warned. Ask away." I wondered what I was letting myself in for.

"Well…okay. Are you involved with anyone back in Iowa?"

"Involved as in, romantically?"

"Yes."

I drew a deep breath, trying to buy time while I considered what to say…specifically, how much to tell Jane about my recent crash-and-burn with Daryl.

"No, I'm not," I said after a moment. "I was, but that ended awhile ago." For some reason I didn't want to tell Jane it had only been a couple weeks.

"I see," she said, and I was afraid she might ask me to

define "awhile ago." Thankfully, she didn't. Instead, she said, "Can I ask you one more thing?"

"Sure."

"Did she know what…umm…you do?"

"No, she didn't. I thought about telling her—thought about it quite a bit, actually—but I never figured out how to do that." I laughed. "It's not the kind of thing you can just drop into a conversation."

Jane laughed also. "No, I'm sure it isn't. But I just wondered if that might have been the reason for your break-up. I mean, if you told her or she found out somehow and couldn't deal with it."

"I used to worry about that also, about how she would handle it if she did find out. But luckily, that never happened."

"Did you ever feel guilty about that? About keeping it from her?"

"No more than eight or ten hours every day."

Jane laughed again. "A hit man who suffers guilt pangs. That has to be something of a rarity."

I couldn't help it. I laughed also.

"Can we change the subject?"

Chapter 34

WE WALKED FOR ANOTHER HALF HOUR or so, mostly in comfortable silence, then turned and headed back. It was about 5:30 when we got to the stile we'd climbed earlier. This time I had remembered to note the nearby landmarks—all of the stiles looked alike to me—but Jane seemed to recognize it anyway.

Before crossing the stile she dropped her flip-flops onto the sand and shuffled her feet into them. I did the same with my topsiders. "Do you always park at this same place?" I asked.

"Usually," she said. "There's another public area a mile or so on down, but this is the one I come to most of the time." She laughed. "Call me a creature of habit."

"Aren't we all," I said.

We climbed the stile and returned to the Subaru. As we settled into the seats she turned to me and smiled. "Thanks for the walk," she said.

"Thanks for the company," I said. "And the lesson on bait balls."

She laughed. "I told you I taught fourth grade. Once a teacher…"

"I get it," I said. "Anyway, I like learning stuff like that. I'm always interested in anything having to do with the outdoors."

She gave me a serious look for a moment. "Hey," she said. "I'm sorry if I was prying when I asked you about being involved with anyone. I mean, that's none of my business and I hope I didn't overstep the bounds."

"No worries," I said. "It's not a big deal."

"Okay." She drew a deep breath. "Any more thoughts on Gaston Stevens?"

"Nothing offhand. But the clock is ticking and I really need to start bearing down and figuring out what I'm going to do. I'm supposed to fly home the day after tomorrow, so I'm running out of time."

"I understand. And I'm sorry if I've held you up in any way."

"Not your fault. You've been helpful and I've enjoyed the time we've spent together"—*did I really just say that?*—"but now I need to focus on doing what you've hired me for."

She nodded. "So what's your next move?"

"Thought I'd go back to the Dive Bar again this evening and see if he and his buddies show up. I'm hoping that if they do, that will give me some idea of how to go about getting close to him."

She nodded again. "Sounds like a plan. I'll keep my fingers crossed that he does show up. Will you let me know if you see him?"

"I will. Want me to call you later?"

"That would be fine. I'm getting together with my brothers and their wives this evening to scatter Sara's ashes. It's just going to be the five of us—the kids bowed out—and we're going out right after dinner. But I should be home by ten or a little after."

"Are you going to scatter her ashes on the beach?"

Jane shook her head. "No. Sara would have liked that, but there are federal laws prohibiting it. The ashes can be scattered at sea, but you have to be at least three miles from shore."

"Really. I didn't know that. Three miles sounds pretty far."

"Yes, it does. It's actually three nautical miles, whatever that means. I don't know the difference between a nautical mile and a regular mile."

I didn't, either. I'd heard the term but like Jane, I was clueless as to the difference. "It sounds far, regardless," I said.

"Right," Jane said. "Bruce chartered a boat to take us out. There are quite a few regulations, actually, and you also have to get a permit. Bruce handled all of that." She smiled. "We'll be out for about two hours. It's supposed to be calm this evening—Bruce checked with the boat captain this afternoon—so I'm hoping I don't get seasick."

I smiled in return. "Good luck."

"Thanks. Like I said, I should be home by ten or a little after."

"Got it."

"If I don't pick up when you call, just leave me a message and I'll call you as soon as I get home."

"Okay, will do."

BEFORE JANE TOLD ME she was getting together with her brothers and sisters-in-law to scatter Sara's ashes, I had been about to ask her to have dinner with me—this despite what I had said about needing to bear down and concentrate on how to deal with Gaston Stevens.

I couldn't deny I was disappointed that I would be eating dinner alone again.

It was a few minutes before six when she dropped me off at the Hampton. I had at least a couple of hours to kill before returning to the Dive Bar so when I got back to my room I decided to check with Rachel James and Mike Stevenson and see how things were going in Des Moines. I thought about texting then decided what the heck, I wouldn't mind hearing a couple of friendly voices from back home.

I called Rachel first.

"Hey you," she said when she answered. "How's it going in North Carolina?"

"It's beautiful down here," I said. "I toured the sea turtle rehab center with Jane yesterday and I met one of her brothers at their sister's celebration of life this afternoon. Otherwise, I've been putting in some serious time walking the beach." Before leaving Iowa I had filled Rachel in on the details of the assignment—and that I had tentatively agreed to meet Jane in person—so I knew she wouldn't be too surprised to hear any of this.

"Beach time is good!" Rachel said. "I'm envious. But so I have to ask: How is Jane?"

"Oh, she's fine," I said, hoping I sounded somewhat offhand. "We had dinner together my first night here, and she's been showing me around. We drove past Gaston

Stevens' house this afternoon after the celebration."

"Have you seen him yet?"

"One quick glimpse is all. We actually drove by his place twice and he stepped out on his front porch just as we were going past the second time. Jane was driving and she just kept going so I don't think he noticed us or paid any attention."

"Well, that's good. Any ideas on how you're going to handle things?"

"Not so far. I'm going back to the bar tonight where he and his buddies hang and I'm hoping to see them. Maybe that will give me some ideas. I was there last night but they were no-shows."

"Good luck with that. I hope they show up."

"Me too. How are things on the home front?"

"All good in the 'hood. You have a stack of mail on your kitchen table but nothing that looks urgent."

"Okay, cool. Thanks again for taking care of the mail and keeping an eye on things."

"No problem. Good luck with Gaston Stevens." She laughed. "And with Jane."

I laughed also. "Thanks."

"And let me know if you need any help down there. Happy to hop on a plane."

I laughed again. "I'll keep that in mind."

"Do that."

MY PHONE CALL to Mike Stevenson confirmed that everything was fine at his place as well. I caught him driving home from work, and he told me Preacher and Rusty were getting along famously (his words) but I should be warned that his wife and daughters probably weren't going to let me take Preacher home when I returned. Just as I'd anticipated, they were spoiling her every chance they got and she had, of course, met their overtures more than halfway.

I laughed and said I was happy to hear things were going so well but he should remind them that I lived by myself and would be mighty lonesome without my dog. He said he'd tell them but doubted they would be convinced. I told him to give it his best shot and he promised he would. I hung up feeling good knowing Preacher was in such good hands, but I also felt a twinge of homesickness and found myself wishing again that she was here to walk with me on the beach.

I shook my head to clear my thoughts and stood up from the armchair in which I'd been sitting in the corner of the room. It was time for dinner and I made a quick executive decision to go back to Agave Azul, the restaurant where I'd eaten the previous evening. (Go ahead; twist my arm and make me eat Mexican two nights in a row.) It was only a few minutes away from the hotel and a margarita suddenly seemed like a very good idea.

It must be the salt-sea air, I told myself.

THIS TIME I ORDERED a combo platter of fajitas—beef, chicken and shrimp—and they were served sizzling, with plenty of smoke coming off the metal plate when the server set it down before me. I hadn't bothered to change out of the t-shirt I'd worn to the beach that afternoon and I knew it was probably going to smell like smoke for the rest of the evening. Somehow I doubted this would be a problem with the patrons at the Dive Bar.

I took my time eating and managed to kill a little over an hour at the restaurant. It was a quarter to eight when the server brought me my check. I paid, left a generous tip and stepped outside. Dusk was beginning to set in and I wondered if Jane and her brothers and sisters-in-law were already on the boat, heading out to scatter Sara's ashes. I guessed they probably were.

I climbed into the Impala and headed for the Dive Bar. I was beginning to learn my way around Schnock's Harbor and it took me less than ten minutes to get to the bar.

When I pulled into the parking lot one of the first vehicles I saw was Gaston Stevens' black Dodge Dakota.

Chapter 35

THERE WAS NO question it was his truck.

I hadn't noted his license plate when we had driven past his house earlier and the truck was sitting in the driveway. But I saw the plate now and immediately knew it had to be his. The plate read GASSED and I remembered what Jane had told me about his nickname.

How precious.

I drove past the Dakota and parked at the far end of the lot. I climbed out of the Impala and thumbed the key fob to lock the doors. Then I paused for a moment, scanning the parking lot and contemplating my next move.

I had been hoping I would find Stevens at the Dive Bar and it appeared my wish was being granted. I had very little doubt I would find him inside, with or without his buddies. The question was, now that I was this close to him—the word target again came to mind—how did I want to play it?

I decided just to go inside, see if I could get a seat somewhere close to him, and then let things develop as they might. Let go and let God, in other words.

Ha-ha.

LIKE THE PREVIOUS NIGHT, the bar was crowded, mostly with young people… younger than me, anyway. But because I had been here before I felt less self-conscious about coming in alone and a little more confident about blending in. As I pushed through the door I gave the crowd a quick scan and almost immediately spotted Gaston Stevens and his friends.

There was no missing Stevens with his red hair. Equally conspicuous was Dave Sonderheim, the friend Jane had described as being nearly covered with tattoos. They were standing next to a booth near the pool table, and just as Jane had said, Sonderheim had full sleeves on both arms and large multi-colored tats from his thighs to his ankles. At this moment, he was, in fact, showing off a new tat he had apparently just added to his collection.

On his belly.

Sonderheim was lifting the bottom of his t-shirt and rippling his abs to make the tat move. I couldn't make out the design from where I was standing, but his actions were drawing laughs and admiring comments from the surrounding onlookers. Stevens stood beside him and was laughing also.

I wondered if there was any way I could get closer to them so I could overhear their conversation.

None of the booths or tables near them were empty so I took another look around the bar and spotted a couple of unoccupied stools close to where I had sat the night before. For want of a better idea, I decided to sit at the bar and hope for some kind of break. Worst case scenario, I could observe Stevens from a distance and maybe see something, anything, that might be helpful. Helpful in plotting his demise, that is.

I slid onto one of the empty barstools and only then noticed that the young woman next to me was Julie, the volunteer from the turtle rehab center. A couple of the other volunteers I'd met that afternoon—a guy named Pete and a woman named Melanie—were seated on the other side of her. As I sat down Julie looked my way and laughed.

"Well, hey, Rob," she said. "Long time no see!"

"Right," I said. "It's been all of, what? Five or six hours?"

She laughed again. "Seems like a lifetime."

"At least," I said, remembering what Jane had said about Julie being something of a character. I couldn't deny there was something irrepressible about her that you couldn't help liking. Plus, seeing some familiar faces and having someone to talk to put me at ease and I felt less conspicuous.

"So," Julie asked, "what brings you to the Dive Bar, and where's Jane?"

"She told me she was getting together with her family this evening," I said. I didn't know who Jane might have told about them scattering Sara's ashes at sea, or whether she would want that generally known, so I didn't elaborate. "But she mentioned this place to me and I just thought I'd check it out since I had the evening to kill."

"Got it," Julie said, smiling. If she suspected there was more to the story, she didn't ask. Instead, she said, "You're welcome to hang with us if you'd like."

"Thanks, I appreciate that. It's always nice to see a friendly face when you're a stranger in town."

Slipping into my harmless old geezer routine once again.

AFTER TEN OR FIFTEEN MINUTES of small talk with Julie and her friends, I decided to take a chance.

Gaston Stevens and his buddies—I assumed the third guy with him and Sonderheim was Grady O'Neill, the other friend Jane had told me about—were still holding court back by the pool table. The nearby patrons were laughing and joking with them and while I couldn't hear what any of them were saying, it was clear everyone was having a good time. A rowdy good time.

Following a particularly loud outburst of laughter, I nudged Julie and said, "That group back by the pool table…do you know any of them?"

Julie glanced at them and then quickly looked back at me with a surprisingly dark expression. "Oh yeah," she said. "I know some of them." She shook her head. "Do I ever."

"Oh?" I said. I tried to look curious—which I was— hoping she would elaborate.

"The redheaded guy is Gaston Stevens. He's the son of a congresswoman, Maggie Stevens. Jane must have told you about him. He's the one who killed her sister." There was no mistaking the bitterness in her voice.

"That's the guy who killed Sara?" I hoped I sounded surprised. Incredulous, even.

"Yes, he's the one who ran her down with his ATV. Of course he tried to claim it was an accident. He said she panicked and jumped in front of him. But that's bullshit. Jane saw him do it and swears it was no accident."

"Wow," I said. "Jane did tell me about that. I think she

said he was charged with manslaughter?"

"That's right. And we all hope he's found guilty. We all loved Sara and we're afraid his mother will be able to get him off somehow. Use her influence or something."

"Huh," I said. "When is the trial?"

"Not for several months. Sometime early next year, I think. In the meantime, he's out walking around, free as a bird and having a good old time." She shook her head again. "It makes me sick."

"I'll bet." I waited a moment then asked, "Who's the guy with all the ink?"

"Dave Sonderheim. He's Gaston's best friend. And the other guy is Grady O'Neill, another good friend."

"You seem to know them pretty well."

"Not by choice, I can promise you. But they've hit on me and my friends several times. Not successfully, I should add. But anyway, yeah, I know them." She turned back toward the bar and took a long drink of her beer.

Call me a shameless opportunist—maybe shameful is more like it—but I wanted to keep her talking. After a moment I asked, "Do you really think his mother will try to use her influence to get him off?"

Julie snorted and said, "It wouldn't surprise me. She has a history of shady deals…or at least, there are plenty of rumors to that effect. And he's gotten away with things in the past, DUIs and that kind of stuff that most of us wouldn't have been able to walk away from."

Jane had already told me this, but I didn't mention it. Instead, I said, "When Jane told me about him, she said she'll have to testify against him and she thinks they'll try to discredit her testimony." I realized I was opening up quite a bit here, maybe more than Jane would have liked, but I was gambling that she might have already discussed this with some of her friends, especially the rehab center volunteers who knew Sara.

"Yes, she's told us the same thing," Julie said, confirming my conjecture. "They'll try to do something to discredit her, make the jury question her testimony." She paused, then she added, "Knowing his mother, if they get desperate it wouldn't surprise me if they even tried to bribe her not to testify. Or change her story, at least."

I laughed and said, "Good luck with that."

Julie smiled and said, "Yeah, no kidding."

Chapter 36

WE SAT IN SILENCE FOR A COUPLE minutes, both nursing our beers. I wondered if I could ask any more questions about Gaston Stevens without appearing more interested than would seem normal. I was trying to figure out what my next question might be when Stevens himself saved me the trouble.

"Well, hey there, Julie," he called out as he and his two buddies approached the bar. They were all carrying longneck beer bottles, presumably empty, and coming over for another round.

Julie turned on her stool to face them and so did I. Julie stared at the trio but said nothing. Gaston started laughing and said, "What's the matter? Cat got your tongue?" Mr. Original.

"I have nothing to say to you," Julie said slowly before turning back to the bar and picking up her beer.

"Aw, c'mon," Gaston said. "It wouldn't kill you to at least say hi."

Julie gave her head one quick shake but refused to turn around and face him again. I was still facing Gaston and his friends but after a moment I turned back toward the bar also. *Be cool*, I told myself. *The last thing you want to do is put yourself on their radar.*

Gaston stepped closer.

"Aw, c'mon," he said again. "You're not still pissed about the accident, are you?"

Julie didn't turn but she did reply. "Of course I'm still pissed. It wasn't an accident."

"Whoa!" Gaston said, feigning outrage. "Were you there? Did you see what happened?"

Now Julie did turn to face him. "No, I wasn't there. But Sara's sister was, and she saw what you did. There was nothing accidental about it."

"And you believe her?" Still playing the outrage card.

"Of course I believe her."

"Of course I believe her!" Now he was mocking her in a ridiculous falsetto.

Julie's voice dropped toward the opposite end of the scale. "Fuck you, Gaston," she said in a low growl.

"Hey, that's not very friendly," Sonderheim said, chiming in for the first time. "Do we really need all this hostility? Here, let us buy you another beer. And your friends here too." He looked directly at me, taking in my t-shirt with the turtle rehab center logo. "Are you with them?"

Fuck.

There was no way I could avoid answering in the affirmative unless I tried to pretend I didn't know Julie and the other volunteers, which would look pretty damned craven. I wasn't about to do that, regardless of how much I might want to go unnoticed.

"Yes, I'm with them," I said easily. "But you don't need to buy us a round. Thanks anyway."

Sonderheim stared at me for a moment, apparently surprised that I'd turned down his offer. Then he smiled and said, "Okay, anything you say, old man. Just trying to broker some peace here."

Before I could respond, Julie said, "Shove your peace, Dave." I was pretty sure her pun was intentional. "We don't need your charity. Take your money and your tats elsewhere."

"C'mon, guys," O'Neill said, joining the exchange. "It's pretty obvious we're not wanted here." I wondered if he was the trio's designated diplomat.

"Yeah, we can take a hint," Stevens said. "Let's let the turtle huggers continue communing with nature. It's all they know how to do."

"Better than communing with the likes of you," Julie said, obviously seething.

"Hey, believe what you want to believe," Stevens said, his voice rising again. "The old lady panicked and jumped in front of me. I tried to swerve to miss her. If her sister says otherwise, she's lying. And that will all come out in the trial. We'll see who the jury believes." He smirked as he said this, almost as if the jury's verdict was a foregone conclusion.

Maybe for him, it was.

"C'mon," O'Neill said again. "Let's get out of here." Yep, he was definitely Mr. Peacekeeper.

But Stevens wasn't quite ready to let it end. He looked at me again and said, "I haven't seen you in here before." There was no mistaking the challenge.

"That's right, you haven't," I said, hoping I sounded agreeable and non-threatening. "I'm just visiting."

"Well, you need to find a better class of friends," he said.

I should have let it drop, should have laughed it off and continued to play the toothless tiger. But instead I said, "I'll take that under advisement."

"Oooh, take it under advisement. Listen to you, Mr. Big Talker."

It was then that Steve, the burly bartender I'd met the previous evening, leaned over the bar between Julie and me. "That's enough, Gaston," he said. "Either knock it off or leave."

Gaston regarded him for a moment without speaking. Then his common sense—presuming he had some—must have prevailed. He turned to his buddies and said, "Let's get out of here."

That should have been the end of it, but Gaston couldn't resist taking one last shot. Maybe he was attempting to save face, or maybe he was just one of those punks who felt like he always had to have the last word. As he turned to leave he looked back at me and smirked again.

"Watch yourself, old man," he said. "You don't know who you're dealing with."

Once again, I should have let it pass. But I didn't.

I smiled and replied, "Neither do you."

I HAD JUST DUG MYSELF into a deep, deep hole.

Momentarily satisfying as it had been to return Gaston's parting jab, I knew I shouldn't have done so. Any hope I had of remaining unnoticed had just gone right out the door with Stevens and his pals. I was on their radar now and there wasn't anything I could do to change that.

I tried to tell myself I hadn't had much choice. I couldn't have anticipated Stevens coming over to us and accosting Julie, or that the conversation would so quickly take a hostile turn. Other than confirming that yes, I was with Julie and her friends, I hadn't really said anything incriminating.

But now I was known to Stevens, which meant my chances of getting close to him without arousing suspicion had just plummeted. That in turn meant staging his death to look like an accident was going to be a hell of a lot more difficult. If he saw me again he would immediately be on guard, and given what I had seen of his personality, he might even welcome another confrontation.

Not good.

I REALIZED JULIE had just spoken to me.

"Sorry about that," she said.

I shook my head. "Not your fault. But you were right. The guy's definitely a prick, if you'll pardon my French."

She laughed. "Oh no, that's all right. I can think of a lot worse things to call him. *Have* called him, in fact." She shook her head and picked up her beer.

I glanced over at Steve the bartender. He was standing back with arms crossed and a satisfied look on his face. I was pretty sure he had enjoyed rousting Gaston. Apparently there was no love lost between the two of them.

"Thanks for your intervention," I said, smiling. "I'd have hated to punch out a congresswoman's son and have it caught on video." I nodded at the security camera behind the bar and laughed as I said this, hoping my remark would be taken as a joke.

"Oh, no worries," Steve said, laughing in return. He nodded toward the camera. "Our cameras haven't worked in months. You'd have been fine."

"Good to know," I said, picking up my beer and taking another pull.

PETE AND MELANIE had remained silent

throughout the entire exchange with Stevens but now Melanie spoke up. "He's an asshole," she said, as though further confirmation was required.

"Right," Pete seconded. "Let's hope he gets hit by a truck sometime between now and the trial."

This drew a laugh from Julie and Melanie. "Could we be that lucky?" Melanie said.

"You mean, could Jane be that lucky?" Julie said. "That way she'd never have to testify. I feel bad for her, having to face him in court and go through all that. You know the attorneys are going to beat up on her, big time."

"I'm sure you're right," Pete said.

Julie gave it a moment's thought, then she brightened and said, "Actually, it wouldn't take a truck."

"Wouldn't take a truck? What do you mean?" Melanie said.

"It wouldn't take being hit by a truck," Julie said. "Something else would work. Something a lot smaller and just as lethal."

Chapter 37

THERE WAS A MOMENT OF SILENCE, then Melanie asked hesitantly, "Are you talking about…a gun?"

Julie laughed again. "No, nothing that obvious. Or noisy. I was thinking more along the lines of a wasp. Or a honeybee."

"What?" Pete was obviously perplexed. So was I.

"Sure," Julie said. "Pete, I don't think you were here that night a few months ago, but you were, Mel. Remember when those three came in and Dave started showing off his latest tattoo? Kinda like he was doing tonight?"

Melanie gave it a moment's thought, her brow furrowing. "Okaay…"

"And then Dave started razzing Gaston about when was he gonna get his first tat, and Gaston said he couldn't risk it. Said with his allergies and his fair skin, he couldn't risk having a bad reaction to the ink and getting some kind of dermatitis or infection. Dave called him a pussy and said he was just afraid of needles, and then Gaston said something about the time he nearly died from a bee sting.

"He said he'd gone into anaphylactic shock—pretty sure that's what it's called—and barely survived. That's why he always carries an EpiPen now. And why he always wears a full wet suit when he surfs, because he can't risk any jellyfish stings."

"Okay," Melanie said again. "I do kinda remember some of that. Wow."

"Right," Julie said. "So if we could just arrange for a wasp to pay him a visit, and make sure he doesn't have his EpiPen handy…" She trailed off and the three of them started laughing.

I laughed too, but my mind was already racing ahead, contemplating ways I might be able to make something like this happen.

"SO TELL ME EVERYTHING."

Once again, we were sitting on Jane's screened porch. I had finished my beer and left the Dive Bar shortly after Julie suggested they arrange for a wasp to visit Gaston Stevens, and I had called Jane from the parking lot to tell her the evening had been a success and I'd gotten my first look at him. She said she wanted to hear all the details so if I wanted to swing by, she would have a pitcher of margaritas waiting.

Talk about an offer you couldn't refuse.

The pitcher and our glasses were sitting on the small table beside us and we were sitting as we had two nights ago, with Jane on the hanging swing and me on a chair at an angle in front of her. Also as before, her bare foot was on my knee and I was giving her a foot rub. This time I had suggested it— it seemed like a fair trade for the margaritas—and she hadn't needed any extra persuading.

"Okay," I said. "When I got there, I spotted Gaston and his buddies right away. They were back by the pool table and Sonderheim was showing off his new tattoo, something on his belly. He kept lifting his t-shirt and rippling his abs to make it move."

"Oh, geez. How juvenile can you get."

"Right. But everybody was laughing so I guess it must have been pretty funny. I couldn't make out the design from where I was."

"Probably something obscene, knowing him."

"Yeah, maybe. Anyhow, they all seemed to be having a good time. I looked around and saw a couple of empty seats at the bar so I went over and sat down and it turned out Julie and a couple of her friends were right next to me. Pete and Melanie."

"Oh, I know Pete and Melanie. They were at the celebration this afternoon. They're nice kids."

"Yes, they are. That reminds me—not to be switching the subject, but how did it go this evening?"

"Oh, it was fine. It was the five of us—my brothers and their wives and me, like I said—and it went okay. The boat captain took us out three miles and the water wasn't rough at all, luckily. Bruce opened the urn and he leaned over the side of the boat and scattered about half the ashes, then he handed it to Edward and he scattered the rest.

"None of us had ever done this before so it was maybe a little awkward, but it was okay. Bruce said, 'Goodbye, Sis,' and I cried a little but otherwise it was fine. We even kinda joked about it after we got back to the marina and were walking back to our cars, saying that now Sara would be with her beloved turtles forever."

"I'm glad it went well."

"Thanks." She took a sip of her margarita. "Now, tell me what happened next at the bar."

"Okay, so I'm sitting there with Julie and her friends, and after a few minutes, Stevens, Sonderheim and that other guy, O'Neill, all came over to where we were. Pretty sure they were coming for refills on their beer. As they got closer Stevens called out to Julie.

"She didn't answer, so he started giving her a hard time about not being friendly. Then he asked her if she was still pissed about the accident, and she said she was, and that it wasn't an accident."

"Oh, wow." Jane took another sip of her margarita. I took a break from rubbing her foot for a moment to pick up my glass and do the same.

"Right," I said, setting my glass back on the table and resuming the foot rub. "So then he started accusing her—mocking her, actually—about not being there so she couldn't know what happened, and that she shouldn't believe what you said about it not being an accident."

"Oh, man. I'm sorry Julie got caught in the middle of this."

"Well, she stood her ground, no doubt about that. She said of course she believed you. And it was about then that Sonderheim jumped in and offered to buy us all a round. Said there was no need for so much hostility, or something to that effect. Then he asked me if I was with them."

"Oh, geez. What did you do?"

"I said I was with them and thanked him for the offer but said he didn't need to buy us a round."

"Then what happened?"

"Julie told him to take his money and his tats elsewhere. That's when O'Neill spoke up and said they should get out of there. Then Julie and Gaston got into it again and he said you were lying, and that when it went to trial the jury would decide in his favor. He said it like it was already a done deal."

"He probably thinks it is."

"Exactly what I thought."

"So then did they leave?"

"After another minute or so, yeah, they did. Steve the bartender told Gaston to knock it off or leave, and that's when they left." I didn't mention my last exchange with Stevens, or my comment to the bartender about punching out the son of a congresswoman.

Jane shook her head. "What a mess. I'm really sorry about Gaston giving Julie such a hard time, but I appreciate her standing up for me." She paused then laughed and added, "At least you got a close-up look at Gaston."

"Yes, and he's every bit the arrogant little bastard you said he was."

"That's for sure. Interesting what he said about the jury. I wonder if he knows the fix is already in, somehow."

"Funny you should say that. When I first sat down by Julie, I asked her who the guys were back by the pool table. I'd already recognized Gaston by his red hair and Sonderheim by his ink, but Julie didn't know that. She told me who they were and that Gaston was the guy who'd killed your sister. That started us talking about the trial, and she said she knew they were going to try to discredit you."

Jane snorted. "I'm sure they will. Try, I mean. The fuckers." She smiled. "Sorry."

I smiled. "No worries. Julie also said Gaston's mother is known to have pulled some shady deals and they might even try to bribe you to change your story."

"Oh, boy. This just gets better and better. All I can say

is, I wish they would. Try to bribe me, that is. If I could record it, I could really bury them. Gaston *and* his mother."

"Julie and I agreed they wouldn't have much luck trying to bribe you."

"That's for sure." She shook her head.

Neither of us spoke for a minute and we both took another drink of our margaritas. Then I patted her foot and eased it off my knee and said, "Time for the other one."

Chapter 38

JANE SHIFTED SLIGHTLY ON THE swing and brought her right foot—the one with the turtle tattoo on the instep—up to rest her heel on my knee. As I began massaging her sole she sighed and said, "You really should consider changing careers."

I laughed. "That'll have to wait a little while. Right now I'm in the middle of an assignment."

She laughed also. "So now that you've met Gaston, do you have any ideas on how you're going to complete that assignment?"

I hesitated before answering; the usual reservations about sharing too much information with a client immediately coming to mind. But Jane was obviously much more than another one of my typical semi-unknown clients with whom I had only long-distance contact. While I was still reluctant to let her play any kind of active role in Gaston Stevens' elimination, I realized she might be helpful in formulating a plan.

"As a matter of fact, Julie said something that gave me an idea," I replied. "I haven't figured out the details yet, but I may have a place to start, at least."

"Really! What did Julie say?"

"She said that Gaston carries an EpiPen at all times because he nearly died from a bee sting years ago. Apparently he went into anaphylactic shock and it almost killed him."

"Really!" Jane said again. "How did Julie know about that?"

"She said she and Melanie were in the bar a few months ago and they overheard Sonderheim asking Gaston when he was going to get his first tattoo. Gaston said he couldn't risk it because he might have a bad reaction to the ink. Something about his fair skin and allergies. Then I guess he brought up the bee sting and mentioned that he can't take a chance on anything like that; said that's why he wears a full wet suit when he surfs, because he can't risk jellyfish stings."

"Huh! That's wild. I know jellyfish stings can be dangerous and people can have bad reactions to them, but I didn't know any of that about Gaston Stevens having allergies or that he had nearly died from a bee sting." She laughed and added, "Well, why would I know that?"

"Right, why would you. But now that we do know, I'm trying to think of some way to take advantage of it."

"Like what?" She laughed again. "Hiding some jellyfish in his bed?"

I laughed also. "That doesn't sound very doable. Julie suggested stealing his EpiPen and then having a wasp pay him a visit. That's maybe a little less far-fetched but it would still be hard to pull off. Finding a cooperative wasp could be tricky."

"No kidding."

"Still, I think there might be something there I can work with. I've been thinking all along that Gaston's death needs to look like an accident. Otherwise, if his mother thinks he was killed, she's sure to call for all kinds of investigations."

"I'm sure you're right about that. She'll want to find and punish whoever killed her precious baby."

"No doubt. And the best way to avoid that is to make it look like Gaston died accidentally."

"So…any other ideas on how you might do that?"

"Not yet."

We sat in silence for a couple minutes. I continued massaging her foot and I wondered if Jane was considering ways we might arrange to have Gaston stung by something venomous. She was reclining against the back of the swing with her eyes closed. Then, after another minute or so, she suddenly sat up straight, eyes opening wide, and said, "Hey. I've got an idea."

"I'm all ears," I said.

She grinned. "Okay, tell me what you think of this," she said, and she proceeded to lay out a plan that immediately reminded me of something Rachel James might have come up with.

When she finished I laughed and shook my head. "Not bad! Maybe you're the one who should consider making a career change."

"No, that's okay," she said. "I'm happily retired from teaching and I'm not looking for a job. I'll leave the hard stuff to you. But what do you think?"

"I like it," I said. "And I think it just might work. Thanks!" Impulsively I lifted her foot and kissed the little turtle tattoo.

Jane laughed and said, "You're welcome." She hesitated a moment, then she reached over and took my hand. "C'mon," she said, standing up from the swing.

And leading me back to her bedroom.

"SHOULDN'T WE BE SMOKING cigarettes? Like lovers in those old-time black and white movies?"

I smiled in the dark. "Are you really old enough to remember those?"

I was lying on my back enjoying the cool breeze provided by the ceiling fan and Jane was lying beside me with her head on my shoulder. "I've seen a few of them, yes," she replied. "More than a few, actually." She laughed. "Back in the days before they started showing sex onscreen, that's how you knew what had happened. If they were lying there smoking cigarettes, that was the signal that they'd just had sex."

I laughed also. "So do you have a pack handy?"

"No, sorry. We'll have to pretend."

There was a minute or two of silence and Jane shifted to snuggle a little closer. Then she said, "What you said earlier about Gaston thinking the fix is in… do you really think that's what he believes?"

I drew a deep breath. "It sure sounded like it when he was talking to Julie."

After another moment of silence, she said, "So are you really going to do what I suggested? To Gaston, I mean?"

"I think I can make that work, yes. I still need to work out a few details but your idea beats anything I've come up with."

She punched me lightly on the chest. "Flatterer."

"Hey, you know what they say about flattery."

"Yes, and it seems to be working very well for you." She lifted her head from my shoulder and kissed me.

A little while later, as I was drifting toward sleep, it crossed my mind that our conversation about Gaston was without a doubt the strangest pillow talk I'd ever taken part in.

I'm pretty sure I was smiling when I fell asleep.

Chapter 39

I PROBABLY DON'T HAVE TO TELL you that I never made it back to the hotel that night.

I woke to the smells of fresh-brewed coffee and frying bacon. I continued to lie there in Jane's bed for another minute or two, then I got up and put on the clothes I'd been wearing since yesterday afternoon. When I pulled my t-shirt over my head I could still smell the smoke from last night's fajitas.

I shuffled my feet into my topsiders and headed out to the kitchen. Jane was standing at the stove, stirring a skillet of fluffy scrambled eggs. She looked up and smiled. "Good morning." She was barefoot and—I was relieved to see this— also wearing the same t-shirt and shorts she'd been wearing last night.

"Good morning," I said, smiling in return. "That all smells wonderful."

"The cornbread is ready to pull out of the oven, so grab yourself a cup of coffee and go ahead and sit down. We can eat in just a minute."

"Sounds good." Jane had already set the table and I picked up a mug and crossed the kitchen to the coffee maker on the counter next to the refrigerator. I poured myself a cup and returned to the table. I added a dash of half and half from the small carton Jane had placed next to the sugar bowl.

"Is there anything I can help you with?" I asked.

"Nope. Everything's ready. Just sit yourself down." She spooned a generous portion of scrambled eggs onto a plate, added three strips of thick-sliced bacon and a large square of cornbread, then placed the plate in front of me.

"Wow," I said. "This looks terrific."

"Well, just for the record, I don't fix big breakfasts like this very often. But"—she laughed—"I thought you might need some fortifying."

I laughed also. "Well, just for the record, I don't eat big breakfasts like this very often," I said. "But I'm not about to turn one down when it's put in front of me. And yes, I could probably use some fortifying."

Jane smiled and returned to the table with her own plate. She sat down and we dug in.

WE LINGERED OVER BREAKFAST for more than an hour, and I couldn't help reflecting that there seemed to be none of the morning-after awkwardness that so often occurs between first-time lovers. Instead, we chatted almost like—pardon the hoary cliché—an old married couple.

Except that much of our talk centered on Gaston Stevens and how we were going to implement the plan Jane had come up with—hardly the kind of subject most couples normally discuss over breakfast. Or normally discuss anytime, for that matter.

Once again, I was reminded of Daryl. But only briefly.

One of the biggest challenges we faced was the time factor. I was booked to fly home the following day, which meant—theoretically, anyway—we would need to execute Jane's plan sometime within the next twenty-four hours. We both agreed this simply wasn't doable. Which meant my stay in North Carolina was going to have to be extended.

Not really a big deal, actually; I would just need to go online and cancel my return flights—I decided I would wait until the assignment was completed to rebook them—and I was confident the Hampton Inn would rent me my room, or maybe a different one, for a few more nights. Ditto the car rental agency if I told them I needed the Impala for a few more days. Assuming they hadn't already reserved the car for another customer, I should be good to go.

I was also confident that if I called Mike Stevenson, he would be okay with taking care of Preacher for a little while longer. Remembering what he had told me about his wife and daughters, I knew this wouldn't require a hard sell on my part.

When Jane and I were discussing all of this and I mentioned extending my stay at the Hampton, she smiled and surprised me by saying, "Why don't you save yourself some money and just stay here?"

Why not, indeed. Since I now seemed to be tossing precedents out the window on a regular basis, what difference could one more make?

AFTER HELPING JANE clean up after breakfast and load the dishwasher, I told her I needed to get back to the Hampton for a quick shower and change of clothes before I checked out. I had nearly two hours before the hotel's 11:00 check-out time and I planned to use part of that time to cancel my flights and make the necessary phone calls. I told her I would try to make it back to her place before noon and we could have lunch on me at a restaurant of her choosing. She happily agreed.

It was a quarter past nine when I got back to the hotel. I stopped at the front desk where Stacy, the tall blonde who had checked me in three days earlier, was on duty again. I explained that I was going to be checking out later that morning, one day early, and she asked if there was a problem with my room. I assured her there wasn't; it was just a matter of something unexpected coming up that required me to shorten my stay. She said she hoped it was nothing serious but she understood and the early checkout wouldn't be a problem.

The first thing I did when I got back to my room was shuck off yesterday's clothes and head for the shower. While I stood under the warm water I replayed the conversation Jane and I had had over breakfast. We had refined her plan a bit, testing one option against another as we attempted to nail down all the details and make things as foolproof as possible.

Of course foolproof is a relative term, seldom absolute. When you're planning to kill someone, it's always a good idea to remember Murphy's Law.

We still had a couple of issues to resolve but I had an idea or two that I thought might work. I planned to discuss them with Jane over lunch and I hoped she would be amenable to what I had in mind.

I CHECKED OUT of the Hampton Inn at 10:45. Stacy said she hoped I had had a pleasant stay and would visit them again sometime, and I thanked her and said I would certainly keep them in mind if I was ever back in the area. I loaded my luggage into the trunk of the Impala and drove the now-familiar route to Jane's house, hoping I wasn't going to be getting back to her place too early.

Before checking out I had called Mike Stevenson and he confirmed what I had guessed, that keeping Preacher a few more days wouldn't be a problem and his wife and daughters would be only too happy to hear the news. I thanked him and said I owed him big time and he laughed and said he planned to collect.

I had also cancelled my flights and got an extension on my car rental. For the moment everything seemed to be falling into place, but once again I reminded myself of Murphy's Law.

And its waggish follow-up: "Murphy was an optimist."

Chapter 40

DRIVING BACK TO JANE'S FROM the Hampton Inn, I was suddenly assailed with doubts and a serious case of cold feet.

Not for the first time—or even the tenth—since taking this assignment, I asked myself what the hell I was doing. Just a couple hours earlier I'd rather blithely accepted Jane's invitation to give up my hotel room and stay with her. Now, I couldn't help thinking I might have made a serious mistake.

The list of never-befores I was compiling, beginning with my agreeing to have dinner with Jane on the night of my arrival, was steadily growing. Was I so gobsmacked by Jane's attractiveness that I'd lost all reason?

It was beginning to look like it.

Then again, she had proven helpful in getting me close to Gaston Stevens and in coming up with a workable, even ingenious, plan for his elimination. If nothing else, she had shortcut the process by which I usually handled assignments. Without her help I probably wouldn't be this close to completing that assignment, so I had to give her credit.

Still, I also couldn't help wondering about her own motives. Sure, she wanted to avenge her sister's death and see justice done, but that needn't have included sleeping with her hit man. I remembered the old saying, that weddings and funerals cause people to do crazy things, and I wondered if last night's love making was at least partially a reaction to the celebration of Sara's life earlier that day.

I was still pondering these questions when I pulled into Jane's driveway.

JANE ASKED IF I was okay with having lunch at the Crab Shack again and I said that was fine; she didn't have to twist my arm and I could already taste another blackened catfish sandwich. She shook her head, laughing, and said, "You and your catfish."

As I was unloading my luggage from the trunk of the Impala and moving it inside, she asked me if I would mind driving us to the Crab Shack and if, after lunch, we could swing by the shop where her Jeep Cherokee had just had its radiator replaced. She said they had called her a little earlier and told her it was ready to be picked up. "If you wouldn't mind dropping me off and following me home afterwards," she added.

"Sure, happy to," I said. Thinking, *could we be any more domestic?*

LUNCH AT THE CRAB SHACK was every bit as good as the first time we'd eaten there. The place was fairly crowded so we kept our conversation light, not discussing anything related to Gaston Stevens that might be overheard. Afterwards we picked up Jane's Cherokee and I followed her back to her place, wondering if she was planning to keep both the Cherokee and her sister's Subaru—remembering she had told me the latter was going to be hers as part of the estate settlement—or if she might decide to sell one of them.

"I really don't need two cars," she said, almost as if she'd been reading my mind, as soon as we parked in her driveway and exited our vehicles. "But Edward and Bruce didn't want the Subaru, and neither did their wives or any of the kids. We considered selling it at auction, and I might still do something like that. But for the moment I'll just keep it for backup in case I have any more problems with my Jeep."

"Sounds like a plan," I said, and I momentarily considered telling her I might be interested in buying the Forester if she decided to sell it. My aging Equinox was rapidly approaching the 100,000-mile mark so I knew I would be thinking about replacing it sometime within the next year or so. But for the moment I held off. I had more immediate matters to resolve.

"What do you want to do this afternoon?" Jane asked.

"How about another walk on the beach?" I said. "We still have some things to finalize if we're going to put your plan into effect."

"Perfect," she said, her smile widening into a grin.

I DROVE US TO THE BEACH and we parked at the same place as before. We crossed the same stile, paused long enough to remove our footwear, then started ambling southward along the base of the dunes. I glanced at my watch and saw it was 2:15.

We walked in silence for a couple minutes, then Jane said, apropos of nothing, "Here's a sea turtle fact I bet you didn't know."

"Just about anything you tell me about sea turtles is going to be something I didn't know," I said, laughing. "I'm afraid my knowledge of marine biology is pretty limited. Well, except for the bait balls you told me about yesterday."

"Well, it's time we start educating you," she said. "Like I said before, once a teacher…"

"Right," I said. "Go ahead and lay your turtle fact on me."

"Okay, here goes. Sea turtles are TSD."

I laughed again. "What the heck does that mean?"

"It stands for temperature-dependent sex determination." There was no missing the enthusiasm in her voice, reminding me again of how devoted Jane was to the turtles, just as her sister had been.

"Okay," I said. "I'm still clueless. What does that mean?"

"It means that the sex of the baby turtles is determined by the temperature of the sand in which the eggs are laid and incubated. I don't remember the exact degrees, but if the temperature of the sand is below a certain degree, the babies will be males. If the sand is warmer, the babies will be females."

"Really!" I said. I'd never heard of this. "So the sex of the baby turtles isn't determined at fertilization?"

"No. It's determined by the temperature of the sand. It's the same for alligators and crocodiles."

"Wow," I said. I was having a little trouble getting my brain around this. One thing was certain—Jane had been correct when she said I probably didn't know this fact about sea turtles. Or alligators and crocodiles, for that matter. And I thought of myself as some kind of outdoorsman.

"Pretty remarkable, isn't it?"

"I'll say. But I gotta ask, does that mean that all of the turtles in a nest will be the same sex? Or just the majority of them?"

"I'm not sure. We could ask Julie about that. She'd probably know. But I know that at least the majority of them will be the same."

"That's incredible."

"I think so too."

We walked on in silence for another minute or so, then Jane said, "Here's something else about turtle nests. There can be up to a hundred eggs or more in a nest, and they all hatch at once. When the first one hatches, it triggers all the others and they hatch almost simultaneously. When they begin climbing out of the nest it's called a turtle boil because with all that activity, the nest looks like a pot of boiling water."

I couldn't help laughing at this. "So 'turtle boil' has nothing to do with…"

"No, it doesn't refer to cooking the turtles, if that's what you're thinking. It's not like a shrimp boil." She laughed and punched my arm. "Shame on you for thinking such a thing."

"Sorry."

"It's okay. I told you, didn't I, that Sara had just found a turtle boil when she was killed?"

"Yes, you told me that."

Jane shuddered. "I'll never forget it. That bastard Gaston killed some of the baby turtles with his ATV. I watched one of them die right beside me."

"I'm sorry," I said again.

She gulped. "It's okay. Well, no, it's not okay. I mean, it's something I'll never forget, but I'll have to learn to live with it." She paused, then added, "Do you think I'll feel better after we…" She didn't finish, but she didn't have to.

"I don't know," I answered honestly.

WE WALKED FOR ANOTHER HOUR or so before turning and heading back to the car. Having broached the subject of Gaston Stevens, we spent much of that time going over Jane's plan again, testing various options and discarding most of them before finally arriving at something we believed would work and, at the same time, minimize the risk to ourselves.

By the time we returned to the Impala, we had agreed on a course of action. We drove back to Jane's house feeling pleased with ourselves and I realized many of the misgivings I'd had earlier seemed to have dissipated. I told myself to stop overthinking things and just go with the flow.

As we were walking into Jane's house she turned to me with an impish smile. "All of that exercise and fresh air has made me sleepy. How about a nap before dinner?"

Another one of those offers I couldn't refuse.

Chapter 41

WE DIDN'T DO MUCH NAPPING.

You knew that.

By the digital clock on Jane's nightstand, it was 4:45 when she sighed deeply and said, "I want to shower before dinner." Like the night before, she was lying with her head on my shoulder. Then she added, "Do you like Italian?"

"Yes, I like Italian. What do you have in mind?"

"There's a restaurant we haven't been to yet. It's called Nick's. Not too far from here. Or if you'd like, we can just stay in and I can fix something."

"No, the restaurant sounds fine. Let's do that."

"Okay, that's settled." She laughed. "Now, change of subject. Do you mind if I make a personal observation?"

"No, go ahead."

"Well…I'm now fairly positive you don't have any tattoos. Unless there's one hidden in some secret place I haven't yet discovered."

I laughed in return. "No, I don't have any tattoos, hidden or otherwise. Why?"

"Oh, I'm just curious. Have you ever wanted one? Or—don't tell me. You're afraid of needles."

"No, I'm not afraid of needles. That's not the reason."

"What, then?"

I hesitated, then I realized I had no reason not to be honest with her. She already knew my biggest secret.

"A tattoo is an identifying mark," I said. "When you try to remain unnoticed like I do, you don't want anything that will draw attention or make an impression that someone might remember."

Jane considered this for a moment. "Okay," she said. "That makes sense. But you could still get one someplace discreet. You know, where it would be covered by clothing."

"Yes, I guess I could. And the truth is, I have considered it from time to time, but I've just never gone through with it."

"Really! Do you know what you would get?"

"Yes. An eagle. Probably on my shoulder."

"An eagle?" She had lifted her head from my shoulder and was lying beside me with her elbow bent and her chin propped in her hand. She was grinning and I was pretty sure I knew why.

"Yes, but not like you might be imagining," I said. "Not something fierce with a huge beak and wicked talons. Or anything military looking."

Her expression changed to puzzled. "What, then?"

"It would be something small, almost in silhouette. The eagle would be in flight, with a mountain range behind it. And underneath would be the words 'A Catskill Eagle.'"

"Really! A Catskill eagle? What's the significance of that?"

"It's from a quotation. A passage from *Moby Dick*."

"Really!" she said again. "What's the quotation?"

I paused for a moment, wanting to make sure I got the wording correct. Then I said, "'And there is a Catskill eagle in some souls that can alike dive down into the blackest gorges, and soar out of them again and become invisible in the sunny spaces. And even if he forever flies within the gorge, that gorge is in the mountains; so that even in his lowest swoop the mountain eagle is still higher than the other birds upon the plain, even though they soar.'"

"Wow. That's beautiful."

"I think so too."

"So is that how you see yourself? As a Catskill eagle?"

I smiled and shook my head. "Hardly. It's more like something I aspire to, but I fall short most of the time."

"Why do you feel like you fall short?"

"I dive into the gorge often enough, but many times I have trouble getting out of it, and I certainly don't soar so high that I become invisible in the sunny spaces." As I said this I realized I had never had a conversation like this with Daryl Nelson.

"But the part about the gorge being in the mountains…

even if you always fly in the gorge, you're still higher than the lesser birds on the plain, right?"

"Well, it would be nice to think so, but I can't flatter myself like that. Like I said, it's something I aspire to, but I'm not likely to ever achieve."

She leaned down and kissed me. "I think you're being too hard on yourself," she said. With that, she flipped off the sheet covering us, stood up and padded off to the shower. But just before she passed through the bedroom's doorway, she paused and looked back over her bare shoulder.

"And," she said, "I think you should get that tattoo."

NICK'S PIZZERIA DELIVERED.

Not just in the literal sense—although they did that also—but also more figuratively in providing wonderful Italian cuisine.

It was a small restaurant, almost a cubbyhole, and I had to smile when we entered. The tablecloths were red and white checked vinyl, and there was a candle standing upright in the neck of an empty wine bottle on each table. I noticed that the candles were lit only at those tables where patrons were seated.

The table we were shown to was midway to the back of the room. Our server, a smiling, slim young man with dark curly hair and a nametag that said Louis, leaned forward and flicked a disposable lighter to light the candle at our table. Then he placed the two menus he had tucked under his arm in front of us and asked if he could bring us something to drink.

Jane ordered a glass of pinot grigio and I opted for a whiskey sour.

I opened my menu and said, "What do you recommend?"

"Everything I've had here is good," she said. "My favorite is the linguine with clam sauce. That's what I'm going to have. Unless you'd rather share a pizza. Their pizza is excellent also and I'd be fine with that."

I studied the menu for a moment and said, "I might have my annual serving of fettucine alfredo. I haven't had any yet this year so I'm about due."

Jane laughed. "Your annual serving? Really?"

"Well, you know what they say. It's not called heart attack on a plate for no reason. So I try to limit myself."

She laughed again. "Go for it," she said.

WE WERE ABOUT HALFWAY through our meal—which was as excellent as Jane had predicted—when she said, "I'm still thinking about that Catskill eagle quote."

"Really? What about it?"

"Well, mostly what you said about often diving into the gorge." She hesitated, then continued. "I'm not quite sure how to put this…I guess I'm wondering if the gorge is related to what you do."

I thought for a moment before answering. Then I said, "It can be, yes. There are always problems and concerns to be dealt with, and I can't deny that's stressful. Sometimes almost overwhelming. But…I've always found a way to deal with it. I don't mean that boastfully; I'd be the first to admit that a lot of times resolving those problems has mostly been a matter of luck. I've had several close calls."

"Okay, I get all that. But I was thinking more in terms of guilt. Is that ever a problem for you?"

"No, not really. Again, I don't mean that boastfully, nor do I want to sound callous. But as a rule—" I lowered my voice—"I don't take an assignment unless I'm convinced the person deserves what I'm being hired for. That pretty much eliminates any guilt."

Jane nodded. She took a sip of her wine and I had a sudden question of my own. A disquieting one.

"Are you having second thoughts?" I asked.

She smiled and shook her head. "No," she said. "I was just curious, that's all. But no, I'm not having second thoughts." She paused, then added, "I never had second thoughts the last time, either. What I remember feeling the most was relief."

"I'm happy to hear that."

"You saved me from an untenable situation. This may

sound awful, but the only regret I had was that I didn't hire you sooner." She laughed. "My hero," she added.

I laughed also. "Hardly," I said. I lowered my voice again. "Killing people for money…there's really nothing heroic about that."

Jane's expression abruptly turned serious. Her sea-green eyes became almost fierce in their intensity, and she studied me for a long moment before speaking. Then it was a single harsh word.

"Bullshit," she said.

I was startled by her vehemence. Too startled to reply.

After another long moment she spoke again, firmly but less vehemently. "You do not do what you do for money. Something else motivates you." She paused, then added, "Something from your past."

Again, I was too startled to respond.

She took a deep breath and added, "I'm right, aren't I?" There was no mistaking her certainty.

"Well, I…"

"It's okay if you don't want to tell me. But it's not okay for you to pretend you're something you're not."

I shifted in my seat. "You're making me pretty uncomfortable."

"I don't mean to. And again, you don't need to tell me the details." She lowered her voice also. "But don't try to tell me you only kill people for money. There's more to it than that. A lot more."

I tried to deflect. "I don't consider myself any kind of hero," I said.

"Okay, maybe hero isn't the right word. And like I said, I'm not going to pry. But I know I'm right about the rest."

Wow. Just wow.

Chapter 42

IT PROBABLY SOUNDS CORNY OR cliché or even downright ridiculous to say that someone has looked into your soul. But that's exactly how I felt after Jane's pronouncement.

In simplest terms, she nailed it.

How she had so quickly and correctly identified my motivation—especially without knowing the details, as she herself admitted—left me marveling at her…what? Intuitiveness? Powers of observation? Aptitude for making lucky guesses?

Maybe all of the above.

She was spot-on correct about my motivation being related to something in my past. My hatred of bullies—and by extension, injustice—stemmed from the death of a high school classmate, a fellow named Milton Mulberry. (Yes, his was a rather unfortunate name.) Milton had been bullied relentlessly until, following one especially humiliating incident when we were juniors, he had committed suicide.

I could have intervened during that incident, but I hadn't. After months of agonizing over my failure to act, I determined I would never again stand by if I saw someone being oppressed and I could do anything to prevent it. Having made that determination, my eventual transition to contract killing became almost inevitable.

Rachel James knew all of this because I had shared the details of Milton's story with her years earlier. That Jane had divined this, after knowing me personally for just a few days, left me shaken.

WE SHARED A LARGE SLICE of tiramisu for dessert. Like the rest of the meal, it was wonderful. And I won't deny I was relieved when we were deciding what to order and Jane said she didn't care for crème brulee. You guessed it—that was Daryl's favorite.

I wondered how much longer it would be until, as my

old philosophy professor had maintained, the universe began to ease up with the Daryl reminders. Or more precisely, my brain stopped defaulting to thoughts of her.

It was about 8:30 when we got back to Jane's house, and we quickly settled into what was becoming a nightly routine—drinks on her front porch, accompanied by a foot rub. Despite my earlier unease over Jane's uncanny assertion during our dinner conversation, I now felt curiously relaxed and at peace.

Maybe that was due to the combination of alcohol and all the carbs I'd eaten. Still, I couldn't help feeling like this was exactly where I was supposed to be at this moment and, more importantly, Jane was exactly the person with whom I was supposed to be sharing that moment.

We hadn't spoken for a couple minutes and I was reflecting on how comfortable we both seemed to be with sitting quietly, without the need for idle conversation. We hadn't discussed anything directly related to Gaston Stevens at dinner, as if we had tacitly agreed to give that subject a rest for the evening. I was fine with that.

But after taking another sip of her wine—I had switched to beer—Jane said softly, "Hey. I think I might owe you an apology."

"For what?"

"For bearing down on you so hard at dinner about what motivates you. I realize it's really none of my business, and I didn't mean to come on so strong."

"It's okay," I said. "No harm, no foul."

"Are you sure? You looked somewhat…alarmed by what I said."

I took a deep breath. "Okay," I said. "I'll admit I was a little surprised. Actually, more than a little."

"Surprised? Why?"

"Because you were right. Money isn't the primary reason I kill people, and yes, it does have something to do with my past. You were correct about all of that, and I guess I was just surprised by the accuracy of what you said. And by how certain you were, even though we've only known each other for a few days." I laughed slightly. "You got it in one, as the expression goes."

Jane smiled. "I knew it," she said softly. "But I promised I wouldn't pry, and I won't."

"That's okay," I said. "It's something that happened a long time ago, and maybe someday I'll share it with you. But in the meantime, I am curious—how did you know?"

Jane paused before answering. She turned her head and gazed out through the screen toward the street. Then she turned back to me and said, "I've become very good at reading people. It's actually a skill I've tried to develop. After what happened in my marriage I was determined I would never again let myself be fooled by anyone's words or promises. It's their actions that matter, and I've made myself start paying close attention to what people do, not just what they say."

"Okay, I get all that," I said. "But I'm still not sure how that applies to me, or how you were able to figure out what you did about my motivation."

"I'm not sure I can explain that myself. It's mostly just a sense I was getting. A vibe." She laughed. "You have to admit, we've gotten very close in the past couple days. Literally very close."

I laughed also. "Can't deny that," I said.

"I think I just sensed that in spite of what you do, you're not ruthless. Focused and determined, yes, but not ruthless. That's why I asked you if you ever felt any guilt. Does that make sense?"

I nodded. "I've never heard it explained quite like that, or thought about it in those terms, but yes, that makes sense."

"I also remember you asking me that first night after dinner if I was sure it was Gaston that I had seen run down Sara. You wanted to be positive and not make the mistake of killing someone who didn't deserve it."

"Right, and you reminded me that Gaston had already admitted to being on the beach that night, but he claimed what happened was an accident."

"Right. And like I said, I'm certain of what I saw, and it was no accident. But the fact that you had to be sure says a lot about you. It you were just doing this for the money, you wouldn't be that concerned about whether or not I was mistaken. You'd just do the job, take the money, and be done with it."

Once again, I couldn't help marveling at her reasoning. Or the astuteness of her observations.

Before I could respond, my phone rang.

It was sitting on the small table next to my bottle of Dos Equis. I picked it up and saw that the caller was Rachel James. I thumbed the icon to answer and said, "Hey you."

"Hey you," she said. "I got your message. Sorry I'm so late getting back to you, but I was up at Summer's this evening for a cookout. What do you need?"

I had texted Rachel earlier that afternoon when Jane was in the shower.

"Reinforcements," I replied.

PART THREE: DISPATCH

Death walks faster than the wind and never returns what he has taken.

Hans Christian Andersen

Chapter 43

RACHEL JAMES ARRIVED IN Wilmington three days later on the same afternoon flight I had flown in on previously. Jane and I were both there to greet her.

We had driven two vehicles, Jane's Cherokee and my rental Impala, to the airport. Jane pointed out that since we also had Sara's Subaru Forester at our disposal, there was no need for me to keep the Impala any longer and continue paying for its rental. I couldn't argue the point, and besides, I was hoping for a chance to drive the Forester. I was still thinking of making Jane an offer if she decided to sell it.

Rachel's flight was on time and while we waited at the baggage claim area for her, Jane suddenly laughed and shook her head. "What?" I asked.

"I was just thinking of what George Carlin said about the silly language airlines have come up with, words like deplane."

I laughed also. "Yeah, I remember that."

"Right. He was a genius when it came to pointing out the absurd." She laughed again. "So, do you think Rachel has deplaned yet?"

"Yes," I said, nodding toward the concourse. "That's her coming now."

Rachel broke into a wide grin—I've often said her smile reminds me of Sofia Vergara's—when she spotted us. She quickened her pace and I noted she was wearing her usual flying outfit, a sleeveless, comfortable black shift that hit her just below the knee, along with black ballet flats. She was carrying a black, knee-length, crushed velvet jacket over one arm—she always complained about how cold airplanes were—and she was pulling a small rolling carry-on with the other. I knew she always traveled light, and I'd seen the same outfit several times previously when she was flying to Kansas to visit her mother and I'd dropped her off at the airport in Des Moines.

"Hey you!" she said as she got close.

"Hey you," I said. "Jane, this Rachel. Rachel, Jane." "Nice to meet you!" they said simultaneously, then they both laughed. Rachel dropped the handle of her carry-on and we shared a three-way hug.

"Welcome to North Carolina," Jane said. "How were your flights?"

"Oh, they were fine. Cold, as always, but otherwise fine."

"We can get you warmed up soon enough," Jane said. "We're in the mid-80s today, and a little beach time should help you get rid of the chills."

"Sounds great!" Rachel said, and they both laughed again.

I was already feeling outnumbered.

INCLUDING RACHEL IN OUR PLAN was a mutual decision.

Jane and I had discussed various options and we kept returning to the realization that we needed the help of someone Gaston wouldn't recognize, preferably someone neither he nor his friends had ever seen before, and someone who had no links whatsoever to Jane or her family.

Rachel, who had already volunteered her help, fit the bill perfectly. And as she had already told me, she was quite happy to jump on a plane and make the trip to North Carolina. It took a bit of fast footwork on her part—getting several days off work on short notice—but she pulled it off with her usual alacrity. And now here she was.

"Al really wanted to come also," she told us during the hour-long drive from Wilmington to Schnock's Harbor. "But he's overseeing that plant expansion where they're adding two new production lines, and he just couldn't get away." Rachel's husband was a troubleshooting engineer at the huge Hormel facility in Osceola, about forty-five minutes southwest of Des Moines. He and Rachel had both played active roles in Greg Fletcher's elimination the previous summer, so he too was familiar with our deeds. Or misdeeds.

"I appreciate his willingness to pitch in," I said, "but I think the three of us should be able to handle it. Here's hoping, anyway."

"Oh, I'm confident we can pull this off," Jane said. "I mean, what could possibly go wrong?"

We all laughed. What, indeed?

WE STOPPED AT THE BEACH on the way home so Rachel could rid herself of the lingering chill she'd felt on her flights and, as she put it, feel some sand between her toes. The three of us strolled for about an hour, during which Jane and I outlined the details of our plan. Rachel listened attentively, asking a few questions and adding a refinement or two of her own.

By the time we got back to Jane's house it was nearing dinner time so while Jane showed Rachel to her guest room, I pulled Jane's Weber grill out of her garage and prepared the charcoal. Yes, Jane was a purist like me; I was relieved that I wasn't going to have to fool with propane.

Dinner consisted of T-bone steaks, baked potatoes (foil wrapped and also done on the grill) and tossed salad. Jane had made yet another pitcher of margaritas and while I usually drink beer with my steak, I wasn't about to argue or complain. As we settled in at the table, I reflected for the thousandth time that this assignment was shaping up like no other I'd had in the past thirty-plus years.

But my misgivings were diminishing. This was no doubt partly due to Rachel's presence—she and I had collaborated, so to speak, on quite a few of my previous assignments, so having her on hand was definitely a confidence-booster.

On the other hand, she was once again going to have to play an active role, just as she had done with Greg Fletcher, and this had me concerned for her safety. Of course we were going to do everything we could to minimize the risks to Rachel and ourselves, but there were always those unknowns that could crop up and wreak havoc.

Still, after the conversation we'd had during our walk

on the beach, I was feeling reasonably confident about our plan, and I suspected this confidence was also at least somewhat related to the ease with which I had settled into what was quickly becoming a real relationship with Jane.

Just a few days earlier I would have scoffed at—totally rejected, actually—the thought of becoming romantically involved with a client...I *had* rejected that thought, in fact, and resolved I wouldn't let it happen.

Which shows you how good I am at prognosticating. And standing firm on my convictions.

AFTER DINNER WE PILED BACK into Jane's Cherokee. Jane drove, Rachel rode shotgun and I took the back seat. This was primarily a recon mission aimed at familiarizing Rachel with the area and the locations where our plan would take place. Because our time was limited, we hoped to begin implementing it the following evening.

We started with a pass by Gaston Stevens's house. Admittedly this was something of a risk, but we gambled that Gaston probably wouldn't be home—we figured he'd likely be out with his buddies—or if he was home, that he wouldn't be outside. We got lucky.

Like before, the door of Gaston's garage was open—I wondered if he ever bothered to close it—and his red Mustang and Polaris ATV were still parked inside. The black Dodge Dakota with the GASSED license plates wasn't in the driveway, which was a pretty good indication he was out for the evening.

Next we headed for the Dive Bar. I was hoping we would find the Dakota in the parking lot but this time we weren't so lucky. There was no sign of the truck and I hoped that Gaston hadn't been spooked when Steve the bartender had ordered him to leave a few nights earlier. I voiced this concern to Jane.

"I don't think so," Jane said. "Gaston's a hothead and he and his buddies are long-time regulars at this place. Something like that wouldn't be enough to cause him to stop coming here. In fact, that's probably not the first time Steve has had to tell him to cool it."

"Okay," I said. "We'll hope he hasn't decided to do his drinking elsewhere."

"Nah," Jane said. "He'll be back. He's a creature of habit."

We all laughed. Then Rachel spoke.

"You're sure I won't have any trouble recognizing him?"

"Positive," Jane said. "You can't miss his red hair, and remember, he'll be wearing an ankle monitor. Plus, one of his buddies, Dave Sonderheim, is covered with tats. If he's with Gaston, they'll be easy to spot."

"Okay."

I leaned forward from the back seat. "Did you decide on a name?" I asked.

"Yes," Rachel replied. "Selene."

"Selene?"

"Goddess of the moon."

Chapter 44

GASTON STEVENS WAS HUNGOVER. Massively so.

He groaned as he rolled over in his bed and groped for his cell phone on the nightstand. He hadn't bothered to put it on the charger before falling into bed sometime around two in the morning—it hadn't occurred to him to do so and he probably wouldn't have been coordinated enough to connect the cable anyway—but the phone still had enough power to be operable and tell him the time.

It was almost noon, 11:48 to be exact. So he'd slept for nearly ten hours. It didn't feel like enough.

His head was pounding and the bright sunlight streaming through his bedroom windows—he also hadn't bothered to close the blinds last night—wasn't helping. He flopped back over on the bed and lay there with one arm across his eyes. He told himself he really needed to get up and get and moving. Instead, he drifted back to sleep.

The next time he awoke, it was just past 1:30. This time he forced himself to sit upright and swing his legs off the bed. Then he bent over and sat with his forearms resting on his thighs and his head—still pounding—hanging. Looking down, he studied the monitor on his right ankle.

That fucking monitor.

He'd seriously considered cutting the fucking thing off, but everyone from his buddies to his mother (and her attorneys) had warned him not to do so. His father hadn't specifically told him not to cut it off but in his typical milquetoast fashion had told him just to make the best of it.

You're not the one who has to clump around with the damned thing on your leg, Gaston had thought, but he'd kept it to himself. He was counting on his parents' help—especially his mother's—to get him out of his latest trouble and he couldn't risk alienating either of them right now. Better to play it straight, at least for the short term.

As for the trouble…Gaston was confident he wouldn't be convicted of manslaughter; that the attorneys his mother had hired would get him off. They had explained to him that manslaughter—in this case, involuntary manslaughter—was a very serious charge. Not as serious as murder, which required an element of premeditation, or even as serious as voluntary manslaughter, which required some sort of provocation. But it shouldn't be taken lightly, they warned him, because involuntary manslaughter covered those instances when someone's death was caused by another person acting recklessly, which seemed to apply in his case.

Gaston wasn't entirely clear on the difference between premeditation and provocation, but he understood that he had been charged with involuntary manslaughter because he hadn't planned to kill the old woman beforehand. It was a spur of the moment impulse (although he hadn't told the attorneys this, and he never would) and he still believed that he could avoid conviction if he could convince the jury that the woman's death was entirely accidental.

He knew the attorneys were going to launch an all-out attack on the old lady's sister, who claimed to have seen him run down the old lady on purpose. It would be the sister's word against his and he planned to stick to his story that he'd tried to swerve and the old woman had panicked and jumped in front of him. He'd already said the bruises on his forearm were caused by him trying to push her out of the way, not by deliberately clipping her as the sister claimed, and he would stick to that line as well.

With no other witnesses, he was confident his story would fly. Or at least be enough to create reasonable doubt in the minds of the jurors. Some of them, anyway, and it would only take one to hang the jury. And what the hell, he thought; she was an *old* lady. Her life was pretty much over anyway.

In the meantime, however, the ankle monitor was a major pain. He'd gotten used to showering with it but he hadn't tried surfing since it had been locked around his ankle, and he still felt self-conscious about being seen with it. He always wore shorts in the summer so there was no way to hide it.

Looking down at it now, he once again thought about cutting it off. Maybe he could claim it was irritating his skin or something and removing it had been necessary for medical reasons.

No, he decided after a moment, better not. Besides, annoying though it was and self-consciousness aside, he had to admit he was beginning to feel like the monitor gave him a sense of notoriety that he kind of enjoyed. If nothing else, it was a good conversation-starter.

Like it had been with the girl he'd met last night at Boomer's Tap. He wasn't a regular at the place so he wasn't as well known as he was at, say, the Dive Bar, but he'd decided to drop in for a beer or two and see if he recognized anyone. He was on his own for the evening; Sonderheim was off somewhere doing God knows what—maybe getting another tattoo—and O'Neill was out with a girl he'd recently met.

Flying solo for a change, Gaston hoped he might get lucky.

The girl's name was Nancy and she appeared to be in her early twenties. She had long, straight black hair and a trim body and she was sitting by herself at the bar when Gaston entered the place. He took the empty stool on her right and when she glanced at him and smiled, he said, "Hi."

"Hi," she replied. She had beautiful straight white teeth and large gray-green eyes. She also had a tiny black metallic ring through one nostril that Gaston thought looked cute. He considered complimenting her on the ring but wasn't sure how she might take it, so he didn't say anything.

She studied him for a moment then spoke. "I think I know you," she said. "You're Gaston Stevens, right?"

"That's right," he replied. "But I don't recall us meeting. You are…?"

"Nancy."

He nodded. "So, Nancy, how do you know me?"

"You were in the news recently. Something about accidentally running down an old lady on the beach. Your mother is Congresswoman Maggie Stevens."

"That's right," Gaston said, pleased that Nancy had

referred to the beach incident as an accident but a little put off by her reference to his mother. "But I didn't realize I was that well known."

She laughed. "You're kinda hard to miss with your red hair and that ankle monitor." She pointed down to where he had tucked his right foot under the bar stool.

He smiled. "Good eyes," he said, thinking, *this chick is sharp. I need to be careful.*

"So tell me what happened on the beach," she was saying. She didn't seem intimidated by what he had done, nor was there anything accusing in her tone.

"Oh, that," he said. "Well, like you said, it was an accident. It was dark and I came up on her kinda fast on my ATV and I tried to swerve around her but she must have panicked because she jumped right in front of me. I reached out to push her out of the way, but…" He let his voice trail off and he shook his head, hoping the rest was self-explanatory and she wouldn't press him for more details.

"But I think they said on the news you were arrested?"

"Yes, but that's all a misunderstanding. My attorneys"—he almost said "My mother's attorneys" but he caught himself—"said that once the facts come out at the trial, I should be in the clear." The attorneys hadn't really said that, at least not in so many words, but he didn't want to get into the whole business about the lady's sister claiming he'd killed the old woman deliberately, and how the attorneys planned to attack the sister's testimony.

Nancy looked thoughtful. "I see," she said after a moment. "Well, good luck!" She sounded like she was ready to be done with the subject.

"Thanks." He hesitated, then decided to press his luck. "Now, can I buy you another beer?"

She shrugged. "Sure," she said. "Why not?"

ONE BEER LED TO ANOTHER, and another, and somewhere along the line they did two or three shots of Fireball as well. Gaston thought things were looking promising until Nancy checked her phone and said, "Oh, geez. I have to get going. I work tomorrow." She stood up from her stool and slipped the phone into the pocket of her shorts. "Nice talking with you. Thanks for the drinks."

"Leaving so soon?" Gaston knew he was well on the way to being totally shitfaced and he was surprised the girl wasn't feeling the same. "Are you sure you're okay to drive?" Trying to sound concerned.

"I should be fine," she said. "I only live a few blocks from here and my car knows the way home all by itself. I just need to get in and start the engine."

It took Gaston a moment to process her joke, during which she moved away from him. "See ya around sometime," she said, turning and heading for the door.

And just like that, she was gone.

Well, fuck me, he thought. *So much for getting lucky tonight.*

He signaled the bartender for another beer.

HE WOUND UP CLOSING the place. Now, the morning after—no, make that the afternoon after—he felt like shit warmed over and at loose ends. He pushed himself up off the bed and headed into the bathroom to piss. Then he downed three extra strength Tylenol and wandered out to the kitchen.

He opened the refrigerator and pulled out a half-gallon carton of orange juice. He drank straight from the carton, remembering how his mother used to bitch at him when she caught him doing that at home. "Use a *glass*, Gaston!" she'd say in that high-pitched voice he despised. Plenty of times he'd been tempted to flip her off, but he'd never had the guts to do so.

He put the orange juice back in the fridge and stood for a moment, wondering what the hell to do with himself for the rest of the day. He thought about going back to bed.

Later he'd try to get ahold of Sonderheim, see if he was up for something this evening.

Like hitting the Dive Bar. They hadn't been there for several days, and maybe he'd have better luck than he'd had at Boomer's.

Chapter 45

JANE, RACHEL AND I SPENT THE NEXT day on further fine-tuning. While there's always the danger of overthinking things—and I'm a big believer in the rule of KISS—there is also always the risk of overlooking something critical. Another old saying, that Fate favors the prepared individual, came into play here. We wanted to be as prepared as possible and leave very little to chance.

After a late breakfast of pecan waffles and spicy pork sausage, the three of us went for another long walk on the beach. The temperature was in the low eighties, the sun was shining and the waves were steadily rolling in as we strolled along the water's edge. Rachel paused every so often to pick up a seashell that she added to a small canvas beach tote Jane had loaned her.

It was an ideal morning, marred only by the knowledge that our reason for coming together in this setting was to administer justice—rough justice, to be sure—by killing someone. Once again I wondered if Jane might be having any second thoughts.

If she was, she kept them to herself.

It also occurred to me that I had been through variations of this same exercise almost more times than I could remember. Rachel had played a key role many of those times, especially in the past few years, but usually in a planning capacity. That she was going to be a participant this time, as she had been last summer, once again had me concerned for her safety. Big time concerned.

I voiced my worries to the two women.

To their credit, neither of them told me I was being paranoid or unduly anxious. Rachel admitted she was feeling a little bit nervous but she quickly added that she was confident she could handle her part of the plan. Given what I'd seen of her in action previously, I didn't doubt this.

Still, there remained the danger of things spinning out

of control, especially if Gaston Stevens didn't react as we were anticipating. This was the unknown that posed the biggest threat, and we wanted to be ready.

We walked in silence for a couple of minutes until Jane said, "What about this?" Then she followed up with a suggestion that sounded like something borrowed from an early James Bond movie.

I couldn't help laughing. But I also couldn't deny that it would probably be effective.

"Yes," I said. "That would probably work."

AFTER OUR BIG BREAKFAST none of us was feeling particularly hungry at lunchtime. We briefly considered swinging by the turtle rehab center on the way home from the beach but decided against it. Rachel said she would love to see the turtles but we agreed that if Julie or Melanie was working and they met her, that could seriously derail our plans. We needed to keep Rachel's identity a secret, at least as much as possible. We couldn't risk her meeting either of them and then possibly seeing one or both of them again that evening at the Dive Bar.

So we headed back to Jane's house. Jane had to make a phone call and then, if the other person was receptive, she and Rachel would be running an errand without me. I'd cool my heels at Jane's house while they took care of this one piece of business.

Do I need to tell you I was starting to feel slightly superfluous?

JANE'S PHONE CALL, which she made shortly after we got back to her place, was to a fellow named Matt Lewis, the scuba-diving enthusiast she had dated briefly a few months earlier. Before making the call Jane assured Rachel and me that she and Matt had parted amicably after agreeing that, aside from a mutual love of the ocean, they didn't have a whole lot in common. Jane didn't scuba dive (although Matt had offered to teach her) and as he was looking for a full-time diving partner, that pretty much finished off the relationship.

"Why didn't you want to try scuba diving?" Rachel asked.

Jane laughed. "This probably sounds a little crazy, but I'm terribly claustrophobic about a lot of things. I love to swim, but the idea of being underwater, zipped up tight in a wet suit with a mask on my face and carrying those big tanks on my back…no, thanks. I could feel an anxiety attack coming on just thinking about it."

"Got it," Rachel said. "And I don't think it sounds crazy at all. I know what you mean about being claustrophobic." She paused to shake her head and laugh. "A few years ago I tried on a sport bra that didn't have any hooks or clips, one of those numbers you just pull on over your head. I took it back to the dressing room and got it about halfway on with it covering my head, and my elbow got stuck.

"I couldn't figure out how to move so I could either get it back off or all the way on, and I just freaked. I was almost paralyzed and I really thought they were gonna come in and find me collapsed and hyperventilating on the floor of the dressing room."

By now they were both laughing, and so was I. I'd never heard this story before and I'll admit I was having fun picturing Rachel—well-endowed as she was—literally stuck in this predicament.

"So what did you do?" Jane asked.

"I finally managed to get my elbow free, thank God," Rachel said. "But if I hadn't I was ready to rip or tear the damned thing to get it off, I was that desperate. I would have paid for the damages."

"I understand completely," Jane said, still laughing. "I'd have done the same thing."

Female bonding. You had to love it.

I DIDN'T OVERHEAR Jane's phone conversation with Matt Lewis but she told us afterwards that he had agreed to her request. Like Jane, Matt was retired, and she and Rachel were supposed to meet him at his house in an hour. To avoid any possible awkwardness, I was going to remain behind at

Jane's house.

I planned to use that time doing a little follow-up research online. I could have done it on my phone but Jane volunteered the use of her laptop. It was one more case of my wanting to make sure all the i's were dotted and the t's were crossed. Mostly I was looking for further reassurance that the plan we had come up with—Jane's plan, actually—stood a good chance of succeeding.

If it didn't, that's when the item Jane had convinced Matt to loan us might come in handy.

Chapter 46

"SO HOW LONG HAVE YOU known Rob?" Jane asked.

She and Rachel were on their way to Matt Lewis's house in North Topsail Beach, no more than a fifteen or twenty-minute drive from Jane's home. She hoped she could use that time to learn more about Rob without seeming too inquisitive, although she doubted Rachel would be fooled.

"Let's see," Rachel replied. She thought for a moment then added, "I guess it would be a little over twenty years. You know he was the editor of *American Wingshot* magazine, right?"

"Right, he told me that. He said he retired last year, right before Christmas."

"That's right. Well, when he was first hired as editor, the magazine was owned by Stryker Publishing in Des Moines. Stryker had two other magazines besides *Wingshot*, and I was the circulation director for all three of them."

"I think Rob said the magazines were sold a few years after he came?"

"That's right; they were. Stryker sold the books to a company called Trimedia. They're based in New York but they asked Rob to stay on as editor of *Wingshot*. They set him up to work out of his home. Our other editor, a guy named Roger Stark, stayed on and worked out of his home also. The rest of us in the office kinda scattered and found other jobs."

"I see. What do you do now?"

Rachel told her and Jane replied, "Wow. That's quite a switch."

"I was ready for a change."

"I get it. When I was teaching fourth grade all those years, there were quite a few times I thought about trying something different. But I never did." She paused. Then: "So you and Rob met on the job. And you just hit it off?"

"Pretty much, yeah. Not long after he started, we were

talking about dogs one day—I think we were going through a bunch of puppy pictures readers sent in for the spring issue of *Wingshot*—and he commented that if he didn't work in publishing, his ideal job would be training guide dogs for the blind. He said nothing warmed his heart like seeing a guide dog performing its duty, and I knew right then we were going to be good friends."

"Ah. So I take it you're a dog lover also?"

"Oh, yeah. Lifelong. We currently have a Saint Bernard named Alexander the Great."

Jane laughed. "That's a fitting name for a Saint Bernard."

"We thought so too."

"Okay, so now I have to ask this. You said you've known Rob for a little over twenty years…how long have you been helping him with his…um, assignments? Or is that information classified?"

It was Rachel's turn to laugh. "Let's just say I've been doing it for a while. Usually I just help him with the planning, but once in a while, I play a more active role."

"Like now."

"Right. Like now."

They rode in silence for a couple minutes, then Jane said, "Can I ask you another question?"

"Sure."

"This is a little awkward. But I'm sure you've noticed that Rob and I are more than just…hit man and client."

Rachel nodded, smiling. "Yes, I've noticed. Sharing a bedroom is a pretty obvious giveaway."

"Okay," Jane laughed. "And let me just say that wasn't something I planned. It just sort of…happened. But what can I say, I found him attractive. And now I can't help wondering about something else. A few days ago we were walking on the beach and he told me he's not involved with anyone back in Des Moines."

Rachel hesitated, then answered. "That's right, he's not."

Jane briefly glanced away from her driving to check

Rachel's expression. Rachel was staring straight ahead and frowning slightly, or at least Jane thought she appeared to be frowning. "That's good to know," Jane said. She smiled. "In fact, I'm relieved." She hesitated, then added, "Can I ask something else?"

"Sure."

"He also told me that he had been involved with someone, but that had ended."

"Yes, that's right also."

"So I can't help wondering…how long ago was it that he was involved with her?"

Rachel turned to look out the passenger door window. She stared at the passing scenery for a moment then turned back. "I'm not sure how much of this Rob would want me to tell you. He tends to play things pretty close to the vest."

"Yes, I've noticed." Jane paused. "I'm sorry if I'm overstepping the bounds."

"It's okay; no need to apologize." Rachel smiled. "I understand why you're asking." She sighed and added, "Okay, I'll tell you this much. Rob was involved with a woman named Daryl Nelson, but she burned him pretty badly. And he took it hard."

Jane nodded. "Burned him how?"

Rachel hesitated again. Then she blew out a sharp breath and added, "Daryl was seeing another guy while she was involved with Rob." She shook her head and gave a short laugh. "Al and I saw her having dinner with the guy and it was obvious they were more than casual acquaintances. She didn't see us, and we're the ones who blew the whistle on her…well, I was, anyway. I've been friends with Rob a lot longer than I've known Daryl, so my loyalty is to him, not her. I wasn't going to keep her secret and let her play Rob for a fool."

Jane smiled. "That's admirable. I'm sure he appreciated that."

"Well, I hoped so when I told him. That was really difficult."

"I'm sure it was."

"And like I said, he took it really hard."

Jane nodded. "Can I ask how long they were involved?"

Rachel did a quick calculation. "I'd say a little over a year. Probably about a year and a half."

"And how long ago was it that you told Rob about seeing her with the other guy?"

Once again, Rachel hesitated. "Not all that long ago, actually," she said after a moment.

"I see." There was no mistaking the concern in Jane's voice.

"If you're wondering if Rob is just doing some sort of rebound thing with you, I don't think so," Rachel said. "He's really not that type. He takes relationships seriously. If anything, he's probably a little too cautious when it comes to getting involved."

Jane smiled, but wanly. "Well, that's reassuring, at least. And I've noticed how cautious he is. I can understand why he'd feel the need to be."

"Right."

"This other woman…Daryl? Rob told me she didn't know anything about his second job."

"No, she didn't. And in fact, I think that was beginning to trouble him. The fact that he was keeping such a big secret from her."

"He mentioned that. He said he was starting to feel guilty about it."

"I'm sure he was. It probably sounds paradoxical, but Rob really values honesty in a relationship."

Jane nodded. "Well," she said, "that's one secret he doesn't have to keep from me."

Rachel laughed. "No, he doesn't."

Jane was silent for a moment. Then she said, "I really appreciate you sharing all of this."

Rachel smiled at her and said, "Isn't it obvious? I'm rooting for you."

"Thanks. I *really* appreciate that." Jane took her right hand off the steering wheel and extended it toward Rachel. They high-fived, then Jane turned off the street into the driveway of a bungalow with moss-green siding.

"We're here," she said.

MATT LEWIS CAME to his front door in a sky-blue t-shirt, khaki shorts and flip-flops. He was tall and lean and deeply tanned, with silver hair cut short, just a little longer than a buzz. He smiled as he opened the door and said, "Come in, come in."

Jane and Rachel followed him into his living room and Jane made the introductions. "Matt, this is my friend Rachel; she's visiting from Iowa, like I told you on the phone. We really appreciate you doing us this favor."

Matt laughed. "I have to say, you kinda caught me by surprise with your request. But you're welcome to borrow my speargun as long as you promise not to shoot anyone. Or yourself."

"No worries on that score," Rachel said, smiling. "I just want to see if I can hit anything underwater. It's one more item to check off my bucket list."

"Jane said you're gonna do some snorkeling?"

"That's right. I'm not into the whole scuba thing, but I do snorkel and this looked like an ideal time to give spearfishing a try. Jane said if I'd happen to connect on a nice sea bass, she'd grill it for dinner."

Matt grinned and glanced at Jane. "That's kind of a tall order." He turned back to Rachel. "But I'm curious—where do you snorkel in Iowa?"

"We actually have quite a few clear-water lakes, but my husband and I also go to Florida every winter, and sometimes Orange Beach in Alabama."

"I see," he said. "When are you heading out to the beach? Here, I mean?"

"Probably tomorrow afternoon," Jane said. "Is it okay if we keep the speargun for a couple days? You won't be needing it?"

"No, I won't need it, and you can keep it for a couple days, no problem."

"Thanks."

"Sure. I'd volunteer to go with you tomorrow and show you a couple of choice reefs where you might find that sea bass, but I have another commitment. I'm teaching a class at the Y, in fact."

"Thanks," Rachel said. "I appreciate the offer, anyway."

Matt nodded toward the door. "C'mon," he said. "Most of my gear is out in the garage. Let's go out and I'll get the speargun and show you how to load it and fire it."

Chapter 47

"WILL IT SOUND WEIRD IF I SAY I think it's kinda cute?"

Rachel's question drew a quick laugh from Jane. "Actually, I was thinking the same thing," Jane said. "It is kinda cute, in a wicked sort of way."

They were driving back to Jane's house after picking up the speargun Matt Lewis had loaned them. The gun, a Cressi Apache 45, was about 30 inches long, black and silver and, according to Matt, perfect for someone new to the sport of spearfishing. It was lightweight, easy to load and fire, and its latex rubber tubing propelled a stainless steel Tahitian-style flopper shaft. This last detail registered in the TMI category for both women, and they didn't ask Matt to elaborate.

"I have several spearguns," Matt had said as he unlocked the side door to his garage and ushered them inside. "But the one I have in mind for you is simple to use and easier to load than one of the pneumatic models." He'd picked up the Apache from a workbench—the garage was filled with scuba equipment and a full wetsuit hung from a rafter—and handed it to Rachel.

"Its effective range underwater is about ten to twelve feet," Matt told them. "That may not sound like a lot, but it should be plenty for what you're planning to do. If you see something farther than that, try to get closer or just don't shoot."

"Got it," Rachel said.

"Okay, please keep in mind that for safety reasons, we always recommend you only load your gun in the water when you're ready to start fishing, not on land beforehand. Of course we're not in the water, obviously, so we'll have to practice here in the garage." He paused, then added, "Also, just like with any firearm, you always want to make sure you keep it pointed in a safe direction at all times, and that there's no one in front of you when you load it."

"Of course," Rachel said.

After showing them how to load the gun, he had insisted they try shooting it at an old cardboard box against the far side of the garage. The gun had proved surprisingly accurate and Rachel and Jane had both hit the box on their first try.

"See?" Matt said, grinning. "Nothing to it."

"What about refraction?" Rachel asked. "My brother Dean used to bowfish for carp in the creek on our farm in Kansas and I remember him talking about needing to hold under the fish when he aimed because of refraction. Will I need to do that?"

"That's a good question, but no, you won't. Refraction shouldn't be a problem," Matt said. "When you're snorkeling you'll be underwater yourself, so you're in the same medium as the fish. It's only if you were standing out of the water and shooting down into it, like your brother would have been doing when he was bowfishing, that you'd need to compensate for refraction."

"Oh, sure," Rachel said. "That makes sense."

Matt had wished them luck and after warning them again to be careful, he said he looked forward to hearing if they scored on a sea bass. They had collected the gun and three shafts—"Please try not to lose those," Matt said—and thanked him. Then they had climbed into the Cherokee and headed home.

"That was pretty good, that bit about refraction," Jane said. "Especially since we're not actually going to be underwater when we use the gun. Did your brother really bowfish like you said?"

"He did, and I went with him a couple times. That's how I knew about refraction. I thought throwing that out couldn't hurt. Maybe make us sound a little more credible, like we halfway know what we're doing."

They both laughed. "Good thinking," Jane said.

They drove in silence for a minute or so, then Rachel asked, "Do you have any empty boxes at your place?"

"I might," Jane said. "Why?"

"Because," Rachel said, smiling. "We need one for a target. You know as soon as Rob sees this speargun, he's gonna want to try it."

GASTON STEVENS GOT OUT of bed again a few minutes after four o'clock. His headache had subsided—finally—and he headed into the shower. While standing under the spray of warm water he thought about what a wasted day this had been so far. He wondered what he could do to salvage it.

Nothing immediately came to mind.

The problem with not having to work for a living—Gaston had thought about this quite a few times, actually—was that you often had too damned much time on your hands. The few jobs he'd ever tried to hold hadn't lasted long, or more specifically, *he* hadn't lasted long. The jobs were a menial lot and he'd usually been fired after no more than two or three months, typically for insolence, tardiness or failing to show up altogether.

Fortunately, he had parents who were willing to support him in his undisciplined lifestyle. Although they occasionally still asked if he was having any luck job hunting—and he assured them that although he hadn't, he was diligently looking—they didn't pressure him on the subject. Well, not much, anyway.

Gaston suspected they had pretty much given up on him and resigned themselves to the fact that, unlike his older brother Dylan, who was a successful CPA, he was never going to set the world on fire. One of his favorite t-shirts boasted "Genius by birth, slacker by choice," and he thought that summed up the situation nicely. Why work if you didn't have to?

But that attitude still left him with too much time on his hands.

He sighed as he toweled off after the shower. The first order of business was finding something to eat. Then he'd try to get ahold of Sonderheim or O'Neill, or both, and see if they were up for hitting the Dive Bar later. They hadn't been back since they had had the run-in with Julie Thompson and her turtle-hugging friends, including that older bald guy with the beard.

Age notwithstanding, the guy had stood his ground, Gaston remembered. If Steve the bartender hadn't intervened…

Gaston almost found himself hoping for a rematch.

Chapter 48

SHOOTING THE SPEARGUN was a total hoot.

It was just past four o'clock when Jane and Rachel got back from Matt Lewis's place. The speargun—Rachel said it was a Cressi Apache 45—was a sleek, black and silver model that, when cocked and loaded with one of its stainless steel shafts, looked seriously lethal.

I couldn't wait to try it out.

We adjourned to Jane's garage, where she found an old Amazon shipping box. She positioned the box against the back wall of the garage and we stepped back five or six paces. "Matt told us the effective range underwater is only ten to twelve feet, but we shot it from farther than that in his garage, so this should be about right," Jane said. She laughed and added, "Not to put any pressure on you, but Rachel and I both hit the box on our first try. Let's see what kind of marksman you are."

I had never fired a speargun before but after they showed me how to load it—slipping the shaft down its track until it clicked into place on the release catch, then bracing the butt of the gun against my sternum and pulling back the wishbone-shaped rubber tubes with both hands, palms down, to the notch on top of the shaft—I clicked off the safety, extended my arm and pulled the trigger. There wasn't much recoil and the shaft flashed across the garage and buried itself in the box. By chance I hit the second "a" in the Amazon logo.

"Oh, sure," Rachel said. "Now you're gonna tell us that's what you were aiming at."

"Of course I was," I lied.

"Uh-huh," she said, punching me on the arm, and we all laughed.

I reloaded the gun with another shaft and tried again. I hit the box a second time and couldn't deny that shooting the gun was instantly addicting. When Jane had initially suggested it, I'd thought of the climactic underwater speargun battle in *Thunderball*. Now, reminding myself that we had procured the speargun primarily for intimidation purposes, I knew it was unlikely I would need to shoot Gaston Stevens with it…in fact, given that we were hoping to make sure his death looked like an accident, it would be far better for us if I *didn't* fire the gun.

Damn it, anyway.

WHILE JANE AND RACHEL were at Matt Lewis's I had gone online and done some additional research on a couple of subjects that were the cornerstones of our plan. Prior to Rachel's arrival Jane and I had already read up on these same subjects so this was mostly an exercise in reassurance. Okay, I'll admit it—I was letting my OCD tendencies get the best of me.

According to what I read, the odds were in our favor…if, and this was a big if, we could maneuver Gaston Stevens as needed. Much of that maneuvering was going to depend on Rachel playing her role successfully, but it was also going to require a fair amount of compliance on Gaston's part. This latter was the biggest unknown factor, but I was hopeful that Rachel's—ahem—powers of persuasion would bring about that compliance.

I'd seen her perform in a similar situation the previous summer, and that left me feeling confident.

OBTAINING THE SPEARGUN was necessitated by the fact that we had no other real weapons on hand. Jane didn't own any firearms and my decision to fly rather than drive to North Carolina had pretty much dictated leaving the cold Colt Python locked in my gun safe. Rachel had offered to try smuggling it through on her flight but I wouldn't let her risk it. So we were, as the old expression goes, seriously undergunned.

I had no source in North Carolina for untraceable firearms, which made Jane's suggestion that we borrow a speargun from Matt our best option. Best case scenario, as I've already stated, I wouldn't have to use it. But having it along as backup, especially if things took a turn for the unexpected, seemed prudent.

After taking turns firing at the box a few more times—like I said, shooting the speargun was addictive—we headed back indoors to start prepping for the evening at hand. Jane was planning to make shrimp tacos for dinner; Rachel needed to get into costume, so to speak, and I…well, I actually had very little to do besides worry about how events would play out in the next few hours.

AFTER SEVERAL TRIES, Gaston Stevens finally managed to connect with Dave Sonderheim. He'd had no luck reaching Grady O'Neill, whom he suspected was still tied up—or tied down, haha—with his new girlfriend, Linda something. But Sonderheim had answered his cell the third time Gaston called, and he had agreed to hit the Dive Bar with Gaston later that evening. Sonderheim worked at one of those quick oil change places and said he would meet Gaston at the bar at around eight o'clock, after he got off work and had a chance to go home and clean up and grab something to eat.

Which still left Gaston with a couple hours to kill.

Sitting at his kitchen table, he decided to drive up north a ways and visit the beach where the accident had happened. He was determined to keep thinking of it as an accident, reminding himself that the key to beating the manslaughter charge was standing firm on his story and not wavering.

He had thought this through a hundred times and he always came to the same conclusion. He knew that, in addition to watching his attorneys destroy the old woman's sister on the witness stand, he was going to have to convince the jurors that the old woman had panicked and jumped in front of him. That meant first convincing himself that that was what had happened.

Even though in his gut he knew differently.

He wondered about that also. *Why* had he done what he had done? He hadn't come up with a real satisfying answer. He knew it had been an impulse thing, that seeing the old lady wandering alone on the deserted beach that night had triggered an urge to do something really reckless, to take a chance and do something he'd never done before. Namely, kill another human being.

Why?

Had he become so bored with his life that doing something violent was the only outlet remaining? Was he that desperate for thrills?

Or was this partly a reaction to the pressure he always felt from being a congresswoman's son? In some twisted way, had he wanted to do something so over the top, so outrageous, that his parents—his mother, especially—would be shocked and forced to acknowledge his individuality?

He didn't ordinarily allow himself to think along these lines, and he didn't want to dwell on those thoughts now. Still sitting at his kitchen table, he rolled a joint and lit it. The weed would take the edge off before he drove up to the beach and revisited the scene of the accident.

He took a deep hit on the joint and held in the smoke. *The accident*, he told himself. That was what he needed to remember.

It had all been an accident.

Chapter 49

"YOU LOOK SERIOUSLY BADASS."

Rachel laughed at my comment. "That's the idea," she said. She had just emerged from Jane's guest room and come out to the kitchen. Jane, standing at the stove, gave her an appraising look and laughed also.

"Rob's right," she said. "You look like you're ready to kick ass and take names. Or maybe not worry too much about the names, but definitely kick ass, regardless."

Rachel was dressed in a tight black t-shirt—there was no missing the fact that she was braless—skinny dark blue jeans and black ankle boots. A wide black leather cuff circled her left wrist and a plain silver chain circled the right. "Thanks," she said in reply to Jane's remark.

"Nice job with the make-up," Jane added, and they both laughed. I'd noticed Rachel's make-up also, lots of eye shadow and dark eye liner that gave her a rather sinister look. Her eyebrows were also darker and more sharply defined than usual. Jane was right; Rachel looked ready to kick ass.

More than ready, actually, and also fully capable of doing so.

RETURNING TO THE BEACH where he'd killed the old lady had been a mistake, Gaston realized, and not just because the fucking ankle monitor made him feel lopsided and walking in the soft sand more difficult.

He'd parked in the public lot, crossed the dunes on the stile and started walking northward, thinking that seeing the place again might somehow help him clarify his thinking about the whole incident. But the farther he walked, the more he realized further clarification wasn't going to happen. Or if it did, it was only going to make him feel guiltier.

He could continue to tell himself that what had happened had been an accident, and in some ways he could almost make himself believe that was true. Running down the old lady certainly wasn't something he had planned beforehand—he'd had no idea she would be on the beach when he decided to do a little joyriding on the Polaris that evening—so in that respect, it *was* an accident, or at least a coincidence, a matter of her being in the wrong place at the right time.

Still, that in no way changed the fact that he'd made an impulsive decision to run her down. And killed her in the process.

Okay, so he'd had several beers before he saw her. He admitted to himself the beers had probably made him reckless, even more so than usual. And that in turn had undoubtedly triggered his action, almost as if he had dared himself to do it. One of those split-second decisions from which there could be no going back.

And that, he realized now, had probably been part of his motivation. It was as if he had *wanted* to get himself into trouble, more trouble than he had ever been in before.

He considered whether embarrassing his mother—the all-powerful congresswoman—had been the reason. Once again he wondered if his actions had been an attempt to assert himself, to break free from her never-ending over-protectiveness.

He kicked at a piece of driftwood half buried in the sand and thought, *fuck it. What's done is done. There's no going back and nothing to be gained by spending any more time thinking about it.*

He would play it out as he had already decided. He really had no other choice.

End of story.

LIKE THE OTHER MEALS she had prepared, Jane's shrimp tacos were excellent. I tried to show some gentlemanly restraint by stopping after three, but I noticed Rachel didn't seem to have much of an appetite. "Nervous?" I asked.

She took a sip of her margarita before answering. Then she smiled and said, "Yes, a little, I guess." She took another sip and added, "Okay, maybe more than a little."

I couldn't blame her, but I also couldn't think of anything reassuring to say that wouldn't sound lame. Luckily, I didn't have to.

Jane reached across the table and patted Rachel's forearm. "You're gonna be fine. Remember what I said a little while ago about kicking ass? That's what's going to happen. Gaston Stevens will never know what hit him."

"I hope you're right."

"I know I'm right. Remember, he isn't the sharpest knife in the butcher's block. Until now he's been cruising along thinking he has nothing to worry about. So my guess is, what you tell him will throw him into a panic."

"Let's hope so."

"At the very least, it's going to rock his boat. He's going to have to rethink a lot of things."

"That's right," I chimed in. "We need him off-balance, and that's what your story will do to him. He's going to walk out of the Dive Bar feeling a lot less sure about things than he was when he walked in."

"I just hope he's there tonight," Rachel said. "And that I can convince him."

I smiled at her. "Fingers crossed that he's there. As for the rest…I'm confident you can convince him. Just imagine he's another Greg Fletcher."

Rachel grinned. "Right," she said.

"Who's Greg Fletcher?" Jane asked.

"A former acquaintance of ours," I said.

"Emphasis on former," Rachel added.

Jane smiled.

Chapter 50

SONDERHEIM'S JEEP WRANGLER wasn't in the parking lot when Gaston arrived at the Dive Bar. It was still a little early, a few minutes before eight o'clock—Gaston had driven straight to the bar after leaving the beach—and Sonderheim was usually late anyway. That was no big deal; Gaston knew he'd show up eventually. In the meantime, he could scope out who was here and see if there was anyone else he knew.

He pushed through the door and paused for a moment to scan the crowd. None of the turtle huggers were present, but he saw a few folks he recognized and he nodded toward their tables and raised a hand in greeting. A couple of them waved in return. Gaston decided to grab a beer and join them. He could kill a little time catching up with them while he waited for Sonderheim to get there.

He moved over to the bar and was about to order when he glanced down to the far end and saw the tall woman standing there. She appeared to be by herself—there was a martini on the bar in front of her and she wasn't talking to anyone—and she caught his eye as he looked at her. A slight smile touched her lips, almost as if she was amused by the sight of him.

What the fuck.

Needing a moment to collect his thoughts, he turned back toward Steve the bartender, who was standing there wearing what Gaston thought was an amused expression of his own. Gaston wanted to ask him what was so fucking funny, but he decided against it. He didn't need another run-in with Steve right now.

Still smiling, Steve said, "Came in by herself about fifteen minutes ago." He paused, then added, "Your usual?"

"Make it a boilermaker," Gaston said on impulse.

"You got it," Steve said. He drew the beer and poured a healthy shot of Jack Daniels into a shot glass. He set both glasses in front of Gaston.

Hoping the woman was watching, Gaston downed the shot and set the glass back on the bar. He picked up the beer and took a pull. Still trying to gather his thoughts, he asked, "What's that she's drinking?"

"A filthy goose martini," Steve said.

"What's that?"

"Grey Goose vodka with a lot of olive juice and three jumbo olives." He laughed. "Want to send her one?"

"Maybe in a few minutes." Gaston wasn't sure he wanted to pursue anything with the woman; from this distance she appeared attractive but he could see she was older than he was. He wasn't good at estimating women's ages but he guessed she was probably in her late forties or early fifties. If that was the case, that would make her nearly twice his age. Too old for him, he told himself.

Still, there was no denying—he hoped he wasn't being too obvious as he checked her out—that she was damned good looking.

He took another pull of his beer and stared at his reflection in the mirror behind the bar, willing himself not to look in her direction again. He decided to stick with his original plan and join the people he knew. He was about to pick up his beer and move back to their table when he sensed motion beside him. He glanced over and saw the tall woman standing next to him, holding her martini in her left hand.

She was still wearing that amused smile and yes, up close she was very good looking. She had long, wavy brown hair and she wore a lot of dark eye makeup that gave her something of a hard, edgy look.

He also couldn't help noticing her large breasts, unrestrained by a bra under her tight black t-shirt. He tried not to let his gaze linger.

He smiled at her, but before he could speak she said, "You're Gaston Stevens, right?"

"That's right," he answered, thinking, *it must be that fucking ankle monitor again.* "And you are…?"

"Selene."

He nodded. "Like Celine Dion?"

"I spell it differently," the woman said. She didn't elaborate but gestured toward one of the empty booths at the back of the room. "We need to talk."

"Oh? About what?" Gaston said, wondering now who the hell this woman was and what she wanted with him.

"About you killing that old woman on the beach."

"YOU THINK SHE'LL BE all right?" Jane asked.

"She'll be fine," I replied. "If there's one thing I'm sure of, it's Rachel's ability to take care of herself."

We were sitting in the Subaru Forester at the back of the parking lot. We had chosen the Forester because we thought it was less likely to be recognized than Jane's Cherokee by Gaston or any of his friends or the other Dive Bar patrons. We had dropped Rachel off about twenty minutes earlier, and Gaston had arrived just a few minutes ago. We'd watched him park his Dakota and enter the bar.

I wondered if Rachel had already made contact with him.

"I hope you're right," Jane said. "I wasn't worried earlier but now I am. I mean, she's completely on her own in there with no backup."

"She'll be fine," I repeated. "Gaston isn't going to try anything funny in the bar or do anything dangerous. Steve the bartender will see to that. Worst case scenario, Gaston blows her off and doesn't bite. In which case we'll have to come up with another plan."

I hoped Jane believed what I was saying and didn't think I was just blowing smoke. Because the truth of the matter was—my confidence in Rachel notwithstanding—I was worried about her also.

GASTON SHOOK HIS HEAD. "I didn't kill anyone," he said. "Not intentionally, anyway. So fuck off."

The woman still had that irritating smile on her face. "I'm not going anywhere," she said pleasantly. "But do you really want to continue this conversation here at the bar? Or shall we discuss this where we won't be overheard?" She gestured toward the empty booth again.

Gaston regarded her for a long moment before answering. "There's nothing to discuss," he said. "Like I said, I didn't kill anyone, at least not deliberately. The old woman's death was an accident. End of story."

"Not quite. In a few months you're going to be tried for manslaughter. That's not quite as serious as murder, but if you're found guilty, you'll still be looking at some serious prison time. *That's* the end of the story."

"Yeah, well, that's not going to happen. I won't be found guilty."

"Sure of that, are you?"

"Look, lady, I don't know what you want or what you're selling, but I'm not buying. So leave me the fuck alone."

"Okay, then," she replied. "I'll see you in court." She turned to leave.

That got his attention. "What do you mean, you'll see me in court? Who are you, anyway?"

"I'm the person who can corroborate the testimony of the old woman' sister. I was on the beach that night and I saw what happened." She paused, then added, "And you and I both know it was no accident."

Chapter 51

"YOU DIDN'T SEE SHIT," Gaston said, feigning certainty. "There was no one else on the beach that night."

"Wrong. I was there. There was enough moonlight for me to recognize you and your Polaris Razor. And to see you deliberately run that woman down. I'm willing to testify to that in court. Unless..." The woman smiled again without finishing.

"Unless what?"

She gestured toward the booth a third time. "Let's talk over there." She turned and started walking away from him.

Leave it alone, Gaston told himself. *Get the fuck out of here, now!*

But his curiosity got the best of him. He followed her to the booth.

"THIS IS DRIVING ME CRAZY," Jane said. "Having to sit here not knowing what's going on."

I felt the same, but I didn't want to show my uneasiness. "The fact that they're both still in there is a good sign," I said. "I'd guess by now Rachel has made contact and she's in the process of reeling him in."

"You really think he'll buy her story?"

"I think so, yes. We coached her—well, you coached her—on all the details, and we rehearsed it plenty of times at your house. Unless Gaston comes up with something totally off the wall that she's not prepared for, I think she'll nail it. Or nail him, rather."

Jane laughed. "You're still hoping we get to use the speargun."

"You know me too well."

"I DON'T BELIEVE YOU."

The woman shrugged. "I don't really care what you believe. But I know what I saw, and like I said, I'm willing to testify to it in court. When I do, it will be a case of two against one—my word plus the old woman's sister's—and I'd bet the jury will believe us, not you. Which means they'll come back with a guilty verdict."

"Not necessarily."

"Really?" She smiled that irritating smile again. "Are you planning to win them over with your charm?"

Gaston studied her for a moment before answering. More than anything, he longed to reach across the booth and slap the smile off her face. But he knew he couldn't do that and he told himself to cool it and not let his anger show. He also felt confused by her claim to have seen what happened. He'd been certain there was no one else on the beach that night and now he wondered where she had been.

Hoping to cover his confusion, he asked, "If you're so sure you saw what you claim, why didn't you come forward sooner?"

Still smiling, she said, "Because I wasn't sure I wanted to get involved. In fact, I was sure I didn't. But now I don't have a choice."

"Why is that?"

"We'll get to that in a minute. In the meantime, you just need to know that I meant what I said about being willing to testify. And here's the thing. The fact that you recklessly ran the woman down is enough for a conviction in a manslaughter case. They don't need to prove motive or premeditation, like they would if you were charged with murder."

How the hell could she know all this? Feeling even more confused, he asked, "Why did you change your mind about testifying?"

The woman paused, but only for a second. Then she said, "Simple. I need money."

Gaston snorted. "So that's what this is all about? You need money? And you think I'm going to pay you to be quiet?"

"That's right."

"Like I said before, fuck off. I'm not going to pay you

jack shit. And I still don't believe you were there that night."

"Then take your chances. I'll be happy to take the stand and tell the court what I saw and heard. That you gunned the Polaris as you were bearing down on the old woman. That she was standing there waving her arms and you deliberately swerved toward her. You didn't attempt to miss her and she didn't jump in front of you. You stuck out your arm and clipped her in the neck as you went by."

"That's not what happened."

"That's exactly what happened. I had just climbed the stile and was standing at the top of the steps when you went roaring by. So I had a perfect view of everything. The woman's sister was already at the bottom of the stile and started running toward her when she fell but you didn't stop. You just kept on going."

"I panicked. That's why I didn't stop. But it was an accident."

"Keep telling yourself that. Maybe you can make yourself believe it. But no one else is going to."

"They'll believe it."

"No, they won't. You're not a credible witness."

"Why do you say that?"

"Because you're a known hothead. Your reputation precedes you. You've been in and out of trouble all of your life, and everyone knows it. You're in the public eye. That's what comes from being the son of a congresswoman."

Gaston bristled. "Leave my mother out of this."

"Is that what you're planning to do? Leave her out of this?"

"She's got nothing to do with this."

The smile again. "I'd bet she has a lot to do with this."

"You're wrong."

"No, I'm right. You're counting on her to get you out of trouble, like she has so many times before."

Hating her for nailing it, he narrowed his eyes in what he hoped was a menacing expression. "Lady, you have no idea who you're dealing with," he said, falling back on one of his favorite lines and trying to steer the conversation away from his mother.

The woman laughed. "I know exactly who I'm dealing with," she said. "You're just a little tit-baby who's hoping his mommy can save his butt, almost like changing your dirty diaper. But guess what. That's not going to work this time. Not when I tell what I saw."

Gaston shook his head, seething. "And you want money to keep quiet."

"That's right."

Gaston hated himself for asking the obvious next question. But he had to know. "How much?"

"I'm not greedy. But I'm in a bind right now and I need three large to get out of it."

"Three large?"

"Three grand. Three thousand."

Gaston shook his head again. "You're nuts. I don't have three thousand bucks."

"Then you'd better figure out a way to get it."

"HOW LONG HAS IT BEEN?"

I glanced at my wristwatch. "Not quite a half hour. Since Gaston got here, I mean."

Jane sighed. "I don't know how much longer I can stand this." She turned toward me. "Are things always this…intense?"

"Not always," I said. "But sometimes, yeah. Depends on the circumstances."

"Wow. I couldn't do this for…well, you know, on a regular basis."

Few people could, I thought. But I was reassured to hear her admit this. "It's worse because it's Rachel who's in there," I said. "We're not the ones at risk, at least not directly, and that's what's driving us crazy. We can't help worrying about her." I'd given up trying to hide my concern.

"It's not just the chance of physical danger," Jane said. "I don't like the fact that she'll be guilty of attempted blackmail when she asks him for money."

Props to Jane for recognizing this. "I don't like that,

either," I said. "But she volunteered and we have to hope Gaston doesn't tell anyone. Especially his mother."

"What if he does?"

I shook my head. "I have to believe Rachel will be able to read him. And put the screws to him in such a way that he'd be ashamed to go running to Mommy."

"I hope you're right."

"You and me both."

"WHAT KIND OF BIND are you in?"

The woman shook her head. "Not your concern. So quit trying to stall. All you need to think about is coming up with the money."

"I told you, I don't have three thousand bucks."

"And I told you, you'd better figure out a way to get it."

"I can't go to my parents."

"Congratulations. That's the most mature thing you've said so far tonight."

Gaston hated her more by the moment, and he hated himself for having let things go this far. He should have walked away, should have shut her down at the get-go. But now it was too late. He glanced toward the door. *Where the hell was Sonderheim?* A diversion would be welcome about now.

"Are you expecting someone?"

Gaston faced her again. "A friend is supposed to meet me here."

The woman laughed. "And you're hoping he'll show up and rescue you?"

"No, I'm not hoping he'll rescue me. I don't need rescuing."

She laughed again. "Yes, you do. But even if your friend shows up, it's not going to do you any good. In fact, you'd better hope he doesn't show up for a few more minutes. Because if he does, I'm out of here, and I'll be going straight to the DA tomorrow."

"What?" Gaston was reeling, trying to make sense of

what she had just said.

"That's right. If your friend shows up before we finish our business here, the deal is off."

"I already told you I don't have three thousand bucks. I for sure don't have that much with me tonight."

"And I already told you, you need to come up with it." She paused, then added, "I'll give you twenty-four hours."

Chapter 52

"TWENTY-FOUR HOURS? Then what? We just meet back here and I hand you the money?"

The woman shook her head. "No, we're not going to meet back here. I'm not coming back to this place."

Gaston sneered. "What's the matter? Not classy enough for you?"

"Classy has nothing to do with it. But we need to conduct our transaction in private. Someplace where we won't be seen."

"And where's that?"

"On the beach."

"On the beach? You mean where the old woman died?"

"No. I have somewhere else in mind."

"MAYBE THIS WASN'T such a good idea."

"It's a little late for second thoughts," I said. "At this point we're committed."

I hoped like hell Jane hadn't suddenly been stricken with guilt while contemplating the course of action we had embarked upon. Even as I thought this, however, I realized we could still pull the plug and walk away. Assuming Gaston bought Rachel's story and agreed to pay her for her silence, we could simply be no-shows. If he went to the location Rachel designated and she wasn't there to meet him, that would end things in his favor. He'd think he had dodged a bullet and would probably be all too willing to put the whole matter behind him. I was certain he wouldn't try to find her again.

Call me ruthless, but that wasn't the resolution I wanted. Having invested this much time and effort into avenging the death of Jane's sister—and confirming that Gaston was indeed the spoiled, arrogant little prick Jane had claimed him to be—I wanted to see our plan through. I hoped

Jane still felt the same.

"I know that," Jane said. "In for a penny, in for a pound, right? It's just that the longer this goes, the more worried I am for Rachel, that's all."

"She's going to be okay," I said. "And it shouldn't be much longer."

We sat in silence for another few minutes. Then I saw a bright red Jeep Wrangler pull into the parking lot and park near Gaston's Dakota. The driver climbed out and as he passed in front of us, I could see he was covered with tattoos.

I recognized him immediately but before I could speak, Jane said, "Oh, shit. That's Sonderheim."

"SO THAT'S IT? I somehow scrape up three thousand bucks and then meet you at this place on the beach and just hand it off? And then we're done?"

"Simple, right?"

"Except like I already told you, I don't have three thousand bucks and I can't come up with it by tomorrow night."

The woman stared at him steadily. She was no longer smiling. "Then you're SOL," she said calmly.

"Can't you at least give me more time?"

"No. Like I told you, I'm in a bind myself and I don't have more time. I need the money by no later than tomorrow night. You either deliver it like I told you, or I go to the DA."

"If I don't give you the money, how is talking to the DA going to get you out of your bind, as you call it?"

"I'll tell him I think I might be in danger. That I know your reputation as a hothead and that's why I didn't come forward sooner. That I'm worried about what you and your mother might try to do. Maybe he can get me some kind of protection. Until I can come up with the money to resolve my other problem, that is."

Gaston shook his head. "This is crazy." He couldn't think of anything else to say.

"No, it's not crazy. Just think of it as a simple business transaction. You pay me what I've asked, and I walk away and you never see me again."

"How do I know you won't go to the DA anyway?"

"I already told you, I don't really want to get involved. But I will if I have to." She picked up her martini and finished it.

"And that's it? How do I know you won't come back again and hit me up for more money?"

"You're overthinking this. After tomorrow night you won't see me again." She smiled once more. "You'll have to trust me."

Gaston looked down at the tabletop and shook his head again. Then he raised his eyes to hers and said, "Okay. I'll try to come up with the money. And I'll meet you there tomorrow night at nine o'clock, like you said."

"And you're sure you can find the place I told you?"

He nodded. "Yeah. I know the beach you're talking about. I surf there sometimes."

The woman started to slide out of the booth. "All right. I'll see you there tomorrow night." She stood up and looked down at him. "One more thing," she added.

"What's that?"

"Come alone. If I see anyone with you, I disappear and the deal is off. And I go to the DA."

Gaston sighed. "Okay," he said. "Anything else?"

"No." She turned and headed toward the door.

Gaston watched her leave, thinking, *you fucking bitch.* And, *what have I gotten myself into?*

DAVE SONDERHEIM WAS JUST REACHING for the door to the bar when it was pushed open from the inside and Rachel stepped through. Both Jane and I sucked in our breath as they did an awkward little dance to avoid bumping into each other. Sonderheim said something, probably excusing himself, and Rachel smiled and said something in return. Then he entered the bar and Rachel hurried across the parking lot to the Forester.

She pulled open the back door and jumped in. "Let's get out of here," she said.

Jane already had the engine running. She quickly shifted into drive and made a tight turn in the lot. We were on the street in seconds.

I turned to look over the seat at Rachel. "How'd it go?" I asked.

She smiled her Sofia Vergara smile. "It went fine," she said. "He bought it."

"Woohoo!" Jane said. She kept her eyes on the road but raised her right hand from the steering wheel to do a fist-pump. "You rock, girlfriend!"

"Well, I hope so," Rachel said. "Now the big question is whether he'll actually show up tomorrow night. But he said he would."

"That's all we can hope for," I said.

"Fingers and toes crossed," Jane added, and we all laughed.

So much for my misgivings about her having second thoughts.

"HEY, MAN, SORRY I'M LATE."

Sonderheim slid into the booth opposite Gaston. He pointed to the empty martini glass in front of him and said, "Who's this belong to?"

Gaston paused for a moment before answering. "Someone I was just talking to," he finally said.

"Oh? Care to elaborate?"

Gaston sighed. He wondered how much, if anything, he should tell Sonderheim.

He also wondered if he could hit Sonderheim up for a loan.

Chapter 53

BY FOUR O'CLOCK THE FOLLOWING afternoon, Gaston Stevens had amassed twenty-four hundred dollars of the three thousand the woman—Selene?—told him he would have to pay her for her silence.

The majority of the money had come from what remained of the monthly stipend his parents provided. (Gaston preferred the word stipend to allowance because the latter sounded so juvenile; never mind the fact that he was old enough to support himself. Slacker by choice, right?) When he checked his bank account he'd seen that he had a balance of a little more than twenty-five hundred dollars, and that had to last him another two weeks.

If he used eighteen hundred of that balance to pay off Selene, he should be able to get by on the remaining seven hundred-plus. He had already paid his rent for the month, and if he ran out of cash, he had a couple of credit cards he could use for gas and food…that is, assuming they weren't both maxed out. He wasn't good at keeping track of that stuff.

The additional six hundred dollars he'd borrowed from his brother Dylan, the rich CPA. He had stopped by Dylan's office but he hadn't had the nerve to ask Dylan for the full twelve hundred he still needed. He cut the amount in half and told Dylan he had to have some transmission work done on the Dakota and he didn't want to ask their parents for the money.

Predictably, Dylan had ripped into him about not getting a job, living irresponsibly and always expecting others to bail him out, etc., etc., but Gaston had put on his best hangdog look and Dylan had acceded in the end. He had pulled out a bottom drawer of his desk, opened a small metal lockbox and counted out six one-hundred dollar bills, leaving Gaston wondering how much more was in the lockbox (maybe he should have asked for the full twelve hundred!) and if all CPAs kept a ready supply of cash on hand. Knowing Dylan had such a stash was worth remembering, Gaston told himself.

Now, six hundred dollars short of his goal, Gaston considered whether Selene would settle for what he had. Sitting at his kitchen table and smoking another joint, he briefly wondered if the problem she had alluded to was drug-related. Tough as she appeared, she hadn't looked like a hard-core user, but…well, whatever. Now he regretted not asking Sonderheim for any money, even a hundred or two, the previous evening.

He had decided not to tell Sonderheim about his encounter with the woman, thinking the less that was known about the whole matter, the better, especially since she had—he hated to admit this—gotten the best of him. He had passed off her empty martini glass as belonging to someone with whom he'd had a brief conversation, nothing more, and Sonderheim hadn't pressed him for details.

By the time Gaston finished the joint he decided to swing by an ATM and withdraw another one hundred dollars. That would give him twenty-five hundred to take to the meeting with Selene, and he hoped that would suffice. He'd tell her that was all he had been able to raise in the twenty-four hours she'd allotted him, and she could take it or leave it.

He guessed she would take it. Let her worry about coming up with the rest of what she needed to get herself out of the trouble she was in. Whatever that trouble was, he told himself she deserved it.

The bitch.

BY FOUR O'CLOCK the following afternoon, the three of us had just about exhausted all the ways we could come up with to keep ourselves busy. With another five hours to go until Rachel's rendezvous with Gaston Stevens, we were struggling to keep our worries at bay. We'd gone over our plan repeatedly, probing for potential problems and playing the game of "What if?" as we tried to anticipate any slip-ups or ways in which Gaston might throw us a curve.

Our biggest worry, of course, was whether Gaston would show up at all. He'd told Rachel he would, but it was quite possible he'd said this just to end their conversation. He might have no intention of meeting her at the place she'd specified to deliver the money, but elect instead to take his chances and disregard her threat to go to the DA.

If that happened, we would have to start from scratch and come up with another plan. We couldn't take a chance on Rachel facing him again at the Dive Bar; there was too much likelihood of the other patrons seeing her, remembering her from her initial visit and questioning her interest in Gaston. Especially if he suffered an untimely death immediately thereafter. No, we had already risked exposing her as much as we dared.

So we had to hope Gaston would show up as he'd promised, and that he would come alone as Rachel had stipulated.

We killed time by going out to the garage and taking turns shooting the speargun until the old Amazon box was so perforated it resembled a colander. Back inside, we settled ourselves in front of Jane's television and watched a couple reruns of one those crime dramas with a title consisting of initials. I had a hard time concentrating—my mind kept wandering to the real crime at hand—and I suspected Jane and Rachel were having the same problem.

Later, we drove to the beach and went for another walk, and while the exercise helped ease our tension, it also raised another worry. We were counting on the beach being deserted when Rachel met Gaston later that evening, but of course we had no way to control this. Late-night beachcombers would definitely complicate matters; we obviously wanted no witnesses to what happened.

While I didn't say so to Rachel and Jane, I was beginning to fear our plan had almost as many holes as the Amazon box.

AFTER VISITING THE ATM and withdrawing another hundred dollars, Gaston returned home and pulled an old Nike gym bag out of his bedroom closet. He tossed it onto his unmade bed and began compiling the cash he'd accumulated over the past few hours. With the exception of the six one-hundred dollar bills he had gotten from his brother, the money was all in twenties and fifties because he had made a point of asking for the smaller denominations at the bank. The cash made a fair-sized pile on the bed, but it would fit into the gym bag with no problem.

As he was stuffing the cash into the bag, it suddenly occurred to him that the woman might want to count it, not trusting him to deliver the full three thousand she had asked for…okay, demanded. But after a moment he decided she probably wouldn't want to stand around on the dark beach counting the money. She would most likely want to conclude their transaction as quickly as possible and take her leave.

That led to another realization. Maybe it wouldn't be necessary to tell her he hadn't come up with the entire three thousand. He could just hand her the bag full of cash, imply the full amount was there, then get the hell out of there. By the time she found out the bag was five hundred short, he'd be long gone. He doubted she would look him up again—he told himself that despite her cool act, she was probably as nervous as he was about what was going down—and she would settle for what he'd given her and call it quits. She wouldn't push her luck and risk having the fact that she had blackmailed him come to light.

That was a gamble, but he was willing to chance it. The more he thought about it, the more he liked the idea that he was giving her less than she'd asked for, that he was screwing her over, if only by a little. And if the twenty-five hundred wasn't enough to get her out of trouble, that was just too fucking bad.

Hell yeah. He liked that. A lot.

DINNER WAS A SIMPLE MATTER of BLTs and chips, but none of us had much of an appetite. I knew that most of my nervousness was due to Rachel being the one who was going to carry the ball, so to speak, later that evening. While I didn't think it was too likely that Gaston would try anything violent—that is, if he showed up at all—I was still troubled by the fact that my role in the whole matter was decidedly secondary. If Gaston did do something unexpected, I would have the speargun to dissuade him, but we still hoped that wouldn't be necessary.

At a quarter past seven Rachel went back to the guest bedroom to change into what she would wear to the beach. Jane and I continued to sit at the kitchen table but we said very little. I knew we were both preoccupied with thoughts of all the ways things could go sideways. We had already discussed those possibilities, almost endlessly, and there was no point in rehashing them aloud.

Rachel returned to the kitchen about ten minutes later. She was dressed in the same outfit she'd worn the previous night but she had foregone the dark eye make-up. She gave us a brave smile as we looked up at her.

"All right," she said. "Let's go do this."

Chapter 54

GASTON STEVENS DECIDED TO HIT Boomer's on his way to the beach.

He didn't want to go back to the Dive Bar after his encounter with Selene the previous night. He knew she wouldn't be there—she had told him she was never going to return to the place—but he didn't want to risk having to answer any questions about her, either. He'd managed to dodge the whole matter with Sonderheim but there was a chance Steve the bartender or some of the other regular patrons might be curious enough to ask him about the tall, edgy-looking woman they had seen him talking to the night before.

He didn't want to deal with that. He didn't want to try to explain who she was, what they had talked about or why she had abruptly departed after their brief conversation. Above all, he didn't want to admit to anyone that he was letting her blackmail him to the tune of three thousand bucks...okay, twenty-five hundred. He didn't want that known to anyone, including his parents. Especially his parents.

Thinking about that now, he felt a curious sense of satisfaction, even a touch of pride. He hadn't gone to his parents for the money and when he had told Selene he couldn't ask them for it, she had made some remark about that being the most mature thing he'd said so far. That he hadn't immediately turned to them and was trying to handle this on his own—all right, with a little help from his brother—left him feeling better about himself. For once, he wasn't running to his parents with his problems.

Of course, he was still counting on his mother's attorneys to get him off the hook, once and for all, when his case went to trial. But at least he had taken care of this one matter by himself.

That was worth a beer or two to celebrate, he decided.

He still had some time to kill, and what the hell, maybe he would run into Nancy again, the chick with the cute nose ring he'd seen a couple nights ago.

It was worth a shot.

WE LEFT FOR THE BEACH at a little after seven-thirty. We wanted to be in place a good hour before Gaston was scheduled to arrive. We took the Subaru again and drove to the same parking area Jane and I had used previously. We parked and climbed the stile to cross the dunes. We climbed down on the beach side and began walking southward along the foot of the dunes, skirting the occasional patches of tall seagrass as we went. To keep the speargun concealed, I carried it in a duffel bag we had bought earlier that afternoon.

Dusk was settling over the beach and we passed the occasional beachcomber and several couples and dog walkers as we went. Most of them were walking in the opposite direction, north, which was all to the good. We still hoped to have the rendezvous point to ourselves, and the farther south we walked, the fewer people we encountered.

We had covered about half a mile and had just come up on another thick stand of seagrass when Jane stopped and said, "This is it." Rachel and I stopped as well. We glanced around and there was no one else in sight. It was rapidly growing darker, a gibbous moon was rising and stars were beginning to shine. It was a calm night with a slight cooling breeze coming off the ocean. The surf was rolling in and I hoped the sound of the breaking waves would provide additional cover for our activity.

We were planning to keep our noise to a minimum but we couldn't guarantee Gaston would do the same.

GASTON PUSHED OPEN the door to Boomer's Tap and stepped inside. He scanned the crowd quickly and grinned when he saw Nancy sitting at the bar just a couple stools down from where she'd sat two nights ago. He recognized her by her long black hair and slim body. Like before, she had a tall draft beer on the bar in front of her.

The stool next to her was empty. *My lucky night*, he thought.

He slid onto the stool. As she glanced his way he smiled and said, "Hi, there."

She smiled also. "Well, if it isn't my favorite bad boy," she said. "Have you had any more *accidents* since the last time I saw you?"

Gaston winced at her inflection but tried to keep the smile on his face. He shook his head and said, "No, I haven't." Thinking, *what a little bitch*. But he was determined not to be put off by her snark. Like before, she was wearing that tiny black nose ring he thought was cute.

"Well, I'm glad to hear you're staying out of trouble," she said. She picked up her beer and took a long pull. "What else have you been up to?"

"Not much," Gaston said. "Just chilling." No way was he going to bring up his encounter with the woman named Selene or mention that he was going to be meeting her later that evening. Assuming he could keep Nancy engaged, he'd have to come up with some suitable excuse when it was time to leave for the beach. He glanced at the clock on the wall behind the bar and saw the time was 8:05.

He figured that gave him a little over half an hour to make his play and get something more definite nailed down with Nancy. He wondered if he might be able to excuse himself at, say, 8:40 or 8:45, telling her he had to run a quick errand but that he would return shortly. Then haul ass to the beach, conclude his business with Selene—he couldn't imagine that would take more than a few minutes—and get back to Boomer's before Nancy left.

He knew she would be curious as to why he had to leave. Maybe she would assume he was going off to score some drugs. What other reason could he come up with to explain why he needed to abandon her, if only briefly, if things were going smoothly?

Damn.

Then another thought occurred to him. Maybe he wouldn't have to leave at all.

He thought of the gym bag full of cash that he'd stashed on the floor behind the driver's seat of the Dakota and covered with an old beach towel. Twenty-five hundred dollars that would be fun, a lot more fun, to spend on something besides Selene's silence.

Would she *really* go to the DA if he didn't show up? And even if she did, would her testimony carry that much weight with the jury? Couldn't the attorneys discredit her the same way they were going to discredit the old woman's sister?

The more he thought about it, the more he liked the idea of blowing off Selene. Especially if it meant she wouldn't be able to buy her way out of whatever trouble she was in. Especially if it meant he could get something going with Nancy.

He noticed she had almost finished her beer. "Ready for another?" he asked.

"Thought you'd never ask," she said.

JANE AND I WADED into the seagrass, which was almost shoulder-high. Rachel stayed outside the grass on the sand. She turned away from us and stood gazing out at the ocean. It was now fully dark and the waves were rolling in stronger but they were still breaking and receding a good distance away from our position. Even at high tide I doubted the water would reach us.

"It's beautiful," Rachel said after a moment.

"Yes, it is," Jane replied. "I never get tired of watching the ocean."

I busied myself stomping down the grass to make a hiding place for Jane and me. We planned to crouch in the grass while Rachel met Gaston and we would show ourselves only if he said or tried anything threatening.

Jane had insisted on accompanying Rachel and me to this spot. We had tried to argue her out of coming, saying it would be better if she remained in the vehicle, ducked down out of sight, and texted us when Gaston arrived at the parking area. But she had adamantly refused.

"This is my doing," she said. "I got you both into this,

and I'm not going to miss the final act. I want to see Sara vindicated. And Rachel will be able to spot Gaston when he's coming, even without me warning you." She paused then added, "*If* he comes, that is."

Right. If he comes.

All we could do now was wait.

Chapter 55

GASTON THOUGHT HE WAS MAKING good progress with Nancy until 8:30—he was still keeping one eye on the clock behind the bar—when a tall guy with sandy hair came in and walked directly over to her. The guy immediately put one arm around her shoulders and said, "Hey, babe, sorry I'm late."

Well, fuck me. In addition to the beer Gaston had bought her, they had also done a shot apiece of Fireball. They had talked, nothing too serious, and he had learned that she worked at one of the t-shirt and souvenir shops in Surf City. She had said nothing further about his upcoming trial, nor had she mentioned being involved with anyone. But now…

"No problem," Nancy said. "Gaston here was nice enough to buy me a drink and keep me company while I waited." She smiled as she said this and Gaston felt a surge of resentment.

"Well, Gaston, that was mighty kind of you," the sandy-haired guy said, and despite his smile, there was no mistaking the mockery in his voice.

Gaston nodded and managed to smile in return. "My pleasure," he said, hoping for nonchalance. While Gaston considered himself to be in pretty good shape from all the surfing he did—and also liked to think of himself as something of a badass—the sandy-haired guy had at least two inches and twenty pounds on him, and Gaston was no fool. Or so he told himself, anyway.

The sandy-haired guy nodded and turned back toward Nancy. He clearly considered the matter settled. Gaston picked up what remained of his beer and finished it. He set the glass back on the bar and caught the eye of the bartender. "Cash me out," he said.

The bartender nodded and turned toward the register.

IT WAS JUST PAST 8:30 when Jane, kneeling beside

me in the seagrass, said, "Man, all this waiting is killing me."

Standing a few yards away, Rachel said, "No kidding. What time is it, anyway?"

I glanced at my watch. The luminous hands told me it was 8:34. I relayed this to Rachel. "We still have a little while yet," I added.

"Maybe he'll be early," Jane said. "Could we be that lucky?"

My immediate thought was that we would be lucky if he showed up at all.

But I kept the thought to myself.

GASTON SAT IN THE DAKOTA for a few minutes before starting the engine. He was disappointed and more than a little pissed by what had just gone down. He wasn't sure Nancy had intentionally played him, but he wasn't sure she hadn't, either. Regardless, things hadn't worked out the way he'd hoped, and now here he sat, wondering what to do for the rest of the night.

He thought again about the twenty-five hundred dollars on the floor behind him. Just a short while ago he'd pretty much decided to spend it on something other than Selene's silence. Now he was having second thoughts about that decision. Once again he wondered if she would really go to the DA If he didn't show up. Could he risk it?

He recalled the satisfaction he'd felt earlier from determining he would handle the problem himself and not involve his parents. Sure, it was going to cost him twenty-five hundred bucks—okay, only nineteen hundred of which was his own—but if it kept Selene quiet and no one else was the wiser…

He sighed and cranked the ignition. He shook his head and muttered, "Fuck it" as he shifted into drive.

Might as well see it through.

I WAS SITTING ON MY BUTT IN the seagrass with my knees drawn up and my forearms crossed atop them. On my left, Jane sat next to me in the full lotus position. She had kicked off her flip-flops, crossed her legs and drawn her feet up into her lap a few minutes earlier, and just seeing her in that position made my knees ache. She hadn't spoken for several minutes and I suspected she was trying to calm herself with her deep breathing.

I shifted slightly and took my right arm down to rest my hand on the speargun. After removing the gun from the duffel bag, I had loaded it and laid it on top of the flattened bag. I was confident I could bring it into play quickly if I needed to do so, but I still hoped that wouldn't be necessary.

"What time is it now?" Rachel asked. She had been standing in position for almost forty-five minutes.

"8:55," I said. "Shouldn't be too much longer."

Beside me, I thought I felt Jane shudder slightly.

GASTON PULLED INTO THE PARKING AREA as Selene had told him. There was one other vehicle parked several yards away, a dark Subaru Forester. He wondered if it was hers.

Then again, maybe not. He hadn't really considered what would happen after he gave her the money. Would they just part and go their separate ways? She had told him that after crossing the stile he should start walking south along the base of the dunes. "Turn right when you come down off the steps," she had said, as if he didn't know which direction south was. "Stay close to the dunes and keep walking until you see me. I'll be about a half mile down."

"Why so far?" he'd asked.

"I want to make sure we aren't seen."

He hadn't questioned her any further. Thinking about it now, he wondered if she had parked elsewhere, maybe farther south, and would return that way after he gave her the money. If that was the case, they would be leaving in opposite directions, as he would have to walk back north to get to his vehicle.

Yeah, that was probably it, he decided. He'd almost bet on it.

He climbed out of the Dakota and grabbed the gym

bag from behind the seat. He closed and locked the truck and headed for the stile.

AT 9:03 RACHEL QUIETLY SAID the words we had been hoping to hear.
"He's coming."

Chapter 56

THE DAMNED ANKLE MONITOR MADE walking in the loose dry sand at the base of the dunes even harder, so after the first twenty yards or so Gaston moved out to the edge of the surf where the wet sand was firmer. He figured he could see well enough in the moonlight to spot Selene before he got to her, and what difference would it make if he didn't follow her directions to the letter? He told himself she should be happy he'd shown up to give her the money, end of story.

Walking south with the gym bag in hand, he still questioned whether he was doing the right thing. Even though he was stiffing her by five hundred bucks, he hated the thought of just handing over the cash and walking away. He wondered if her testimony, added to that of the old woman's sister, would be that damaging; if their combined accounts would be enough to sway the jury into returning a guilty verdict.

He reluctantly decided he probably shouldn't risk it. And now, looking ahead, he could see Selene standing about fifty yards farther down the beach, next to a thick stand of seagrass at the foot of the dunes. He started angling her way.

It was too late to turn back.

"HE'S OUT BY THE WATER but he's coming back in," Rachel said softly, almost in a whisper. I had to strain to hear her. "I probably can't say any more."

"That's okay," I said, whispering myself. I wasn't sure she heard me but I realized it didn't matter. We all knew our roles and there was no need to keep talking. Now it was up to Rachel to handle the exchange with Gaston while Jane and I kept hidden in the seagrass to provide backup if needed. It wouldn't be needed if everything went according to plan.

Another big if.

Jane laid her hand on my leg and gave it a quick squeeze. I reached down and squeezed her hand in return. I glanced at her and she gave me a brief, wan smile. Then we both turned our attention back to Rachel.

"I BROUGHT THE MONEY." Gaston hefted the gym bag as he stopped eight or ten feet away from the woman.

"The whole three thousand?"

Gaston hesitated. He'd hoped to just hand off the bag, say something clever about this concluding their business and how he hoped to never see her again, then get the hell out of there. He didn't want to be pinned down about the money and he didn't want to prolong things by answering questions.

He hefted the bag again. "You can count it if you'd like," he said, trying to dodge her question. Once she took the bag, he was going to split, regardless.

"Bring it to me."

He was tempted to toss the bag at her feet. Who the hell was she to be giving him orders? But something told him not to antagonize the woman, to keep his cool just a little longer. He was this close to being done with her, once and for all. He took three steps toward her and held out the bag with his right hand.

The woman reached out and took the bag just as a white-hot needle pierced his right ankle.

"Ahh! Motherfucker!" Gaston jumped back. He looked down and saw fire ants swarming over his topsiders and up both of his bare legs, biting and stinging as they went. Each sting was another hot lancing pain, almost incapacitating, that left Gaston gasping. Instinctively he reached down to brush the ants off his shins but that served only to transfer some of the ants, still biting, to his hands and wrists.

He staggered back from the nest he had stepped into and began fumbling in the pocket of his shorts. The woman had also stepped back several feet as she stood holding the gym bag, watching him with a curiously detached expression. The crazy thought flashed through his mind that she had lured him to the ant nest deliberately.

He managed to free the auto-injector from his pocket but he fumbled and almost dropped it in the sand. "Son of a bitch!" he said, panicking. He was beginning to feel lightheaded and his heart was racing from the effects of the ants' venom. So many bites all at once…he knew he was only minutes away from slipping into anaphylactic shock.

He pulled the auto-injector from its carrying tube but nearly dropped it again. His fingers were growing numb and felt as thick as sausages. "Help me," he said in desperation. He held the injector out toward the woman. She dropped the bag on the sand behind her and stepped forward, avoiding the ant nest. She took the auto-injector from his hand and said, "What do I do?"

Gaston was panting now, barely able to draw a breath. "Pull off the blue cap and pull it up," he managed to say. "Put the orange end here." He punched his right thigh with his fist. "Push until it clicks. Hold it there three seconds." He closed his eyes as the woman placed the injector against his thigh. He thought he felt another sharp prick but it was almost impossible to distinguish from the dozens of ant bites.

"There," the woman said. She stepped back and Gaston, swaying on his feet, opened his eyes. The pressure in his chest was increasing and he was dimly aware that some of the ants were still biting. He groaned and staggered back another few steps.

"Go to the water!" the woman said. "Wash the ants off in the water!"

Now barely conscious, Gaston registered her words and stumbled toward the surf.

JANE AND I ROSE to our knees when we heard Gaston exclaim "Motherfucker!" We paused for an instant then cautiously began getting to our feet, still staying low and keeping our heads below the top of the seagrass.

When we heard him say, "Son of a bitch!" we raised our heads high enough to see over the grass. I held the speargun tightly in my right hand, ready to extend my arm and shoot if it looked like Gaston was becoming aggressive. But he was swaying on his feet and had just pulled what I guessed was an EpiPen from the pocket of his shorts. He pulled the pen from its carrying tube but fumbled it and almost dropped it. That's when we heard him say "Help me" as he extended the pen toward Rachel.

She dropped the gym bag she'd been holding and stepped forward to take the pen. We heard Gaston, gasping for breath, tell her how to use it, and we watched as Rachel placed the pen against his thigh as he'd said. A moment later she stepped back and told Gaston to go to the water to wash off the ants.

Disoriented but apparently heeding her direction, Gaston staggered out to the surf and kept going until he was almost waist deep in the water. Then he fell forward as another big wave rolled in and broke.

He didn't regain his feet but continued to float face down as the wave receded, taking his body with it.

Chapter 57

WE STOOD WATCHING GASTON'S BODY for several minutes as the receding tide gradually carried it farther out to sea.

Eventually we lost sight of it beyond the waves. That's when Jane spoke softly. "We should get going," she said. I thought I heard a trace of something—wistfulness? regret?—in her voice, and again I wondered if she was having second thoughts about what we had done.

Rachel said, "Right," and bent over to pick up the EpiPen's carrying tube from where Gaston had dropped it. She slipped the pen back into the tube and stuck it into the pocket of her jeans. I uncocked the speargun and removed the shaft from its track and returned everything to the duffel bag.

"We don't want to forget this," Jane said, picking up the gym bag that, presumably, held the money with which Gaston had hoped to buy Rachel's—correction, Selene's—silence.

The three of us began walking northward to the parking area where we had left the Forester. I scanned the beach ahead of us, hoping to see no one.

We were lucky. We encountered no late-night beachcombers or strolling couples, and we got back to the vehicle without incident.

None of us spoke along the way.

"I CAN CONFIRM THOSE FIRE ANTS are nasty bastards," Rachel said, breaking our silence when we were settled in the Forester and Jane had started the engine. "I got bitten a couple times myself when I helped Gaston with his EpiPen. Good thing I'm not allergic."

"Good thing," Jane agreed. "Where did they bite you?"

"On my hand. Now the bites are burning and itching like crazy."

"That's what they do. I've got some lotion at home that should help."

"Thanks," Rachel said. "A margarita might help also. Or two."

"That can also be arranged. Definitely."

I thought a margarita—or a couple—sounded like a good idea also. As we pulled out of the parking area I glanced over at Gaston's Dakota. I wondered how long it would take for his body to be found and what the investigation into his death would determine. Aside from footprints—which the wind and the tide would quickly obliterate—I was reasonably confident we had left no trace of ourselves on the beach. But like always at the conclusion of an assignment, I was going over everything that had happened, probing for any slip-ups we might have made or something we might have overlooked.

Offhand, I couldn't come up with anything and, my native pessimism notwithstanding, I had to admit that our plan had worked almost flawlessly, even better than I might have hoped. After learning of Gaston's severe allergic reaction to insect bites, we had chosen the rendezvous point based on the discovery Jane and I had made of the fire ant mound several days earlier. It was Jane's idea to lure him into stepping on the mound, and Rachel had executed that part of the plan perfectly.

We had hoped to make Gaston's death look like an accident—or at least conceal the fact he had been killed deliberately—and this scenario seemed likely to fill the bill. Only the ME's conclusion would ultimately confirm our success, but in the meantime, I felt optimistic about the outcome.

I was shaken from these thoughts by Jane's next question. "So Rachel, I have to ask," she said. "Did you really give Gaston the injection?"

"No, I didn't," Rachel said. "I pinched his skin between my fingernails so he'd feel something, but I didn't push the plunger on the pen."

Damn. And I thought I was the one who was supposed to be the master at this stuff.

WE DROVE IN SILENCE for a few minutes until Jane said, "Rob, you're awfully quiet."

"Just thinking," I said. I was still doing my post-execution analysis. Old habits are hard to break.

She laughed. "Are you disappointed you didn't get to use the speargun?"

I laughed also. "Oh, not really," I said. "It worked out better this way. But considering all those ant bites Gaston got, the speargun might have been more merciful."

"Yeah, no kidding," Rachel said. "These couple of bites I got are bad enough. Several hundred would be terrible."

We lapsed back into silence.

RACHEL SAID SHE WANTED to hit the shower when we got back to Jane's house and while she was doing so, Jane mixed the promised pitcher of margaritas. I had carried Gaston's gym bag inside and while she was making our drinks I told her I was going to count the money. "Good idea," she said. "Let's see if Gaston came through like he promised."

I dumped the contents of the bag out on the kitchen table. Aside from a few one-hundred-dollar bills—I quickly determined there were six of those—the rest of the cash was in twenties and fifties. It took me a few minutes to sort through it and count the lot. "It comes to twenty-five hundred," I said when I finished.

"So he shorted us by five hundred," Rachel said, walking barefoot into the kitchen. Her hair was wet from the shower and she was wearing denim shorts and a gray and black camo-pattern t-shirt that I knew was one of her favorites.

"That's what I count," I said. "I wonder if he did it deliberately, or if that was all he could raise?"

Jane set the pitcher of margaritas on the table next to the cash. She smiled and said, "It doesn't matter. We're twenty-five hundred ahead. And more importantly, we got justice for Sara. Let me get the glasses salted and we'll toast our mission accomplished."

And that's what we did.

DESPITE THE EFFECTS of the margaritas—or maybe because of them—I had a hard time falling asleep later that night.

That was to be expected, actually. I usually spend a restless night after completing an assignment, not because I'm feeling guilty about what I've done, but because my brain stays in overdrive, still replaying the events, still analyzing, and so on. Even after so many years as a contract killer, this has never changed.

But this time my thoughts followed a different path. Instead of reviewing everything that had gone down and looking for any errors or miscalculations, I kept returning to the fact that my involvement this time had been that of a supporting player only. About that I *did* feel somewhat guilty.

There was no denying that it was Jane who had come up with the plan and it was Rachel who had played the primary role in seeing it through. I'd gone along as backup, nothing more, and yes, I found that troubling.

So was this just a matter of my male ego feeling bruised?

I hoped that wasn't the case, and after further reflection I finally decided it wasn't. Rather, I realized that what was troubling me most was knowing that Rachel had run almost all the risks. She had volunteered to do so and had proven supremely cool under pressure, but I didn't like my friend—my best friend—putting herself in harm's way like that.

Once I realized this, I told myself I wouldn't let it happen again.

Right.

As if I could do anything to stop her.

Chapter 58

AT BREAKFAST THE NEXT morning we unanimously decided that our first order of business was getting Rachel out of town as quickly as possible.

We agreed that we couldn't risk her being seen by someone—specifically, any of the patrons of the Dive Bar or Steve the bartender—who might remember her conversation with Gaston in the bar two nights earlier. We knew that as soon as Gaston's body was found, an investigation would be launched and his mother would stop at nothing to get answers. Sure, it would be apparent that Gaston had died from anaphylactic shock or drowning, but that still left a number of questions.

Foremost among these was the matter of the twenty-five hundred dollars Gaston had brought to the exchange. We didn't know where he had gotten the money, but we guessed he might have borrowed all or some of it from friends or family members, maybe even withdrawn some of it from a bank account. Regardless of the source or sources, sooner or later it was bound to attract attention and we knew the police would then adopt the "follow the money" strategy.

They would never know what ultimately happened to the money—we planned to make a series of anonymous donations, spread out over several months, to the Paige Green Turtle Rehab Center—but the cops would undoubtedly discover and zero in on the fact that Gaston had accumulated the cash on the day before his death.

Suspicious? Absolutely. The police would want to know why he had done this, and they would issue their standard call asking anyone with possible information to contact them. But while the Dive Bar folks might recall seeing Rachel talking with Gaston, they didn't know her identity or the subject of the conversation. Even if they did come forward and describe her to the police, they had no real proof that she was directly involved with Gaston's death.

Plus, recalling the bartender's comment about the bar's security cameras not working—something we had taken into account during our planning—there shouldn't be any images of Rachel captured on video that the police could use to identify her with facial recognition technology. Bottom line, we believed the police would have a very difficult—read, impossible—time finding Rachel if she was already back home in Iowa.

We also briefly discussed the fact that the three of us had encountered a fair number of other people during our daytime walks on the beach. None of them, however, seemed to have paid any particular attention to Rachel (or, for that matter, to Jane and me) and they too had no inkling that any of us had any connection to Gaston. They had no reason to suspect us of any wrongdoing or report us to the police.

The only other person who had seen Rachel for any length of time was Matt Lewis, Jane's scuba-diving friend who had loaned us the speargun. Jane had told him that Rachel was visiting from Iowa, so again, he had no reason to suspect she had any connection to Gaston. Jane told us she would return Matt's speargun in another day or two and thank him for the loan. She would also tell him that Rachel had returned to Iowa and, if he asked, that they hadn't managed to score on a sea bass.

We were confident that if we got Rachel out of Schnock's Harbor and out of North Carolina in the next few hours, any possible recollection or mention of her by anyone would ultimately lead to a dead end.

Sorry about the awful pun.

AFTER CHECKING THE VARIOUS flight options online, we decided to drive Rachel to Charlotte, where she could catch a direct flight to Des Moines that evening. We could have opted for a connecting flight from Wilmington to Charlotte (a reverse of the route Rachel and I had both taken to get down here) but in the interest of keeping Rachel out of the public eye—and multiple airports—as much as possible, we chose to drive to Charlotte, which would take about four and a half hours.

Her flight departed at 7:20, so we planned to leave Schnock's Harbor by noon or a little after. Barring any problems along the way, that would have us at the Charlotte airport in plenty of time for Rachel to check in and grab something for dinner before she boarded.

I briefly considered trying to book a seat on the same flight...after all, my work here in North Carolina was done. But I decided against it because I wanted to stick around for at least another day or two to see what might transpire with the investigation into Gaston's death.

Or that's what I told myself, anyway.

The real reason was that I wanted to spend a little more time with Jane.

You knew that.

WE SPENT THE REST of the morning periodically checking news programs, watching for reports on the death of Gaston Stevens.

The first one came in at a few minutes after nine. During a break in the *Today* show for a local news update, a blonde woman newscaster reported that they had just received word that a body had been recovered along the beach about a mile south of Schnock's Harbor. Apparently a drowning victim, the body had been carried in by the morning tide and was that of a young adult male whose name was being withheld pending notification of family members. Further details would be reported as they became available.

We were certain it had to be Gaston.

Subsequent reports throughout the morning proved us correct.

BY THE TIME WE LEFT for Charlotte, Gaston's name had been released, along with the fact that he was the 26-year-old son of Congresswoman Maggie Stevens and had recently been charged with manslaughter in the death of Sara Lawson, another resident of Schnock's Harbor. Gaston's cause of death was thought to be respiratory failure caused by anaphylactic shock, the result of more than two hundred fire ant bites visible on his body. The police investigation was continuing and—just as we expected—they asked anyone with information about Gaston's recent activities or whereabouts to contact them at the phone number shown on the screen.

One report included comments by a local physician who explained how anaphylactic shock, brought on in this case by a severe allergic reaction to fire ant venom, could cause respiratory failure and death in a matter of minutes. While it was initially supposed that Gaston had drowned, the doctor explained that it was likely Gaston was already having extreme difficulty breathing when he entered the water, which he was presumed to have done to rid himself of the ants. The doctor added that cardiac arrest was also a possibility, and only a complete autopsy could determine the exact cause of death.

No mention was made of the cash Gaston had accumulated, and a police spokesman stated that at this early stage of the investigation they had no explanation for why Gaston had gone to the beach or how he had happened to suffer so many fire ant bites. Hearing this, we surmised that either the police hadn't yet discovered the money connection or they were holding this information back, hoping to match it to those tips phoned in to their hotline.

For the moment, at least, the fire ants were getting all the blame for Gaston's death.

Just as we had hoped.

Chapter 59

We left Jane's house at 12:15 and took Route 17 south to Wilmington, where we picked up US-74 and began traveling northwest toward Charlotte. This time we were in Jane's Cherokee and she was driving with Rachel riding shotgun. I sprawled across the back seat, content to be alone—well, semi-alone—with my thoughts.

Jane kept the Cherokee's radio tuned to a news channel and from time to time we caught updates on the investigation into Gaston's death. Not surprisingly, the death of a congresswoman's son was one of the day's lead stories, especially given the unusual circumstances and Gaston's notoriety.

Much of what we heard was a rehash of the earlier reports we had seen on television, with a few additional details coming to light. Search teams had been deployed to the beach where Gaston's body had been found, and his Dodge Dakota had been discovered in a public parking area about a mile north of there. Hearing this confirmed for us that his body had drifted southward for a half mile or so after he entered the water.

The police were still advancing no theories as to why Gaston had gone to the beach, and they repeated their request for anyone with possible information to contact their hotline, giving the number on the air and promising anonymity.

We wondered if the search teams had found the fire ant mound, and if so, whether it had yielded any further evidence. Gaston's footprints were probably still visible on the mound, but Rachel had been careful to avoid the mound and stay in the loose dry sand, rendering any of her footprints almost indistinguishable. Jane and I had done the same.

So far, so good.

WE STOPPED FOR GAS and a restroom break at Lumberton, about halfway to Charlotte. It was just past 2:30

when we got back on US-74, and we caught the end of another newscast. Nothing significant was mentioned that we hadn't already heard.

We had driven for maybe another fifteen minutes, mostly in silence, when Jane said, "Do you think Gaston told Dave Sonderheim about Rachel?"

It was a good question. I had wondered the same thing but hadn't brought it up, not wanting to fuel any further worries with the two women. Jane and I had seen Rachel and Sonderheim nearly bump into each other as Rachel was leaving the Dive Bar after talking to Gaston. We had assumed Sonderheim was meeting Gaston, so it was natural to suppose Gaston might have said something to him about the encounter he had just had with the woman who called herself Selene.

"Maybe not," I said, hoping I sounded optimistic. "Rachel, you said you made sure you told Gaston to come to the beach alone. Based on that, let's hope Gaston decided to keep the whole matter to himself."

"Would he really do that?" Jane said. "I mean, considering what a loudmouth he generally is…er, I mean, was?"

"Hard to say," I said. "He might, if he was embarrassed about it. He probably wouldn't want anyone, especially his best friend, knowing that he was letting a woman shake him down."

"I wish now I had told him to keep it to himself, but I didn't think to do that," Rachel said. "My bad."

"Not a big deal," I said, trying to sound reassuring. "Even if Gaston told him about you, Sonderheim didn't get more than a passing look at you as he was going into the bar. And even if Gaston did tell Sonderheim and he tells the police, there's still very little likelihood they'll ever be able to find you. In a few more hours you'll be long gone."

"I just need to remember not to come back to North Carolina anytime soon," Rachel said, and we all laughed.

A bit nervously.

WE GOT TO CHARLOTTE Douglas International

Airport at a quarter to five and parked in one of the short-term parking lots. Rachel said it wasn't necessary for us to go into the terminal with her; that it was okay if we just dropped her off, but Jane and I both insisted on seeing her off. Her flight wouldn't board for another two hours, which gave us plenty of time to have one last meal together.

We picked a combination restaurant and bar on the outer concourse in the main terminal. Rachel ordered her favorite filthy goose martini, Jane ordered a margarita and I went with a Goose Island IPA, the same beer I'd had here several days earlier. The menu was limited to salads, sandwiches, fries, and pizza, which was fine with us. Rachel commented that she didn't like to eat a big meal before flying and Jane and I said we wanted something light also, thinking of the four-and-a-half-hour return drive to Schnock's Harbor we would be making later that evening.

Our conversation during the meal was equally light. The restaurant was crowded so we didn't risk talking about Gaston's death, although newscasts on the television sets above the bar occasionally provided updates. Congresswoman Maggie Stevens had released a statement thanking the public for their support and understanding at this most difficult time and imploring anyone with information that might aid the police in their investigation into her son's death to come forward.

There was still no mention of the twenty-five hundred dollars.

We finished our meal in a little over an hour and Rachel said, "I should probably check in and get through security." Jane and I waited while Rachel made her way to an American Airlines kiosk to get a printed boarding pass—like me, she refused to use her cell phone to board—then we walked with her to the first security checkpoint.

We stood together somewhat awkwardly for a moment, then Jane threw her arms around Rachel, hugging her fiercely. "Thank you for *everything*," Jane said. "I really, *really* appreciate what you've done."

"You're welcome," Rachel said, smiling. "Thank you

for your hospitality. Come see us in Iowa sometime."

"I just might do that."

Rachel turned to me and gave me a quick hug. "See you back in Des Moines, Rob," she said. Then she laughed and added, "You are coming back, aren't you?"

I laughed also. "Oh yeah, I'll be back," I said.

"Okay," Rachel said. "See you soon."

"See you soon. And…thanks again."

Rachel nodded, then she turned and walked off toward security, pulling her small rolling carry-on behind her.

WE WATCHED AS RACHEL passed through security, then Jane took my hand and squeezed it. "Wow," she said. "What a wild few days."

"Indeed," I said, squeezing her hand in return.

Jane sighed and gave me a wistful smile. "I'm ready to go home. Would you mind driving?"

"I'd be happy to," I said, and we turned and left the terminal.

Chapter 60

JANE AND I GOT BACK TO SCHNOCK'S Harbor at about 10:30 that night. We didn't talk much during the drive. We agreed we had heard enough news reports on Gaston's death for one day so Jane tuned the Cherokee's radio to an easy listening station that played songs like Jim Croce's "Time in a Bottle" and James Taylor's "Fire and Rain."

The music seemed to suit our mood. For the moment, anyway, we were done speculating about what the police might yet turn up in their investigation, whether Gaston had told Sonderheim about his conversation with Rachel or if anyone from the Dive Bar had mentioned her or their conversation to the police. Any further updates could wait until tomorrow.

About an hour before we got to Schnock's Harbor my cell chimed with an incoming text. I took my eyes off the road for a moment to give it a quick look. The text was from Rachel, telling us she had just landed in Des Moines and Al was on his way to pick her up. I handed the phone to Jane so she could read Rachel's message.

"Do you want to reply?" Jane asked.

"Yes," I said. "Maybe just a thumbs-up emoji and something like 'Thanks again.'"

"Got it." She tapped in the message and hit send.

NEXT MORNING, THE NEWS programs had the expected follow-ups on the investigation into Gaston's death, although again there was very little we hadn't already heard. There was still no mention of the money, and apparently no one had come forward with a description of Rachel. All good.

About mid-morning Jane asked if I was up for a walk on the beach. "I'm feeling restless," she said, and I told her I was also and a walk sounded good.

"I need to get in as much beach time as I can while I'm still here," I added. A little earlier I had gone online and booked my flights for tomorrow. I was going to depart from Wilmington on an afternoon commuter flight to Charlotte—there were a surprising number of these—then take the evening flight to Des Moines that Rachel had just flown.

We took the Cherokee to the beach and parked at the same public area as two nights earlier. Gaston's Dakota was gone, either driven away by a family member or towed. I wondered if the police might have impounded the truck as part of their investigation, treating it as a crime scene. Then I reminded myself that according to the news reports we'd heard so far, it hadn't been established that any crime had been committed. Gaston's death was still being treated as an accident, the result of anaphylactic shock.

Nevertheless, as we were climbing out of the Cherokee I also remembered the old axiom about criminals always returning to the scene of their crime. I didn't mention this to Jane.

We crossed the stile and hesitated for a moment, then Jane said, "Let's walk north." That was the opposite direction of the fire ant mound and I was fine with that, although I was still curious as to whether the police had found the mound and if so, how much time, if any, they had spent investigating it. Nothing besides Gaston's footprints should have been present, which meant the reason he had gone to the beach would still be unknown.

I hoped it remained that way.

WE STROLLED IN SILENCE for a few minutes, then Jane said, "Do you think the cops will ever find out about the money?"

"I'd guess they will," I said. "In fact, they may already have done so. They could just be sitting on it and waiting to see if anyone comes forward with information that might tie into it and give them a lead."

"What kind of lead?"

"Something that would explain what Gaston was going to do with the money. Part of that could depend on where he got it. If he borrowed it from, say, friends or family members, they might have some idea of what he was going to use it for…or what he *told* them he was going to use it for, anyway."

"Do you think he would have told them the truth?"

I thought about that for a moment. "I kinda doubt it," I said. "Like we said yesterday, he probably wouldn't have wanted it known that he was letting anybody blackmail him for their silence. The embarrassment, for one thing, plus the fact that agreeing to pay them would almost be a confession of sorts, an admission that he was guilty and needed to do whatever was necessary to protect himself."

"But what if he did tell someone what the money was for? Really for, I mean." There was no missing the worry in her voice.

"I still think it's a dead end," I said. "Remember, no one knows Rachel's real name, so even if someone does report seeing her talking to Gaston at the Dive Bar, that's not going to lead anywhere. The people in the bar don't know for sure what they talked about, and the cops aren't going to be able to find anyone around here named Selene who matches Rachel's description."

"Oh, right."

"Plus, if Gaston did borrow the money but didn't tell anyone what it was for, there are other possible explanations."

"Like what?"

I shrugged. "Drug buy? Gambling debt? Who knows?"

Jane pondered all of this for a moment, then she smiled and asked, "Do you *always* analyze everything this extensively after an assignment?"

I grinned, probably sheepishly. "Pretty much, yeah. I try to anticipate whatever might happen so I can be ready for the worst. Or try to be ready, anyway."

"And does that work?"

"Sometimes." We both laughed.

We didn't say anything for another minute or so, then Jane said, "I guess you really do have to be careful and try to anticipate everything. You can't afford to be careless and overlook something."

I nodded. "Years ago I worked with a guy named John Schroeder. We got to be good friends, and he was, by his own admission, the company's resident curmudgeon. We all kidded him about that but he'd say, 'Hey, I live life pessimistically, and I don't apologize for it. Once in a while, I'm pleasantly surprised. The rest of the time, I'm at least partially prepared.'"

Jane laughed. "Kind of like the old joke about the guy who said, 'I'm not paranoid. I'm just extremely alert.'"

"Right," I said. "Same sort of thing."

WE WALKED ON for another couple minutes, enjoying a breeze in our faces and the sound of the surf to our right. Then Jane said, "Speaking of money, we need to discuss your payment."

"Okay," I said, although I had really been hoping we could avoid the subject, at least for the time being. I was still feeling guilty that Rachel had been the key player in this exercise and she had borne almost all the risk. I had actually done very little, so I felt that if anyone deserved to be paid, it was Rachel, not me.

Also, I wasn't comfortable with the idea of taking ten thousand dollars from this woman with whom I had become intimate. Sure, a deal's a deal, but for obvious reasons I could no longer regard our relationship as strictly business. In simplest terms, I didn't want her money.

Before I could voice any of these concerns, Jane spoke again. "Last time I sent a check to your P.O. box, made out to your proofreading LLC. Is that how you want to handle this again? I mean, we can skip the mail part, but I'll be happy to write a check to the LLC that you can take home with you. Will that work?"

I sighed. "Yes, that would work, but let's talk about this for a minute." I hesitated, then went on. "The truth is, I don't really feel like I've done much to earn it. Rachel carried the ball this time while I mostly just stood by and watched. If anyone deserves to be paid, it's her."

Jane considered this for a minute or so, then she said, "What about splitting it? There's no way I'm not going to pay you for your time and effort, and the same goes for Rachel. Don't sell yourself short; you did plenty by coming down here and setting things up."

I had to laugh at that. "I'm not sure how much setting up I did, either," I said. "You're the one who came up with the plan involving the fire ants, remember?"

"Okay, but I wouldn't have known about Gaston's allergy if you hadn't heard Julie talking about it with Pete and Mel in the bar. You're the one who came up with that critical piece of information."

"That was just luck," I said. "Right place, right time."

"Yes, but you were the one who was there, not me. You're also the one who contacted Rachel and told her we needed reinforcements. I couldn't have done that, either."

I sighed again. "I'm not going to win this one, am I?"

Jane laughed. "No, you're most definitely not."

Chapter 61

NOT SURPRISINGLY, OUR PARTING at the Wilmington airport the next day was bittersweet.

My flight to Charlotte left at 4:10 in the afternoon and we got to the airport about an hour and a half before that. Tucked into a zippered pocket in my battered old steel gray briefcase was the check for ten thousand dollars Jane had written to my LLC.

"Remember," she said as she handed me the check, "You're to split this with Rachel. Promise me you will."

I laughed and said, "Are you afraid I'm going to keep the whole thing for myself?"

"No, I'm afraid you're going to try to give the whole thing to Rachel."

Damn it to hell, anyway. This woman had me pegged, coming and going.

JANE INSISTED ON PARKING and coming into the terminal with me, rather than dropping me at the curb. We decided we had time for a quick drink before I checked in so we found a bar and ordered a glass of pinot grigio for her, another Goose Island IPA for me.

We sat at a small table in a far corner of the bar. "I'll keep watching the news and let you know if anything important develops," Jane said quietly.

"I'd appreciate that," I said. We had already discussed this before leaving Schnock's Harbor and had agreed we would limit our conversations concerning Gaston to phone calls. Call me paranoid (again) but I didn't want anything put in writing, not even in texts between cell phones. I didn't know how readily such texts could be accessed, but I was reasonably certain they could.

At the same time, I was fairly confident neither Jane's cell nor mine was tapped—why would they be?—so I figured we would be safe enough talking about Gaston if anything further came out in the investigation. As long as no one was listening in and recording our conversations—unlikely, as neither of us was a suspect—we should be fine.

Jane took a sip of her wine and smiled at me. "I'm going to miss you," she said.

"I'm going to miss you too," I said. "I really like it down here. The beach, the turtle rehab center, the whole area. And of course, those blackened catfish sandwiches at the Crab Shack."

"Maybe you should think about relocating. You know, to someplace warmer so you don't have to deal with those Midwest winters."

"I have the same thought every January or February when I'm blowing the snow out of my driveway and the windchill is below zero."

"Ouch. That sounds brutal."

"It is."

We fell silent again and I sensed a certain awkwardness, like both of us wanted to say more but we were afraid of overstepping the bounds.

What bounds?

This assignment had played out like no other I had ever undertaken. I had violated my first rule of contract killing— no personal involvement—in ways that just a couple of weeks ago would have seemed unthinkable. I had met and become intimately involved with a woman who was attractive, bright, witty and resourceful. And, oh yeah, my client.

Wow. What bounds, indeed.

Jane was studying her wine glass as she rotated it on the tabletop. I picked up my beer and took a pull. I set the glass back on the table and said, "Hey."

She looked up and I saw her eyes glistening. "Oh, hell," she said. "I wasn't going to do this." She brusquely wiped a hand across her eyes. "Sorry."

"It's okay," I said. I reached across the table and squeezed her hand.

She took a deep breath and shook her head. "No, it's not okay. I need to be an adult about this. Of course you have your life back in Iowa and I have my life here. That's the reality of the situation."

"Well, for what it's worth, I'm not liking this, either," I said. "This turned into something more than just another assignment for me. A lot more." *Good Lord, did I just say that?*

That brought a smile. A rather wan smile, to be sure, but a smile nonetheless. "Thank you for that," Jane said. "And, for what it's worth, I feel the same."

"Then let's keep our options open. Remember, Rachel invited you to come see us in Iowa. I second that invitation."

"Okay, deal," Jane said. She laughed and added, "I've always wanted to try a corn dog."

I laughed in return. "I'm sure that can be arranged."

WE FINISHED OUR DRINKS and Jane walked with me to the American Airlines desk so I could check my large rolling bag. The briefcase, of course, I was going to carry onboard.

After checking the bag and getting my boarding passes, we ambled off toward security. When we got there, Jane reached up and gripped my shoulders. "Thank you for everything," she said. Then, before I could respond, she pulled me closer for a long, deep kiss.

She stepped back and gave me another smile. "Stay in touch, Hit Man," she said.

"You too, Turtle Lady."

We both laughed and shared one last kiss. Then I turned and headed toward the security check-in.

I WAS HALFWAY BACK to Des Moines later that evening when I realized I had never gotten around to asking Jane about buying her sister's Subaru.

Chapter 62

My reunion with Preacher the next morning was joyous.

I had texted Mike Stevenson while waiting in the Charlotte airport to catch my flight to Des Moines. I told him I would be getting home later that evening and would plan to swing by and pick up Preacher in the morning. He replied that that was fine and he would do his best to break the bad news to his wife and daughters. He ended his text with a laughing emoji.

I headed over to Mike's place at a few minutes after nine. It was Saturday so I knew his wife Janice and their daughters, Jessica and Emily, would be there. Recalling what Mike had told me about how they had spoiled Preacher and didn't want to give her up, I hoped I could reclaim her without things becoming awkward or difficult. I knew Mike had been joking—well, mostly, anyway—but I also knew how quickly people could become attached to a dog in their care, especially one as likable as Preacher.

Luckily, it turned out to be less of an ordeal than I anticipated…not an ordeal at all, in fact.

When I stepped into Mike's house Preacher greeted me with a salvo of wild barking and began bouncing around before rearing to put her forepaws on my chest and attempting to lick my face. This was accompanied by whimpering that, I can't deny, put a lump in my throat.

"Yes, I'm happy to see you too," I managed to say. I ruffled her ears and glanced past her to see Mike and Janice and the girls all smiling.

"Well," Janice said, "there's no question about whose dog she is," and we all laughed.

Rusty, Mike's yellow Labrador, stood next to the girls wagging his tail and apparently also happy with the proceedings. While he and Preacher generally got along just fine, I wondered if he might be pleased that she was going home so he would no longer have to share his family's affections with her. Then again, maybe he would miss having a live-in playmate.

"I really appreciate you watching her while I was gone," I said. "She looks great."

"We were happy to do it," Janice said. "She's a well-behaved guest, and she's welcome to come back anytime."

"Well-behaved?" I said. "Are we talking about the same dog?"

AFTER THE GIRLS had said goodbye to Preacher—they both hugged her and kissed her forehead—Mike helped me carry her dog food and dog bed out to the Equinox. I put Preacher's ramp in place against the back bumper and she trotted up it and settled herself in the cargo area like always.

"We need to be getting her and Rusty out for a few workouts before much longer," Mike said. "Duck season will be here before we know it."

"Right," I said. "Maybe next weekend if it's not too hot?"

"Sounds good. Let's plan on it."

I thanked Mike again and we shook hands. Then I climbed into the Equinox and cranked the ignition. I backed out of the driveway and into the street. I flipped up a hand to wave at Mike, then Preacher and I headed out to Maffitt Reservoir.

All the time I'd recently spent walking on the beach with Jane notwithstanding, I was feeling a little homesick for our old stomping grounds. It would be good to ramble around at the lake again and do so accompanied by my dog.

THE WATER LEVEL at the reservoir was down, not uncommon this late in the summer, so that the sandy shoreline extended out a good ways beyond the grassy banks. The morning was already warm, in the upper seventies, and I wanted to stay close to the water so Preacher could splash around to cool off as needed.

We parked on the west side of the lake and walked

down the grassy hillside to the shoreline. I was carrying one of Preacher's retrieving dummies, planning to toss it a few times for her to fetch from the water. But when we climbed down from the bank and started walking along the shoreline, Preacher trotted on ahead of me, investigating various scents, and I decided to let her set our course.

I also reflected that the low water level made the extended shoreline almost a mini-beach of sorts, which of course immediately reminded me of Jane.

I wondered what she was doing this Saturday morning, and whether there were any further developments concerning Gaston Stevens' death. I had texted her when I got home last night, and she had replied a minute or two later that she was happy I'd made it safely. She ended her text, "Miss you…talk soon," and I replied with the thumbs-up emoji and the words, "Me too."

It also occurred to me that just as I had missed having Preacher with me when I had walked on the beach with Jane, now I was missing Jane while walking with Preacher.

The ironies just kept on coming.

I DECIDED ON CHARLIE'S BARBECUE for dinner that evening.

After staying at the lake for about an hour, Preacher and I headed home. I spent most of the day catching up on the various tasks that had accumulated while I'd been in North Carolina—sorting through the pile of mail on my kitchen table and paying a few bills (yes, I still write checks, and why are you not surprised), answering several emails from friends, doing a couple loads of laundry and mowing the lawn, front and back.

I waited until late afternoon to tackle this last chore, when most of the yard was in shade, but I still worked up a good sweat. Standing in the shower afterward, I told myself I had earned a night out.

I got to Charlie's at a little after six. I took my usual seat at the bar and Anita smiled when she saw me. Without asking, she began drawing a tall Blue Moon.

"Long time, no see," she said as she set the beer in front of me. "You look like you've been getting a lot of sun somewhere."

"North Carolina," I said. "Just got back last night."

"Ah. Vacation?"

I nodded. "Visiting a friend," I said. "Spent quite a bit of time on the beach."

"Nice."

"Yes, it was."

"Well, I have to say, it seems to have agreed with you. You look a lot better than the last time you were here."

"Thanks," I said. I hesitated, then added, "I *feel* a lot better." As I said the words the reality hit me. I *did* feel a lot better.

"Happy to hear that. Do you need a menu?"

"No, I'll go with my usual."

"Catfish fingers, fries and coleslaw," Anita recited as she punched in the order on the register's computer screen. Unlike *Jeopardy!* contestants, she did not phrase it as a question.

"Geez, I'm so predictable."

"That's right," Anita laughed. "You are."

THE CATFISH FINGERS of course reminded me of the blackened catfish sandwiches I'd enjoyed at the Crab Shack.

"This friend you were visiting," Anita said, snagging a French fry off my platter and dipping it in my coleslaw. "Male or female?" She kept some of the slaw balanced on the fry as she popped it into her mouth.

"My, my, aren't we nosy?"

"Don't make me hurt you to get the answer."

I laughed and was about to respond when a young blonde server named Blake (as stated on the little wooden pig-shaped nametag pinned to her t-shirt) approached Anita carrying one of those handheld point-of-sale devices that look like an oversized cellphone. She held up the device so Anita could see its screen and began describing some problem trying to run a customer's credit card, none of which made any sense to me.

Anita listened for a minute then sighed and said, "Do you want me to come back to the table with you?"

"If you would, yeah," Blake said. She looked at me and said, "Sorry."

"No problem," I said. In fact, I welcomed the interruption because it would give me time to figure out how much—or little—I wanted to tell Anita about Jane.

The two of them walked away and I ate another couple of catfish fingers while they were gone. Anita returned a few minutes later, shaking her head.

"Problem resolved?" I asked. I picked up my beer and took a long pull.

"Yes, but these young kids we hire," she said, shaking her head again. "I swear, I'm the mother to so many children from different vaginas."

Geez Louise, she could have given me some warning. I nearly snorted Blue Moon out my nose.

Chapter 63

AFTER FINISHING DINNER at Charlie's I made my usual swing by Half Price Books but I didn't find anything that caught my eye or, in the case of my favorite authors, that I hadn't already read. I left the store empty-handed and got back home at about 8:30.

I let Preacher out to make her nightly patrol of the back yard and grabbed a bottle of Blue Moon from the fridge. I smiled as I uncapped the bottle, recalling Anita's remark about being the mother to so many children, etcetera. I told myself to remember to share that with Rachel the next time we talked.

I hadn't spoken to Rachel since getting home from North Carolina but I had texted her to let her know I was back. She had replied with a smiling emoji and the words "Welcome home." I sent her a thumbs-up emoji—I was relying on emojis more and more, I'm ashamed to admit—and that concluded our exchange. I suspected we both needed a little time to decompress after the events of the past few days.

It was a calm, clear evening and I followed Preacher outside. I had just settled myself in one of the deck chairs when my cell chimed with an incoming text. I thumbed the icon and saw that the message was from Jane. It said, "If you're not out carousing on this Saturday night"—I smiled—"are you up for a call?"

I replied, "Sure. Just sitting on the deck with a cold one."

A few seconds later my cell rang. "Hey there," I said.

"Hey there," Jane said. "How are you?"

"I'm doing okay," I said. I was happy to hear her voice. She sounded like she was in good spirits. "How about you?"

"I'm doing okay also. I have a couple of things to share that I thought you might be interested in."

"Go for it."

"Well, first of all, Gaston's mother has made another statement. She was on the news today and they're now offering a fifty-thousand-dollar reward for information pertaining to his death. She didn't come right out and say she suspects foul play but she did say she couldn't believe Gaston didn't have his EpiPen with him since he's been carrying one for years, ever since he nearly died from that bee sting."

"Really," I said, remembering that Rachel had picked up the EpiPen's carrying tube that night before we left the beach. She had stuck it in the pocket of her jeans, along with the EpiPen itself, and I knew they were both now in Jane's trash and would soon be on their way to a landfill. "Did the police say anything about the EpiPen?"

"They're being pretty careful with their statements, probably because of her position as a congresswoman. But they did mention the possibility that he might have just forgotten his EpiPen that night. That's what other people seem to think."

"What other people?"

"Well, Matt Lewis for one. I returned his speargun this afternoon and one of the first things he said was, 'Did you hear about Gaston Stevens?' I told him yes, I had heard, and then we talked about it for a few minutes."

"What else did he say?"

"Oh, mostly just that the way Gaston died was pretty strange, alone on the beach that night. Apparently there's quite a bit of talk going around. Everyone is wondering what he was doing there."

"And there's still been no mention of the money?"

"Not so far. Or not that I've heard, anyway."

I didn't say anything for a minute, thinking over what Jane had just told me. It sounded like the police still hadn't turned up anything beyond the obvious, that Gaston had died from anaphylactic shock caused by a severe allergic reaction to the fire ant bites. Why he had gone to the beach that night—and now, why he wasn't carrying his EpiPen—was still a mystery, and I wondered how much longer this would continue. I also wondered if the family's reward offer would bring anyone forward, and if it did, what they might say.

"Rob? Are you still there?"

"Yes, I'm still here. Sorry. Just thinking about what you said."

"What do you make of it?"

"At the risk of sounding callous, I'd say so far, so good."

"That's what I was thinking also."

"Did Matt Lewis have anything else to say?" I told myself I wasn't asking this question out of jealousy.

"Oh, just something about how he'd bet I was relieved that I wouldn't have to testify against Gaston now. He kinda laughed as he said it and I just smiled and said yes, I was relieved. I really didn't want to keep talking about that, or sound like I was happy that he died."

"Smart. Did he seem okay with that?"

"Yes. I was afraid he might bring up Sara's death and say something about Gaston's death being karma, but he didn't. Then we talked a little bit about Rachel. I told him she had gone back to Iowa but we'd had fun with the speargun even though we hadn't gotten any fish. I thanked him for letting us borrow it, and that was pretty much it."

"That's good."

"Yes, I was only there for a little while. Probably no more than fifteen minutes or so."

"Good deal." I wondered if she could hear the relief in my voice.

"So," Jane said, "Have you seen Rachel since you got back?"

"No, I haven't. A couple of texts is all. We'll probably get together sometime next week."

"Well, when you do, be sure and thank her again for me. And remember to split the check with her. The amount, I mean."

I laughed. "I'll do that. I haven't forgotten."

"In the meantime…" she hesitated, then continued, "is it okay if I tell you again that I miss you?"

"It's fine," I said, and I knew I was grinning. "I miss you too."

I heard Jane sigh, then she said, "I'll bet your dog was

happy to see you."

"Yes, she was. I picked her up this morning and we went out to the lake. We had a good long walk and then I came home and paid some bills and mowed the lawn."

"Wow," she said. "You've been productive."

"Well, I had some catching up to do after being gone."

"And are you all caught up?"

"Pretty close, I think."

This time it was Jane who fell silent. I gave her a minute, then said, "Hey."

"Yes, I'm sorry. Just thinking."

"About...?"

"Oh, everything that's happened in the past few days. I can't quite believe it's...over."

"Let's hope that it is," I said. "Over, I mean."

"Right. I'll let you know if anything more develops."

"Yes, keep me posted."

Another moment of silence, then Jane said, "I guess I should let you go." She paused, then added, "I wish you were here and we were sitting on the porch drinking margaritas."

I laughed again. "I'd like that also. As it is, I'm making do with a Blue Moon on my deck."

"A Blue Moon, huh? Is that your preferred beer?"

"It's one of them, anyway. At least in the summertime."

"I'll have to remember that. I'll try to have some on hand the next time you're down this way."

"Deal."

She sighed again. "Okay, I'll let you go. Good night, Rob."

"Good night, Jane."

Chapter 64

I wondered when that would be. Or *if* it would be.

My relationship with Daryl Nelson having recently gone to hell like it did, I couldn't help feeling a little pessimistic about my romantic prospects. There was no denying that I was strongly attracted to Jane, and it certainly sounded like those feelings were mutual. But if I couldn't successfully maintain a relationship with someone local, what were the odds of my being able to do so with a woman who lived halfway across the country?

Then again…

The geography factor couldn't be ignored, but it wasn't totally insurmountable. And the fact that Jane and I had recently collaborated on an assignment—okay, killing someone; let's not mince words—bound us together in a way that Daryl and I had never known.

There it was again, rearing its ugly head, the big secret I had withheld from her during the entirety of our relationship. With Jane, as I had already observed, I would never have to worry or feel guilty about that. In some ways, she and I had already established more trust in just a few days than Daryl and I had in eighteen months.

Wow. Talk about cutting right to the chase.

PREACHER RETURNED TO THE DECK and sprawled next to my chair. I finished my Blue Moon and decided one more wouldn't hurt. It was Saturday night and I had no special plans for the next day, so why not. I went inside, grabbed another beer from the fridge and returned to my chair.

As always, I started replaying the conversation I'd just had with Jane. Although I had told her that for the moment everything sounded okay regarding the situation with

Gaston—"so far, so good," I had said—I was concerned about the fifty-thousand-dollar reward the family was now offering. That was bound to attract some attention and it wasn't unlikely that some of the Dive Bar patrons might come forward, hoping to collect.

Whether they would offer anything substantial in the way of information remained to be seen. They might be able to provide a description of Rachel but none of them knew her name, and beyond the fact that she had talked to Gaston, they would not be able to offer much else. The police could search for the mystery woman as a person of interest, but that was likely to be a dead end.

Or so I told myself.

I continued to mull this over.

If someone did come forward I wondered if the police might employ a sketch artist to do a rendering of Rachel, based on the description of the witness or witnesses, and then circulate the sketch through the media. I gave this a little more thought and decided that even if this happened, it wasn't likely to generate any solid leads.

First, from what I'd seen, such sketches often had a rather generic, "every person" quality and they frequently bore no more than a passing resemblance to the actual perpetrator. Also, there was the matter of all the makeup Rachel had worn to the bar. It had altered her appearance pretty significantly, such that any description based on how she looked that night was likely to be at least somewhat skewed.

Finally, I thought it highly unlikely that a sketch circulated in North Carolina—or even the surrounding states—would attract any attention in Iowa. And even if it did, I doubted it would lead to Rachel being identified.

Nevertheless, once again I regretted letting her play such an active role, and I gave myself another mental kick for not having weighed the risks more carefully. I wondered if this lapse in judgment had been caused by my attraction to Jane. Not only had I violated at least one of my inviolate rules—no personal involvement--but I had also gotten careless, maybe even downright sloppy. Worst of all, I had endangered someone besides myself by doing so.

I sighed and took a long pull of my beer. For the umpteenth time I told myself it was well and truly time to retire.

WHEN PREACHER AND I returned from the lake the next morning, the message light was blinking on my old landline phone. After feeding Preacher her morning meal, I went back to my office and punched the play button on my answering machine.

The message was from Daryl Nelson.

Speak of the devil.

"Hey, Rob," she said. "You're probably out at the lake with Preacher and I know you don't want to talk to me, but I wondered if you might want those books you loaned me. If you do, I thought maybe we could meet for lunch one day this week and I'll bring them with me. Let me know…thanks."

The books she was referring to were a couple of hardcover novels, one by John Sandford and the other by Michael Connelly, if I remembered correctly. Early on we had discovered a mutual love of crime fiction and we had occasionally traded books back and forth. I had loaned her these a couple months earlier.

I still had no desire to see Daryl…or so I thought, anyway. But now that she had reminded me about the books—given everything that had happened recently, I had pretty much forgotten about them—I realized I actually would like to have them back. I'm a confessed bookaholic and I tend to regard my good hardcovers the way many people feel about their fine jewelry. I treasure them.

On the other hand, getting the books would require seeing Daryl again, something I had vowed I wasn't going to do. I supposed I could ask her to send them to me, but that seemed a little silly, even petty, in that we lived in the same city. If I wanted the books, it just made sense to get together with her.

Of course, I also had the option of telling her not to

bother returning the books; that it was no big deal and she could keep them. If I really wanted the books for my collection, I could buy new copies.

There again, however, that seemed a little petty or spiteful. I wanted to avoid giving her that impression. Besides, I told myself, I could keep our meeting brief. Lunch should take no more than an hour, and then I could walk away once and for all.

So why was I feeling so apprehensive? Was I testing myself? Did I need to prove to myself that I could stand firm on my conviction to cut things off with Daryl entirely? Even as I pondered this I told myself I wasn't going to be persuaded into agreeing to remain friends with her, or any such nonsense.

But I also had to admit there was an element of curiosity involved. Given everything that had recently happened with Jane, did I need to confirm I no longer felt any attraction to Daryl?

I believed these were all good questions—legitimate questions—but I knew if I discussed them with Rachel, she would tell me I was overthinking this; that I should just meet Daryl, grab my books and be done with it. And she would be right.

I picked up the phone to return Daryl's call.

Chapter 65

WE AGREED TO MEET AT THE STAR Bar on Ingersoll Avenue at 11:45 on Tuesday. That gave me almost exactly forty-eight hours to continue overthinking the matter…or to put it in more colorful terms, mind-fuck myself thoroughly.

I told myself there was no reason to get bent out of shape about this. I'd done nothing wrong, at least as far as Daryl was concerned, so meeting her for lunch so she could return my books was no big deal. There was no reason to feel nervous about seeing her, something I'd done hundreds of times before.

Of course, now the circumstances were decidedly different.

I also reminded myself to keep a cool head when I saw her and not make any bitter or snide remarks caused by any lingering anger I might be feeling. I still regarded myself as the wronged party insofar as our relationship was concerned, but I didn't want to come across as wounded or resentful. I hoped I could remain detached.

Until I saw Daryl, I would take Preacher to the lake, keep busy with whatever tasks needed my attention on the home front and stay in touch with Jane. Not only did I want to continue monitoring the Gaston Stevens situation for any new developments; I also hoped to keep the romantic spark alive between the two of us.

Pretending otherwise was just fooling myself.

JANE AND I TALKED again on Monday evening. We'd had a couple text exchanges on Sunday and another on Monday afternoon, then she called me at about 8:30. As usual, I was sitting on the deck, Blue Moon in hand, while Preacher made her patrol of the back yard.

"Hey there," I answered my cell.

"Hey there," Jane said. This had become our standard greeting, much like the "Hey you" Rachel and I used. "I have another update on Gaston Stevens if you're interested."

"You bet. I'm all ears."

"Okay. Well, first of all, I volunteered at Paige Green this afternoon for a couple hours, and Julie Thompson was working. She started talking about Gaston almost immediately, and she said some of the same things Matt had said on Saturday. That she thought I must be relieved by what had happened, and so on."

"Right," I said. "What did you say?"

"I told her that yes, I was relieved I wouldn't have to testify against him, but I also said that the descriptions I'd heard of how he died sounded pretty awful. I didn't want to give her the idea that I was actually happy about what happened."

"Smart."

"Thanks. Then she went off on why he was on the beach that night. Oh, which reminds me—the police have started talking about the money, finally. They released a statement saying they had learned that Gaston made two withdrawals from his bank account totaling nineteen hundred dollars on the day he was killed. Plus, his brother came forward and said Gaston borrowed six hundred from him that same day, saying he needed some work done on his truck."

"Interesting. We knew they'd get to the money eventually."

"Well, they have. And as you'd imagine, that's caused all kinds of speculation. What he wanted the money for, and so on."

"That's not surprising. Did Julie have anything to say about that?" I was willing to bet she did.

Jane laughed. "Oh yeah. Julie said she's sure he wanted the money to buy drugs. She's convinced the whole beach thing was a drug deal gone bad. That Gaston went to the beach that night, stumbled into the fire ants, and whoever he was supposed to meet just took the money and left him there."

I didn't reply for a moment while I considered what Jane said. Julie's conjecture was an almost too-perfect explanation that would account for Gaston's death without implicating any of us. I couldn't deny something like that was exactly what we had been hoping for. I wondered how many other people shared

Julie's opinion.

"Does anyone else think the same thing?" I asked.

"Yes. Some of the other volunteers at the rehab center heard us talking and they said they agreed. That seems to be the general consensus, in fact."

"Wow," I said. "Are the police looking into that?"

"I think so, yes. And that reminds me of something else. Maggie Stevens is trying to downplay the whole drug thing, saying her son wasn't a drug user, but I don't think anyone believes her. But there is one other thing I need to tell you about."

"What's that?"

"Well, I told you about the reward Maggie Stevens, or the family, is offering for information. That evidently got some attention. Several people from the bar have come forward and said they remember seeing Gaston talking to a strange woman one night earlier. The night before he died, I mean."

"Uh-oh." I felt my scalp beginning to tingle.

"Right. But so far it hasn't led anywhere. Or at least the cops aren't saying much. They're still asking for more information."

"Have they released a description?"

"Only a general one. Tall, middle-aged, lots of makeup."

I couldn't help laughing at that. "Let's hope they stay focused on the makeup," I said.

"Let's hope," Jane said. "Do you think you should tell Rachel?"

"I will, yes. But so far it sounds pretty vague. And we know she wasn't caught on video because the bar's cameras weren't working."

"That's right. We got lucky there."

"Yes, we did."

Neither of us spoke for a moment, then I asked, "Is that everything about Gaston?"

"For the moment, anyway. I'll let you know if anything further develops."

"I'd appreciate that. In the meantime, let's hope people buy into the drug theory. Especially the cops."

"Right."

Another pause, then Jane asked, "So, what have *you* been up to?"

"Oh, the usual," I said. "Just taking care of things here at home, getting my dog out to the lake for exercise, that kind of thing."

She laughed. "Sounds exciting."

"Almost more than I can stand."

"Have you seen Rachel?"

"No, still haven't seen her. But I probably will later this week."

"Well, don't forget…"

"I know, I know. I'll split the payment with her, I promise."

"Okay."

We talked for another couple minutes, saying we missed each other and then wishing each other good night. After ending the call I sat and reflected on the fact that I hadn't said anything to Jane about meeting Daryl for lunch the next day.

There was no reason to have brought that up, I told myself. It was nothing more than a quick get-together so Daryl could return my books, after which we'd go our separate ways. There was no need to upset or alarm Jane.

Still, I disliked keeping those kind of secrets. I thought once again of that old saying, that if you're doing something you wouldn't be comfortable telling your partner, you probably shouldn't be doing it.

During the entirety of my relationship with Daryl, I'd been haunted by the fact that she knew nothing of my contract killing.

Jane knew all about it, so that would never be a problem. But I didn't want our relationship to be marred by secrecy of any kind.

Assuming it *was* a relationship, that is.

Chapter 66

MY LUNCH DATE WITH DARYL went smoothly, almost surprisingly so.

I was reminded of Mark Twain's oft-quoted comment, "I am an old man and I have known a great many troubles, most of which never happened." I'll admit I'm still reluctant to refer to myself as old, but I can attest to the wisdom of the rest of that statement…i.e., most of our worries beforehand are for naught.

That's how things played out with Daryl.

The Star Bar is only a few minutes from Daryl's office, and she was already at the restaurant when I got there at a quarter to twelve. She was seated in one of the booths along the wall opposite the door and my books were on the table in front of her.

I couldn't deny that she looked good. She was wearing a crisp white blouse and khaki slacks and as always, her dark hair was gleaming. She smiled as I approached and as I slid into the seat across from her she said, "You've been spending quite a bit of time in the sun."

"As a matter of fact, I have," I said, but I didn't elaborate. No way was I going to tell her anything about my recent adventure in North Carolina. I'd let her assume I'd gotten my tan right here in Iowa.

"Well, I brought your books," she said, placing one hand atop them. "Thanks for the loan."

"You're welcome. I appreciate you returning them."

There was a moment of awkward silence—I'd anticipated there might be a few of those—but we were saved by the arrival of the server, a young woman named Alicia. She placed menus in front of us and asked, "Can I bring you something to drink?"

"Iced tea for me," Daryl said.

"I'll have the same."

"Lemon?" Alicia asked.

"Yes, thanks," Daryl said.

"Sure," I said.

Alicia left and Daryl said, "No beer?"

"It's a little early," I said, smiling. We both knew I wasn't opposed to the occasional beer at lunchtime, but Daryl didn't pursue it.

Instead, she said, "So, what else have you been up to, besides working on your tan?"

I smiled again. "Oh, the usual. Yard work, taking Preacher to the lake, washing the SUV, that sort of thing. How about you? How are things at the *Register*?"

"Oh, pretty much same old, same old."

"Nothing exciting happening right now?"

She laughed. "Not unless you consider the state fair coming up in a few weeks exciting."

"A lot of people think it is."

"That's right, they do."

Before our conversation became more banal, Alicia returned with our iced teas and said, "Are you ready to order?"

"Better give us a couple more minutes," I said. "I haven't looked at the menu yet."

"No problem," she said. "I'll be back."

We both picked up our menus and sat silently for another minute or so. Then Daryl said, "I always have a hard time deciding. Everything here is good."

"Yes, it is," I agreed. I scanned the menu and suppressed a smile when I saw, under the "Big Plates" section, a blackened catfish entree. I hoped Daryl hadn't noticed my double take.

Alicia returned a few minutes later. "Do you know what you're having?" she asked. As usual, the restaurant was crowded and the majority of patrons, judging by their business-casual attire, were from various downtown offices. I suspected Alicia hoped we had made up our minds and weren't going to require her to come back again.

Thankfully, Daryl answered immediately. "I'll have the turkey Caesar wrap," she said.

"And your side?"

"The wasabi potato salad."

"And you, sir?"

"I'll go with the Monte Cristo. And I'll have the potato salad also."

"Very good," Alicia said. "I'll have those out to you shortly."

ANOTHER MOMENT OF SILENCE.

Then Daryl gave me a wan smile and said, "Thank you for meeting me."

"It's okay," I said. "Thank you for remembering the books."

She sighed. Then she shook her head and laughed. "I wouldn't have blamed you if you'd told me to stuff them," she said.

I laughed also. "I wouldn't do that," I said. "You know how much I value my books. I'm happy to have them back."

She shook her head again. "Okay," she said. She hesitated, then added, "I hope you don't think I was using the books to bribe you into seeing me. But there is something else I wanted to tell you."

"Go ahead."

She took a deep breath. "I'm not seeing Craig Wilkinson any longer."

"Really?" I hadn't been prepared for that, and I was surprised by her frankness. "What happened?"

"It's complicated, but the bottom line is, I'm pretty sure he was also seeing someone else. In fact, I'm certain of it."

Why are we not surprised, I thought. But I didn't want to sound sarcastic or, for that matter, insensitive. Nor did I want to betray too much interest, although I was curious as to how she had found out. So I just said, "Sorry."

"Really?" Daryl sounded like she didn't believe me.

I shook my head. "I don't wish anything bad for you," I said. "And yes, I'm sorry it didn't work out."

Daryl sat staring at me as if she still didn't believe me. And, I suppose, who could blame her. I had told myself beforehand that I didn't want to come across as bitter or spiteful, but I was a little surprised myself that I wasn't feeling any sense of satisfaction after what she had just told me. I had suspected all along that Wilkinson was a player, and I was sorry that Daryl had been hurt by him.

She gave me another wan smile and said, "I guess it's true what they say, that if someone will cheat with you, they'll also cheat on you."

"Yes," I said. "I suppose there's quite a bit of truth to that."

We were spared further discussion, at least for the moment, by Alicia's arrival with our food.

THE REST OF THE MEAL passed pleasantly enough, with small talk about how good the food was, a few semi-guarded comments about the upcoming fall elections—remembering that Daryl had told me she first met Craig Wilkinson at a fundraiser for one of our representatives, I sensed we were both treading lightly here—and each of us asking the other about the health of our respective pets. As we were finishing eating Alicia came back to refill our glasses with more iced tea and ask us if we wanted anything else. We told her no and then she asked if we wanted one check or two.

"One." Daryl answered before I could speak. "And I'll take it."

"Okay, I'll be right back," Alicia said.

As she walked away I said, "You don't have to buy my lunch."

"It's okay," Daryl said. "I invited you, remember?"

"Then at least let me get the tip," I offered.

"No, I'll take care of that also."

"Well…all right, then. Thanks."

"My pleasure."

AS WE LEFT THE RESTAURANT Daryl said, "I parked in back."

"So did I," I replied. I didn't mention that my Equinox was next to her blue Corolla.

We walked down the sloping driveway to the parking lot behind the restaurant. "Oh, you're right next to me," Daryl said.

"Yep."

We stood facing each other and Daryl said, "I need to get back to the office. Thank you again for meeting me."

"Thank you for lunch. And for returning my books." I had them tucked under one arm and I shifted them slightly.

"You're welcome," she said. She smiled and then stepped forward to give me a quick hug. She stepped back and said, "Take care, Rob. And…give me a call if you'd like to get together sometime."

I smiled. "I'll do that," I said.

We both knew that was never going to happen.

Chapter 67

"PLEASE TELL ME YOU'RE NOT GOING to do that." Rachel looked seriously concerned.

It was a few minutes after nine and we were sitting on my deck with our usual beers, a Miller 64 for her and a Blue Moon for me. Despite the darkness the temperature was still in the low eighties and because of the heat, Rachel had left Alexander the Great at home and walked over to my house alone.

This was our first get-together since we had returned from North Carolina. I had suggested Al join us but Rachel said he was turning in early because he had to be at work by five a.m. He was still overseeing the installation of the two new production lines at Hormel.

"No, I'm not going to call her," I said. I had recapped my lunch meeting with Daryl and told Rachel about Daryl's parting invitation. "In fact," I added, "I'm sure she knows I won't."

"Well, hold that thought."

"Will do."

We sat in silence for a couple minutes then Rachel asked, "Are you happy about what happened with Craig Wilkinson? That Daryl got burned, I mean?"

"If you'd asked me that a couple weeks ago, I'm sure I would have said yes. But now...no, I can't say I'm happy about it. In fact, I actually feel kind of bad for her."

"Not bad enough to give her another chance, I hope."

"No, I already said I'm not going to call her. And I won't."

"Good. No backsliding."

"I promise."

We both took a hit of our beers, then Rachel asked, "Have you heard from Jane?"

"Yes, a couple of times. We talked last night, in fact. She called to give me an update on what's going on with

Gaston Stevens."

"Oh? What's the latest?"

I filled Rachel in on what Jane had told me about the police finally bringing the whole money issue to light, how that had triggered a lot of speculation about Gaston using the money for a drug buy, and that the family's reward offer had brought several people from the Dive Bar forward who told the cops about seeing Rachel talking to him the night before he died.

"Uh-oh," Rachel said. "Did they describe me?"

"Yes, but according to Jane, the description was pretty vague. Just that you were tall and wore lots of makeup."

Rachel laughed. "Well, that doesn't narrow it down a whole lot. But I'm glad they noticed the makeup. Who knew that was going to be such an effective disguise."

"Right. If that's what they're focused on, I'd say you're in the clear."

"I hope so."

"Plus, even if they had a more accurate description, I don't think they could track you down up here in Iowa. Not without actual photos or video, I mean."

"I think you're right."

"That reminds me of something else, though," I said. "Before I left, Jane wrote me a check for ten thousand dollars. She made me promise to split it with you."

Rachel shook her head. "No way," she said. "That's your fee. I'm not going to take any of that."

"Jane insisted. And I have to say, I agree with her. You did most of the work and took all of the risks this time. Plus, you had expenses getting down there and back. Plane fare, etcetera."

Rachel thought about this for a minute. Then she said, "Well, as a matter of fact, Summer was just telling me that Sam is going to need braces, and she's not sure how much of the cost their insurance will cover. So…"

"There you go," I said. "That settles it."

I HEARD PREACHER whine from inside the back

door, asking to be let outside. I stood up to let her out and I asked Rachel if she was ready for another beer. "Sure," she replied.

I let Preacher out and stepped inside. I grabbed two more beers from the fridge, uncapped them and returned to the deck.

When I had settled into my chair again, Rachel said, "So, besides the stuff with Gaston, what else is going on with Jane?"

"That's a good question," I said. "We've been texting quite a bit, and like I said, we've talked a couple times." I hesitated, then added, "We've been saying we miss each other." I'm sure I laughed a little sheepishly as I said this.

"Aww," Rachel said. "That's nice. Are you making plans to see her again? Maybe invite her to come up here for a visit?"

"I haven't done anything like that yet. Truth is, I'm still pretty uncertain about the whole thing." Seeing Daryl had rekindled a lot of self-doubt, I suddenly realized.

"Why are you uncertain?"

"Oh, a lot of reasons. The distance, for one thing. I mean, there's half a country between us."

"That's not that big a deal. Flights are pretty cheap right now, and you could take turns. You could even drive it if you didn't want to fly. What would it take? Two days?"

"Yes, but regardless of whether we fly or drive, how often could we realistically expect to see each other? Maybe six or eight times a year? What kind of relationship would that be?"

"A perfect one," Rachel said, laughing.

I laughed also. "Okay, but still...I can't help wondering if the whole thing is somehow...I don't know. Jinxed?"

Rachel shook her head. "Jinxed? How so?"

"Well, consider the circumstances. How we met. Or maybe I should say, *why* we met. Coming together to kill someone...is that really a good basis for romance?"

Rachel laughed again. "Why not?"

"Okay, okay. I'll admit I'm probably overthinking this."

"Gee, ya think? I swear, if the Olympics ever added an event for overthinking, you should be on the team for the U.S. You'd have a lock on the gold."

"Thanks."

Neither of us spoke for another minute or so. Then Rachel said, "I'm gonna stick my neck out here and tell you what I saw."

"All right," I said.

"I spent several days with the two of you, and I can tell you that the connection between you and Jane was a lot more than casual. In fact, I'd even go so far as to say the two of you were connected in a way that you never were with Daryl."

"Really?" I said. "You saw that?" Even as I spoke I was remembering Jane's comments about what motivated me as a contract killer, how she had unerringly zeroed in on the fact that I didn't do it for money.

"Yes, I saw that."

"Huh," I said. "So you really think I should try to pursue this? Not worry about the distance or anything else, and just go for it?"

Rachel smiled and shook her head again. Then she gave me that unwavering look I had come to know so well over the years. "Permission to speak frankly?" she asked.

I laughed. "Of course."

"Rob, get your head out of your ass."

Epilogue

WALKING ON THE BEACH IN THE moonlight, Jane Trehorn smiled as she thought about her last phone conversation with Robert Vance.

They had talked three nights earlier. She had called to apprise him of the latest details in the investigation of Gaston Stevens' death, not that there was much new information to relate. Despite the family's reward offer of fifty thousand dollars, the investigation was apparently stalled.

Those Dive Bar patrons who had come forward and told the police about seeing Rachel talking to Gaston had provided a description of her, and a couple of them had subsequently worked with an artist to produce a sketch of Rachel that was then circulated.

Rob had asked if the sketch looked like Rachel, and Jane told him it didn't. He had a good laugh when she said it looked like a cross between a vampire and a Goth girl, to which he'd responded, "Oh, Rachel would love that, especially the vampire part."

"No doubt," she had replied, laughing also.

Besides the bar's customers, the police had questioned the bartender, Steve Fulton, but he hadn't been especially forthcoming. He said he remembered seeing the woman talking to Gaston but he hadn't paid much attention to them. The only other detail he provided was that she had ordered a martini.

Jane suspected that Steve might have been holding back. She knew he hadn't had much use for Gaston or his buddies and was quite possibly not upset by Gaston's demise. Regardless, the cops had come away with little additional information after talking to him. All good.

Jane glanced at her Smartwatch. It was a quarter past nine and she had been walking for about forty-five minutes. As during her last walk with Rob a little over a week ago, she had walked north, opposite the direction of the fire ant mound where Gaston had met his fate. The previous night, she had walked south—the first time she had done so since his death—and after passing the fire ant mound she had moved out to the edge of the surf and stood gazing up at the moon for several minutes.

Most of her thoughts at that moment were of her sister.

She had wanted to avenge Sara's death, and thanks to Rob and Rachel, that had happened. But as satisfying as Gaston's death had been, she was still filled with a keen, sometimes almost overwhelming sense of loss and grief; and she knew those feelings would always be with her. They might diminish in time, or at least become more bearable, but she knew they would never leave her completely.

And that's okay, she had told herself as she turned away from the surf and began walking back to her vehicle. *Sara, I did the best I could for you.*

Now, one night later, she was once again thinking about Rob. Although they hadn't talked for three days, they had exchanged quite a few texts, mostly recounting their daily activities, and they always ended those messages by saying they missed each other. Jane wondered if Rob was thinking of inviting her to come up to Iowa anytime soon. In one of his texts he had mentioned that the state fair would be starting in a few weeks and she had smiled when she recalled her comment to him about wanting to try a corn dog.

She wondered if she should drop another hint or two.

She had almost reached the stile opposite the parking area where she'd left her Cherokee when she saw something approaching out of the darkness. A moment later it resolved itself into the figure of a large dog.

The dog came trotting toward her, its paws making a soft scuffling sound in the sand. Obviously friendly, it approached with its head held high and its tail wagging. It came right up to her and she could see it had a wiry coat, gray-white with large dark brown patches, that gave it a somewhat scruffy appearance. With its bearded muzzle and bushy eyebrows, it wore a rather comical expression, and Jane couldn't help laughing as she reached down to pat the dog's bristly head.

"Well," she said, "Where did you come from?"

A man's voice—which she instantly recognized—called out, "She's with me."

Jane looked up to see the man silhouetted at the top of the stile. She felt herself breaking into a wide smile but before she could speak, he called out again.

"Her name is Preacher."

Acknowledgments

As many authors before me have noted, writing and publishing a book is never a solitary endeavor. Lots of people contributed their support, expertise and encouragement to make Robert Vance's third outing a reality, and it's my pleasure to recognize them here.

I'll begin, as always, by thanking my first readers, Jamie Lamb and Randy Clark. Jamie and Randy read each chapter as it was completed, assiduously pointing out anything that needed to be corrected, clarified, explained, or, in some cases, eliminated. Additional props to them for providing input and details on such matters as wardrobe, dialogue and menu items (Jamie) and various automotive repair costs and the make, model and specs of Gaston's ATV (Randy).

Thanks also to Doug Clark and Ryan Clark, Randy's brothers and my cousins, for helping me out on such diverse subjects as Scriptural passages and hockey positions, and for providing a steady supply of laughs via video clips, jokes and ribald commentary.

Next, thanks to Tracy and Greg Christiansen, D.O., for their hospitality during my visit to North Carolina. Their generosity and efforts in showing me the sights, educating me on such phenomena as bait balls and king tides, and treating me to fine meals at local restaurants (plus some wonderful meals cooked by Tracy) provided much of the detail for Vance's own visit. More thanks to Greg for his input on fire ants, their toxicity and the symptoms of anaphylaxis; any errors, inaccuracies or exaggerations in this area are mine alone.

I also want to thank several good friends for agreeing to become fictional characters in this work. Included in this august group are Shawnna Wathen and Aleasha Biondi (bartenders "Anita" and "Biancia," respectively), John Schroeder, and Steve and Stacy Fulton. Here's hoping I've done right by all of you and you enjoy your characterizations.

In a related vein, thanks also to Heidi Schnock, another good friend, who lent her last name to the fictional town in this story, and to Paige Green, Jamie's cousin, for letting me borrow her name for the turtle rehab center.

Karen Hodges Miller of Open Door Publications once again guided this project through to completion, helping me navigate the countless ins and outs of getting a book into print as well as doing her usual masterful job of copy-editing and polishing my writing, which included pointing out (tactfully) a couple of key areas that needed revising to keep Vance and Jane on track and out of trouble. A writer herself, Karen recently published a memoir titled *Hibiscus Strong*, featuring a cast of proud, independent women and a wealth of colorful anecdotes--some humorous, some poignant, all entertaining— in short, a highly recommended read.

And speaking of fine writing, special thanks to Joe R. Lansdale, one of my favorite authors, for granting me permission to refer to his Hap Collins and Leonard Pine series, and specifically, one of the titles in that series, *The Elephant of Surprise*. Like Robert Vance, I love that play on words, and I heartily recommend the entire series if you haven't yet made the acquaintance of Hap and Leonard. Ditto Joe's many stand-alone novels.

Jaycee DeLorenzo of Sweet 'N Spicy Designs nailed, on her first try and with laser-like accuracy, the concept I suggested for the cover of *Beach*; and Lisa Snyder of Silver Hoop Edge, LLC, who initially designed my website, ProudPointPress.com, handled all of the necessary updates to keep both Robert Vance and myself current. Thanks to both of you.

I also want to give a shout-out to Pageturners Bookstore in Indianola, Iowa, and to Beaverdale Books in (you guessed it) the Beaverdale neighborhood of Des Moines. Proprietors Kathy Magruder and Alice Meyer, respectively, and the staffs of their indie bookstores have been tremendously supportive in sponsoring book-signing events and helping to get Robert Vance before the public. If you happen to be in the area of either of these fine shops, be sure to stop in. And buy something!

Additional thanks to Megan Reuther, host of *Hello Iowa!*, which airs weekdays at 11:00 a.m. on WHO-TV, Channel 13, in Des Moines. Megan graciously invited me to appear on the program to discuss Vance's previous two adventures, and I can attest she is the consummate host, immediately putting her guests at ease and asking all the right questions. A link to the video clip of our interview can be found on the ProudPointPress website.

And finally…two very special groups of people deserve thanks for their ongoing support and encouragement during the entire writing process; it's not an exaggeration to say that this encouragement provided much of the impetus needed to get the project across the finish line, for which I am profoundly grateful.

The first group is Jeanna Ginn's Tuesday Night Supper Club, a band of regulars who fill the seats at the bar of the SE 14th Street Applebee's every Tuesday evening. In addition to her duties as bartender, Jeanna emcees these get-togethers; the usual suspects include Russell Burnett, Barry Cermak and Shari Fransen, Chad and Heidi Chatham, Steve and Stacy Fulton, Bret Halls, Gary and Judy Ireland, Troy Keeney, Taylor Millikan, Rick Monteon, Jake Phillips, Chantele Pliler, Victoria Pliler, Matt and Anie Rehbein, Rachael Roeder, Jeff and Julie Runyan and Robert Smith. These folks held me accountable on a weekly basis by checking on the book's status; I wouldn't have dared tell them I ever spent a week not writing anything.

A second and equally important group consists of family members and long-time friends who, like the folks just mentioned, offered ongoing support, also regularly inquiring about the book's progress and asking when it would be available. I apologize in advance for anyone I've failed to mention, but this group includes Jayden Bailey, John Brynda, Tom Burek, Michelle Carr, Dave Carty, David Chase, Janet Cressy, Danielle DeCamp, Jo Eckert, Gail Fitch, Joe Freeman, Sandi Gamage, Steve Gash, Linda Gibson, Cheryl Hoffman,

Debbie Horney, Kathleen MacMurray, Dave Moeller and Karen Muelhaupt.

Also: Kerry and Becky Nielsen, Tammy Norris, Barbara Pamp, Frances Paterik, Bree Silvia, Terry Simpson, Loren Spiotta-DiMare, Nichole Staker, Tom Stephenson, Julie Sterling, Marla Talbott, Pam Teslow, Annie Troxell, Sandy Tryon, Tom Weaver, Ryan Werner, Julie Williams and Steve Wilson.

Again, my heartfelt thanks to all of these folks, and to you, gentle reader. It's extremely gratifying to know that Vance's adventures have been so well received. While it's tempting to suppose he might now settle down with Jane Trehorn and live happily ever after in retirement, we all know that bullies and injustice will continue to haunt the world in which we live. And so…

Robert Vance will return.

About the Author

Rick Van Etten is a former college English instructor, corporate communications professional and retired magazine editor whose work has appeared in *Gun Dog, Wing & Shot, Sports Afield, Ducks Unlimited, Game & Fish, Petersen's Hunting, Farm & Ranch Living* and *Reader's Digest*. An Illinois native and lifelong upland bird hunter, Rick now lives in Iowa. *The Killer on the Beach* is his third novel.

You can find more information about Rick's books at www.ProudPointPress.com.